something like forever

Jay Bell Books
www.jaybellbooks.com

Did you buy this book? If so, thank you for putting food on our table! Making money as an independent artist isn't easy, so your support is greatly appreciated. Come give me a hug!

Did you pirate this book? If so, there are a couple of ways you can still help out. If you like the story, please take the time to leave a nice review somewhere, such as an online retail store (my preference), or on any blog or forum. Word of mouth is important for every book, so if you can recommend this book to friends with more cash to spare, that would be awesome too!

Something Like Forever © 2017 Jay Bell / Andreas Bell
ISBN: 978-1978411371

ALL RIGHTS RESERVED. This book may not be reproduced in whole or in part without permission. This book is a work of fiction and any resemblance to persons, living or dead, or events is purely coincidental.

Cover art by Andreas Bell: www.andreasbell.com

This book is dedicated to Ben, Tim, Jace, and all the other characters who have made this series such a pleasure to write. Thank you for keeping me company during the lonely times. I'm sorry for all that I've put you through. Maybe that's why I feel the need to finally set you free. Before we begin this final dance, please know that I love each of you dearly. May your strength and resilience help inspire those going through similar struggles.

-=Books by Jay Bell=-

The *Something Like...* series

#1 Something Like Summer
#2 Something Like Autumn
#3 Something Like Winter
#4 Something Like Spring
#5 Something Like Lightning
#6 Something Like Thunder
#7 Something Like Stories - Volume One
#8 Something Like Hail
#9 Something Like Rain
#10 Something Like Stories - Volume Two
#11 Something Like Forever

The *Loka Legends* series

#1 The Cat in the Cradle
#2 From Darkness to Darkness

Other Novels

Kamikaze Boys
Hell's Pawn

Other Short Stories

Language Lessons
Like & Subscribe

Something Like Forever

by Jay Bell

Part One:
Acapulco, 2014

Chapter One

This is the end of our story. Looking back, it's hard to understand how we reached this point. Infatuation led to a rollerblade accident, and from there... love. While it lasted. Although now I see that it never went away. Separation doesn't cure a broken heart. Meeting a guy in the clouds sure helped, but like all angels, his feet only touched the ground for so long. When all hope seemed lost, that old love from my youth returned, bringing more than comforting nostalgia. What followed in his wake was new. A dream reborn. A second chance.

Ben Bentley looked up from his phone, the cold digital screen a stark contrast to his surroundings. He was standing on a beach, warm sand slipping between his wiggling toes. Directly ahead, waves crashed into the shore, reminding him again of how all this had begun. Ben's eyes moved to the water where he spotted a bobbing head with dark hair and striking silver eyes. Tim Wyman was the man who, if the fates were kind, Ben would spend the rest of his life with. They were married now. This was their honeymoon! But as Ben watched the water pull away from the sand, he was reminded that vows and rings were no guarantee of a happy future. Anything could happen, no matter how heartfelt their wishes or adamant their promises.

"Hey!"

Maudlin thoughts disappeared at the sound of that voice. Ben turned to see someone special walking toward him. His son! The newly bestowed title lifted his spirits and filled him with pride. Jason Grant wore nothing but a pair of wet swim trunks that clung to his legs. His shoulders were broad, his build was slender. His hair stuck to his forehead in damp brown tangles, the blue eyes intense and locked onto his own. Jason was handsome in his own way, although Ben didn't feel attracted to him in the slightest. He always assumed that biologic connections made such things impossible. Ben certainly wasn't attracted to his sister—obviously—or any of his male cousins, but they were blood. Jason wasn't, but he *was* family. Legally now. The adoption papers had been signed, although their family bond had started long before then. Five years ago. Funny, because it already felt much longer. An age difference of nearly ten years separated them. People would probably mistake Ben and Jason as brothers for the rest of their lives, but when it came to their relationship, the roles were that of a parent and child.

Ben had experienced a lot. Not just the loss of one great love and the rediscovery of another. His heart had been put through the wringer in many other ways, but he had overcome each obstacle until his life settled down into a peaceful rhythm. Jason was still finding his way and often needed guidance. Judging from his current expression—the brave smile forced—now was one such occasion.

"You're crazy," Jason said, nodding at the phone. "I know how addictive those things are, but this is paradise!" He spread his arms wide, as if presenting the world.

He wasn't wrong. The sun was setting, the fiery sphere seeming to touch where the waters of the bay met the Pacific Ocean. Orange and blue intermingled in the heavens above, the colors darkening as the day drew to a close.

"Do you get a signal out here?" Jason asked, coming to a stop in front of him and looking down at the phone. "Mine's barely worked since we landed."

"Not really," Ben replied. "I've got one bar, which is just enough to give me false hope before it times out."

Jason angled his head to see the phone better. "Then what are you doing?"

"Oh." Ben held it up to show him before pocketing the phone. "Just writing. I used to all the time when I was younger. Always felt like it helped me work through things."

"Uh oh."

"Uh oh?" Ben repeated.

Jason shrugged. "People don't need to work through things if they're happy. This is your honeymoon!"

Ben laughed. "I *am* happy. A little overwhelmed too. So much has changed. I just got hitched and gave birth to a twenty-four-year-old man!"

"Gross!" Jason said, grinning broadly. "Still, it's not like you guys weren't already living together, and I've been around for ages now, so I don't see what's really changed." The smile faded. "Oh."

Ben forced his own smile to remain, despite how he felt. "I'm going to miss you."

Jason nodded, eyes becoming watery and Adam's apple

bobbing as he swallowed. Then he turned to look beyond the waves at the gently swelling water. Tim wasn't alone out there. Two silhouettes could be seen, heads that faced each other and talked between bouts of action. Arms moved in arcs and feet kicked to propel them forward in a friendly competition. Ben had no trouble telling who was whom. The man who often threw back his head to laugh, or who would launch into the air with arms pressed to his sides before plummeting beneath the surface like a stone—that was Tim. The name alone made Ben flash back to a small desk in a Texas high school where he had scribbled that name into a notebook over and over again. Next to this he had written his own name, making himself a Wyman, but never truly believing that dream would one day come true. But it had! All except for the last name. Ben was too used to being a Bentley, and he didn't want Tim's name to change either.

As for the other swimmer, the person who moved through the water with practiced precision—the one who kept a watchful eye whenever Tim performed a potentially harmful stunt—they didn't come much sweeter than him. William Townson was a good man. Ben had no doubt about that. He only wished his profession wasn't quite so heroic. William was a Coast Guard rescue swimmer, and while that was noble and necessary, the job came with risks. His line of work was dangerous, and if anything should ever happen to him... Ben knew that pain all too well, and would do just about anything to shield Jason from it. Aside from depriving Jason of the love that he so deserved. Not that he wasn't tempted. William's occupation required him to live near an air station, which they definitely didn't have back home in Austin. This meant changes were necessary. William wanted to resume his career with the Coast Guard. Jason wanted that for him too. Because of that, they were moving to the other side of the county. All the way to Oregon.

"I can't do it."

Ben's attention whipped back to Jason. Between the crashing waves and the gradually stirring nightlife behind them, he wasn't sure if he had heard right, so he simply shook his head.

Jason took a deep breath, chest heaving. "I know you said that you're proud of me, but I can't. It's like someone gave me everything I ever wanted but then asked me choose only one thing to keep. Most of it is easy, but not when you get to the people. Emma is my best friend, and you…" His voice squeaked. "You're my dad."

"Come here," Ben said, opening his arms.

Jason accepted, squeezing desperately and sniffling over his shoulder.

Ben patted his back, then rubbed it to comfort him. "We'll *always* be here for you. You know that. Moving to Astoria won't change how we feel about you. Nothing can."

Jason pulled away, head shaking. "I wish I had never come up with the stupid idea. I know William wasn't happy being a paramedic, but most people don't like their job, right?"

"It's more than that," Ben said. "You told me how important it is that William can be where he's needed. To do what?"

"To save lives," Jason said with a glum sniff. Then he looked hopeful. "Paramedics save lives too. He just doesn't get to swim while doing so."

Ben resisted a smile. "You also explained how few rescue swimmers there are. Not everyone can do what William was trained to."

"No," Jason said grudgingly.

"And what about his daughter?" Daisy had been an unexpected surprise, but Jason had reacted with patience and love. "You want her to have both parents near. Oregon will make that possible."

"Yeah," Jason said, wiping his eyes on the back of his wrist. His voice wavered. "What about me? When do I get to have my family close again?"

"We'll be with you," Ben said, feeling emotional himself. "That's one of the best things about family. Nothing can break that bond, no matter how big the distance between us, or how much time goes by. I promise."

Jason bit his bottom lip, perhaps to stop it trembling, and shook his head as if Ben couldn't possibly understand. He was right. Ben didn't know what it was like to grow up without parents. Jason had seen his family crumble and fall apart, so of course he questioned Ben's claim. He needed to do this though. Jason needed to live for himself and risk the happiness he had in the hope of gaining even more. Ben had learned that lesson and benefited from it. Jason should too.

The only problem was that Ben didn't actually want him to

go. "Maybe you should give this a try," he said, pulling out his phone again.

Jason moved closer to see, seeming eager for a distraction. "What were you writing about?"

"All of it." Ben sat and patted the sand next to him so Jason would do the same. Then he unlocked the phone and handed it over. "I started shortly after Tim and I got back together. I wanted to make sure I was doing the right thing, so I wrote out my thoughts. That meant delving into our past, and then what happened when we were apart—"

"You're writing an entire book on your phone?"

"No!" Ben laughed. "Normally it's my laptop, but I'm not writing a book. Am I? I don't know what I'm doing exactly, but it helps me gain perspective. When you get all the facts down along with your feelings, it's easier to take a step back and see the whole picture. That might help you too. At the very least, it's cheaper than therapy."

Jason nodded. "I'll try, but again, this raises the question of why you feel like you need therapy on your honeymoon."

"Oh." He looked to the water where Tim spread his arms wide and flopped backwards. William reacted with surprising speed, grabbing Tim and pulling him toward the shore. Only a demonstration of rescue swimmer techniques and not a real emergency. William got along great with Tim, which was crucial because he would probably become their son-in-law. Thank goodness. Not only because Ben liked him, but because William was just as physical as Tim. Ben could never keep up with all the jogging and weightlifting and Tim's need to wear himself out every day. Only in the bedroom were they evenly matched. The thought made him smile. Ben was happy. Truly so! He had a new husband, a cozy home, and a growing family. Strange, then, that he still longed for more. "I've got a lot of years ahead of me," he said, trying to enunciate the yearning inside. "Four decades. Maybe more. What am I supposed to do with all that time?"

"The same thing you're doing now," Jason replied.

He didn't sound certain, which showed that he was growing up. Jason was right to doubt the status quo. Ten years ago, Ben's life had been completely different. And yet, it had been strangely similar. Ben had just gotten married then and was looking toward the future with bright hopes and unshakable optimism. Maybe he had done some growing up too, because Ben no longer assumed that everything would work out okay. Whatever the future held, he would have to be on his guard and strive to ensure things went the way he wanted. But first he had to figure out exactly what that was. Starting now. His heart's desire was for Jason to stay, but it was the job of any good parent to know when to push a baby bird from the nest. Only then would his son learn to fly.

"Honeymoon! I freaking love my honeymooooon!"

Tim sang this as he strutted into the bedroom. His shorts were somewhere else in the suite (tossed carelessly on the floor, no doubt) and his tank top was being pulled over his head seductively. That was the intent, at least. He tripped over the clothes Ben had abandoned on the carpet (okay, so he shouldn't judge), but Tim managed to recover before falling. The shirt came off the rest of the way, mussing the black hair, and making his doofy expression all that much more endearing. Of course it didn't hurt that Tim was left wearing only a pair of maroon boxer briefs.

Ben watched all of this while sitting up in bed, sheets bundled around his waist and an open book in his lap. He did his best not to look impressed.

"Fun fact," Tim said, hands gripping the ornate footboard of the bed. "Nookie is guaranteed every night of a honeymoon."

"Oh really?" Bed said, making sure he didn't sound convinced.

"Yup! Matter of fact, it's the law."

"It's definitely not."

"Maybe not back in the United States," Tim said, "but here in Mexico, it's different. Seriously."

Ben crossed his arms over his chest. "You're full of it."

"I'm not!"

"What's this law called?"

"*Es puro cuento*," Tim said without hesitation.

Ben let his arms drop. "Really? That's a law?"

Tim smirked. "Yeah, but I understand if you need a break. Not everyone can keep up with the Wy-machine."

"The *Wy-machine*?" Ben repeated incredulously. "How long did it take you to come up with that?"

"It's a work in progress," Tim said, making his pecs bounce.

"Do you think Wyman-machine sounds better? Or I was trying to think of some way to use the '-man' part, like 'I put the man into Wyman.'"

"How about I put my man-part into Wyman instead?" Ben teased.

"Not a chance," Tim said.

"There's an American law that says you have to. It *is* our honeymoon. Maybe it's time we switch things up."

Tim was barely paying attention. He snapped his fingers, like he'd come up with a good idea. Then he turned his back to Ben, hooked his thumbs in the band of his underwear, and looked over his shoulder. "Honey?"

"Yes?"

"Moon!"

The underwear came down.

Ben got the joke and shook his head. "I'm *so* glad I married a frat boy."

"I bet you are," Tim said, sauntering toward his side of the bed, naked now and increasingly hard. "Isn't that every gay guy's fantasy? Not all of them, maybe, but the quiet bookish types who don't have muscles of their own and wish they could find out what they feel like."

"Okay, that is pretty hot," Ben said, pulling down the blanket so Tim could climb inside. "Although outside the bedroom, those bookish types like meaningful conversations."

"About art?" Tim asked, sliding between the sheets. "Or architecture. Or how about a lecture on Mexican culture?"

Ben grinned. "You're the complete package, baby!" He leaned over for a kiss.

Tim reciprocated, scooting nearer. "So who are you in the mood for tonight? Tim the artist, or Tim the frat boy?"

The frat boy, but Ben hesitated. "Do you think it went okay with William today?"

Tim shook his head, not understanding. "Is this about our bet to see who could eat the most *ceviche*? I know we looked like pigs, but you saw how Jason couldn't stop laughing. Especially when I coughed and an entire shrimp came flying out... Which, now that I think about it, wasn't very classy. Sorry."

"It's fine," Ben said with a smile. "I love all your different sides. And I know you tipped the waitress well."

"She was a good sport."

"Yeah." Ben took a deep breath. "I meant when you and William were alone. When you were out swimming, or went for that bike ride together, did he say anything about him and Jason having problems?"

Tim scooted down to rest his head on Ben's stomach while still looking up at him. "Nope. He kept talking about their Oregon plans. He's really excited about the move. Why? Is everything okay?"

"I don't know," Ben admitted. "We shouldn't say anything, but Jason is acting like he's changed his mind."

"About the proposal or—"

"Oregon. I think he wants to stay in Texas."

"With William?"

"Yeah."

Tim looked confused. "But what about—"

"I know. Oregon is a good idea, isn't it? William can return to active duty and be close to his daughter, and Jason..." Ben exhaled. "Tell me he needs to broaden his horizons."

"He needs to broaden his horizons," Tim said earnestly, pushing himself up on an elbow. "This is about us, isn't it? Jason doesn't want to leave us behind."

"Exactly!" Ben said, not hiding his surprise. "Did he talk to you about it too?"

"No, but whenever we hug lately, he's got a death grip on me. I could barely breathe the last time. I thought it was him being excited about the adoption, but then I caught him looking at you the other day when we were out shopping. He was staring across the store at you like his heart was about to break."

"Stop," Ben said, feeling like his own was also in danger of cracking.

"All of this is normal," Tim said. "When I left Kansas— Bad example. I couldn't wait to get out of there because I didn't have any friends left. Same when I left Houston, but I still felt sad about leaving you behind. I know we hadn't talked for a year at that point, but just the idea that we would be even farther apart made me sad. Sometimes you feel the distance, even while you're still close."

Ben reached for him, so Tim flopped back down, using him as a pillow again and grinning while Ben stroked his hair. "I suppose I felt that way before I moved to Chicago. It seemed like a really good idea until a few days before it was time to leave. Then I panicked."

"Jason is feeling the same thing," Tim said. "He'll keep freaking out, and we'll keep reassuring him. No way is he letting William get away. Not this time. You've seen them together. Remind you of anyone?"

Ben chuckled, causing Tim's head to rise and fall. "You're right. I'm worrying for nothing."

"Exactly. I'll be sure to talk to him anyway. Just to make sure he knows that we'll always be there for him."

Ben felt a swell of emotion. "You're the best. You know that?"

Tim grinned in response. "No, but I sure like hearing it."

"Remind me, what was that honeymoon law called?"

"*No hay nadie más guapo que tú,*" Tim said, eyes smoldering as he pushed himself up again.

Ben peered at him. "Is that what you said before? It sounded different this time."

"No more talking," Tim said, face moving closer.

Silver eyes locked onto his, and Ben knew he couldn't resist them, so instead he closed his own. When their lips met, he felt like he could melt into those arms and spend the rest of the trip tangled up in the sheets. Or at least the rest of the night, which is exactly what they did.

Honey-freaking-moon! At times the thought had Tim blissed out. He was married! To Benjamin! It wasn't all that long ago that his chances seemed ruined. Life was full of surprises though, not all of them bad, because here they were on their honeymoon. Acapulco might not enjoy the glamorous reputation it once had, but Tim still adored it. He made sure they got the most out of the trip, dragging them up to the Chapel of Peace for tranquility and the breathtaking view, and down to Zocalo for the flea market stalls and restaurants. Ben seemed to enjoy himself, as did Jason and William, but Tim still worried it wasn't enough.

This wasn't Ben's first marriage, nor his first honeymoon. Normally that didn't bother Tim, but at times he found it hard to compete. Acapulco versus Paris. Man… Then again, he was pretty sure that Paris didn't have gorgeous beaches or nearly as much sunshine. As for the food, considering that they both had simple tastes, Ben had to prefer enchilada suizas over snails or whatever. Hopefully. But when it came to culture, Tim knew that Paris had most cities beat. The cabarets, art museums, fashion boutiques, rivers, and of course a certain famous tower. Both cities offered interesting architecture, but Acapulco had been hit hard by a hurricane the year before and was still recovering. Then there were local issues with drug violence. More than once Ben had read aloud a news headline, then looked to him in concern.

Tim stuck to the same answer each time. Acapulco was a great place full of good people. He was determined to prove that. Visits to the local museums helped prove that this too was a city rich with culture, and a few hours spent at *El Fuerte de San Diego*—a fort built to protect the port from pirates—asserted Alcapulco's historical significance. Still, those lingering doubts persisted. When Tim took Ben to a giant mosaic dragon, a mural by Diego Rivera, they marveled over the colors and symbolism. But could it really compete with the Mona Lisa? Tim knew which piece of art he preferred, but one was a household name, and more likely to be bragged about when they returned home again.

"Having fun?" Tim asked. They had taken a bus close to La Quebrada to see the cliff-diving spectacle there, but first they had done some shopping and explored the local neighborhoods. Today was their last day in Acapulco, and he intended to make it memorable. As they walked toward the cliffs, he couldn't help noticing that Ben was quiet, so he asked why.

"I'm good," Ben said, expression pensive. "Just a little tired."

"Want me to carry you? Never mind. Why am I even asking?" Tim moved like he was going to pick Ben up. His boyfriend—no, his husband!—protested and shoved him away while laughing. At least his smile had returned.

"You can carry me," Jason said from behind them.

"You've got your own muscle," Tim said over his shoulder. "Ask him."

"I don't mind," William said, shielding his eyes to look at Jason, "but only if I can use you as an umbrella. Actually, do we have any sunblock left?"

They had already gone through an entire bottle, Jason lubing up William at frequent intervals. At first Tim thought this was an excuse for them to get touchy-feely, but William was fair-skinned and had grown increasingly red as the trip went on.

"We're out," Jason grumbled. "How much farther?"

"Where's that water you promised?" Ben murmured to himself.

"Could we walk in the shade?" William asked. "If there's any around here, that is."

Crap! The trip was a disaster! If they had gone to Paris, they would probably be riding in a horse-drawn carriage while feeding macaroons to each other between sips of champagne. Tim looked around and spotted a convenience store ahead. He could already hear the rumble of an overworked air conditioner. The interior seemed nice and dark.

"Follow me!" he said, picking up the pace.

Twenty minutes later, the situation was much improved. Everyone had a cold drink, Jason had smeared half a bottle of newly purchased sunscreen on William, and a taxi had just pulled up to carry them the rest of the way.

"This is really nice," William said once they were all crammed inside.

"Hard to imagine how it could get any better," Tim said, leaning forward to check on his husband. Not that he was in the front seat. Jason had called shotgun. The rest of them were in the back. William insisted on being in the middle, which didn't make sense because Ben was the smallest and would have fit better there. And that would have allowed Tim to snuggle with him a little. Instead, William was grinning while glancing back and forth between them. He tended to get a little excited when around them both. Tim thought it was sweet. "You okay, babe?"

William opened his mouth like he was about to answer, then turned even redder and leaned back so Tim could see across the seat. Ben smiled, appearing more relaxed. "This is nice. Can we have him drive around for the next half hour?"

Tim was sure it was a joke, but after checking his watch, he saw that they still had plenty of time. He asked the driver to take the most scenic route possible. They drove through crowded commercial areas and neighborhoods with narrow winding streets, the day-to-day stress outside the car not touching them inside their bubble. By the time they reached the destination and climbed out of the taxi, they were all eager to stretch their legs. Just a short walk brought them to the cliffs, a breeze cooling them along the way.

Most tourists watched the spectacle from the patio of a nearby restaurant, but Tim guided his family to a platform lower down. From there they had a better view and a finer appreciation for the height of the cliffs, which stretched craggy and unforgiving toward the sky. The rocky wall directly ahead of them sloped outward the further down it went, ending in a pool of frothy churning water, azure waves rushing in from the Pacific. Five dark-haired heads could be seen floating below. The performers. Tim made sure that everyone was pressed against the rail for the best view, then pointed as the five bodies below swam for the cliffs and began climbing.

"They're barefoot!" Ben gasped.

"They should be using climbing gear," William said with concern. "Harnesses, helmets, gloves…"

"Take it easy, Coast Guard," Tim said, beaming at the display. "They know what they're doing."

"They're pretty hot!" Jason added.

They definitely were. Brown muscles glistened and strained as each person continued to climb. Two stopped at a lower outcrop, walked to the very end of the ledge, and looked down. Even there, they were well above eye level.

"They're not going to jump!" Ben cried. "They'll hit the rocks!"

"Only if they get the timing wrong," Tim said. "They have to wait until a wave comes in or the water below isn't deep enough."

"I'm calling the Mexican Coast Guard," William said. "What's their number?"

"Just watch," Tim said, nodding as one of the performers raised his hands above his head in a classic dive position. Then he jumped, managed a flip, and plummeted toward certain doom. A wave rushed in to catch him at the last second, but was the water deep enough? The audience breathed out in shared relief when the diver surfaced again unharmed. This was repeated by the second performer, then all attention went to the very top of the cliff, which was twice as high.

Ben grabbed Tim's arm, clutching him close. Tim allowed himself a satisfied smirk. Acapulco was pretty damn cool! All three performers at the top of the cliff jumped at once, tumbling through the air like they had been cast out of Heaven. One flipped twice, the other two seemed intent on belly flops, but as the water neared, they straightened and entered like a syringe plunging into skin.

"That's beautiful," William breathed. "It scared the hell out of me, but it's beautiful."

"You've jumped from higher than that," Jason said. "Right?"

"No way!" William said, looking wide-eyed as the performers started climbing again. "What is that? A hundred feet? More?"

"Yeah, but you jump from a helicopter." Jason said.

William shook his head. "Only after it descends as close to the water as possible!"

"It's still cooler," Jason said, unwilling to admit that William was anything less than amazing. His eyes were shining, even as the show went on, but the smile faded when he looked instead at Ben and then at him.

Tim offered a reassuring smile, trying to show that it was okay. Jason returned the gesture, but without as much certainty. Tim led by example and turned his attention back to the show. They experienced vicarious jolts of panic and spikes of adrenaline while watching, and when the demonstration finally ceased, they all felt like they had narrowly escaped death, despite having only been in the audience. Tim made sure they stuck around long enough afterwards to tip the divers, and to translate, because William had a slew of questions for them. Despite his initial concerns, it was clear that his future son-in-law had enjoyed himself. Tim hoped that Ben had too.

"What did you think?" he asked as they were walking away.

"I loved it!" Ben admitted. "But if you *ever* try anything like that, I'll kill you. I don't care if that makes sense or not."

Tim laughed. "Fair enough. What now? It's a little early, but we could grab dinner."

This resulted in a chorus of not-hungrys.

"I wouldn't mind going back to the hotel," Ben said. "We can rest, refresh, and then go out."

Tim summoned another taxi to make this wish a reality. Once they were in the hotel lobby, they consulted each other for direction.

"The pool here has a high dive, doesn't it?" William asked.

"Saw that coming," Jason said. "Looks like we're going swimming. Again. Don't you ever get tired of the water?"

"It's like that movie, *Splash*," Ben said.

Tim laughed. The other two looked at them blankly.

"Daryl Hannah?" Ben tried. "She's a mermaid who goes to the city and gets legs, but she has to soak in a bathtub occasionally to stay healthy."

"Must be before our time," Jason said with a snort.

"Whatever," Ben said. "I'm sure it'll get remade soon enough, and then you can see it."

"That's right," Tim said, backing him up. "We actually had original ideas back in our day."

Jason held up a palm. "You guys have fun watching silent movies in your room. We're going swimming."

Tim waited until he and Ben were in the elevator alone before he laughed. "I love that boy."

"I do too," Ben said. "I'm so glad we brought them with us."

"Me too, although privacy is nice."

"Yes," Ben said wistfully. "It can be."

Looks like they would indeed be having sex every day of their honeymoon. Not that Tim was keeping track. Okay, he was. He knew quality beat quantity, but he was thrilled nonetheless. Except when they got back to their room, Ben turned around at the door like someone saying goodnight at the end of a date.

"I think I need a little Daryl Hannah time," he said.

"You want a bath?"

"Yeah."

Tim nodded. "No problem! I'll run one for you."

Ben remained motionless.

"Oh." Tim said. "You need some alone time."

"Just a little," Ben said. "The quiet sounds good. That way I'm ready for tonight."

Tim wanted to pout and beg for sex or at least ask to sit on the toilet and keep Ben company, but he had learned that the payoff was double if he played it cool. Even if that wasn't his first instinct. "No problem," he said. "I'll join the boys at the pool."

"No flips or anything fancy!" Ben scolded.

Tim just grinned. If Ben didn't love him, he wouldn't be so worried all the time. "Enjoy yourself," he said, stealing a kiss. "I'll see you in an hour."

Before he left, he changed into his swimsuit, which involved walking into the bathroom naked to fetch it from the shower rod where he had hung it to dry. He could have gotten it before undressing, but he wanted to remind Ben of what he was missing. He hoped it worked like subliminal advertising. A flash of the wiener now might lead to a trip to the concession stand later for a hot dog.

After leaving the hotel room, Tim banished such thoughts from his mind and instead looked forward to diving into cool water. Texas was hot, but Mexico was hotter, and even he was getting a little tired of the sun. He took the stairs instead of waiting for the elevator, only hesitating when nearing the indoor pool. What if Jason and William were enjoying their privacy? Without the parents around, so to speak. Tim shook his head. Nothing figurative about it! He was a parent now, meaning his presence was probably a big downer. The door to the pool area had a diamond-shaped window, so he peeked through it. William was climbing the ladder to the diving board. Jason was sitting on one of the deck chairs, skin and hair dry despite wearing swim trunks. Buds were in his ears, the green wires snaking down to his phone, which was no doubt streaming a horror movie or maybe a YouTube video.

Future, meet your past, because the scene wasn't so different from what he and Ben often did. Hanging out together while engaged in separate tasks, although Ben would be reading by the pool instead of watching videos. No longer feeling he would ruin a romantic moment, Tim pushed open the door. Jason wasn't surprised to see him, nodding before looking back at his phone. William's reaction was a little more enthusiastic, a sheepish grin followed by blushing cheeks. On this trip, he had done the same thing every time Tim showed up in a swimsuit. The reaction was flattering, and frankly, if Tim wasn't already happily married and Jason wasn't so in love with William, he would have no trouble returning the attention. As it was, he considered whatever fleeting attraction William had as harmless and cute.

"Learn any tricks watching those divers?" he asked.

William perked up. "They make it look easy, don't they? I tried doing a flip and failed miserably."

"Just takes practice," Tim said. "We can do it."

They had a few false starts, Tim landing on his back for one of them, which smarted. He got it on the next try, realizing that he just needed a lot of bounce. This was less intimidating on the low dive. He managed to flip on three separate attempts, each easier than the previous. Then he coached William until he too was able to do it.

"I'm surprised they don't teach you this in the Coast Guard," Tim said when climbing out.

"Diving boards and helicopters don't mix," William retorted. "Not unless you're looking for a haircut."

"Maybe we should try it from the high dive," Tim suggested.

"I'm game!" William replied, grinning at him.

This earned them a small audience. Jason rose and walked closer to take photos and record a video. A handful of a little kids sat on the edge of the pool and clapped or called out numbers, like scorecards from an Olympic judge. "¡Nueve! Cinco. Ocho." Or if they were really lucky, "¡Diez! ¡Diez ¡Diez!"

Even a backflip didn't earn them a perfect score. Only a cannonball would do the trick, the kids giggling if they got splashed enough, or once, William kept jumping up and down on the board until he had a ridiculous amount of air. Tim was certain he almost hit the ceiling. Eventually the kids got tired of sitting on the sidelines and started participating, but on the lower diving board instead. Only one of them was brave enough to attempt the high dive. He just happened to be the smallest one too. The kid couldn't have been more than six years old. Tim stood on the sidelines and watched, unsure if he should feel impressed or concerned. He looked over, trying to find the parents, and saw a woman on her cell phone. She seemed to be arguing with someone about a travel reservation. Then she looked up and shrieked.

Tim followed her terrified eyes, turning just in time to see the little kid plummet toward the water. The boy hadn't dived or pulled his limbs in. He looked more like a skydiver, arms and legs spread wide. Not good. The boy hit the water facedown and flat, a painful smacking sound echoing throughout the hall. He didn't come up again. Not quickly enough. Tim braced himself to dive in, but a blur blew past him before he could. William shot beneath the water like a torpedo, only breaking the surface again when a small bundle was in his arms. Then he began swimming backward, dragging the child along, just like he had demonstrated to him the other day.

Tim got down on his knees so he could pull the child free from the water, wishing desperately that he had refreshed himself on CPR, because the kid was making a terrible choking noise. Then the boy started coughing instead, thank goodness.

"¡Mi bebé! ¡Mi pobre bebé!"

The mother rushed to her child. Tim made room for her and turned to William, who was out of the pool and looking like he meant business.

"He's okay," Tim informed him. "He's breathing."

"He just got the wind knocked out of him," William said. "Same thing happened to me once."

The mother turned, spluttering emotional thank yous. Tim translated for William, who had some emotional words of his own. They were politely phrased and softly spoken, but ultimately boiled down to the mother needing to keep a closer watch on her child. That was less fun to translate, but the woman took it well, thanking him again. Then she alternated between scolding her son and smooching the boy on his cheeks. Tim chuckled at this display, then looked over to check on his own son. Jason was standing there shocked and pale. Tim thought he knew why, but he waited until they were upstairs in the hall before he said anything.

William had slipped into his room, Jason about to follow when Tim grabbed his arm.

"Hey! Just a sec."

Jason looked surprised, then murmured something to William before pulling the door mostly shut. "What's up?"

"Funny how life works," Tim said. "Sometimes it sends you a sign too clear to ignore."

Jason searched his eyes. "Ben told you."

"Telling one of us is telling the other," Tim said. "Unless you swear me to secrecy."

Jason exhaled. "I know that I need to let him go."

"Right. William belongs in the Coast Guard where he can keep helping people," Tim said, "and you need to go with him. For support."

"But—"

"Ben and I have each other," Tim said. "You made sure of that by forcing us to get married." He leaned forward and in a conspiring whisper added, "and I'm really glad you did."

Jason flashed a smile. "It had to happen eventually."

"Yeah. You've taken good care of us. We'll miss you, but we

won't be lonely. Now it's your turn to figure out who you want to spend the rest of your life with."

"I already have," Jason said.

"Then on to step two, which is actually spending your life with him. You'll see us again. A lot. We won't let you get away that easily."

Jason just stared. When his lip started trembling, Tim grabbed him in a bear hug. "You're doing the right thing. Don't let fear trip you up. Trust me. I speak from experience."

Jason nodded against his shoulder, then sniffed and pulled away. "I'll try."

"That's my boy," Tim said, ruffling his hair. "Send me a text when you guys are ready and we'll end this trip with the biggest meal you've ever seen. Better bring a bucket to barf in, because it's going to be ridiculous!"

"And suddenly I'm not feeling so hungry," Jason said, shaking his head, but he smiled and looked as though a weight had been lifted from his shoulders. Reassured that he would always have a home, hopefully now he would focus on creating one of his own.

Chapter Two

Home again. Ben fumbled for the right key, already missing the sound of claws on linoleum from beyond the door. And if *he* was missing Chinchilla, that meant—

"Maybe I should go pick her up real quick." Tim grabbed the luggage, ready to enter, but looked with transparent longing toward the drive that led away from their house. "Allison's got her hands full already with Davis. She might have forgotten that we're home today."

"She's stopping by later," Ben said, opening the door, although only a crack. Force of habit. When he remembered that no over-excited dog was going to make a break for it, he opened it the rest of the way.

The air that drifted out, despite being a little stale, smelled reassuringly familiar. For the previous six years it had been home. Good memories had been made here and a few bad ones too, but mostly the house hidden away on the outskirts of Austin had been his sanctuary, which he never expected to find again after—

"Hey," Tim said before Ben could enter. "Quick question."

Ben turned to face him. "What's up?"

Tim's smile was unusually bashful. "Is it always going to feel like this?"

Ben shook his head, not understanding. "What do you mean?"

"Being married. The wedding was way better than I expected. Now I wish we had done it sooner. The honeymoon was awesome—"

"I liked it too!" Ben had felt a little worn out at the end, but not in a bad way.

"Yeah. I just didn't think it was possible to love you more than I already did. So are we just riding a high, or is always going to be like this? You've been married before. I figured you would know."

Ben thought about mornings spent at a small kitchen table, the sound of a laugh that he still missed, and a hand that always sought out his before they fell asleep at night. "That's up to us," he said, a little misty-eyed. "It's our job now to hold on to this feeling for as long as we can."

"I won't let you down."

Ben smiled. "You're adorable. Hey, do you remember our first day here? How you wanted to carry me across the threshold?"

"You wouldn't let me," Tim said. Then he perked up. "You said it was marriage stuff."

"Did I?" Ben said demurely.

Tim dropped the luggage. Ben was pretty sure he heard a souvenir breaking, but he didn't care. He was already laughing as Tim scooped him up, chest puffed up with pride as he sauntered into the house. Sure he misjudged and bumped Ben's head against the doorframe, but love hurt sometimes. Tim set him down in the entryway and they kissed, but before it could turn into anything more, they both pulled away.

"It's muggy in here," Tim said.

Ben nodded. "I'll turn up the air."

Married life! So perfectly domestic. Tim brought their suitcases inside and shut the door, and when Ben was done fiddling with the thermostat, they went together to the living room.

He watched as Tim walked to the sliding glass door and peered out at the backyard. "It's bad enough that Jason doesn't live here anymore," he said. "Without Chinchilla, it doesn't feel like home."

"Empty nesters," Ben said. "I'm sure it won't be long before someone shows up. Speaking of which, when does Marcello get back in town?"

"I don't remember exactly," Tim admitted. "He could be back already."

They looked at each other and grinned.

"Should we check the Marcello detection device?" Ben asked.

Tim nodded and they hurried to the kitchen. They had spent the last ten days out of town, so there was no reason that any of their friends should have stopped by, but when they checked the refrigerator, sure enough something had changed.

"I like how he left the bottle in there," Tim said, holding up the champagne, "even though the cork is gone and it's empty."

"He could fit four of this house into his own," Ben said, shaking his head. "Why would he need to come here when he already has *everything*?"

"Probably likes going through our underwear drawers," Tim murmured. "Hey, there's an idea! We'll put champagne bottles in our underwear drawers and see how long they last."

"I'd rather not know," Ben said, filling the electric kettle to make tea.

Tim was still poking around in the refrigerator, looking unsatisfied. "We need fresh stuff. I want to start juicing more. As in smoothies. We don't get enough fruit."

"Too easy," Ben said.

"Wanna hit the store?"

"I was planning on unpacking and doing some laundry."

"I'll run then," Tim said, shutting the fridge.

"Okay." Ben made sure to keep his tone neutral, even though he really liked the idea, because there was something he wanted to do. A thought had been nagging him for the last two weeks, but he needed to be alone for it. Probably. Tim was cool about everything these days, but Ben would feel a lot less silly without an audience.

He started the first load of laundry, straining to hear over the sound of the washer filling. When the front door closed and the buzz of an engine faded away, he went to peek out the entryway windows. No sign of Tim. Ben almost wished that the car would return, because now he felt nervous. Then again, how bad could this possibly go? Unless objects started floating around the room and smashing into things, but even that would be welcome, because at least he would be here.

Ben went upstairs to the office. Tim rarely used it, preferring to work in his studio, which was now a converted shed elsewhere on the property. That meant the office was mostly Ben's. That's not why the framed photo was kept there. He wasn't hiding it away, although he did move it out of the bedroom because it was awkward to be in the heat of the moment and look over to see that face again. Too awkward, and at times, too tempting, but no fantasy could ever count as cheating. Not when it involved him.

Ben sat in the office chair and faced a framed photo on the desk. It showed a flight attendant looking debonair in his uniform. The man's eyes shone with pride, love, and everything else good that he had embodied.

"Hello, Jace." Ben choked back tears and shook his head. "Sorry, I know you don't like it when I cry. At least, I know you wouldn't have liked it. Ugh. This is stupid."

He looked away, but only for a second. Then his attention

returned to the photo and a few small knickknacks he kept next to it. Reminders. One was the nametag Jace had worn while working, which by coincidence, shared the same name as his son. Jason. Later the airline had changed their policy and allowed Jace to use the name everyone called him, but Ben kept this one for sentimental reasons. Jace had been wearing it when they met. Ben caressed the nametag with the tip of a finger, looking next to the ceramic fortune cookie that Jace had never seen with living eyes, but that Ben had bought because it always made his heart fill with affection. Now was no different.

"Sorry," Ben said, addressing the photo again. "You know I don't usually do this. I just really need to tell you something, and I'm not sure where else to go. I thought about flying out to Warrensburg but—" Ben shook his head to clear it. "I got married. Tim and I, obviously. I know you didn't want me to be alone. You also wanted me to be happy, and I really am." Ben wiped tears from his eyes. "I can imagine how this looks, but I mean it. I'm doing really well, even though I wish you were still here. No idea how that would work, but you always said that emotions didn't have to make sense. I just want you to know that we're still married." Ben held up his left hand where he had been wearing the same ring for ten years. "Tim's okay with that. He gets it. It makes me a bigamist, but I don't care. I love you. I will *always* be your husband. No matter what."

Try as he might, he couldn't help sobbing a few times. Then he got himself under control. Ben forced himself to think of the happy memories they had made together. Feeling better, he grabbed the framed photo, kissed it, and set it down again. Then he rose, walked to the door, and looked back with his hand on the light switch. "I love you, Jace. If you're out there, I hope you can feel that."

He waited for an answer—just in case—and when it didn't come, he turned off the light and went back downstairs to continue his life. And the laundry.

Ben went to answer the door, hearing muffled thumps and a few choice cuss words. When he opened the door, Allison stood there looking disheveled. A leash was twisted around her ankles and a squirming baby wiggled from one arm. Or a toddler, technically speaking, because Davis was officially mobile.

Currently he was reaching for the dog at Allison's feet, his hands opening and closing as he burbled something. He could speak, although Ben always wished the kid came with subtitles because he never understood a word.

"Is he saying gimmie?" Ben asked, "or live meat?"

"He's saying he wants you to grab him before I fall over!"

"Oh sorry." Ben took Davis, who looked extremely offended by this and quickly worked himself up into tears. "Uh..."

"He's fine," Allison said, twisting around until she was free of the leash. Then she brushed past him. "Air conditioning!" she moaned. "Ours broke down yesterday."

"Wow, that sucks," he said over the sound of wailing. "Can we switch?"

She handed him the leash and took Davis, walking with her son deeper into the house. Ben shut the door, then squatted to set Chinchilla loose. The dog wagged her stubby tail, noticed Davis watching her, and fled. Ben had never seen her move so fast as she disappeared around a corner.

"I think she likes it better at Marcello's place," Allison said. "I know he was in Japan, but doesn't he have—I don't know—servants who could have taken care of her?"

"Blame Tim," Ben said. "He wanted her to be with someone she knows, so—" He winced, because the wailing continued. "Would orange juice help?"

"You could shove an entire dinner roll in there and it wouldn't make a difference," Allison said. "Do you have a full-length mirror. He's really into his own reflection lately."

"In our bedroom," Bed said.

They made their way upstairs. Sure enough, when Allison set Davis on the carpet in front of the mirror, he was instantly mesmerized.

"Thank god," Allison said, sitting on the edge of the mattress. "It's a testament to the power of love that I would lay down my life for this little beast. In fact, I'm pretty sure he'll be what kills me. And soon."

Ben plopped down next to her. "You'll be fine," he said warmly. "Admit it, you love every second you get to spend with him."

"True," Allison said instantly. "Twisted, but definitely true. So anyway, tell me everything about the honeymoon!"

He did, even pulling out his phone to show her photos and videos, and while she was interested, she seemed to be expecting more. He soon found out why.

"So everything is okay?"

He nodded happily. "Yup!"

"Are you sure?"

Ben shrugged. "Yeah."

"No problems you need to discuss with me? You're not struggling with being married to someone other than Jace? You're not second-guessing yourself, or putting Tim through unfair comparisons?"

"Nope. I've got it all under control."

Allison narrowed her eyes. "Where is my best friend and what have you done with him?"

Ben laughed. "He's right here. You're not my therapist!"

"Could have fooled me," Allison said. "I don't like this. You're supposed to be the troubled and tortured one, not me."

"Are there problems you need to tell me about?" Ben inquired. "Go on, pretend this bed is one of those therapy couches."

Allison grinned, kicked off her sandals, and scooted back on the bed so she could recline. "I like this! Let's see. What sort of troubles do I have?"

Ben sat on the edge of the mattress and angled himself so he could still see her. "What about your son?"

"He's perfect," Allison said dismissively.

Ben nodded, pretending his palm was a notebook that he was writing in. "Patient is in denial." When she looked like she wanted to pounce, he quickly added, "Because nobody is perfect, although Davis is really *really* close." This pacified her enough that he could continue. "Let's talk about your relationship."

"Brian?" Allison asked. "Yes! We're overdue a bitching session about our spouses. Okay, let's see…" Her tongue was sticking out of the corner of her mouth as she tried to dredge up something bad about one of the nicest guys in the world. "I know! You won't believe what he said to me the other day. We were getting busy for the first time in weeks, and he comes at me with the following line." She held up her hands. "Brace yourself. He said, 'We don't have to have sex, honey. We can cuddle instead.'"

Ben scribbled furiously in his imaginary notebook. "Was he having performance issues?"

"No! He never does. We were both riled up and ready to go, so what the hell?" Her eyes shot over to where Davis was smearing the mirror with clammy hands. "Heck! What the heck."

"Tim said the same thing to me once," Ben admitted. "The timing was strange too because he was practically humping my leg."

"Practically?"

"Okay, literally, but I'm sure he meant well. I think our guys are just trying to tell us that—even though they love bedroom time—what they feel for us goes beyond the sexual. You know? Like they would still want us even without the sex. For most guys, I think that's a big deal."

"That might be true," Allison retorted, "but I *want* Brian to want me. I want him to go crazy and beg if I'm holding back the cookie jar. Not that I ever would."

"Cookie jar?" Ben repeated with a grimace.

"Oh stop. How many of your weird terms have I had to hear over the years? Especially with Tim. What did you call it? He's on the metric system?"

"The European standard," Ben said with an embarrassed chuckle. "And I didn't make that one up."

"You sure liked repeating it."

Ben eagerly changed the subject. "You and I have it good, don't we?"

"Oh absolutely," Allison said, stifling a yawn. "We have the best men imaginable, and now that we've settled down, we get to kick back and enjoy the rest of our lives with them."

"It's the 'rest' part that I've been thinking about lately." Ben abandoned playing therapist so he could scoot onto bed with her. "We've both been through a lot since we were teenagers. Now it feels like all the drama is over, and I'm asking myself what comes next. Everything feels so stable. I'm not used to that and don't know what to do."

"Enjoy it," Allison suggested. "And speak for yourself. My life consists of daily drama." She sat upright. "You should adopt again! A baby this time. Could you imagine? We'll raise our children together! How cute would that be?"

He leaned forward to check on Davis, who was now licking the mirror. "I'm not sure I'm ready. We're still focused on Jason and trying to figure all of that out."

"Smart decision," Allison said, relaxing again. "I just wanted someone to commiserate with. We could still share the experience. How about you start babysitting Davis overnight? That way we can compare notes, and I could get some sleep."

"I'm up for that," Ben said. "Do you want to take a nap?"

"No," Allison said, but her eyes were closed. "Maybe just for a few minutes…"

Ben smiled and slid off the bed. He approached Davis, who looked at him warily, like he was ready and willing to start crying without further notice. "Hey, little guy," Ben tried, reaching for him. "How would you like to go downstairs for a pudding cup?"

The face started to crumple.

"We could share it with Chinchilla," he added, mentally apologizing to the dog. "How's that sound? Do you want to help me give Chinchilla a treat?"

Davis reconsidered, his face breaking out into a gap-toothed grin. Instead of picking him up, Ben offered his hand and helped him stand. "Take a nap," he said to Allison. "We'll be okay."

His friend didn't respond. She was already softly snoring. Ben considered her fondly. Then he recorded a quick video to humiliate her with later, because that's what friends were for.

Goodbye. Tim hadn't expected that they would need to say it so soon. Just a month after the honeymoon, he and Ben were at the airport, hanging back to give Jason and William their privacy. Waiting with them was Kate, William's mother, who was already dabbing at tears. The young lovers stood in front of the security checkpoint, oblivious to the people impatiently swarming around them to reach their gates.

"I should have kept making babies," Kate said. "I should have made as many as this body could handle and home-schooled them all. If I had it to do over, I'd never let them leave the house."

The funny thing was, Tim could relate. He didn't want Jason to go and was thankful that day hadn't yet come. William was flying ahead to Astoria to set up their new life. Once he had, he would send for Jason. Just the idea tugged at his heartstrings. He could only imagine how much worse it was for Kate, who had carried a child for nine months and raised him every day for eighteen years and beyond. Tim was surprised how quickly a stranger had become family. He had always assumed that, if someone adopted, the child would need to be young for any sort of bond to form. This wasn't the case. He didn't care how ridiculous anyone found it. Jason was his son.

"I was thinking about locking ours in his room," Ben confided. "Just for a few years, maybe a decade. Or two. Then we'll let him out."

"Kidnapping my own child!" Kate said. "Now why didn't I think of that?"

"It's good you didn't," Ben said, "or William wouldn't have saved all those lives. You must be proud."

"Prouder than I ever imagined," Kate said, eyes watery as she watched her son. "That has made every second of missing and worrying about him worth it."

"He'll be fine," Tim said. "Good heart, good head—and man can he swim!"

The person in question looked in their direction, then waved them over. They walked as a group, Tim focusing on Jason, who appeared absolutely miserable. While the other two were busy saying goodbye to William, Tim moved closer to his son.

"You'll be all right," he said, putting an arm around Jason. "Just think of last time. You were facing four years of being apart! This time it'll be... what?"

"A month, maybe two," William said, having overheard. "I'll get things figured out up there, and then?" He smiled, waiting for a response.

Jason had a harder time matching his expression. "Then I'll fly to you and we'll be together."

"Exactly," William said, coming in for a hug.

Tim started to move away, but one of those big pale arms pulled him close as well.

"The rest of you get in here too," William said. "We're all family now. Or will be soon. Right?"

This was directed at Jason, who laughed and clamped his mouth shut with a shake of his head. This was a running joke between the two. Ever since William had proposed, Jason had declined to give his answer until four years were up, wanting to be certain. William didn't seem to mind, playfully attempting to find out sooner, despite everyone knowing what his answer would be. When it did happen, that would likely take their lives in all sorts of directions. For now, things were still simple and

Tim was content to wait, preferring to bask in the sensation of them all being together while he still could.

"Don't be mad at me."

Tim looked up from the painting he was working on, surprised by the figure standing in the doorway. Any visitor was unusual. Since he had bought the shed and converted it to a studio with William's help, it had become a private sanctuary. Ben occasionally poked his head in, asking if he was hungry or to let him know he was going somewhere. More often he texted, not wanting to disturb Tim's work. This was beneficial to his art, since interruptions could throw him off, although the current visitor was just what he needed.

"Stay there," he said to Jason, eyes darting over the silhouette of a body framed by outside light. He was tempted to take a photo, but that felt like cheating. Instead he checked the canvas. The painting was of Jason, standing much like he was now. William was down on one knee, holding up a life-saving medallion instead of a ring. The backdrop was an airport rather than their yard where the proposal had actually taken place. Tim wanted to superimpose the two events. The security checkpoint was represented by lifeless gray lines, the impassive crowd of travelers a blur of color moving around the only two static figures. "One more second," he said, looking up again and making a quick adjustment. "Okay."

Jason came the rest of the way inside, closing the door behind him. He looked around the space, no doubt taking in the mess of canvases, paint tubes, and drop cloths, but hey, that's what a studio was for. Behind him was the loveseat where Tim sometimes napped and a giant set of flat-file cabinets where he kept his best work. Jason moved closer, already straining his neck to see what he was working on, but Tim held up a hand to ward him off.

"Uh-uh. You know I don't let anyone see a work in progress."

Jason rolled his eyes and smiled, but worry soon weighed down his expression. "I need you to tell Ben something for me."

Tim set his brush aside. "Why?"

"Because you know how. And because it's easier to tell you because you're not perfect like he is. No offense."

"None taken," Tim said with a chuckle. "For the record, Ben

isn't perfect. He just looks that way when compared to me." The joke fell flat, the worried expression persisting, so he added, "What's going on?"

Jason broke eye contact. "I wrote William a letter."

Tim let this sink in. He considered different possibilities, but only one seemed likely. "You're bailing on your plans?"

His son nodded.

"Jason! Why?"

"Because!" Jason shot back, voice terse. "He's where he needs to be and so am I!"

Tim took a few deep breaths and shook his head. "You're not. You really aren't. You might have a good life here, but—"

"It's you," Jason said, voice croaking. "And Ben. That's who I belong with."

"Really?" Tim hated to do it, but he couldn't think of any better way of making his point. He grabbed the easel and turned it around so Jason could see the canvas. The bright blue eyes widened, then filled with tears. "That's who you belong with. Maybe not forever. Some relationships last, others don't, but until you've given it a shot, I bet you won't be happy."

Jason shook his head. "You don't understand."

"I do about this, because I was dumb enough to say goodbye to Ben once, and I spent a long time regretting that decision. Don't make the same mistake."

"It's more complicated than that," Jason said, trying to glare his tears out of existence.

"Then we'll figure it out," Tim said. "Together. Until then, don't send the letter."

Jason continued to glower. "I already did. Last week."

"Do you know if he's gotten it?"

Jason nodded sullenly, pulled out his phone, and held it up. Tim came closer to read the screen. The most recent text from William was short.

Four years.

Tim sighed. He had already watched Jason go through a period of separation that long and had seen how miserable it made him. The clouds only disappeared when William returned for brief visits. Even when Jason had tried to move on, and seemed to, he wasn't as happy. Not like he'd been during their most recent time together.

"We need to talk to Ben about this."

Jason nodded. "I couldn't figure out how to tell him. I figured… You've made a lot of mistakes."

"Thanks!"

"Sorry, but you know the best way to do it without him getting mad."

Tim thought about it. "That usually involves me being shirtless, which somehow, I don't think is going to work for you."

"Definitely not."

"He'll be upset," Tim said, "but he won't be angry. I promise. You really should tell him yourself, *but*… I suppose I can do it for you. Just this once."

"Are you going to take your shirt off first?"

"Oh hell yes," Tim said. "This one might require the full monty. I'll tell him when I get out of the shower."

"Thanks." Jason nodded to the canvas. "Do I really look so scrawny next to William?"

"You complement each other. You'll be depriving the world of something beautiful if you don't change your mind."

Jason wasn't swayed. He could be stubborn, and when he was, nothing could move him. Not even Ben. For this situation, they would need reinforcements.

"Welcome to your—" Allison sized them up. "—first of many family counselling sessions."

Tim resisted a groan. Allison was rarely wrong, and while he wasn't looking forward to this becoming a regular occurrence, he would do whatever was necessary to get Jason's life back on track. Not that his son seemed pleased about the situation.

"There's going to be more than one of these?" Jason complained, arms crossed over his chest.

"She's only kidding," Ben said calmly. "Aren't you?"

"I'm in for as many as it takes," Tim said.

Jason slumped deeper into his chair. "Some of us have to work."

"I work!" Tim shot back. "Who do you think is paying for this?"

"He didn't mean it like that," Ben said, "but your schedule is a lot more flexible than either of ours."

"And that means I shouldn't have a positive attitude?"

"No, but you know he's only—"

A fluttering noise followed by a thwack attracted their attention. Allison had tossed her notebook into the air and it had landed in the center of the circle. Or the square, since there were four chairs, each facing the middle.

"That's better," Allison said, rising briefly to fetch the notebook. "There aren't a lot of rules for what we're about to do. Don't interrupt when someone else is speaking. You'll each have your turn. The one exception is when this hand goes up." She raised it to demonstrate. "That means you stop talking and listen to me. Any questions so far?"

They eyed each other and shook their heads.

"Good." Allison's lips twitched. "One more thing before we begin. I just want to say how happy I am that things have returned to normal. I've been getting a lot more sleep lately, and Ben is back to needing me. Just how it's supposed to be."

"Are you seriously gloating?" Ben asked, fighting down a smile of his own. "Don't act like things are perfect at home. Brian told me that he's losing what little hair he's got left."

"Blame an excess of testosterone, not stress," Allison replied. "I like my men virile."

"Are you saying mine's not, because—"

"Guys," Tim said. "Can we focus?"

"Professional," Allison murmured to herself. "Right. Sorry." She cleared her throat. "Now then, Jason, we're here because we all care about you. We have the best intentions, but only you get to decide what path your life takes. All we can do is offer our advice. With that in mind, why don't you explain the situation to us."

Jason's arms remained crossed, but now he seemed more like he was hugging himself. "William moved to Oregon to return to active duty, which I want. I was supposed to go with him, but—" His eyes darted first to Ben, then to Tim. "My home is in Austin."

"One of your homes," Allison said. "It's possible to have more than one. Ben and I are from The Woodlands, and even though we haven't lived there since our high school days, I still consider it home. Don't you?"

"Yes," Ben said. "Absolutely."

"Tim, do you still feel like Kansas is home?"

No, not at all, but he nodded along anyway. "Yup."

"So there you go. Even though we all live in Austin and consider it home, we're still capable of returning to a different one."

"I'm sorry for asking this," Jason said. "I don't mean it to sound harsh, but did The Woodlands feel less like home after your father died?"

"Yes," Allison said instantly. "It sure did. Less so when my mother died. Once they were both gone, I didn't feel as anchored. You've been through that too, haven't you?"

"Yeah," Jason said. "I also know what it's like to be taken from my home and not be allowed to return."

"We would never do that to you," Ben said. "Ever! You'll always be welcome here."

"Then why are you pushing me away?"

Ben's mouth moved, too shocked to speak, so he looked to Allison for guidance.

"Tell him how you feel," she suggested.

"I love you," Ben said to Jason.

"I know," Jason responded. "I love you too, but I don't get—"

"I'm trying to help you!"

"We both are," Tim added.

Allison held up her hand. "Ben, what you said is good, but try telling him how this situation in particular makes you feel."

Ben leaned back in his chair, eyes unfocused as he seemed to search for the right words. "It feels like I'm holding you back," he said. "When you first came into our lives, the goal was to help you get back on your feet. Now you are, but you're scared to use them."

Allison looked at him. "Tim?"

"I just want you to be happy."

"I *am* happy," Jason stressed.

Tim shook his head. "Not as much as you could be. When you're with William, it's like you're on drugs. Wait, *are* you on drugs?"

Jason laughed. "I get why you guys worry, but I've got it figured out. I've thought about this. It's not like I made the decision while drunk and emotional one night."

"Then explain your reasoning to us so we can understand," Allison said.

Jason nodded. "William and I have been apart before. Four

years." He clenched his jaw and had to collect himself. "Nothing changed between us. We still felt the same way, so we'll be fine."

"He could meet someone," Ben said. "I never thought that anyone could get to me like Tim did, but then I met Jace. You know I love Tim! With all of my heart, so imagine my surprise when it turned out I could love more than one person. I agree that William won't stop loving you, but what if he meets someone else he loves too? Someone who can be there physically and not just emotionally."

"Then I'll wait," Jason said, looking to Tim. "Like you did."

"Trust me," he said. "That gets old. You think four years is bad? Try ten! And no matter how nice the new guy is, it's still absolute torture."

"Was it?" Ben asked, looking concerned.

Allison raised her hand. "Let's stay focused. You lovebirds can rub beaks later. So it sounds to me, Jason, that you feel like William is a sure thing."

"Yeah. He won't stop loving me."

"Okay. Are you implying that Ben and Tim will stop loving you?"

Jason looked to them both again, this time with a guilty expression. "Yes."

"We will *never*—" Ben began, but the almighty hand of Allison cut him off.

"Please explain to us why you think that Ben and Tim might stop loving you."

"Because that's what people do," Jason said. "I know you don't want to believe it, Ben. We've talked about this, and maybe you're right, but that's romantic love. It's stronger. People always act like—" Jason turned to Allison. "Would you do anything for Davis? Would you die for him?"

"Without a second thought," she replied.

"Why?"

"Because I'm his mother."

Jason nodded as if satisfied. "And if someone was hurting him. If Brian started drinking again and started hitting Davis—"

"That isn't fair," Ben protested.

"It's fine," Allison said. "I think I see where you're going with this, Jason, but why don't you expound for us. Tell us about your experience."

"You all know the story," Jason said. "I was taken away from my mom because her boyfriend was abusing me. But she didn't come save me. She didn't ditch him and get clean so she could have me back. And I know none of you believe this, but she was a good mother. She loved me! At least up to a certain point. I don't know what happened after that. She gave birth to me, raised me with love, and still abandoned me. I wasn't the only one. I met tons of kids in foster care in the same situation, so I'm not going to screw this up." Jason's chin trembled. "William will keep loving me, even if I can't be with him, and I know you're disappointed in me now, but I'll make it up to you, so—" His voice cracked and he started crying.

Ben rose instantly and went to him, massaging Jason's shoulders and whispering comforting words. Then he looked to Allison for help.

She nodded, like everything was under control. Tim hoped she knew what she was doing, because he was feeling down now too. He couldn't help wondering if Jason was right. His own parents weren't great. Tim hadn't realized how emotionally starved he was until he met Ben. He knew that Allison's father hadn't been a good parent either. He drank too much and was abusive. Ben's parents were amazing, but not all were. Jason wasn't being unreasonable. Some people loved conditionally, and only if they got their own way.

"Bad things happen," Allison said. "None of us can deny that, but we can't allow misfortune to stop us from living our lives. Cast your mind back a few years. Jason, you and Ben were eating breakfast when that little… when Ryan broke into the house with a gun. What happened was horrific. I wasn't even there, and I still didn't feel safe in my own home afterwards. The experience had to be even more traumatic for you all. Tell me, did you ever eat breakfast in that kitchen again?"

They nodded in unison.

"Why?"

Tim knew the answer, but the question wasn't directed at him. Instead he waited for Jason to figure it out.

"At first because I wanted to protect you guys, in case it happened again." Jason furrowed his brow. "I might not be very tough, but I wouldn't let him shoot anyone. I'd do whatever it takes."

"You wanted to take care of your family," Allison said approvingly. "Is there another reason you kept eating breakfast in that same kitchen?"

Jason nodded. "I didn't want to upset Ben, so I put on a brave face. I knew if I acted like everything was normal, he wouldn't worry as much."

Allison leaned back. "To summarize, something bad happened, but you didn't let that stop you from doing what you needed to do. Did that get you shot? How many other Ryans have broken into the house since then? Four? Five?"

"None," Jason said with a chuckle. "I get what you're saying. Ben and Tim aren't the same as my mom. They might not do what she did, but isn't it smart to learn from bad things when they happen?"

"Yes. It's okay to be cautious, as long as it doesn't make you paralyzed."

"I'm not," Jason said. "I moved out on my own."

"He did really good too," Tim said. "We kept guilt-tripping him to stay, but it didn't work."

Jason smiled. "It nearly did."

"That's excellent," Allison said. "So you're able to live away from Ben and Tim without feeling like it will jeopardize your relationship with them."

"We're still in the same city," Jason said. "The same state."

"There's a big difference between Texas and Oregon," Allison said amiably. "That makes sense. Do you ever get so busy with work and friends that you don't see Ben and Tim as often as you'd like? Has, oh I don't know, a week gone by that way?"

Jason nodded. "Yeah, but we still text and stuff. And I know they're not far away."

"Good." Allison made a quick note. "So if you're comfortable spending a week apart, as you've already proven, maybe you would be willing to do so again?"

Jason shrugged. "Sure."

Allison's face remained neutral, but Tim swore he could see a gleam of victory in her eyes. "Right now you're facing a lot of unknowns. Nobody could blame you for being apprehensive about visiting a new state. Why don't you take a week off and go up there? You'll get to see William and spend time with him. Even if you decide to stay in Austin permanently, at least you'll know what Astoria looks like. You won't have to imagine where he lives. You'll have seen it for yourself. Wouldn't that be comforting?"

"Yeah," Jason admitted, seeming open to the idea.

"Excellent," Allison said. "Now then, does anyone have a question they want to ask or something else they need to say? We'll take turns. Let's start with you again, Jason."

The therapy session went on, but Tim's focus kept returning to Jason. He had never realized how much they had in common, how they both came from broken homes, albeit in different ways. Going forth, no matter what Jason decided for himself, Tim was determined to be there for him. Not only to love him in a way his own father never had, but to guide him toward the happiness Tim had found, and that he knew Jason could discover too.

Chapter Three

Christmas had come around again, which couldn't be right, because Ben swore the last one was only a few months ago. Had each year gotten shorter? Had someone trimmed days off the calendar without him noticing? He could still remember being young, when a year had felt like an eternity. Ben supposed that, to someone who was ten, a year was a significant portion of their life. Now it was just a sliver of his own. He refused to do the math. Not with forty looming so close.

Instead he considered the house. He hadn't gone overboard this year, keeping the decorations confined to the living room. Tim had wanted to string up lights on the roof and put creepy animatronic robots on the lawn, including a life-sized Santa who supposedly danced, but to Ben's eye, looked more like he was thrusting. The live display at a hardware store had given him flashbacks to Chuck E. Cheese's and its nightmarish singing animals, so he talked Tim out of it, which wasn't easy. His husband insisted this might be their last family Christmas for a while. Ben had his doubts.

Jason wasn't making progress. In fact, he seemed to be getting worse. Ben had seen him go through this when William first joined the Coast Guard. Jason would throw himself into his work and try to keep himself as occupied as possible. During the rare instances when he had time off, he would be depressed until he found a new distraction. Today would be rough on Jason. With both the pet store he managed and the shelter where he volunteered closed, he would be forced to think about the man he missed. Even worse was that William wasn't able to come home for the holidays, still too low in the pecking order of his new air station. Maritime accidents didn't take a day off, and the Coast Guard couldn't either. Ben almost wished he had let Tim go overboard with the holiday festivities, but then again, this could be for the best. Jason feeling sad might finally motivate him to take action.

"Can we open some presents now?"

This was asked by Tim, who stood next to the Christmas tree in the living room. He wore a cream sweater with navy blue snowflakes the same color as his jeans. The scene looked like something from a catalog, complete with model. Ben pulled out his phone and snapped a photo, Tim's expression increasingly impatient.

"Wait until Jason gets here."

"Just one present," Tim pleaded, putting on his best smile. "Or two."

"Do you see any presents with your name under the tree?"

"No," Tim said, his grin widening. "I wonder why."

"You must have been a naughty boy." Ben went to the kitchen to check on the food. He had prepped a number of dishes in advance, easy things like scalloped potatoes that he knew he couldn't mess up. A ham waited in the oven, already cooked to perfection, thanks to the grocery store where he had bought it. Ben wanted to enjoy the holiday instead of stressing, and he didn't have the best record with meat. He was tempted to go vegetarian, just so he never had to deal with it again.

"He's here!" Tim cried out, sounding like a little kid who had spotted Santa Claus.

Ben felt excited too. Jason keeping himself busy meant that they hadn't seen each other much. The irony wasn't lost on Ben. Jason refused to leave town so he could stay close to them, but the emotional turmoil of not leaving town made him work hard enough that they didn't see each other anyway. This had to stop. Today.

They met Jason in the entryway, where he was treated like a star. Chinchilla hopped around his legs, Tim had him trapped in a hug, and Ben fussed with getting his jacket off and hung up.

"Too much love!" Jason said, laughing at their antics.

Tim finally released him. "We're just excited you're here so we can finally open presents."

"Oh man," Jason said, turning around. "I left mine in the car."

"I'll go get them," Tim offered.

"No!" Ben and Jason shouted at the same time.

Tim seemed puzzled by this. Was he already suspicious?

"I'll get them," Jason said. "I had the heater turned up too high and that coat is crazy thick. I need to cool down."

Tim remained confused. "If you're sure."

"Let's get Chinchilla started on her stocking," Ben suggested.

"Oh right! Yeah!" Tim excitedly moved toward the living room, whistling for Chinchilla to follow.

Once they were far enough away, Ben whispered, "Did you park the car?"

Jason nodded. "Behind the garage, just like you said."

"Perfect."

"Do you think he knows?" Jason asked.

"He thinks he knows, and that's what will make it all the more delicious."

Jason laughed and nodded toward the interior. "Better keep him distracted."

"I will," Ben said, but concern had his feet glued down. "Are you doing okay?"

"Yeah!" Jason said, his upbeat tone sounding false. "Great!" Then his shoulders relaxed and he seemed more himself. "It's good to be home."

"It's good to have you here," Ben said. "Hurry back."

He went to find Tim, who was on the floor with Chinchilla, a slew of dog toys and treats surrounding them. Once again he had gone overboard.

"Did you use Jason's store discount?" Ben asked.

"Yes dear," Tim droned. "Now stop worrying about money and get over here. It's Christmas!"

His grin was infectious. Ben only paused to stream holiday music from his phone to the stereo system. Then he sat next to his husband. Jason soon joined them. They tore through presents, Tim patient through all of this. He received new cologne from Jason, which was a running joke between them, ever since the time Tim had refused to share his. He also got a stocking that Ben had stuffed full of little knickknacks, but nothing too substantial. That was it. Tim mostly sat and smiled as they opened their presents from him, like a pair of three-hundred dollar sunglasses that Ben had discovered at the mall but refused to buy due to the extravagant price. Some of Tim's other presents were a little odd though, like a rainbow-striped beach towel, or an individually wrapped bottle of sunscreen.

"I'm beginning to detect a theme here," Ben said.

"Really?" Tim asked, handing over another box.

Ben opened it. Inside was a wooden instrument.

"A ukulele!" Jason cried, snatching it from him. "So cool!"

"It's yours," Ben said. "I have a feeling it's not the real present."

"I'm taking you to Hawaii," Tim murmured, expression amorous. "You said you wanted to go on a trip with me. I didn't buy tickets yet so we can plan it together, but I'll take care of everything else."

"I love it," Ben said, leaning forward to kiss him. "I love you!"

"Hawaii!" Jason said, sounding excited. "Can I go too?"

"No kids this time," Tim said, wagging a finger. "You guys cramp my style."

The joke about the honeymoon was just enough of a reference to William for Jason to grow somber.

"Here," Ben said, reaching for a thin flat package. "This one is for you."

Jason opened it, his expression a little wounded when he saw the homemade present. Ben had a feeling it was the subject, rather than the quality of the gift, that had him upset. He had wanted to buy a travel guide, but Astoria wasn't exactly a tourist destination, so Ben had settled for doing research online and printing out a book of his own. He wasn't *that* cheap though. "Look at the bookmark."

Jason flipped through folded and stapled pages until he reached an envelope. Confused, he opened it and examined the contents. "A flight?"

"Just a visit," Ben assured him. "We thought you'd like to go see William, especially since he hasn't managed to visit Austin lately."

"I don't know if I can get time off."

"Which is why we booked it for two months from now," Tim said.

They had anticipated this response. Jason always used his work as an excuse.

"February fourteenth?" Jason said incredulously. "Valentine's Day?"

"That's the day you normally spend with the person you love," Ben said, "although most people look happier about the prospect."

Jason was sitting cross-legged, the tip of one foot thumping the floor nervously as he nibbled his lip and stared at the airline ticket. The words must have finally sunk in because he looked up and laughed. "I'm ridiculous, aren't I?"

"Just a little," Ben said warmly. "I know it's a surprise, but I hope you like the idea."

"I love it," Jason said, seeming determined now to be positive. "Thanks! I love you guys!"

"We love you too," Ben said.

"Yup," Tim agreed, eyes on the tree. "Sooo..."

"I think there's one thing for you here," Ben said, reaching for a card.

It wasn't anything special, or even store-bought. Much like Jason's present, Ben had created it on the computer and printed it out. Tim looked excited when he saw the image on the front. A black muscle car. A Dodge Camaro, to be precise.

"A Dodge Challenger!" Tim enthused.

Close enough. They had discussed the vehicle earlier in the year, Tim saying he wanted it for Christmas. Ben didn't have that kind of money. Sure they shared a bank account and everything else they owned, but they both knew that Ben's paycheck wasn't enough to pay for most cars, especially a new one. Tim had countered by saying he only wanted permission, so that's what Ben had decided to give him. The card contained a single word inside. *Permission*.

The thing was, Tim hadn't waited for permission. He had already bought the car in secrecy. That didn't bother Ben in the slightest, but he still wanted to have some fun.

Tim hopped to his feet. "I've got another surprise for you guys!"

"Really?" Ben asked, pretending to be confused. "What?"

"Get your jackets on and I'll show you!"

Ben exchanged a covert glance with Jason, who looked equally amused. Then they resumed their act. They went to the entryway, got bundled up, and followed Tim outside.

"Where are we going?" Ben asked. "Tell me you didn't buy that dancing Santa!"

"Nope!" Tim led them around the house, keeping outside the privacy fence and following it to where the woods began. They didn't have to travel deep to find a tarp on the ground, obscured by pine needles and dried leaves, and too flat to hide anything but the earth beneath it. Tim rushed toward this, picking up one corner and spinning around. "Where did it go? Oh man. Oh fuck!"

"What's wrong?" Ben asked.

"The new car! I bought it last week and hid it out here so—" He noticed Ben's expression and dropped the tarp. "You knew."

"I heard you park it back here," Ben said. "I was in the yard with Chinchilla. I thought someone was hunting on our land."

"Did you take it back to the dealership?" Tim looked crestfallen. "I only bought it early because I knew you would let me. I wanted to have it today. Hey... Where's Jason?"

Ben spun around. Their son was nowhere in sight. He was starting to wonder if the flight to Oregon had been a grave miscalculation when they heard an engine revving closer to the house. Jason had decided to reveal the surprise in a grand fashion!

"It's out front?" Tim said, looking first gleeful, then concerned. "No way! He is *not* driving my new car!"

Tim took off in a sprint. Ben laughed and then gave chase. The Dodge Challenger was parked outside the house and freshly washed. Jason had made sure of that, taking it to a place to be detailed. Every surface gleamed like it had just rolled out of the factory. A few other details had changed too.

"The plates!" Tim said, noticing them. "How did you get them so soon? Oh my god."

He had noticed the vanity license plates. Ben was particularly proud of this touch, since they looked cool. Unlike the boring white plates with black letters and numbers, these were much more stylish. The background was black, a large white star intruding from the right. As for the personalized characters Ben chose, he only had six to work with and had settled on GRDITO.

"Gordito!" Tim declared. His childhood nickname. "I love it!"

"I wanted to give you something more than just permission," Ben explained.

He had paid attention during the many times Tim raved about what he would do if he got a new car. Ben always pretended not to care, merely grunting in response, when really he had been making a mental list of all the accessories Tim wanted.

"Rubber floor mats!"

A special kind created from digital scans of the car, so they not only fit perfectly, but protected every inch of the floorboards. Ben had chosen air fresheners that plugged into the vents, bought emergency equipment for the trunk, and even splurged on a performance tuner, which was some sort of little computer that did something. Whatever it was, it sure made Tim happy! After rummaging around in the interior and declaring his excitement over and over again, Tim finally climbed out of the car with shiny eyes.

Then he noticed Ben standing there and tried to play it cool. He leaned against the car and jerked his head toward it. "So... What do you think?"

"It's a very sexy car," Ben admitted.

"Yeah, but..." Tim jerked his head toward the car again and winked.

"What?"

"Black sports car. Me. Bring back any memories?" Tim managed to swagger just by shifting his weight to the other foot.

Ben tried to roll his eyes but they refused, too charmed by the display. "It does remind me of this teenage guy I had a crush on. Not that he ever noticed me."

"Oh he did," Tim said. "Probably was too scared to ask if you wanted to go for a ride."

"O-kay," Jason said, eyes wide. "I'll be inside with Chinchilla. You guys have fun. Or whatever."

"We're not going to do it in the car," Ben laughed. "You can go for a ride with us."

"That's okay," Jason said. "I promised William a video call. I'm not sure if I'm going to tell him about the plane tickets yet. Maybe I'll surprise him."

"Mm-hm," Ben said distractedly. When Tim turned up the heat—with a mere gaze!—those silver eyes were practically hypnotic.

"I'm definitely outta here," Jason said, making a hasty retreat.

Tim sauntered around to the passenger side and opened the door. "What do you say, Benjamin?"

"Just have me back before curfew!" Ben said, climbing inside the vehicle.

Once the door was shut behind him, he breathed in, happy he had chosen a musky scent. Manly. The interior was slick, black with subtle red accents, such as the seatbelt straps. Ben settled into the bucket seat and had to admit he was impressed. The Bentley that Tim used to drive (and had promised to sell) was nice, but felt too stately. It seemed more suited to Marcello than a cocky guy who often forgot that he wasn't twenty anymore.

"Nice," Tim said, sliding into the driver's seat and caressing the steering wheel.

"What's SRT stand for?" Ben asked, noticing the letters on the dashboard.

"Street racing technology."

"Oh! Great! You can race it right back to the dealership."

Tim chuckled. "I'm not racing this baby anywhere. I love her too much. No risks."

"I like the sound of that," Ben said. "If you're telling the truth." He braced himself as Tim started the car and put it into drive, but his husband kept his word. They cruised at a reasonable speed down the drive and onto the street.

"This feels good," Tim said, gripping the steering wheel and grinning. "I don't want to be one of those sad people who try to stay young by buying a sexy-as-hell car, but..."

Ben shook his head. "But?"

"Never mind. That's exactly who I want to be!"

He pressed down on the pedal. The car shot forward. Ben was momentarily terrified until adrenaline shot through him and, like a rollercoaster ride, he found himself caught up in the thrill. The roads were fairly empty anyway, most people inside and enjoying the festivities. It certainly didn't hurt that they lived outside the city. They cruised around, Tim trying out different settings and pushing buttons while grinning gleefully.

"I take it you didn't drive the car much before now?"

"I drove it straight home from the dealership," Tim said. "Didn't even take it for a test drive first. Salesman probably thought I was crazy."

"He probably thought you were a dream come true," Ben said. "He's not the only one."

Tim shot him an appreciative smile. "It's funny what you said earlier. About how we're not going to do it in the car. Do you remember saying the same thing when we were teenagers? That always seemed weird to me. We did it everywhere else."

"I was sick of you making me duck anytime you thought you saw someone from our school. That's why."

"Oh. Sorry."

"Ancient history," Ben said. "I didn't want to give you any ideas. A way to keep me hidden and get laid at the same time? You never would have let me come up for air!"

Silver eyes met his, questioning. "And now?"

Ben laughed. "I should have seen that coming."

"You still can," Tim said.

Ben bit his bottom lip. "These seats aren't really designed for that."

Tim hit a button, reclining just enough that his lower body was more available. "Better?"

"It'll do," Ben said, looking around once for any police cars before undoing his seatbelt and leaning over. "Just keep your eyes on the road," he said while unbuttoning the jeans.

"You know why they call me Gordito?" Tim asked, voice husky.

"Because you were a fat baby?" Ben retorted.

"Yeah, but the nickname still fits. Wouldn't you say?"

Ben pulled down on the underwear's elastic band, reaching in to pull Tim's cock free. It certainly was beefy! Not the thickest Ben had ever seen. That honor went to some guy in college, and while it had made an impression visually, it had also hurt his jaw and definitely wouldn't fit anywhere else. Ben greatly preferred what Tim had. He rolled back the foreskin, admiring the russet head. Ben pumped a few times. Tim lifted his hips so his jeans and underwear could be shimmied down. Then Ben went to town.

He had done this thousands of times over the years. Maybe not in the car, but sex with Tim only got better. That had everything to do with love. Little had changed between them physically. They had always been compatible in this way, but the deeper they got into their relationship, the more Ben's affection for him grew. This resulted in pure infatuation. He had always been crazy about Tim's body, and despite them getting older and more flawed, he only found Tim that much more attractive. He hoped that would always continue. Ben already felt like he could do this all day.

"Jesus," Tim said, gasping. "Go easy! You're like a vacuum cleaner!"

"Watch the road," Ben reminded him before continuing his work. He allowed himself to play more, caressing the balls, biting the base of the cock playfully, or just stroking while using the tip of his tongue to make sure the head stayed lubed. Maybe it was his imagination, but the car seemed to be picking up speed.

"Uh," Tim said. "Don't get any on the seats. Actually—" He pressed down on Ben's head, forcing himself deeper inside. "—you better swallow."

Ben *always* swallowed. Unless he wanted to see. Still, having Tim tell him to do so, hand still on his head as he began to thrust, was a huge turn on. The car was definitely going faster, but Ben couldn't exactly tell him to slow down. Instead he reached out and thumped Tim's right leg until he got the message.

"Okay okay," Tim said, the car slowing. Then his hand pressed down harder, just before he exploded in Ben's mouth. Straight down his throat, in fact. Ben was too much of a pro for this to trip him up. Running out of oxygen was his only concern. After a few more thrusts and a long groan, Tim relented. "Seriously," he said, not pulling out completely. "I need you to swallow every single drop."

Ben glared and freed his mouth long enough to say, "You're lucky I think this is hot!" Then he kept going, making sure that Tim was drained and clean.

"I'm the lucky one," Tim said, still moaning. "Yeah. Definitely the lucky one!"

Once Ben had him put away and the jeans zipped, he sat up. "We should do that more often."

"Deal!" Tim said, chuckling madly. Then he glanced over at him, eyes lingering on the bulge in his pants. "Wanna take the wheel? You just gotta tell me when to speed up and when to break."

"You're not going to blow me from the driver's seat!" Ben said. "Don't worry about me. I'm fine. Sometimes it's fun to keep wanting." After they rounded a corner he added, "Unless you want me to drive. That could work."

"Uhhh," Tim said, the limits of his love clearly tested. "Your car has so many dings!"

"So? You've got insurance, right?"

"Yeah," Tim said grudgingly. "I do."

Ben sniffed, as if hurt. "I guess we don't feel the same way about each other."

"We do!" Tim said, hitting the turn signal and starting to pull over. "You can drive it all the time if you want."

Ben laughed and reached for the wheel, gently guiding the car back to the center of the road. "I just wanted you to say I could."

"You really can," Tim said, even more eager now that he knew Ben wasn't likely to accept.

"It's fine," Ben assured him. "But the next time you're a passenger in my car…"

"I'm up for that!" Tim said with a grin. A moment later, he reached over to take Ben's hand. "This is what I want for Jason, you know? Not just the sexual stuff, which I definitely do *not* think about him doing, but the simple things too. Going for a drive together, or messing with each other, like when you moved the car from where I hid it. When we're together, everything is fun. Even the boring stuff."

"It is pretty awesome," Ben agreed. "What did you think of his reaction to the tickets? He seemed upset at first."

"Yeah, he did. But then you made him realize he's being silly. That'll probably keep happening until he's up there. Then he'll realize how good it feels to be with William and he'll stay."

"I hope you're right," Ben said, although if he was truthful, not all of him wanted that. The logical part that understood what was best, yes, and most of his heart too. But not all of it.

Tim pulled up to the mansion, the automatic gates clattering shut behind him. He ignored the large garage and the paved parking area, instead cruising up to the entrance. The car windows were down, allowing in the first temperate weather of the new year, although the evening was growing chilly. Tim parked and trotted up to the large front doors to let himself in.

Marcello didn't have a butler. That had always seemed weird, since the man hired maids and groundskeepers and called in private chefs like other people ordered pizzas. Then again, butlers were all about rules and enforcing them, which went against the philosophy of the person living here. Marcello was more trouble than a teenager, despite being many *many* decades beyond that age. He had even managed to get Tim arrested recently, although the charges had been dropped, so no harm done.

As Tim closed the doors behind him, he chuckled to himself and shook his head. No harm done? He always let Marcello get away with murder—not literally, as far as he knew—and that had everything to do with Eric Conroy. Mentor, savior, father figure, and the second greatest love of his life. Eric had been a lot of things to him, and his death had left a void in Tim's life that he thought would never be filled. No doubt Marcello felt the same, having lost his dearest friend too. That had given them enough in common to start a relationship of their own, and they now shared a longer history than Tim had with Eric. That was a strange thought, but not a sad one, since he valued their friendship like nothing else.

Tim had missed the big guy. This was Marcello's second recent trip to Japan. This one had lasted three weeks, but to Tim, it felt much longer than that. He paused in an entryway larger than his master bedroom. He stood still long enough to listen for Marcello and heard light music ahead, so that's the direction Tim went.

He entered the living room at the rear of the house, the one with tall windows that provided a view of the pool and, farther out, Austin's sparkling skyline. The lighting here was low, hidden LEDs providing a warm orange glow. Now that Tim could hear the music better, he recognized it as Barry White. What really drew his attention was the voluptuous form on the couch, draped in a pale green silk robe, the white floral pattern unmistakably Japanese.

"Why, hello there," Marcello said seductively as he rose gracefully and slinked toward him.

"Hello yourself," Tim said, voice husky, as he too moved forward.

As soon as they were close enough to touch, they both laughed and threw their arms around each other.

"I'm so glad you're back!" Tim enthused.

"No matter how delightful the distractions in Japan," Marcello replied, "my heart belongs in Austin with you. How could I not return?"

Pure flattery, but also the way Marcello expressed his affection.

"Come," the large man said, gesturing to the couch. "Join me for a drink."

"I'm driving," Tim said.

"And I'm pouring," Marcello replied. "I'll make sure you get home safely."

"Japanese champagne?" Tim asked, eyeing the bottle and glasses curiously.

"Saké," Marcello said, twisting off the bottle's cap and pouring. "On previous trips, I discovered that while saké is an acquired taste, it isn't one I necessarily long for. Then, during my most recent travels, a young man—my goodness, he was delicious—introduced me to this latest trend. Sparkling saké! Here, I'm dying to know what you think."

Marcello handed him a glass, then sat back on the couch. Tim joined him. After clinking rims, he took a sip. The drink had a faintly milky taste, but he already liked it more than he did normal saké.

"It's good!" he said, following up with a braver gulp.

"Everything is better with bubbles, wouldn't you agree? I dare say I have carbonation to thank for my bubbly personality. My trip took a turn for the better after this little discovery. Not just because of the companionship which filled that particular night, although it certainly didn't hurt. But no, it was this ambassador of drinks which helped bridge any cultural gaps. The sparkling saké flowed like wine, and a number of very lucrative deals were made."

"That's awesome!" Tim said, raising his glass again. "Just tell me you aren't moving there."

"Ah," Marcello replied enigmatically. "Wouldn't that be something?"

Tim frowned. "If that's where this conversation is headed, at least wait until I finish the first drink."

"You'll get no argument from me," Marcello said, taking another sip. "I heard you stopped by the studio while I was gone."

Studio Maltese, the headquarters of Marcello's media empire. Officially he dealt in photography, although his future successor, Nathaniel, had the studio increasingly involved in video production. The respectable kind, like commercials and online content designed to go viral.

"Was there something you needed?" Marcello added.

"I might have missed you," Tim said. "A little bit. You should have seen Nathaniel. Dude was a mess."

"Oh?"

"Yup. He was totally stressed and said that you never look like you're doing much while you're at the office, but that you must be holding back the tide somehow because he was drowning."

Marcello barked laughter. "Never let the blood show."

"Huh?"

"Charles Eames," Marcello explained. "One of the greatest designers of the twentieth century, along with his wife, Ray. No matter how badly the audience wishes to know the manner in which a magician performs his tricks, it's always better to maintain the mystery. I'll be opening a new studio in Japan."

Marcello said this casually. No abracadabra or waving of a wand. His sleight-of-hand was too good for anything so showy.

"I'm ready for a refill," Tim said after draining his glass.

Marcello reached for the bottle. "Always take your pleasure seriously. Another of Eames' little gems, one I've made part of my personal philosophy."

Tim didn't reply. He was too busy trying to imagine what Austin would be like without Marcello. Forget the city. The idea that really upset him was his friend moving away. At times Jason's refusal to leave Texas seemed childish, but on an emotional level, Tim understood. He also wanted the people he loved to remain as close to him as possible.

"Don't appear so downtrodden," Marcello said. "I meant it when I said my heart belongs here."

"So you're not moving to Japan?"

Marcello cocked his head. "I'm tempted to lie, simply so that darling expression of yours will remain. But no. This client is impressed by my business model and wishes to replicate it, with my help."

"Including the escort service? And the porn movies?"

Marcello tittered happily. "I only wish. No, they are blissfully unaware of that aspect."

"This is big," Tim said. "It could mean a lot of things."

"I'm aware of that," Marcello said. "Why do you sound more concerned than excited?"

"Because if you set up a studio for them, they won't need you anymore."

"Not quite," Marcello said, his expression sly. "While I'll admit some details have been lost in translation, what they truly desire is a studio accessible to the community. Keep in mind, this client was once the market leader for photography equipment. No doubt they have plenty of studios of their own, but the media they produce is too technical. It lacks artistic flair or the more guerilla photography of today's youth. The current generation is content with the cameras in their phones, and it is hoped that a community studio will allow them to come into contact with more sophisticated— Yes?"

Tim had raised his hand, feeling like he was in another family therapy session with Allison. "You lost me. Give me the 'our plane is about to crash and we've got two minutes left to live' version."

"In that scenario, I'm not certain I'd be interested in talking," Marcello said, letting his eyes wander. "Very well, when we were young, the latest fashion or hottest cars helped determine status and popularity. These days, it's how many followers you have on Instagram. What better way to get the upper hand on your peers than with superior photo equipment in a studio designed to be—forgive me, this isn't my choice of words—selfie heaven."

Tim thought about it and laughed. "Sorry, I'm just trying to imagine Uncle Marcello surrounded by dozens of Japanese teenagers as you teach them how to take a decent photo."

"Hundreds of teenagers. Perhaps even thousands. The budget and scope for this project is monumental. That's why I need your help."

"I'm not that good with a camera," Tim said. "You should be talking to Kelly Phillips. Out of all your photographers, he's got the most artistic eye."

"I plan on doing so," Marcello said, "but you have another type of expertise that I require. They want this studio to have a certain sensibility, a mixture of Western and Eastern cultures, and that includes the interior design. Not just the furniture or accessories, but also the paintings on the walls, and perhaps even a tasteful sculpture or two."

Tim remained still, not wanting to get excited until certain he understood. "They're going to need a lot of art."

"Indeed they are. If only I knew of a gallery willing to accommodate such an enterprise."

Any gallery would leap at the opportunity. Marcello didn't need a favor, he was offering one. They had set up the Eric Conroy Gallery together, but Tim was the one who ran it, interacted with customers and artists, and did the bookkeeping. Marcello helped with fundraising, and boy would this raise some funds!

"Wait, they're willing to pay, right?"

"Oh absolutely," Marcello said, eyes twinkling as he took

another sip. "They want to start with twenty or so pieces, but I'm certain I can talk them into twice that many."

Tim laughed maniacally, thinking of all the artists this would help. Not just financially. Simply being able to say that one of the biggest companies in the world had bought and was displaying their work... That would be good for resumes, wallets, and egos alike! "That's why you had me bring the portfolio."

Marcello nodded. "Did you forget?"

"No! Laptop is in the car. I'll go get it."

Marcello gestured for him to remain seated. "There will be time for that later. I'd like to present you with another idea. These talks were very inspiring. The idea of a community studio has me intrigued. What if we pursued the same goal here?"

Not just for photography, but other mediums of art too. They had discussed the concept before, Tim even looking for a suitable studio space to rent. He still remembered how, for much of his youth, he didn't have a place to paint. Not one where he could leave canvases to dry, or where he didn't need to worry about getting paint on the floor and walls. Only when his father repurposed an office space for him did he gain that freedom. Few artists were so lucky. "I just need to find a place we can rent that doesn't mind a bunch of eccentric types coming and going, or demand a ridiculous security deposit."

"We already have a space," Marcello said. "The back rooms of the current gallery. Two are used for storage. We can relocate the contents elsewhere."

"That could work," Tim said, nodding slowly. "As long as it doesn't disturb the customers."

"Incorrect. The customers would be invited to *tour* the studio space! We'll make it a feature that sets the Eric Conroy Gallery apart. Where else can you see art in progress, or offer to buy a piece even before its completion?"

People would love that! Sales would skyrocket. Tim was starting to worry they wouldn't have any art left to exhibit, but that was a good problem to have. He only had one lingering concern. "Never let the blood show."

Marcello smiled. "That only refers to my own. Most artists are already bleeding all over the place. I simply want to help them earn a living while doing so. I've changed my mind. I'm too excited to wait! Would you mind fetching your laptop?"

"I'll be right back!" Tim said, hopping to his feet.

"I don't suppose your own art is included in the portfolio?" Marcello called.

Tim stopped and turned around. He did keep digital images of his paintings, simply because it was easier to browse a file folder than to yank open drawer after drawer in search of a particular piece. "Yeah, most of it is on there. Why?"

"I'm a fan of your work," Marcello said pleasantly. "I can't imagine not including a piece or two in this endeavor."

His art? Hanging in a Japanese studio? Yeah, this was definitely going to be good for a few egos, including his own! His only concern was, when it came to Marcello, few things were as simple as they first seemed.

Chapter Four

Ben stood in the left wing of the stage, out of sight of the audience, and fidgeted nervously. Not that long ago, he had wished for the globe to stop spinning so fast. Lately he had been wanting it to hurry up, eager for this day to come. Now he just wanted it to be over. He normally looked forward to Valentine's Day. Ben was all about love, so naturally an entire day dedicated to it was right up his alley. No pun intended.

Of course, most Valentine's Days didn't involve dropping off his son at the airport and watching him try to hide tears while Ben did the same. At least he was finally on his way to Oregon. For just a short trip, but it was progress. While that was positive news, the rest of the day had been frustrating. He usually made sure to have this evening off, but the star of the show had quit unexpectedly, and Ben was the only person dumb enough to take his place. What's worse, this play didn't have any songs. Ben wasn't a good actor. He got by, but the audience was only forgiving when he busted out the tunes. Without his singing voice, he was a lackluster performer whose sole strength was making the other actors on stage look good by comparison.

Jason hadn't texted. Not since they dropped him off. He would have arrived hours ago, so what was taking so long? Ben listened to the actors on stage, trying to determine how far away his next entrance was. Just a few minutes. Was that enough time to run back to the dressing room to check his phone?

"You're doing great!" Brian whispered, patting him on the shoulder. "Thank you for doing this!"

He had said a variation of the same thing every night for the past week. Ben couldn't be angry at the theater owner though. He liked him too much. Brian was a sweetheart who just happened to be married to his best friend. Ben had seen countless times how Brian doted on her, willing to do anything in his power to keep Allison happy. In return, Ben wanted to do the same for him, but he felt he was letting the man down.

"I'm bombing out there," Ben whispered back. "Did you hear how many laughs I got during the dinner scene?"

"Erm, yes," Brian responded carefully. "It sounds like people are having fun."

"There wasn't a single joke in that scene!" Ben shot back. "I'm ruining it!"

"You're doing great," Brian said, eyes on the stage. "You've always been too hard on yourself. Oh! You're up!"

He patted Ben on the back. Or was it a gentle shove? Either way, it got him moving. Ben strolled out on stage and stumbled, but at least that was intentional. His character had stormed out during the middle of dinner and had now returned drunk. Maybe he could hide his lack of talent beneath all the slurring. Setting aside his personal problems, Ben focused on the performance. That was the plan, anyway. His attention kept returning to a table in the front row, where Tim sat sipping a beer, silver eyes never leaving him, even when the other actors were speaking. That was flattering and brought back a few memories, but Ben kept hoping for some sign. A quick thumbs-up or a nod that indicated Jason was okay.

"You're a disappointment," Ben's character snarled at his wife. "An even bigger one than me."

The audience was supposed to murmur in discontent. That's what had happened each time with the previous star. Instead the audience was silent. God he sucked at this! His wife slapped him, then threw herself on the couch to weep. Ben moved to the drink trolley to pretend to pour another scotch, keeping his head down and seeking out Tim in the audience again. His husband was looking at his phone! He wouldn't do that during a performance unless it was important. Jason had finally texted! Ben was so eager for news that he stopped pantomiming. Only when Tim looked up and flashed a reassuring smile did Ben get back into character.

He took his scotch to the center of the room, gestured at his wife with it while saying more horrible things, and then was shoved out of the house (off stage, actually) by the handsome neighbor who his wife would eventually leave him for.

"Good stuff, good stuff!" Brian said, meeting him in the wing.

"I don't know who you're trying to convince," Ben shot back, "me or yourself." Then he muttered a quick apology, because snapping at Brian felt about as good as kicking a puppy. Besides, he was only angry at himself. How many special evenings was he ruining? How many people had bought tickets, thinking they would charm their dates, only to see one inept actor sully the entire play? "I need to sing."

"The next show is a musical. I sent you the script already. Rehearsals start next week."

"I know," Ben said. "I mean I need to sing now. Tonight."

"There aren't any songs!"

"Doesn't matter," Ben said. "I'll recycle one from a previous play. How about *Crystal Tears*? That always got a good reaction from the audience."

"It's about an old man," Brian managed to splutter, looking paler by the second. "And his wife who just died."

"I can make it work," Ben said. "We'll change the words around."

"You're on in five!"

"True." Ben paced back and forth, trying to think of an alternative. "How about that other one? What's it called?" He sang a line as quietly as he could manage. "I'm despicable without your love, a filthy crippled dove."

"*Reprehensible*," Brian said. "That was years ago. Do you still remember it?"

"I sing it in the shower all the time," Ben said.

"But the plot. How does it make sense?"

"The guy makes one last plea for his wife to stay. We'll drop all those lines that I can't deliver and he'll sing to her. That she still chooses to leave him after I bring the house down—which I will—shows just how over him she is. Or how much she loves the other guy." In truth, he didn't care if it made sense at all. He just wanted the chance to redeem himself and maybe save Valentine's Day for some of the people out there. Tim included.

"I don't know," Brian said. "The other actors..."

"I'll take care of them," Ben said. "I've got this. Trust me."

Brian nodded, every bob of his head forced, but at least he had agreed. Ben grabbed a bottle of water to make sure his throat wasn't dry and started warming up by singing under his breath. This he could do! He actually felt excited when making his final appearance on stage. He walked a circle around his wife, like he was sizing her up or dressing her down, when really he just needed a chance to whisper a warning to her. "I'm singing. Your lines stay the same."

The actress glared at him with tangible anger. Ben wasn't sure if she was acting or not. No time to worry about it. He held out a hand to her, one that wouldn't be accepted, and started singing. He wasn't aware of what the audience thought about this new direction. He didn't have the headspace to consider them, Tim, or even the situation with Jason. All of that faded away, the song becoming his entire world. Enough that Ben wept authentic tears as he alternated between self-loathing and a desperate plea for love that he knew he didn't deserve. By the time the song ended, his wife seemed ready to forgive him, as if the actress couldn't resist deviating from the script. Luckily she caught herself at the last moment and tore into him. Ben bore the brunt of her anger, hung his head, and left the stage. Even though he was the villain of this story, the audience burst into applause.

"I love you," Brian said. "I just turned a little gay, I swear. Take me right here, or in your dressing room, or anywhere else you want!"

Ben laughed, gave him a hug, then thought of his phone again. "Sorry, I need to— Sorry!"

He sprinted for the dressing room, and once there, picked up his phone. Nothing on the lock screen. Entering his pin number revealed zero notifications. Nada in his text messages. No voicemail either. He had new emails, but nothing from Jason. Ben thought about calling or sending a text of his own, but if Jason and William were being romantic together—or even if they weren't—Ben would be an unwelcome distraction. Instead he forced himself to be patient. He returned to one wing of the stage and watched the story reach its scripted conclusion. Then he joined the others for the curtain call.

Ben bowed a few times, stepping back and gesturing at the true actors, encouraging the audience to applaud for them. Then, when the curtain was descending, he hopped off the front of the stage, straight into the audience.

"What are you doing?" Tim laughed, standing to meet him.

Ben kissed him. "It's Valentine's Day. I want to be with my man."

"Aw," Tim said, coming in for another smooch.

Ben dodged. "Did you hear from Jason?"

"Oh, I see how it is," Tim said, but not judgingly. "Yeah. He's safe. Where do you want to go? Are you hungry?"

"A little. No details besides that? He didn't say if they're getting along?"

Tim's mouth was still smiling, but his eyes weren't.

"What's going on?" Ben asked.

"That was quite the song!" an elderly voice said. A member

of the audience had come to speak with him. That was flattering, but also frustrating. Ben buried his irritation, not wanting to do anything that would reflect poorly on Brian. A few other people came close to listen to the conversation. Ben explained the situation, how he was a singer, not an actor, and made sure to thank anyone who insisted he could do both. Luckily his husband came to the rescue.

"I think someone has earned himself an ice cream, don't you?" Tim said, making Ben sound like a five-year-old who had participated in a school play, but it worked. Soon they were outside the theater and alone.

"What's going on?" Ben asked.

Tim sighed. "Jason didn't get on his flight."

"We dropped him off at the airport!"

"I know. I'm just as surprised as you." Tim held up his phone. "That's all he texted, aside from about ten apologies."

"Where is he now?" Ben asked, temper rising.

"At home, I guess."

Ben started walking to where the car was parked. "Then let's go!"

He wasn't angry exactly. Frustrated, yes. Exasperated, definitely. The flight was for a short trip! He would have been back in a week. What was the issue?

"Don't be mad." These were Jason's first words when he opened the apartment door. They were practically his mantra as of late. "I have a flight credit, so the money wasn't wasted."

"I don't care about the money," Ben growled.

Jason sheepishly moved aside so he could enter. His roommate, Emma, was on the couch, and had either been comforting him or trying to make him see sense.

"Hi, Uncle Ben," she said, rising to give him a hug. "Go easy on him," she whispered while doing so.

Ben couldn't make any promises, but he tried to calm himself for her benefit. He watched as Emma hugged Tim and exchanged pleasantries. Then she retreated to her room, leaving them alone.

"I know you're not afraid of flying," Ben said. "I also know that you love William. Or am I wrong?"

"You're not," Jason said, slumping into the couch.

Ben remained standing, Tim hovering at his side. "Then why aren't you in Astoria right now?"

Jason remained silent. Maybe he believed he had already said everything he needed to during their counselling sessions. Or perhaps the empty wine glasses on the table had something to do with it.

"This has gone beyond what is normal or acceptable," Ben said.

Jason's head whipped up, expression hurt. "I got scared."

"Of what?" Ben demanded. "You're a grown man! You should be able to get on a flight by yourself. William would have picked you up at the airport! All you had to do was wait in line and sit in a cramped seat."

"I'm sorry," Jason mumbled.

"That's not good enough!"

"Ben," Tim said, touching his arm. "Ease up."

He didn't want to, but he tried anyway. "I don't know how to help you anymore."

"I don't know either," Jason replied, unable to make eye contact.

"Are you hungry?" Tim said. "Let's go out for some grub."

Ben didn't budge. Neither did Jason.

Tim tried again. "Or I could bring back takeout."

"That would be nice," Ben said. "Thank you."

Tim nodded. "No problem. Chinese sound okay?"

"Sure." Ben waited until he had gone. Then he moved toward the kitchen. "Do you have any wine left?"

"The box is on the counter," Jason said.

Ben found two glasses in the cabinet and returned to the couch with them filled. Then he sat next to his son and handed him one.

"Happy Valentine's Day," he said.

Jason glumly accepted the glass, and they drank together.

"This isn't like you," Ben said. "This isn't the boy who risked sneaking into the room of his foster brother, just to watch him sleep, or the one who refused to lie about how he felt when he finally got caught. This isn't the man who wouldn't back down because he knew, absolutely *knew* that he loved William, even though another guy was in the way. So tell me what's changed. Between then and now, what happened to make you so damn afraid?"

"You," Jason said, voice wavering. "For the longest time,

I wouldn't even let myself think of you and Tim as anything but my friends." He shook his head as if it were hopeless. "You shouldn't have adopted me."

"Screw that!" Ben said. "I don't regret adopting you or anything else I've done, and do you know why? Because I followed my heart! Even though it got me into trouble and I made stupid mistakes and hurt the people I love, at least I was being true to myself instead of giving in to fear. Can you honestly say you've done the same?"

"No," Jason said, eyes downcast.

"Then what's your excuse? How did adopting you turn into an excuse for shutting down like this?"

"Because she died!" Jason said, voice cracking. "I kept writing those stupid letters to my mom, waiting every day for a response, and she wasn't even alive! I didn't know. I was at the group home when it happened. They didn't tell me right away, but if they had just let me be with her, if I was still living with my mom when she started dying..." Jason drained half his glass, hand shaking when he set it down again. "Maybe I could have helped somehow. Like I did for Tim."

The images came unbidden. Palms pressing against a gunshot wound, trying to hold back the blood gushing out, but those hands hadn't been his own. Ben had panicked, and Tim might have died had Jason not been there and acted quickly. "It's extremely unlikely that will happen again."

"I'll be here if it does," Jason said, jaw clenching. "You can hate me all you want, but I'll be here if anything bad goes down. I won't be selfish like she was." He shook his head, slow and determined. "I won't."

"Neither will I," Ben said, "and that means letting you go."

Jason looked at him sharply, expression vulnerable. Then his face crumpled, and he leaned over.

Ben opened an arm to take him in, rubbing Jason's back as he cried, and admitted to himself that he no longer understood. Ben had once thought he did, but what Jason had gone through must have scarred him more deeply than he realized. Only now was he discovering the full extent.

"What about William?" Ben murmured. "Aren't you scared of losing him too? He's the one putting himself at risk every day."

"He knows what he's doing," Jason said, wiping at his nose.

"He trained most of his life for this."

"What about emotionally? What if you lose him that way? I don't want anything bad to happen to you either."

"He'll be back," Jason said. "William mentioned that he has time off soon. He'll come back for me."

But for how long? The man might be a saint, but he was still human.

When Tim returned with food, they focused on eating, sticking to subjects that didn't have to do with foster care or far-away boyfriends. Then they said goodbye, Ben reassuring Jason that they loved him, and that they would never stop.

"That was rough," Tim said once they were home again.

"Yeah," Ben said. "I think I'd like to be alone. Do you mind? Maybe we could do something romantic tomorrow instead."

"It's fine," Tim said, kissing him on the cheek. "I'll be in my studio."

Ben smiled at him in appreciation. When the house was his alone, he exhaled and shook his head. He was out of his element. Allison, despite all her success as a counselor, seemed incapable of finding a solution either. Although he *did* know someone who dealt with people like Jason on a daily basis. Michelle, Jace's sister and Emma's mother. The hour was late, but she was forgiving. Usually. Ben went upstairs to the office before calling her, keeping Jace's photo near as a good luck charm.

"Perfectly normal," Michelle said once Ben had explained everything. "A lot of these kids are in survival mode for so long that it's only when they're finally secure and happy that all the bad stuff comes out. They can't afford to deal with it while still in the midst of everything, you know?"

He didn't, but he was starting to get the picture. "When I asked Jason what had changed, he said we shouldn't have adopted him."

"Breaks my heart," Michelle said, not sounding surprised. "It's sunk in by now that he has a family again. Jason already knows what it's like to lose someone he has romantic feelings for. I saw how upset he was when things fell apart with Caesar, and while that devastated him, he bounced back. Losing family… I wasn't working at the home when his mom died, but I know they couldn't place him with a new family for months. He was a wreck."

"Do you know any details?"

"Only what his former caseworker told me. She wasn't the nicest person. She advised me to let him age out of the system, claiming he was too broken to fix."

Ben grimaced, feeling guilty for being so firm with Jason earlier, but he didn't know how else to help him. "So what do I do now?"

"The same as any parent. Smack sense into him with one hand while guiding him with the other. I mean that figuratively, of course. Don't actually slap him around, no matter how tempting it might be. He's too old for spankings, but you can try taking away his toys."

"If only it were that easy," Ben said.

They commiserated a little longer before he thanked her and hung up. Then he sat and stared at Jace's photo, trying to imagine what he would do if forced to choose between his family and the man he loved. No brainer. Ben would have chosen Jace every single time. His family would be fine without him. They had their own lives, so that decision was easy. Especially now that Ben knew the agony of being without Jace. As for Jason, he had lost his mother and assumed that such pain only came from losing family, when in truth, it could apply to anyone who was taken away too soon. Death was the most potent of heartaches.

He'll come back for me.

Ben had an idea, one that didn't sit easy with him. Regardless, he still wanted to find out how the other half of this story was doing, and it wasn't quite as late on the West Coast yet. He placed another call, the voice that answered sounding concerned.

"Hello?" William said. "Ben? Is everything okay?"

"That's what I was calling to ask."

"Oh. I'm all right. How's Jason doing?"

"He's upset. At himself, mostly." Ben rested an elbow on the desk and pinched the bridge of his nose. "I'm sorry if we got your hopes up. I really thought he would make the trip."

"It's fine," William said amiably. "I'm coming home anyway."

"Jason said you might be visiting soon."

"No, I mean for good. I think it's for the best."

"You can't quit the Coast Guard," Ben said.

"I'll have to finish out the year, but when that gets close, I'll talk to my CO and—"

"If you aren't happy, I understand," Ben cut in, "but if you're quitting just to be with Jason, then you need to think again."

"He's more important," William said firmly.

"More important than saving lives?"

The line crackled before the answer came. "Yes."

Ben practically tipped backward in his chair. Talk about dedication! He knew William wouldn't say something like that lightly. This was getting out of hand! Ben weighed what he needed to do, not liking it but pressing on. "I don't think you should. In fact, you shouldn't come home at all. Not even for a visit."

"Why?" William asked.

"Because that's what it's going to take. We both know Jason's original plan was the best one. You get to return to active duty, and he gets to broaden his horizons."

"Yeah, but what would I tell him?"

"The truth! That if he wants to see you, he knows what he's got to do. Or don't say anything at all. That's up to you."

The unease in William's voice was transparent. "I don't want to hurt him."

Ben rubbed his forehead and dropped his hand. "Listen, Tim and I won't always be here. We're not that much older, but we'll probably die before he does. When that happens, I want Jason to already have a life outside of us. I really hope that life is with you, but even if it isn't, this is a lesson he needs to learn. So I'm asking you, even though it makes me sick to my stomach, to stay away. You can keep calling him and remain in touch, but if he wants to see you again, he needs to travel there to do so."

The line was silent for a long time. Ben waited patiently, knowing it wasn't an easy decision.

"Okay," William said at last. "I'll do it."

Ben didn't feel victorious. By the time he hung up the phone, he felt downright ashamed that he really had found a way to take away Jason's toys.

Tim picked up the paintbrush, pointed it at the easel and canvas in front of him, and grinned. After thinking about it briefly, he angled his body so the camera could see him better, expression frozen except for his eyes, which he moved to look at the photographer.

"Just act natural," Kelly repeated, lowering the camera.

"Okay." Tim jabbed at the canvas with his brush, even though no paint had been applied. They were in the new studio space at the Eric Conroy Gallery, which had been an instant success. Over the last few months, dozens of artists had come here to paint, and he knew customers enjoyed the tours because money talked. Sales were up. Way up! Over the past week, promotional photos had been taken and videos recorded to show to the clients in Japan and help convince them of the concept. That's why Tim was facing the lens now.

"You used to model for Marcello," Kelly said. "Right?"

Tim nodded, a grin still plastered on his face. "Uh huh."

"Must have been a long time ago."

"Hey!" Tim scowled instead. "Is that a joke about my age?"

Kelly shook his head. "You've forgotten how to vogue."

"I can vogue!" Tim said, changing his posture. He placed his hand on his chin and focused a thoughtful—perhaps even enigmatic—gaze on the canvas.

"God help us," Kelly said, raising the camera to take a photo. He grimaced while doing so.

Tim let his posture go limp. "I wasn't very good back then either."

"You were," Kelly said. "I've seen the negatives. The best were when you forgot about the camera. The one where a guy is sticking his tongue in your ear is my favorite"

"Get someone in here then. Just don't tell my husband."

Kelly laughed. "I have a better idea. Instead of me taking a photo of you pretending to paint, why don't you paint?"

"Oh." Tim shifted uncomfortably. "That's kind of private."

"Meaning?"

"I usually don't have an audience."

Kelly raised an eyebrow. Then he snorted. "I understand. Tell you what, I'll call Marcello and ask him to send a real artist over so we can get this shoot done."

"I am a real artist!"

"Of course you are, but you can't perform, so we can either cuddle and talk about your feelings, or we'll get someone in here capable of getting it up."

Tim glared, eyes locked on Kelly as he grabbed the nearest supplies and moved a mounted palette closer. He squeezed paint onto this, then went to work. He didn't have many colors handy, just red, black, brown, and orange. Enough to get his point across. He started painting Kelly, coaxing out the shape of his body in broad strokes, and moving upward to work on the face during the brief instances when the camera was lowered. He ignored the sound of shuffling feet and refused to tell Kelly to stand still, wanting to prove that he could paint even with his subject in motion. Soon he had the basics committed to canvas and enough of a mental image that he was able to completely ignore Kelly, who was now taking photos from a distance. Eventually he came close again.

"Let's see it," he said.

Tim continued painting, his strokes furious. "I'm not finished."

"Fine. It's a work in progress. Show me."

"Not yet!" Tim growled through gritted teeth.

"Turn it around for the camera to see!"

"Fine!"

He threw down his brush, grabbed the easel, and spun it around, huffing as he faced the camera. The lens stared back impassively. Then Kelly lowered the device and smiled. "I love it!"

"You do?" Tim looked at his impromptu creation. He had painted Kelly as a sinister figure, lithe body dressed in black and clutching a camera to his chest. The face was handsome, despite the leering grin and scheming eyes. Most striking of all were the two red horns on either side of his head, like Kelly was the devil himself.

"You captured me perfectly!" Kelly said with good humor. "Nathaniel would love this. Actually, I still need a wedding present. Do you think you'd be willing to part with it?"

"I'd need to finish it up," Tim said, appraising the piece anew. It wasn't bad! "Congratulations, by the way. Marcello told me the good news."

"Thanks," Kelly said distractedly, eyes still on the canvas. "You have true talent. I'm not saying that out of vanity either. I went through your portfolio. You've done some stunning work."

"You really think so?" Tim said, taken aback. Then he rolled his eyes. "You're just trying to build me up so I keep going. That way you can take more photos."

"Not at all," Kelly said, lifting the camera from around his neck. "I've got what I need. We're done. All I'm saying is that you make a better painter than a model, and considering how much the camera loves you, that's really saying something."

"Thanks!" Tim said, standing a little taller. "Feel free to stop by anytime to boost my ego."

"I'm coming back for that when it's finished," Kelly said, nodding to the canvas. "Just promise you won't make me look sweet."

Tim laughed, but before he could say anything in response, they heard the front door chime. He left the studio space and went into the main hall. The afternoon was late, the sun filling the room with warm light that had him itching to keep painting. Especially when he recognized the silhouette moving toward him.

"Benjamin! What are you doing here?"

He was answered with a kiss, then a hug that showed him it hadn't been an easy day for his husband. "I miss you."

Tim chuckled. "I'm right here."

Ben pulled away with a hangdog expression. "I know, but rehearsals start in a little bit, so I'll be gone most of the night. All I want to do is go home with you, grab a burger on the way, and sit on the couch while we pig out and watch something stupid."

"We can still do that when you get back," Tim said.

"I wanna do it now," Ben pouted. Then he straightened up and put on a more adult voice. "Oh! Kelly! How are you?"

"I'm exceedingly well," Kelly said, moving through the room with his equipment in hand. "I won't interrupt, don't worry. I have places to be."

"It's nice seeing you again," Ben said.

"You too," Kelly responded, his back against the door. He looked at Tim. "I'll review the images and see if there's anything else we need. I mean what I said about that painting. I'm coming back for it! Just make sure you get my bad side." He grinned wickedly and pushed his way outside.

"Good kid," Tim murmured. Then he looked back at Ben, who had resumed sulking. "You're really over this theater stuff, aren't you?"

Ben dropped the act and scrunched up his face. "What do you mean?"

"You complain about it all the time."

"Really?" Ben winced. "Sorry. I don't mean to be annoying."

"You're not," Tim said, taking his hand. "You can always vent to me. That's in the job description. It's just lately, you seem unhappy whenever you have to go there."

"The new production only has two songs, and Brian wants me to play the lead, who barely sings at all. I'd only get a few lines of each song."

"He's really fond of you," Tim said. "And even a single word of your singing is enough to win over the audience. You'll do fine."

Ben pressed against Tim so he could be held. Then, after a smooch, he put on a brave face and headed for the door. "I'm just going to sing *all* my lines," he said. "I don't care if anyone else does."

"They'll fall in love with you!" Tim called after him. "Just don't forget who got there first!"

Ben stepped out of the gallery and squinted against the afternoon sun. Once his vision had adjusted, he walked to his car. The parking space next to his was occupied, the vehicle's trunk open as Kelly stowed his equipment inside. Ben felt a pang of guilt, just like he often did when they crossed paths. He supposed he always would if he didn't do something about it.

"Hey!" Ben said, approaching him. "Do you have a second?"

"Naturally," Kelly said, closing the trunk. "What can I do for you?"

Now how to broach the subject? "I owe you an apology," Ben said.

Kelly smiled and shook his head, like it couldn't be true. "For what?"

"This is going back a few years," Ben said, exhaling. "When you and William were still together. I was encouraging Jason to do whatever it took to um…"

"Steal William away?" Kelly said. His arms were crossed over his chest, but his expression was amiable. "Sounds like not much has changed. From what I hear, you're still trying to get them together."

"Oh. You and Jason still talk."

"On occasion," Kelly said, dropping his arms. "It's fine. I know you want what's best for him. As for William, we weren't meant to be. That relationship should have ended long before it did, so if you helped usher that in somehow, I certainly have no hard feelings. Had we not broken up, I wouldn't have met—" Kelly smiled, held up his left hand, and wiggled the ring finger, which had a gold band around it.

"That's gorgeous!" Ben enthused.

"Thank you," Kelly said. "For the apology too, but you needn't bother. All the bad things I've been through have led me here, right where I want to be. I wish it worked that way for everyone—that after surviving each hardship life throws at us, we would end up stronger and happier than before."

"That would be nice," Ben said. "I think it's a testament to your strength that you've come through it all so well adjusted."

"Well adjusted?" Kelly said, shooting him a wink. "I'm not sure everyone would agree with you on that, but I appreciate it. How is Jason doing?"

"Good!" Nothing had changed, but Ben had tried to restrain himself the last couple of months. They saw each other regularly, including when they celebrated Jason's birthday, and they generally got along well as long as the subject of William didn't come up. "At least I think he's good. Has he told you anything different?"

"Just go easy on him," Kelly said diplomatically. "I know Jason can come across as this unstoppable force, but he also has a vulnerable side. I never would have believed that when I first met him, but he does."

"Definitely," Ben said. "I'll try my best to take care of him." Their topics of conversation exhausted, he opened his arms. "You take care of yourself too."

"That's never been my forte," Kelly said, "but these days I have someone who keeps me in line while spoiling me at the same time."

They hugged and Ben stood by his car to wave goodbye as Kelly pulled out of the parking lot. Then he looked back at the gallery, wishing for more spoiling and less keeping in line, but Tim's pep talk had worked. Ben got into his car and began the drive to the theater, determined to make one of them proud.

Rainbows. Hugging and crying and cheerful celebrations. Ben stared slack-jawed at the television, occasionally mustering the strength to pull his mouth together for a stunned smile. Then his jaw would drop again, because he simply couldn't believe it. Marriage equality, not just for certain states or a select few, but everyone. Everyone! Including two gay guys who had barely left the bed today.

That was intentional, even before the news broke. He and Tim had an entire day to themselves. No shift at the hospital or performance at the theater for Ben. No gallery openings or studio time for Tim. Just an entire day to waste in any manner they saw fit. So far it had been good. Tim had risen, put on his robe, and gone downstairs, returning with caffeine and two bowls of cereal. They had talked and flirted while eating, Ben switching on the bedroom television afterwards. They didn't use it often. More so when Jason still lived there and they couldn't agree on what to watch, but it was nice sometimes to hunker down and make staying beneath the sheets the only priority.

"Un-fucking-believable," Tim said, equally awed by what the news channels were reporting. The Supreme Court had ruled that marriage was a fundamental right of all people regardless of sexual orientation. "Do you think this will stick? They can't overturn it with another Prop 8, can they?"

"I hope not," Ben said. "I think this is different. The Supreme Court is... supreme."

Tim laughed and reached over to take his hand. They watched a little longer, the same information being repeated over and over again, but the news was so good that Ben didn't think they would ever tire of hearing it. Tim was the first to grab the remote and turn off the television. When Ben looked at him questioningly, he saw a Cheshire grin. Tim rolled over on top of him, arms straight so he could hold himself up while staring down at Ben, the grin not abating. He had lost the robe after returning from the kitchen, meaning they were both naked.

"In the mood to celebrate?" Ben asked, certain of his intentions. Or so he thought.

"I want to marry you," Tim said. "Today."

Ben laughed. "We're already married!"

"Yeah, but not in the eyes of the law." Tim lowered himself for a smooch and pushed himself up again. "Come on. If we hurry, we might be the first gay couple in Austin to get hitched."

Ben laughed again, nervously this time. "I don't need to be

first. And we *are* married, no matter what anybody says."

"I totally agree with you. Still, this way we'll be able to file taxes together and all sorts of boring stuff that we couldn't before. We should show our support, you know? People fought to change the law, and we can show our appreciation by doing what they made possible."

"You're right," Ben said, hoping it would be enough.

Tim nipped at Ben's neck, placing a kiss there afterwards. "Is that a yes?"

Ben honestly wasn't sure, which was an uncomfortable sensation because he usually knew himself so well. Why hesitate? He loved Tim! No doubt about that. Ben knew he wanted to spend the rest of his life with him, so what was the problem? They should rush out and make their marriage official in the eyes of the law. Simple as that. In theory.

The phone on the nightstand rumbled. Tim reached over to grab it. When he saw the message, he laughed and tossed the phone on the sheets. "Marcello is throwing a party to celebrate."

"When?"

"Tonight, although he says people are welcome to show up now if they want."

"I'd rather go tonight," Ben said, stroking the muscles of Tim's arm. "I was looking forward to being lazy with you. I don't want to rush downtown for anything either. Not today. I'd rather do other things."

"Other things?" Tim asked.

Ben started moving his hips back and forth. "If my days of living in sin with you are numbered, I plan on making the most of them. What's our personal record?"

"Four times in one day," Tim said instantly.

"Think we can break it?"

"We'll probably break something if we try!" Tim laughed. "We were teenagers."

"And now we're more experienced. Should be a cinch."

Ben gave himself over to the needs of his body, which was easier than trying to figure out why the idea of marrying the man he loved—the one who for all intents and purposes he was already married to—filled him with unease.

Chapter Five

The good news was like a drug, pure-grade optimism that had been injected into the vein of the gay community, keeping them riding a high that would hopefully never end. Judging from the smell in the air, there were plenty of real drugs too, along with booze and who knew what else. That wasn't unexpected. Marcello's parties always became a little wild. Except the charity fundraisers. Those remained dignified, but when the big guy invited people into the private areas of his home, things tended to get crazy. So far everyone still had their clothes on, although the current discussion of filling the hot tub with tapioca pudding would probably change that. Either way, Ben wasn't ready to go home just yet.

The day had been an exciting one, even if he and Tim hadn't managed to break any personal records. Too many people wanted to call to express their congratulations, and to bask in the good news with them. By noon, they had risen and gotten dressed. Tim insisted on taking them out for lunch. They picked up Jason on the way. Ben even managed to mention William without upsetting anyone.

"If you two ever decide to get married," Ben told him, "I'm happy you'll have the right to."

Jason had grinned his appreciation and asked the most obvious question. "What about you guys? Think you'll get married again?"

"Absolutely," Tim answered for them both.

Ben merely smiled. His mother had made the same inquiry, which was responded to with a vague, "I can't imagine why we wouldn't!" Allison hadn't thought to ask when they spoke on the phone, but she texted afterwards, Ben replying with, "I guess we better talk to our lawyer and get it figured out."

He didn't see any reason to rush. The lawyer who had officiated at their wedding, Adrien York, was a clever man. He had made sure that inheritance wouldn't be an issue, that they had power of attorney in emergency situations, and that they could visit each other in the hospital. They were set. Everything was fine.

Ben turned to look across the living room. He had left Tim's side to get them fresh drinks, but he hadn't made it to the kitchen, his thoughts distracting him. At the moment, Marcello was telling a story and getting big laughs, Tim shaking his head beside his friend and adding details, which were no doubt closer to reality. Ben watched for a minute, then asked himself again, just to be sure. The answer was the same. He still loved Tim. He still wanted them to spend the rest of their lives together. Why not eliminate any last vestiges of doubt by signing one more piece of paper?

If he couldn't figure it out sober, then maybe it was time to get wasted. Ben hurried into the kitchen, grabbing a beer for Tim from the refrigerator before going to a cluster of bottles on the counter and trying to find the wine he had been drinking.

"Congratulations!"

Ben turned to face an older man with white hair and keen eyes. He looked exceedingly gleeful, but then so did most people here. The older man nodded at the bottles. No, at his hand, as it turned out.

"Did you just get married today?"

"Oh!" Ben said, pulling his hand back long enough to consider the ring. "Ha! No, we've been married for about a year now."

"Different state?" the man asked, taking one of the bottles to pour himself a refill. Then he offered to do the same for Ben. The wine was red, so close enough. He nodded and held out his glass.

"No, we got married in Texas. Second time for me, actually."

"Really?" the man said. "Doesn't that beat all! How did you manage? Let me guess, you're friends with the governor."

"Nope," Ben said. "I just refused to let anyone tell me if I could get married or not. I might be not able to give myself the legal right, but that's not why most people get married. They do it out of love, and so did I."

"Can't argue with that," the man said, holding up his drink so they could clink glasses. "Still, I'm relieved it'll be easier for anyone not as brave as you."

"Thanks," Ben said, taking a sip. "And me too. I'm glad today happened." He practically counted under his breath in anticipation of the next question.

"Do you think you and your husband will pay a visit to the courthouse? Just to make it official."

"I don't know that we need to." Sometimes it was easier to be honest with a stranger. "We worked with a lawyer to make sure we have all the legal rights we need. I'm happy that everyone else can get married, but I'm not sure there's any point for us."

"Then again," the old man said. "I know from personal experience how legal documents, such as wills, often need to be updated. Better to have a nice tight knot on any legal loopholes, if you know what I mean. You said you were married once before? To a different feller, I assume."

Ben nodded.

"There's your reason!" the man said, looking pleased with himself. "When you marry your current husband, it'll be more legitimate than that first marriage because the federal government recognizes this one. Just think how good it'll feel to call your ex-husband to tell him that!"

Ben managed to laugh out of politeness, when really his insides had twisted up. He couldn't think about it now though. He needed to get away. "I better take this beer to my husband before he changes his mind and marries someone else."

The old man laughed, wished him the best, and turned to find another conversation partner.

Ben rushed from the kitchen and out of the house, needing to breathe in fresh air. *Just think how good it'll feel to call your ex-husband to tell him that!* He tried to imagine sitting in the office at home and explaining to Jace's photo that he was getting married, for real this time, and that although what they had together might have been a promise, it wasn't legally binding. Ben would be more married than before. He laughed without humor, then pressed his back to the house, sliding down until his rump hit the cold stones of the front porch. He set the beer next to him but kept the wine in hand. He would need it to face this revelation. His hesitation didn't have anything to do with his love for Tim. Instead it was more about how it would make Jace feel. If he was even out there. Ben liked the idea of an afterlife, an immortal soul, and a nice friendly god in the sky. But he didn't know if any of that was real.

Either way, he would still have to live with himself. Ben liked how things currently stood. He had two great loves, and he was married to them both. That was balanced. Healthy. Setting either of them above the other wouldn't feel right.

The front door opened. Tim poked his head out. The rest of him followed when he spotted Ben. "You okay?" he asked. "I was worried you got lost and wandered into Marcello's basement or something."

"I just needed some air," Ben said. "It's all a little overwhelming. Wait, Marcello has a basement?"

"Uhhh," Tim said, wincing slightly. "No?"

Ben laughed and shook his head. "I don't want to know. Here." He handed Tim his beer, then kept his hand extended so he could be pulled to his feet.

"We can go," Tim said. "I know you wanted to have a nice quiet day at home."

"This is a special occasion," Ben said. "I want to celebrate with you and show everyone how beautiful marriage can be. Just in case there are any doubters."

"Marcello already offered to marry anyone who's interested. He's filling out one of those online ministry forms right now." Tim offered his arm. "Ready to make it official?"

Ben didn't hide his horror. "I love you, and we have a lot to discuss, but if we let Marcello marry us, we'll probably find out later that he *really* married us."

"Oh like we'll be married to him?" Tim laughed, then looked concerned. "We better get inside and warn the others!"

"Or just watch," Ben said, accepting his husband's arm.

As they went indoors, he reassured himself that nothing had changed. Two husbands, two weddings. The rest they would figure out later.

Ben walked down the hospital hall, feeling especially proud. He loved his profession as a speech therapist. Helping people learn to speak again, whether they were recovering from a stroke or dealing with a disorder, always left him exhausted but satisfied. His theater work was fine, but it didn't make him feel like he was changing lives for the better. He could do that here, and today was extra special because of the young man at his side.

Jason noticed his smile, too nervous to return the gesture. Instead he puffed up his cheeks and blew out a gust of air. "Will we have time to practice again?"

Ben laughed. "We practiced the entire evening!" That had been fun. Since they had to leave so early in the morning, Jason had spent the night, bringing his favorite pillow with him and of course his guitar. Not the newer electric one he had gotten for Christmas. Jason liked it and enjoyed having more than one to choose from, but for situations such as these, he faithfully relied on the guitar he had grown up with. Having him home again felt good. Ben needed all of his willpower to resist suggesting he move in permanently.

The speech pathology area of the hospital consisted of a consultation room that doubled as an office, and two small adjoining rooms that were used for rehabilitation. Ben reported to the office, as he always did when beginning his shift. Wanda, the resident speech pathologist, was seated behind her desk and focused on paperwork. She was a small and feisty woman, despite her advanced age, and a stickler for the rules. Ben braced himself for trouble as he and Jason filed into the room. Sure enough, Wanda's attention skipped right over him to Jason.

"Who's this?" she asked.

"Jason, my son. He's here to help."

Jason shuffled forward and offered his hand. Wanda shook it, eyes moving back to Ben. "To help?"

"The music idea I told you about," he said.

"That's all I thought it was," Wanda said. "An idea."

Ben felt his face growing red. He dealt with this on a weekly basis, but with an audience present, he found it a lot more embarrassing. "Why don't you wait in there?" he said, turning to Jason and gesturing to one of the rehabilitation rooms. Ben guided him to the door, shutting it after assuring Jason that he wouldn't be long. Then he turned back to Wanda. "I just want to try it out. You know how well Neil responds to music. I thought this would help."

"It's a nice idea," Wanda admitted, "but something we should talk to the board about."

The board! Wanda loved the board. Ben often pictured her like the Log Lady from *Twin Peaks*, but instead of walking around with a gnarly old log cradled in one arm, she would be holding a two-by-four. Her precious board. Of course the one she was referring to was made of directors instead of wood. Ben had never met them and didn't care to. Wanda religiously attended any open meeting, always returning with stories of the issues she had raised with them and their responses.

"Just a trial," Ben said. "Think of it as a bring-your-child-to-work day. Jason is just going to sit quietly in the corner and *maybe* get so bored that he plays his guitar."

"He really shouldn't interact with the patients."

"He won't. Sorry, but my first appointment is in five minutes."

Wanda breathed through her nose and nodded curtly.

Ben grinned in response. "Thank you!" He fled before she could change her mind.

"She seems tough," Jason said when they were alone in the rehabilitation room.

"She's fine," Ben said. "Wanda just wants everything to run smoothly."

"I always pictured you as being the boss."

"Here?" Ben laughed. "Maybe someday." He turned his attention to setting up, thinking of the constant battle for any sort of change, like the iPads that their patients responded so well to. He had spent a year championing those, even sneaking in one from home until the mysterious board finally gave Wanda the green light. Dealing with her was the smallest portion of his day. Ben never let it get him down, preferring instead to focus on his patients.

"Hello!" The door leading from the office opened, a mother guiding her son through.

Janice was his own age, and the best sort of parent because she always stood back and let Ben do the work he needed to do. Her son, Neil, was six years old and on the Autism spectrum. He didn't verbalize much, but over the previous year, they had made progress.

"Hi, Janice," Ben said, shooting her a smile. Then he squatted. "Hello, Neil!"

Neil's focus moved around the room, settling on Jason. Nearly a full minute passed, but eventually he looked at Ben again. "Hello."

As simple as it seemed, this was a big deal. Not only did Neil not speak very much, but he wasn't strong in social interactions either.

"Aaaaand how are you doing, todaaaaaay?" Ben sang.

Neil, whose expression had been impassive, smiled briefly. "Fine."

"That's wonderful news, my friend," Ben sang again. He would be doing so for much of their session, since it was an easy way to get through to Neil, but he always mixed in normal speech too, wanting Neil to respond just as much to that because very few people in the real world would be singing to him. "I have another friend with me today," he said, extending an arm toward Jason. "That's my son! His name is Jason, and do you know what he can do?"

Neil just stared.

"Do you know what he can do?" Ben repeated. "Can you guess?"

Neil shook his head.

This wasn't as good as a verbal answer, but Ben let it slide. "What can you do, Jason?"

"I can play the guitar!" He said this in the sort of voice reserved for little kids, which was adorable because Ben hadn't heard him do that before. Then Jason started playing chords.

Neil's eyes went wide like a hungry tiger had slunk into the room and was stalking him. He might appear terrified, but that's how his excitement manifested. His little arms were shaking too. Ben had already warned Jason about this and nodded encouragingly. Jason played a short little tune, then pretended he was insecure. "Was that good? Did you like it?"

Neil nodded instantly, which was great but not quite enough.

"He can't hear you," Ben said gently. "Was it good?"

"Yes."

"All right!" Ben said. "That's great news! Do you think Jason can stay and help us today?"

Neil needed a little longer, but he answered again. "Yes."

Off to a great start! They went through warmup exercises, Ben following the curriculum just in case Wanda had her ear pressed to the door. Halfway through the session, when Neil's attention started to waver, Ben teamed up with Jason. Together they sang *Apples and Bananas*, a song by Raffi that had a very simple repeating verse, the vowels changing with each round. Apples and Bananas became Ipples and Bininis and so forth. A little confusing for Neil, maybe, but Ben mostly wanted to get him talking. After performing the song twice, they were able to get him to fill in a few words wherever they stopped. Then they returned to the standard lessons until Neil's frustration showed.

Another song calmed him and got him verbalizing again.

"That was amazing!" Janice said at the end of the session. "I'll never get that darn song out of my head, but Neil absolutely loved it!"

"You might want to let Wanda know that," Ben said quietly.

"Will your son be here next time too?"

Ben turned to ask him and saw Neil standing next to Jason, one of his small hands pressed to the instrument, but his attention was on Jason, like he was a rock star.

"Say thank you," Janice prompted.

Neil quietly continued to stare. Then he pulled his hand away, holding it with his other. "I like you," he murmured.

"I like you too," Jason said, chuckling in surprise.

Ben saw his patients out, closed the door behind them, and resisted the urge to whoop with excitement. "That went really well," he said.

"Yeah?" Jason cocked his head. "Better than normal?"

"Absolutely! Neil talked a lot and didn't have a single tantrum. We usually have to take breaks, but he plowed right through the hour this time."

"Cool," Jason said, nodding in satisfaction. "How much does a gig like this pay?"

"I'll take you to lunch."

The next patient was an older guy who was recovering from a tumor. That session mostly went as usual. Ben introduced music toward the end, unsure of how well it would go over, and was glad he left it until last. The man wasn't a music fan. The teenager they saw next was, Jason very generously playing along to a Justin Bieber tune that she streamed from her phone, even though it wasn't his kind of music. The final patient was an older woman who had suffered a stroke, and once she saw the guitar, all she wanted to do was sing. They needed to work on sharpening her articulation, and what better way of doing so than by rocking along with The Rolling Stones? Her choice, and definitely not what they had practiced. Jason was thrilled. Wanda didn't look as happy when she poked her head in the room, but he would deal with that later. All that really mattered was that a patient who normally behaved as if she was being patronized finally showed enthusiasm for her own recovery.

"That was awesome!" Jason said when they were leaving the

hospital together. "I'm quitting my job. I mean it. We'll be the ultimate speech therapy team!"

"I wish," Ben said, grinning in response.

"Hospital jobs pay well, don't they?"

"Yeah," Ben admitted. "They do, but it helps if you're full-time. I'd be making some serious dough if I did this all day."

"Why don't you?"

"I tried." They reached the car. Ben unlocked the doors. "I asked if I could go full-time, but it's not in the budget."

Jason waited until they were both seated in the car before he responded. "So after Wanda retires you'll take over?"

"No. They'll probably just hire someone else and I'll stay the assistant."

"What? Why?"

"Because I'm not qualified."

"That's bullshit! How long have you worked here?"

"Almost ten years," Ben said, putting the car in reverse and backing out.

"How much more qualified can you get? Then again, you probably wouldn't have time for the dinner theater, so it's better this way."

Ben remained silent.

"Or not," Jason said. "If you had a choice…"

"Don't go there," Ben said with good humor. "I had a big meltdown about this a few weeks back, and Allison already had to listen to my sob story. I'm over it."

"But if it were up to you?"

"I'd work here full-time. I looked into music therapy as an alternative. It would help if I could play an instrument, but then again, I really like what I do."

"So start applying at other hospitals," Jason said. "Find a position like Wanda's and take it. You have *ten years* of experience. You'll get hired in no time!"

He shot Jason a smile, appreciating how passionately he felt about the subject. "What I really need is my master's degree. With that I could become a speech-language pathologist and go all sorts of places. I could even open my own practice. Ben Bentley & Son. How's that for a business name?"

Jason laughed. "So why don't you?"

"What?"

"Go back to college."

The idea surprised him so much that he ran a red light. At least he preferred to blame the suggestion, which really was ludicrous. "I'm too old to be a college student again."

"Not for your master's, you aren't," Jason said. "Who cares what anyone thinks? Besides, we look like we're the same age. No one will know."

"I love you," Ben said. "Have I told you that today?"

"Seriously," Jason said, not willing to drop the subject. "Why not? Or do you still want to be Wanda's bitch another ten years from now?"

"I'm not her bitch!" Ben said, shaking his head. "Anyway, where do you want to eat? We could hit the mall."

Jason checked his phone. "That took longer than I expected. I still need to go home and get changed for work. Can we grab a burger on the way?"

"You can. I'm staying away from fast food right now."

"Worried about your figure?"

Ben exhaled. "You try being married to someone who exercises for fun. We were standing in front of the mirror the other day, and... Well, I guess you understand."

"For sure!" Jason said. "At least William likes me skinny, so I don't have to work out."

"Same here!"

They bumped fists, Ben feeling good. William remained a mostly taboo subject, so even this little exchange felt like progress. As they waited for their order in the drive-thru, Ben's head was still spinning from Jason's pep talk. What if he did it? What if he went back to college? He wouldn't be studying general subjects. Most would relate directly to his work, which he was really into. Still, being the one old guy in a classroom full of bright-eyed twinks would feel terrible.

"You coming in?" Jason asked when they reached his apartment complex.

"I'll keep you company while you eat," Ben said, the smell of french fries making him want to drool. He'd have to live vicariously through Jason because he was serious about this diet. He wasn't starving himself, just eating as healthy as possible, which for now meant a side salad and an unsweetened iced tea.

Once inside, he was relieved to see that the living room wasn't too messy. Emma was probably to thank for that. A casual glance toward Jason's bedroom revealed exactly the kind of mess he was expecting. It hadn't been that way with William around. Ben wondered how that situation was going. Tim knew details, but whenever Ben asked, he always replied with, "Ask him yourself! He's your son too!" Normally he didn't, feeling too passionately about the subject to keep his cool. Tim was right though. A parent would ask about such things no matter what.

"So how's everything going?" he tried, sitting on the couch.

Jason was next to him, hunched over the coffee table as he ate. "Fine. Work is boring. Volunteering at the shelter is way cooler. That's my speech therapy, you know? I would do that full-time if I could, but they don't have any money."

"That's a shame," Ben said, poking at his salad with a plastic fork. "How about your personal life?"

"Fine. I've been hanging out with Caesar a lot lately. We have sad bachelor nights over here. Pizza, booze, and telly. Hey, do you ever watch *Doctor Who*?"

"Caesar?" Ben asked, ignoring the question. "Are you sure that's a good idea? And you're not a bachelor. Are you?"

Jason chewed and swallowed, eyes amused. "We just call it that. And don't worry, Caesar and I are just friends. He's got a girlfriend, although he always gives these totally inappropriate hugs. He does it on purpose, just to get a rise out of me."

"A rise?"

"Not like that!"

"Just be careful," Ben said. "Especially if you're drinking together." He thought about leaving it there, but he was too curious not to probe further. "Does William know?"

"About me hanging out with Caesar? Yeah."

"And?"

Jason shrugged, expression unhappy.

"Everything okay between you two?"

Jason shrugged again, concentrating on his fries. That he hadn't ordered a milkshake to dip them in implied that he was watching his figure too. But for which guy?

"You can tell me," Ben said. "I know I wasn't very patient before, but it's only because I care so much about you. If there's anything you need to talk about, please don't hesitate."

Jason nodded. Then he leaned away from his food. "I don't think he's coming back."

"William?"

Jason nodded again. "It's been almost a year. I know he has time off. Sometimes three days in a row. It's enough for a quick visit, but—" His chin trembled and he looked away.

Ben abandoned his salad, too distracted to eat. "You know what I'm going to say."

"That I need to go there, but what's the point if he doesn't want to see me? Maybe he…" Jason shook his head, like it didn't make sense, but he pressed on anyway. "Maybe he met someone new."

Ben sighed. "He loves you."

"I know," Jason said. "But that doesn't mean he can't love someone else. I don't see why else he hasn't come back. It's the only thing that makes sense."

"That's not why he hasn't come back."

"Then what?" Jason said, tone frustrated. "I can't figure it out and it's driving me crazy!"

Ben swallowed. He couldn't keep Jason in the dark any longer. It wouldn't be right and hadn't been from the very beginning. His scheme wasn't working anyway. "He's not coming back because I told him not to."

"What?"

"I thought it would encourage you to finally go to Oregon and…" His voice faltered, the hurt expression on Jason's face causing him to feel just as much pain. "I'm sorry. It was stupid. I was only—"

"You told him not to see me," Jason said, his voice squeaking.

"Yes, but only—"

"Why would he even listen to you?" Jason was clenching his jaw, the sorrow shifting to anger.

"I convinced him," Ben said. "Don't blame William for this because—"

"I don't!" Jason shouted. He looked surprised by his own outburst, but the anger had been unleashed, and there was no reining it in. "Do you have any idea how bad I miss him? Do you even have a clue?"

"Then go see him!" Ben pleaded. "It's been a year! You have a plane ticket you can use any time you want. It's a vacation, Jason. A visit! No one is forcing you to move up there. All we want is—"

"Get out."

Ben remained seated. "I just want you to try. You're nursing wounds that you never let heal. Well what about him? Maybe he's up there feeling just as lost without you. When do you start thinking about William's needs instead of just your own?"

"Get out!" Jason was pointing toward the door, his jaw clenching. "I don't want to see you anymore."

"Jason. Please." Ben sucked in a shuddering breath. "It was stupid of me to get involved. I'm sorry."

"So am I," Jason said, wiping away tears with a hand before using it to point to the door again. "I'm sorry I ever listened to you. Leave."

Ben rose, wanting to defend himself or simply admit again how foolish he had been, but Jason was too emotional for them to discuss this rationally. Ben was too. He knew he needed to go. He forced himself to walk to the door, when all he really wanted was to hug Jason and try to shield him from the hurt, but that wasn't possible. Not when Ben was the one who had hurt him.

"I love you," Ben tried.

This only seemed to make it worse. Jason's face started to crumple before it became a mask of anger. Then he stomped toward him, Ben flinching away, but Jason was only going for the door to throw it open. "Either you leave," he growled, "or I do."

"Okay," Ben said. "We'll talk later. Or you can call Tim. Just make sure you calm down before you drive anywhere."

This was met with steely silence, so Ben slunk from the apartment, feeling ashamed. He had been trying to make things better, but had only managed to make them worse.

"Should have learned from my mistakes," Tim said.

He stood in the living room, hands on his hips. Ben was on the couch, wondering why he had ever thought that Tim being home again would make him feel better. The trip to the buffet sure hadn't, Ben stress-eating his way through plate after plate. He had returned home feeling twice as bad as before. The second Tim walked in the door, Ben had launched into every grisly detail, hoping for commiseration or maybe advice. Instead Tim was standing there and shaking his head.

"This is your letter on the door," he said.

Ben glowered at him. "What's that supposed to mean?"

"You were trying to manipulate events—"

"For the greater good!"

"Hey, that's exactly what I was thinking when I had that kid put a letter on Jace's door."

"A letter that contained a *lie*. No, this is more like my seventeenth birthday, when I put my foot down about you dating Krista Norman. It worked that time. I cut you off and you came rushing back to me. I thought the same thing would happen with Jason and William."

"They aren't teenagers in high school," Tim said, all teasing gone from his voice. He sat on the couch and pulled Ben near. "We should be encouraging them to talk about their problems openly. That's what we try to do, right?"

"Yes, but they need to be in the same room, face to face."

"Video calls aren't good enough?"

"It's not the same." Ben grimaced, his stomach churning. "You're right though. I messed up."

"And we'll make it better again. First we need to let Jason cool down. Then I'll go over there and talk to him. I get where you're coming from, but it might be easier for him to listen if it's coming from me."

"That's a good plan," Ben said. "I just hope that he'll still trust me."

"He will." Tim squeezed his shoulder. "This is exactly why we adopted him. He's stuck with us, no matter how stupid we are."

"I'm the only stupid one," Ben said. "I don't remember the last time you messed up."

"Would it make you feel better if I did mess up again?"

"Yes! Could you?"

Tim exhaled. "Let's see. There's this cute guy who keeps coming into the gallery. Never buys anything, but he always finds an excuse to talk to me. I could have an affair."

"No! Definitely not." He shifted uncomfortably. Stress sure took a toll on the body. Ben literally felt sick to his stomach. "Maybe you should call Jason, just to check on him."

"You said he had to work, right?"

"When he gets home then?"

Tim nodded. "Okay. Maybe you should take a nap. You don't look so good. I can grab something for dinner or heat up the grill."

"Yuck," Ben said. "I ate way too much already."

"What did you have?"

Mongolian barbeque. The kind with an entire buffet of raw ingredients that could be assembled in any combination and given to a chef to stir-fry. He loved it, but kept thinking of the trays full of raw meat, sitting there for hours after the lunch rush was over, pink and warm and exposed to open air...

"Sorry," Ben said, shoving Tim away. He started heading for the stairs, wanting privacy, but didn't have time. He barely made it to the bathroom by the entryway, already puking as he threw open the toilet lid and fell to his knees. Tim showed up soon after, placing a damp washcloth over the back of his neck as the retching continued. "Food poisoning," was all Ben managed to say.

A suitable finale to a messed-up day. How did the old poem go? *This is the way the world ends, not with a whimper—* Ben reached up, grabbed the handle, and pulled. *–but with a flush.*

Ben awoke in the middle of the night, disoriented. He was in his bed, but on the wrong side. Normally he slept closest to the wall where he felt the most secure. Tim was on that side now. Ben felt his stomach flip and remembered why he was nearest to the bathroom, and why the plastic bucket was next to the bed. He wasn't looking forward to using that again, so he forced himself to rise. That's when his phone rumbled, possibly for the second time, if that's what woke him up initially. He saw a text from Jason but wasn't able to read it. Instead he ran with his phone to the bathroom, the meager contents of his stomach coming up again before he dry-heaved. Once this passed, he forced himself to read the text through the tears in his eyes.

I booked my flight. I'm leaving tomorrow.

That was all. Ben stretched out on the bathroom floor, unsure if he felt relieved or upset. Jason was leaving them. This is what he wanted. Just not how.

"Babe?" Tim padded into the bathroom, hair sticking up on one side. He bent down next to Ben and placed a palm over his forehead. "You're burning up! Are you sure this is food poisoning?"

"I don't know," Ben admitted. His thoughts were equally feverish. He struggled to focus, which was upsetting because now more than ever he wanted to think clearly. His son needed him!

Then again, Jason had more than one dad. "Can you call him?"

"Only if you promise to get back into bed."

Ben nodded, but didn't have the strength to move.

"Okay, tiger..." Tim slipped his arms beneath him. "Let's do this."

"I'm fine," Ben protested as he was picked up.

"I can see that."

Ben gave in, resting his head against Tim's bare chest and wishing he could stay there, even though his skin felt too hot. The sheets were damp with sweat when he was set down. Tim noticed this too, pushing away the comforter on the other side of the bed, and then heaving Ben over to it. "In you go," he said, pulling the sheet over Ben. Then he set the bucket on the mattress next him. "I washed it, don't worry. Use it if you need to."

"Where are you going?" Ben asked, fighting to stay awake.

"To call Jason. Then I'll be back. I promise."

Ben wanted to reply. He wanted to get up and call Jason himself! But his stomach was already suggesting that they head back to the toilet instead, and rather than face that prospect, he decided to give in to sleep.

When Ben awoke next, it was morning and he was racing for the bathroom again, unsure if he should sit or kneel. As it turned out, he did a little of both, swearing to himself to never eat again. Then he crawled back in bed, body exhausted, throat aching, and head burning. The next time he stirred, a doctor was standing over him. Tim wasn't far behind, anxious as Ben took a sip of water and answered questions as best he could. He had one of his own that he asked as soon as they were alone.

"Jason?"

"He's fine," Tim said. "Worry about yourself. The doctor says you have a stomach bug. Can you drink more water?"

Ben tried, hoping it would stay down this time. All he wanted was to burrow beneath the covers to escape the light, which only made his head throb more. He was already too hot, so he settled for putting a pillow over his head. Then he drifted in and out of sleep, feeling delirious, but the monotone hum of the airplane cabin helped soothe him. He couldn't remember where he was flying, or why, but at least he had a row of seats to himself so he could stretch out. He felt the thin airline blanket being pulled up to his neck to cover him better, a hand resting gently on his shoulder before moving away. Then the seatbelt sign turned off with a chiming noise, causing his eyes to shoot open.

Ben was in bed. The room was dark, the house silent. Tim lay next to him, his back to Ben, too deeply asleep to stir, even when Ben sat up and braced himself for another sprint to the bathroom. He felt okay. As in, his muscles were still sore, he felt like he had swallowed razorblades, and he was pretty sure he could fry an egg on his forehead, but at least he didn't feel like puking.

He stood unsteadily and went to the bathroom sink, needing to quench his thirst. Then he returned and looked at Tim, who must have been taking care of him since yesterday. Or the day before? Ben didn't know anymore, but he was certain his husband deserved his sleep, so he quietly made his way downstairs. He drank from the kitchen sink, sipping handfuls of water from his palm. Then he sat at the table with his head down, waiting for any sign that the water was on its way back up. When this didn't happen, he rose again, taking a glass from the cabinet and filling it from the tap.

Ben forced himself to drink slowly. He wandered from the kitchen to the living room in search of his phone, because the more his head cleared, the more recent events came back to haunt him. Jason's hurt expression. The trembling hand as he pointed to the door. Ben supposed he deserved that. Now he intended to make it right. If only this stupid bug or whatever hadn't hit him when it had. Jason probably thought he didn't care and had misinterpreted his silence. And now he was gone. Wasn't he?

He spotted his phone on the coffee table and snatched it up. He had text messages from his mother and Allison, but nothing from Jason. His emails didn't reveal anything either. He finally noticed the time. Four in the morning. He thought about sending Jason a text, hour be damned, but worried about waking him, or distracting him from William if they really were together. He could wait a little longer until morning. Ben sat there, sipping water and fighting against nodding off. How could he possibly need more sleep? Seriously!

Eventually his stomach felt moody again and the rest of his body started to shiver. Only an hour had gone by. Maybe sitting around in his underwear wasn't a good idea. Ben decided to wait in bed under the blankets. He slowly made his way upstairs, careful not to wake Tim. He leaned the phone upright against the lamp on the bedside table, so he could see the screen. Then he stretched out, determined to keep his eyes on it, but they wouldn't cooperate. He fell asleep again, and this time it was blissfully black. No disjointed memories of the argument or anything else. When he woke again it was morning, a pale blue sky outside the window, which had been cracked to let in fresh air. Or to blow away his stink. The bed next to him was empty, the lock screen of his phone devoid of notifications, so he forced himself up. He used the toilet as it was intended and then took a shower, sitting in the tub and letting the water wash over him when his legs felt too weak to stand.

Once he was dressed and his teeth were brushed, he went downstairs. Tim was in the kitchen, cleaning up at the sink. When he turned around and saw Ben standing there, his expression was torn between relief and concern.

"How do you feel?"

"Like roadkill," Ben managed, throat still raw. "And a little hungry."

"No problem!" Tim said, springing into action. He raided the cabinets, taking out items that Ben didn't recognize, meaning he must have gone shopping. "We've got applesauce, rice, toast. If you're thirsty we have Gatorade or I can make you a ginger tea. Or some veggie broth!"

"Someone's been playing internet doctor," Ben said, mustering a smile as he sat at the breakfast bar. "Actually, wasn't there a real doctor here? Or did I dream it? Doctors don't do house calls anymore, do they?"

"Marcello's does," Tim said, nodding to the items on the counter. "What'll it be?"

"Applesauce," Ben said. "And a ginger tea. With honey. Please."

"Coming right up!"

He rubbed his eyes, willing himself to wake up, and wondered if Tim would make him a real tea with caffeine instead. Then he remembered his need to contact Jason and started to rise.

"Where are you going?" Tim asked, spinning around like a prison guard.

"To get my phone. I need to text Jason. Or call."

"I heard from him," Tim said, setting down a bowl of applesauce.

"Is he okay?"

"Yeah. Sit and try to get some of this in you."

Ben sat but ignored the food. "How's he doing? What did he say?"

Tim leaned forward, palms flat on the counter. "He canceled his flight."

"What?" Ben's stomach sank, which was better than what it had been doing lately, but this was still terrible news. Their argument had been horrible. The least that could have come from it was Jason actually trying. Instead it had all been for nothing. "I give up. I won't mention William ever again, or try to tell either of them how to have a relationship. I'll just stay out of it and hope for the best, because all I seem capable of is making it worse."

Tim stared at him like he was speaking in tongues. "Jason made it to Astoria. He flew out yesterday."

"But you said he—" Ben felt both hopeful and fearful. "He canceled his flight back."

"Yeah," Tim said, voice hoarse. He turned around to use the sink, although to Ben, it looked as though he was running the water for no purpose.

"You okay?" he asked.

Tim nodded and shut off the water. When he spun around, his eyes were watery and his expression strained, but he forced a smile. "This is what we wanted, right?"

"I guess so," Ben said. "When is he coming home again? Did he say?"

Tim shook his head. "He said he's still figuring it out, but I don't think he's coming back. He sounded too happy. Eat."

"I should call to tell him I'm proud. And that I'm sorry." Ben thought about it for a moment. "Or maybe we should stay away? The less he thinks of us right now, the better."

Tim peered at him, then walked over to press the back of his hand to Ben's forehead.

"What?" Ben asked, pulling away.

"You're still a little warm."

"So?"

"I'm trying to figure out if you have a fever, because our son finally worked up the courage to leave despite fearing that we'll stop loving him, and you think it's a good idea to break off contact. What kind of message will that send?"

"That one of his dads is an idiot."

"Close enough," Tim said, expression vulnerable. "Would you please eat? I need you to get better."

Because even though their roles had seemingly reversed, Tim wasn't the best at remaining strong in emotional situations. Ben was usually the one to comfort him during trying times, and this was one of them. The two most important men in Tim's life had argued, one flew the coop, and Tim was left playing nurse to the other while no doubt fighting off worries of his own.

Ben picked up the spoon and took his first bite in days, determined to regain his strength. He would need it to rebuild bridges that, he hoped, hadn't yet completely burned.

Chapter Six

Tim gripped the steering wheel tighter, pretending he was driving a Porsche 918 Spyder instead of a geriatric Toyota Corolla. He even hunkered down, eyes narrowed in concentration. The curve ahead was tight, but if he took it just right, he could pull ahead of the competition and win this race! When a minivan overtook him to switch into his lane, he sat upright again and abandoned the fantasy.

"Are you sure this is a good idea?" Ben asked.

"Absolutely not," Tim said, refusing to answer the question seriously. The first few times had been fine, but they had crossed the state line into Oregon already. This was their third day of driving! Way too late for second-guessing. They had paced themselves, doing a little over ten hours a day and trying to choose interesting towns to overnight in. "What we should have done is flown up there to buy him a new car. I'm not sure I want Jason driving this hunk of junk."

"It's a good car!" Ben said, patting the dashboard affectionately. The vehicle had belonged to him before they had given it to Jason. Even back then, it had been antiquated. In Tim's opinion, anyway. He always preferred the latest and greatest. "And you know that's not what I mean. What if Jason isn't happy to see us?"

"The guy who chose two old farts over his hot rescue swimmer boyfriend?"

Ben laughed. "When you put it like that…"

"He'll be happy to see us," Tim said. "You could always text him and let him know. Or are you still not talking?"

"We're talking," Ben said.

"Just a text now and again, right?"

Ben nodded.

"Because, after an entire month, you're still trying to give him his space."

"Yes," Ben confirmed.

"Then this is definitely a good idea. You're both being idiots."

"I'm trying to do what's right for him!"

"Screw that," Tim said with a chuckle. "I bug him every single day!"

"Really?"

"Hell yeah! I don't care if he wants to hear from me. I love him too much." He shot Ben an apologetic expression. "I'm not saying you don't. It's just that—"

"I get it," Ben said. "Somehow I let it get awkward between me and him. Seeing each other will help. I hope."

"It will," Tim said. "At the very least, I bet he'll be happy to have all this stuff."

Before leaving they had loaded up Jason's car with essentials like his clothes and winter gear that he would need in Oregon. They had emptied out his bathroom too and were tempted to bring whatever furniture they could squeeze in, but Ben had advised caution. Jason might feel like they were shoving him away. Tim doubted that, but he knew how vacations could wear thin after a while. Jason's enthusiasm for staying in Oregon might wane, in which case, he could still easily load up his car and drive back. With space to spare, because the passenger seat wouldn't be occupied. Nor would one of the seats in the back.

Tim casually angled the rearview mirror so he could see the chubby little bundle in the backseat. Clever girl that she was, Chinchilla raised her head to stare back.

"How's she doing?" Ben asked, choosing to smile over at him rather than check on the dog himself.

"Great!" Tim said. "She needed a vacation. I can tell. She's tired of smelling the same old pee."

"Um. What?"

"Oh," Tim said, laughing in embarrassment. "You know how dogs love peeing on hydrants or whatever? First they always sniff them, so I figure other dogs are leaving messages. It's like the internet. We live out in the boondocks, and I bet that's the equivalent of being on dialup. Chinchilla needs more bandwidth."

"She needs more pee to smell."

"Exactly!"

"I'm surprised you don't pee when you're out walking together, just so she has something new to smell."

"Ha ha. Yeah." That's not why they peed together. They were marking their territory. It was a bonding exercise! "So uh, anyway, she seems a lot peppier since we left."

"She does," Ben said. "She's doing great."

Something in his tone was a little too accommodating. Tim

wasn't in denial. He knew Chinchilla was getting older, but she was no granny. She still ran around the yard, snapped at bugs, and loved playing tug-of-war. Her muzzle was whiter now, but she was doing fine. Just to make sure, he pulled over at the next rest stop, this one a small wooded park next to the highway with restrooms, a few picnic tables, and lots of green grass and trees. Chinchilla got out of the car, sniffed, harrumphed, and opened her mouth in a smile. And to pant, but he knew her well enough to tell when she was happy.

After giving her a moment to warm up, Tim jogged with her a short distance. Mostly for his benefit, since he was sick of being stuck in the car. He also knew it would help her sleep better, and yeah, it proved she was no senior citizen. If Chinchilla was old, she was a modern old lady, still active and vital. No rocking chair for her! She had places to go and people to meet.

As if on cue, a camper van pulled up and a couple of mutts were let out by their owners. Time to socialize! After watching to make sure they were friendly, Tim walked her over so she could sniff butts, run in excited circles, and occasionally bark. All the good stuff that came with being a dog. Afterwards he went with her to the picnic bench where Ben sat on the table, having found a narrow beam of sunlight between trees to bask in.

"This is nice," Ben murmured, eyes closed. "I don't want to get back in the car."

"Me neither," Tim admitted, hopping up next to him. Chinchilla, now worn out, settled down underneath the table. "Three more hours. Then we'll be there." He braced himself for more of Ben's concerns, surprised when the conversation took a different turn.

"Ever think about getting Chinchilla a friend? She looked really happy playing with those dogs."

"I have," Tim said. "She gets tired of it though. I was at Marcello's studio once, and Nathaniel was there with Zero. They get along and I had errands to run, so I thought it would be okay to leave her. Nathaniel agreed to watch her, and I was only gone a few hours, but when I got back..." Tim shook his head. "She ran to me and hid behind my legs. Nothing bad happened. I think she's just too used to being the star."

"That I can believe," Ben said, opening his eyes to smile. "What about other kinds of adoption?"

"A cat? That's more your thing, but we can if you want. I'm open."

"Open to more than just pets?" Ben asked.

"Oh!" Tim exhaled. "Wow. Is that something you've been thinking of?"

Ben shrugged. "A little."

"I'm surprised. Especially with all the stress lately."

Ben shook his head. "I can handle it. So what do you think? Maybe a baby this time?"

"I don't know," Tim admitted. "Let's see how we feel after this trip. Maybe you're just missing him."

Ben thought about it and nodded. "I am. Ready to go see our son?"

Tim felt his heart swell, still loving how that sounded. "Yeah. Let's go."

Astoria was a gorgeous little town clinging to a peninsula that jutted out into the waters of the Columbia River. Most of the land was sloped, the colorful wooden homes reminding Tim of birdhouses. No big skyline like Austin had. Just quiet streets and humble businesses. That was his impression anyway. After living so long in an area of two million people, a town of just ten thousand seemed quaint. He was relieved that it didn't have a creepy vibe like some small towns did. Astoria was just as liberal as the rest of the West Coast. He had researched it to make sure, needing to know that Jason was unlikely to be targeted here because of his sexuality. He felt a little more concerned when pulling up to the apartment building where William lived, which was clearly a repurposed motel.

"Remember the motel in *Breaking Bad*?" Ben said. "The one with all the junkies and prostitutes?"

"It's not that bad," Tim said, mostly for Ben's benefit. People seemed to consider the space outside their doors as an extension of their apartment, since both the lower and upper walkways were filled with various possessions. A cheap plastic playhouse for children, bicycles, grills, and in one case, a rickety old table where three men played cards and drank beer, despite the afternoon still being young. One of the men shouted and raised a shot glass, the other two doing the same. More than just beer, it would seem.

"That's it," Ben said, having spotted the same spectacle. "He's coming home with us."

"He's not," Tim said. "Let's go see. Like most apartments, it's probably nicer on the inside."

They climbed concrete steps to the second floor, Tim able to spot the right door simply because the outside area was clear. William was the tidy one. If not for him, Jason would probably have just as much stuff sitting outside as his neighbors did.

"You didn't tell them about this trip, did you?" Ben asked.

"Nope. I kept it a secret, just like you wanted." He didn't need to ask why. Ben and Jason were a lot alike. Had they announced their visit, Jason would have spent the last few days doing exactly what Ben had done. Worrying. This way he would be caught off guard, which should help them patch things up. Or it could be a disaster.

"What are you doing?" Ben whispered.

Tim had his ear pressed to the door. "Making sure they're not doing it. They haven't seen each other for an entire year. Remember when we got back together?"

"Yes," Ben said. "We took things slow."

"Right. But once we got back into the swing of things…"

Ben smiled. "I'm sure they can tear themselves away long enough to answer the door. Hurry up and knock. I can't wait!"

Tim couldn't either. He hammered on the door, made his voice deeper than usual, and shouted, "Police! Open up!"

Scant seconds later, William threw open the door, looking bewildered. Then his face lit up with joy. "Whaaaat? I can't believe it! Are you serious?"

"Completely," Tim replied, opening his arms for a hug. As much as he liked William, he couldn't help looking for Jason as they embraced, but he didn't see anything over his shoulder except a small but clean apartment. His stomach sank. Wouldn't it be just his luck if Jason had flown home at the same time they were driving up?

"Ben!" William cried, turning to hug him instead.

Tim watched, feeling happy despite his concerns, which he didn't wait to voice. "Jason isn't here?"

"Job interview," William said. "He should be back soon. Come in!"

Tim looked at Ben as they entered the apartment to see if

he was okay. After a reassuring nod, he turned his attention to the interior. Definitely a former motel room. The layout hadn't changed. No walls had been knocked down to create space. The main room had a couch instead of a bed, but the two-seater looked like it converted to one. Past a small dining room table was a kitchenette. All that left was a door to the bathroom.

"Before you say anything," William announced. "We're working on it. We won't be staying long, especially now that…" His smile wavered as he looked at Ben. "What a surprise!"

"We're not here to steal Jason away," Ben said, picking up on his concern. "We only want to show our support. And smooth things over. We didn't part on the best of terms."

"He'll be glad to see you," William said. "I'm sure of it."

Ben didn't seem to share this certainty, but he smiled his appreciation. "So he's at a job interview?"

"Yeah!" William said. "He's having a hard time because this isn't Austin. I think there's only one pet store in town and they weren't hiring. I keep telling him that he has general manager experience. That doesn't mean he has to make sure kitty litter is in stock for the rest of his life."

"Speaking of which," Tim said. "We brought someone else with us."

"Chinchilla?" William guessed.

"Yeah," Tim said. "She's in the car, since we weren't sure if you guys would be home. I figured Jason might be glad to see her."

"You have no idea," William said. "Whenever we're out, he stops to pet every dog we see. *Every* dog. It was cute the first few times. Now I have to make sure we leave the apartment early since it takes forever to get anywhere."

Tim laughed. "I'll go get her."

"I'll go!" Ben said, hopping to his feet. "I left my phone in the car anyway."

"Okay," Tim said, tossing him the keys.

Ben fumbled, glared before picking them up, and left the apartment.

"Married life," Tim said. "You sure you're ready for this?"

"Yup!" William answered. "I know you're crazy about each other. Don't pretend."

"True. Ben's just a little on edge right now. How are things?"

"Great!" William said, but he was sensitive enough to understand what Tim really wanted to know. "Jason is really happy here. He misses you guys, but this has been a fresh start for us. He's not competing with Kelly like when we first met, and I don't have to worry about Caesar, like when we first got back together."

"Ex-boyfriends are such a pain," Tim agreed, not admitting that he had previously been one of *the* biggest pains. "Things sound really positive!"

William nodded. "Yeah! We don't have to worry about the Coast Guard keeping me away now that we're here together. I had my first three-day shift this week. Jason did great. He's keeping himself busy. Only one thing still bothers him, but I think this visit will help with that." He reached for his phone. "He should be here soon."

"How's Daisy doing?"

"Oh my gosh!" William said, beaming proudly even though his attention was still on his phone. "She's getting so big! She can walk now, and talk. Not much. It's mostly gibberish. She calls me poo-poo instead of papa. We're working on it."

"I still call my dad poo-poo," Tim said. "But only behind his back."

William didn't hear his joke. He stared at the phone intently and then looked up. "Jason is here! This thing isn't always right, but it says he's right out front!"

After a sliver of hesitation, they both leapt to their feet, not wanting to miss the show. They hurried outside and looked over the railing. Jason was walking through the parking lot, outstretched arms carrying a large flat donut box. He seemed to be daydreaming, unaware that not far away, someone was getting out of his old car, equally oblivious to the reunion that was about to transpire.

Ben prided himself on his ability to multitask. He had a grip on Chinchilla's leash and was backing out of the car, butt first, while texting his mom to let her know they had arrived safely. He managed to send the message and stand, quickly navigating to the most recent texts he had exchanged with Jason.

Doing a lot of sightseeing? Ben had written, when really he wanted to ask if Jason liked Astoria, but he worried that question might cause Jason to compare it to Austin, get homesick, and come back.

Yeah, Jason had texted back. *It's not very big. I feel like I've seen it all already.*

Ben hadn't responded, feeling the answer was already teetering on the brink of Jason saying he was over Astoria and wanted to come home. Which, if Ben was honest, he wouldn't mind, but only emotionally. Logically, he knew that Jason was where he needed to be. Then again, that motel... Ben turned to look at it, and a few things happened at once. Chinchilla finished sniffing a tire and shook her leash, causing it to jangle. Elsewhere in the parking lot came the dull thud of something hitting the pavement. Ben was orientating on the sound when he saw a rainbow sprinkle donut rolling toward him. This bumped against his foot, and when he looked up to find out where it had come from, he saw his heart's desire.

Scarcely more than a month had gone by, but it was still long enough that Ben cried out Jason's name. His son reacted, leaping over a flat white box and running straight to him. Ben opened his arms, choking back tears of joy as they embraced. Chinchilla leapt around their legs, at least until she discovered an unattended donut and was distracted by another of her favorite things.

Ben let her eat, figuring she deserved a reward for enduring the grueling car ride. This allowed him to turn his full attention on Jason. Ben looked him over and took in every detail, just to assess if he was doing well. He looked great! His skin had sun and his smile was bright, like he had gotten a lot of practice recently.

"What are you doing here?" Jason mumbled, wiping at his eyes.

"We thought you might want your—" Ben started to gesture at the car, then he decided to bare his soul. "I was dying to see you," he said. "That's why we're here. Me especially. I miss you. And I love you!"

Ben held his breath, awaiting a response, because he understood Jason's fear now. After having messed up, no matter how good his intentions, he couldn't help wondering if Jason was happier without him. Ben had gone to great lengths to reassure Jason that his love would never waver, but now he found himself asking the same question. What if Jason stopped loving him back?

He got his answer when Jason hugged him again, squeezing so tight that it hurt, which was better than the pain Ben had lived with during the past month.

"I love you too," Jason murmured. "It's so good to see you. And you," he said, letting go of Ben to squat and pet the dog.

It was a testament to how much Chinchilla loved him that she briefly abandoned the donut to wag her butt and receive kisses on her head. Then it was back to her rainbow sprinkle affair.

Jason stood, looking a little sheepish and uncertain. Ben remembered how much harder it had been at that age to feel comfortable in his own skin. He was sure they could get past this. They simply needed to spend more time together.

"We just got here," he said. "I haven't really seen the apartment. Want to give me a tour?"

"Yeah," Jason said. "Let me just..." He hurried to pick up the box he had dropped. Then he looked back, as if needing reassurance that this was really happening. After another insecure grin, he led the way upstairs and into the apartment. More hugs from Tim followed, and another round from William for them all, before they were seated at a small square table near the kitchenette.

"Tell us about the job interview!" Ben said. "Is that what the donuts are for? Because you got the position?"

"Congrballashins!" Tim said from next to him, most of a chocolate long john stuffed into his mouth. Chinchilla was at his side, looking up with unbreakable concentration just in case any crumbs fell her way.

"I don't know if I got the job," Jason said, "but I found work. I went in to this coffee shop to apply to be assistant manager. While there, I saw flyers for upcoming performers. Musicians and poetry readings mostly. So I asked about that too, and they had a cancellation earlier today. I got the gig!"

"Tuneat?" Tim asked while continuing to chew.

"He wants to know if you're performing tonight," Ben translated.

"Yeah! My first paying job in Astoria. It's just thirty bucks for two hours, plus any tips. Still, I figure we can use the money."

"Absolutely!" William said proudly, reaching over to rub his back. "I can't wait! You don't mind if we're there, do you?"

"Better than playing to an empty room," Jason said. "I'm kind of freaking out. I usually don't do this sort of thing, but I figured it might increase my chances of getting the assistant manager job. Just imagine a manager who can appease angry customers by whipping out his guitar. I wish I had mine here. I'll have to use the guitar at the coffee shop, and it's a little warped. The strings don't even match."

"Back seat of the car," Tim said with a grin.

"You guys are the best!" Jason said, eyes shining. "That'll make it easier to put on a good show tonight. I need this! I want to start earning money before we look for a bigger apartment."

Ben forced himself to hold back, especially when Tim met his gaze. They had money. More than enough, but they had discussed this before. They wanted Jason to be self-sufficient, and Ben knew his son had pride. Jason had never looked to them for a handout. Even getting him to accept Ben's old car had been a struggle. In the end, they had to pretend it was an early Christmas present. Still, that didn't mean they couldn't put a ridiculously huge tip in his jar tonight, or help out in other little ways.

"If you need anything while we're here," he said, "we can go shopping together. Groceries or maybe clothes?"

Jason groaned. "Go ahead and ask."

"I don't know what you mean," Ben said innocently.

Tim had no such reservations. "Since when did you start wearing Polo shirts like William does? Because you might want to choose a smaller size. Or start bulking up."

"Shut up!" Jason said warmly. "The airline lost my luggage. I've got the jeans and T-shirt I flew in and that's it."

"I keep offering to take him shopping," William said. "We aren't broke!"

"No," Jason said, "but we should be careful. Besides, I keep hoping my luggage will show up."

"Do we tell him now?" Tim asked.

Ben smiled. "We brought more than just your guitar. The trunk is full of clothes."

"Oh thank god!" Jason breathed.

"If you're anything like me," Ben continued, "then you probably packed your favorite things for this trip. That's what's missing now, right? Did you file a claim?"

"Yeah, but they want you to prove what was in there and the value."

Ben was about to insist they go shopping, but if recent events had taught him anything, it was that he had to allow Jason to make his own decisions. "I wouldn't mind getting a new outfit. I'm going to a major concert tonight and want to look my best."

"I guess I could get a nicer shirt to wear," Jason conceded. "You're right that all my best stuff was in the suitcase."

"There's a JCPenney in town," William said. "Or some cool vintage shops."

"Vintage," Ben and Jason said at the exact same time. Then they laughed. Yes, they were definitely going to be okay.

The coffee shop was long and narrow, only opening toward the back where Jason had enough room to get set up in one corner. He was sitting on a stool, feet on the upper rung as he worked at tuning his guitar. Ben was especially glad they had made the trip now. Events would have played out the same, except Jason would be using an instrument he wasn't comfortable with, and the area they now sat in would almost be empty. Aside from himself, Tim, and William, only one other person was there, and she was fixated on her laptop.

"Okay," Jason said, looking up. He too noticed the lack of an audience and shrugged. "I feel like we know each other already," he joked. "Like we're old friends. This is my first time doing anything like this, so go easy on me."

He started with an instrumental, which showed his strength. Jason could sing, despite preferring not to, but he knew how to carry a tune, even if his voice wasn't exceptional. That was fine, since it would make it easier for patrons to converse. By the end of the song, two more customers had moved closer so they could watch.

Jason played another pair of tunes, humming to one and working up the courage to sing on the next. The room was slowly filling, three more people having arrived. The girl with the laptop left with an annoyed expression, perhaps needing silence to work. She was replaced by an older couple who bobbed their heads along to the music. Jason was on his fourth song when he did a doubletake, nodded, and smiled at someone. Ben looked over to see an older woman with her arms crossed. The owner, judging from the way she scrutinized the audience, as if assessing how pleased her customers were.

Jason focused more intently on playing, this song another instrumental. Voices could be heard talking over his music. That was fine, since this wasn't a formal concert, but Ben noticed the way Jason's eyes flicked to the audience, his lips sandwiched together as if feeling uncomfortable. When that gaze sought him out, Ben raised his eyebrows and spread his hands in a way that he hoped said, "I'm open to the idea." Jason didn't seem to get the message right away. Not until toward the end of the song when he smiled.

"Thanks," Jason said after some light applause. "What a gorgeous group of people here tonight! I think I recognize one of you in particular. I could be wrong, but is that Ben Bentley I see? The famous singer who brings down the house every night back in Texas?"

The customers started looking around, as if expecting to find a celebrity in their midst. Ben found this more funny than embarrassing and was on his feet the second Jason asked the next question.

"Maybe he'd be willing to accompany me?"

"I might be able to manage a song or two," Ben said as he joined Jason. Then they did what they always did when getting ready to make music together. They haggled. "Lisa Loeb?"

Jason shook his head. "Don't freak, but I never listened to the CD you gave me. How about something by the Doors?"

"Too moody. We need peppy. Cat Stevens?"

"Works for me! *Wild World*?"

"Love it!"

And just like that, Jason was playing and Ben was singing. He hadn't had time to consider the lyrics when Jason suggested the song, but as he crooned, he remembered that it was a song about someone leaving, and a warning about how rough the real world could be. The song could have easily been written by a concerned parent for their child. Was the selection intentional? Only one way to find out. As the song wound down, he decided to leave the next choice to Jason.

"What do you think?" Ben asked, eyeing the newcomers. Five or six people had wandered into the area and taken seats.

"Led Zeppelin," Jason said. Classic rock. Of course. "Do you know *Ramble On*?"

Jason was always making Ben listen to rock songs, and while

he remembered the tune, the lyrics were fuzzy. They were easy enough to pull up on his phone so Ben nodded. The song was a good choice, the guitar dominant. Hearing the intro brought many of the lyrics back to Ben. Another song about saying goodbye, except this one felt more positive to him. Someone was setting out on his own again to find the girl he loved. Or the guy, in Jason's case. Ben was tempted to change the pronouns to match, but Jason was a stickler about such things. *You don't mess with the classics!* he had scolded once.

By the time the song came to an end, the room was filled to a respectable degree and the owner seemed pleased. Jason seemed oblivious to this. He was watching Ben, eyes full of emotion. "You wanna choose?"

"Elton John," Ben said. *"Daniel."*

Jason licked his lips and nodded. They were definitely on the same wavelength. The song wasn't guitar driven, but Jason did an admirable job of adapting it. That meant it was up to him. The real difficulty came in keeping it together emotionally. As he sang about watching someone leave, Ben started fighting back tears. When he looked over to see Jason crying as he played, Ben broke down too. He still managed to get out the last verse, but when the last twang of the guitar faded into silence, he sobbed once. Jason was on his feet, holding the guitar away with one arm and reaching out with the other. Ben had no instrument to worry about. He embraced Jason with all his strength, not wanting to ever let him go, even though he knew he had to. The time had come to stop making music together.

"She's beautiful," Ben said, probably for the tenth time, but it was true. Daisy had her father's blond hair and her mother's almond complexion, which made for a striking combination. He adored her. It didn't matter that every time Ben tried interacting, Daisy would reach for one of her parents, not trusting his presence there. Mere moments later, she would forget about him, stumbling around the living room for another toy or chasing after Chinchilla while squealing at the top of her lungs.

They were leaving. After a wonderful week of touring Astoria and hanging out with Jason and William, now they had to begin the long ride back. Ben wanted to fly, but bulldogs weren't allowed because short-nosed breeds were more likely to die while in the cargo hold. Not that Tim would have allowed her to be checked like luggage. Renting a car to drive back had also provided Tim with an excuse to reserve one of his beloved sports cars. A convertible. Ben would need a hat. For now, he was enjoying the remaining time with his family.

"I guess we should decide if we want one of these," Tim joked. He was stretched out on the floor, back against the carpet. He had remained perfectly still to gain Daisy's trust. His reward? The child was now carrying various toys over to him, placing each somewhere on his body and slowly burying him beneath multicolored plastic.

"Are you thinking of adopting again?" Lily asked. She too sat on the floor as she passed Daisy more toys to entomb Tim with.

"You're replacing me already?" Jason complained. He was on the couch and stroking the face in his lap, William looking like he was in heaven.

"We're just trying to figure out what to do with ourselves now that our little nestling has flown away." Ben sighed and pantomimed dabbing tears away, mostly because pretending he was sad was the easiest way of hiding that he really was. "Think you're up for a little brother or sister?"

"I don't know," Tim answered for him. "The last kid we adopted was a pain in the ass. I don't think I could handle another."

"You'd be sparing the poor child," Jason retorted. "It isn't easy living with such overbearing parents. Oh and did I mention manipulative? And deceptive? And uh... Help me out here, hon. Give me some more negative words."

"Sexy," his boyfriend replied, quickly hiding his face.

"He's useless," Jason said, shaking his head.

"I dunno," Tim chimed in. "I think he's right on the money."

"Anyway," Lily said, sounding exasperated, "I think it's a nice idea. How serious are you?"

Ben considered Daisy, who was adorable and had already made him laugh more times than he could count. Then he looked to Jason, the love in his heart exploding. There was no comparison. "I think we'll wait. I'm pretty happy with the way things are."

"What about your degree?" Jason asked.

"I was just being silly," Ben quickly replied.

"Really? Don't you want to get your master's or whatever?"

"You want to go back to college?" Tim asked.

"No! I was just..." He shook his head. "I was frustrated with my job that day. That's all."

"I get it," Tim said. "Kind of like a few months ago, when you were moving to Thailand to teach English."

Ben laughed. "Shut up! I'm allowed to have a midlife crisis. Here, Daisy, put this teddy bear on Tim's face."

She took the stuffed animal from him with great suspicion and hobbled over to add it to the growing pile of clutter, but sadly, the teddy bear only ended up on his chest.

"Ha!" Tim said victoriously. "Nice try!"

"You sounded serious at the time," Jason said, not letting the subject drop. "With a little more college, you said you could do anything, even open up your own practice. Don't make a face! You're the one who's always bossing me around about my life. I don't get to do it back?"

"That's right," Ben said. "You don't. Bossing is a privilege of being a parent. It doesn't work the other way around. Now go brush your teeth and take a nap."

"Awwww!" Jason whined, like he didn't have a choice. He smiled though, Ben matching his expression, even down to the tinge of sorrow. He would miss moments like these.

They lingered as long as they could. Any later and they would have to stay another day, but Ben had a job to return to. Jason did too, as they had recently learned. He was now assistant manager of the coffee shop with the added duty of arranging more performances, whether for himself or other musicians. The pay wasn't great, but it was a start.

Grudgingly, they made their way outside, loaded Chinchilla into the car, and took turns saying goodbye. All but Jason and Ben, who waited until the very end. Understanding that they needed privacy, Tim got into the driver's seat. Lily and William returned inside with their daughter.

"I don't want to do this," Jason said, hanging his head. Then he hurried to add, "I'm staying. Don't worry. I just don't want to say goodbye."

"Then don't!" Ben said. "We're coming up here every year for vacation. Tim wanted that to be a surprise, so brush off those acting skills when he tells you."

Jason opened his eyes and mouth as wide as he could. "Like this?"

"Exactly like that. We'll fly you home anytime you want. Even if it's just for a weekend. All you have to do is ask. Call all you want too. Or don't, because I'll be calling you anyway. Or we can video conference. Maybe we could send little packages to each other?" Ben brushed the hair away from Jason's forehead, as if it would help it be less messy, when really he just wanted an excuse to touch him. "I hope you know that we weren't serious in there. About adopting. There's no replacing you. Give me a million years and a million kids and it wouldn't make a difference. You're special and—"

"Ben," Jason said. "I need you to stop."

"Too much? Sorry, I just—"

"If you keep going," Jason interrupted, "I'm getting into that car with you. I don't care about the consequences."

"I don't want that," Ben said, shaking his head. Then he sighed. "Okay, I do, but you're doing the right thing. Just know that you're in here—" He tapped on his chest. "—*way* too deep to forget about, or for me to stop loving you. Ever. Do you hear me? I mean it." Ben was crying now but he didn't care. "Never doubt that. Not for one second. I love you."

"I love you too," Jason said, his face crumping.

Then he was in Ben's arms, and it didn't matter that he was a grown man. Sometimes he felt just like a little boy. Ben wished for nothing more than to shield him from the hardships of the world. But he couldn't. Not any longer. Ben let his arms drop and took one step back, surprised by just how difficult this was.

"Take care of each other," Ben said.

"You too," Jason said, cheeks streaked with tears. "I'm going to miss you."

"I'll be back before you know it," Ben said. "I promise." Then he forced himself to turn away.

"You all right?" Tim asked once they had driven to the end of the block. His hand was on Ben's leg, reassuring and warm.

"Yeah." Ben resisted the urge to turn around in his seat for one last look. "You?"

Tim was quiet a moment. "The last time I was this heartbroken was when Eric died."

Ben grasped the hand on his leg, squeezing it tight. "They'll be okay. Right?"

"Absolutely," Tim said. "Are you kidding? He couldn't be in safer hands. A rescue swimmer! William is the nicest guy I've ever met too. He'll be there to make Jason feel better when things get rough."

William was only the second-nicest guy Ben had ever met, and yes, he still remembered how comforting it was to be with someone like that. Wild and elusive also had its perks, even if Tim was a lot more settled these days. "Thank you," Ben said. "For the trip and everything else. You've got this parenting thing down."

Tim slid his hand free to place it over Ben's. "You're pretty amazing too."

Then they grew silent, Tim no doubt doing the same thing as Ben—entertaining worries between revisiting happy memories. They were half an hour into their trip when Tim broke the silence.

"William is a father now."

Ben snorted. "You just noticed?"

Tim wasn't finished. "That means when Jason and William get married, we legally become grandparents."

He mentally tried on the title for size. Grandpa Ben? Or maybe Grandfather Benjamin, not that it was any better. "Do you think it's too late to sabotage their relationship so they break up?"

Tim nodded. "Yeah. Probably."

"Then until that day comes," Ben said with a theatrical shudder, "let us never speak of it again."

Chapter Seven

"Sneak attack!"

A magazine of some sort thwacked the script Ben had been reading. Not that he cared. Every character in the upcoming play was a child, and yet each role was to be played by an adult. That was weird. Ben wasn't looking forward to dressing up like and pretending to be a kid. Even music couldn't save this production, since the songs consisted of compelling lyrics like, *Gumdrop gals and lollipop lads sure are sweet, but ladies and gentlemen, they're not for you to eat!* He had already been searching for any excuse to bail, so he didn't mind the interruption. He looked up at Tim, noticing the shit-eating grin.

"Are you in the mood?" Ben asked. "You can't wait until later? It's fine. Let's go!"

"I *am* in the mood," Tim said, sliding out a kitchen chair to join him. "In the mood to discuss your future! A blowjob would be good too. But only after."

Ben laughed and focused on the magazine, or as it turned out, a catalogue from the University of Texas detailing its graduate program. "Tim—"

"Just hear me out! I know neither of us is eager to go back to school, but you could really benefit from this. I've done the research. If you become a full speech pathologist, the sky is the limit. You'll be able to do whatever you want. I can tell you're getting restless. I know you. And before you shoot me down, think about this: You and I have, what? Thirty or forty more years of work ahead of us? I'm okay with that. I help artists get their work shown in galleries and earn scholarships so they can go to school. I know Eric is up there watching me and proud of what I'm doing. I'm sure Jace is proud of you too but—"

"I can do more," Ben said, already nodding. "I like the idea. I really do, but I've also done the research. Here." He flipped through the catalog, finding the section that estimated cost. Then he turned it for Tim to see. "Eight thousand dollars per semester. Probably more. By the time I'm finished, it'll be over thirty thousand! I can't afford that. I know you have lots of money—"

"*We* have lots of money," Tim said. "When are you going to get that through your head?"

"Okay, we have a lot, but not enough to take a risk. What if, after the first semester or two, I decide graduate work isn't for me?"

"You'll stick with it," Tim said. "I know you will."

"You believe in me, and I'm grateful, but that's no guarantee. I might not have what it takes."

"You do," Tim said easily. "You've already been doing this kind of thing for years now. You'll breeze through these classes while picking up a few new tricks. Easy."

"Money is just one concern. Time is an issue too."

"Quit your jobs so you can study more. It's just for two years. We'll make it work."

Ben shook his head. "I'm not quitting my job at the hospital. I won't abandon any of my patients."

"We can find a way around that too. You might have to give up your theater work. Just for a little while."

Ben looked up. "Say that again."

"The theater work," Tim repeated. "You could take a break from it."

Ben moved the catalog aside to consider the script, spotting another lyric from one of the songs. *You can stick a fork in me, but I'm not done. Let's eat lots of sugar, and have tons of fun!* He looked at the front of the script incredulously. "Who wrote this thing, a Care Bear?"

"Sorry," Tim said, standing again. "I interrupted you. Just think about it, okay? There are only three days left to enroll."

Ben wanted to agree, just to get away from the script, but he held back. Thirty thousand dollars for the chance at a better future? He needed to consider this carefully because Tim was right. Three decades was a long time. Four was even longer. He could spend those years being subservient to Wanda during the day and representing the lollipop guild or whatever at night. Or he could write a new script for his life, one that ended with his dreams coming true.

Tim strolled into Studio Maltese, bringing the optimism of a blue-skied day into the murky gray hallway. He loved visiting here. To him it felt like a second workplace, having all the benefits and none of the drawbacks. Tim never had to worry about clocking in or getting projects done on time. He just had to show up, say hello to Dave the security guard (who always waved him through), and ride the elevator up to the executive office on the third floor.

The ride didn't last as long as usual. The doors opened to reveal a broad-shouldered guy with a permanent scowl. Nathaniel was handsome in his own way and had been a major temptation during Tim's only date with him. That all seemed like ancient history now. Tension between them, be it sexual or otherwise, was nonexistent.

Nathaniel glanced up, surprise easing the grumpy expression into something more friendly. "You're early," he said.

"Better than late," Tim said, grabbing the door so it wouldn't shut.

Nathaniel stepped into the elevator, offering his hand. "Did he convince you to go?"

Tim shook Nathaniel's hand, then his own head. "Huh?"

"Marcello. Did he—" Now it was Nathaniel who grabbed the door. "Are you going up or down?"

"Up."

Nathaniel flicked his arm so the suit jacket pulled away from his wrist. After consulting his watch, he sighed. "Sorry. It's been a long day. I thought you had finished early."

As opposed to arriving early, which meant he knew what this meeting was about. Tim had thought it was just a friendly invitation, a chance to catch up with his closest friend. Instead, it sounded like Marcello planned to convince him of something.

"Got a second?" Tim asked, blocking the other side of the elevator door. Electronic beeping protested this behavior. Or maybe Marcello was up in his office, monitoring them and trying to prevent them from talking.

Nathaniel looked from him to a camera in one corner, then nodded and stepped off the elevator again.

Tim followed. "How's married life treating you?" he asked once the doors closed.

"Good," Nathaniel said, his smile making a rare appearance. "Really good. Kelly is... amazing. I can't believe I almost lost him. I still wake up in a cold sweat sometimes and have to make sure he's really there."

"I know the feeling," Tim said. "Sometimes I think we've got it better than most people. There's that saying about not knowing what you've got until it's gone. Well, both you and I know exactly what we've got while still getting to have it. Does that make sense?"

"Perfect sense," Nathaniel said. "We've been to the brink and back again. Plus, now that I've already screwed up once, I'm confident I won't be so dumb again."

"Speak for yourself," Tim said with a chuckle. "I've still got tons of stupid mistakes left in me. Hey, I'm mad that I didn't get a wedding invite!"

"It wasn't exactly traditional," Nathaniel said. "Our families weren't even there. How about dinner sometime?"

"Just you and me?" Tim said with a wink. "Back to the taco trucks?"

Nathaniel laughed. "Not a chance. Kelly would kill us both. I'm serious about dinner. You could bring Chinchilla. Zero isn't the best host, but we're working on it."

"Sounds great!" Tim said. "She would love that. I would too!"

They both reached for their phones, like cowboys drawing their guns for a duel. They always did this. "Dog photos?" Tim asked.

"Yeah," Nathaniel said with a nod. "Check this one out. During the summer, I had the groomers buzz Zero down. Huskies don't do so well in the heat. I asked them to leave a strip of hair like—"

"A mohawk!" Tim declared gleefully. "You're so lucky. Chinchilla's hair doesn't get long enough to do anything fun."

"Don't say I'm lucky until you see our couch." Nathaniel noticed the photo he was holding up. "That bow is adorable! Zero would never wear anything like that. The groomer tried once and he rolled in the dirt just to get it off. He's hopeless."

"No Halloween costumes then?" Tim swiped his phone and held it up again.

"Huh-uh. No! You dressed her up like a princess? I'm dying!"

This went on for longer than it probably should have. Only when they finished fawning over each other's pets did they think to share photos of the men they were married to.

"He doesn't age," Nathaniel said, scrutinizing a photo of Ben. "I was organizing fundraiser photos recently and saw an old one of him. Looks exactly the same, even though this must have been ten years ago."

"I don't know how he does it," Tim said wistfully. Then he looked at the photo Nathaniel was presenting of a guy sitting up shirtless in bed, the sheets gathered around his waist. "Jesus! Kelly is modelling again?"

Nathaniel shook his head. "Took that one just a few minutes after he woke up."

"Don't let him out of the house," Tim advised.

"Nah," Nathaniel said with a dopey grin. "You've got to trust them. Otherwise, what's the point? Keep that in mind during your meeting."

"I don't have any trust issues with Ben," Tim said, not understanding.

"That's good. What about Marcello? Do you trust him?"

"Absolutely not," Tim said, but he winked to show he was kidding. He loved Marcello, and even though he could be slippery, Tim did trust him. Completely.

"Better not keep him waiting," Nathaniel said, jabbing the button to call the elevator. "I meant what I said about dinner. Anytime."

"I'll let Ben know. He'll love the idea." Tim stepped into the elevator and turned around. "You're not riding along?"

Nathaniel shook his head. "I'll take the stairs. Best of luck."

Nice guy, although not the best at providing reassurance. As the elevator doors shut, Tim felt nervous. What did he need luck for? The little box rose and the doors opened again. Marcello was halfway across the office and moving toward him, a finger waving in the air.

"Lies!" he declared. "All lies! Don't believe a word of what that man told you."

"So his dog *isn't* the handsomest in the world?" Tim teased.

"The most ill-behaved perhaps," Marcello said, peering suspiciously. "He didn't spoil anything?"

"Nada," Tim said. "I'm the picture of innocence."

"They always start that way, but it never seems to last." Marcello gestured to the couches. "Please. Make yourself comfortable."

Now he knew he was in trouble. The couches were where Marcello did his best convincing.

"I have beer," Marcello offered, moving toward the wet bar. "A selection from Germany, although if you're feeling patriotic, I have American brands too."

Beer? Instead of champagne. Yup. He was definitely in trouble. "You killed someone," Tim said. "You killed someone and want help disposing of the body."

"I have people who handle such things," Marcello said dismissively. "Now then, what shall it be? A refreshing Kristallweizen? A fruity Radler? Or how about a robust Kellerbier?"

"Refreshing sounds good," Tim said, taking a seat.

Marcello uncapped two bottles and joined him. "How are things at home?"

"Better than ever," Tim said, putting on a smug expression. "I've been sleeping with this hot college guy."

"Oh really?" Marcello said, attention instantly piqued. "That sounds positively scandalous! While normally my cup of tea, I'm inordinately fond of your husband. What does he think of all this?"

"Ben? He's in the same room while we're getting it on."

Marcello's smile was subtle. "I take it then, that you convinced him to reenroll."

"Busted," Tim said, eyes trained on the golden liquid being expertly poured into each glass. "It really is hot. I know he's the same guy, but I love dropping him off and picking him up from school. He drives himself usually, but sometimes I insist, just to keep the fantasy going. I'm hoping we can find somewhere on campus to uh..."

"I'll make you a list of suitable places," Marcello said, sliding a glass over to him. "You know, I enjoyed our friendship even before Ben came along, but I must admit, I find your relationship with him as inspiring as it is endearing."

"Thinking of settling down finally?" Tim asked.

"Heavens no! Not while I'm still so young." Marcello raised a glass to clink it against his before continuing. "I had rather a different idea in mind, although it's not the one I called you here for. Perhaps now is not the time. You have enough to consider without throwing a movie into the mix."

"A movie?" Tim said, nearly spitting out his beer. "About me and Ben?" He thought about it and laughed. "I get it. One of your pornos."

Marcello pulled back. "I take offense at that term!"

"Sorry," Tim said. "One of your romantic movies that don't shy away from sex because it's... How do you always put it?"

"A revealing part of any relationship. Pun thoroughly intended."

"Fair enough, but I'm not sure I like the idea of being naked on screen, even if it's some actor representing me, and I know Benjamin wouldn't like it."

Marcello nodded thoughtfully. "Perhaps, just this once, I could make an exception. The sex scenes could fade to black, so long as you don't begrudge me a little skin. A family-friendly rating could also mean a larger audience. Just imagine what a service that would provide. Finally, a timeless gay love story to inspire generations!"

Tim snorted. "More like our personal life on parade for everyone to see. We're private people. Not to mention that there are parts I'm not proud of. Things got pretty dark with Ryan."

"Oh we'd leave him out of it," Marcello said. "I wouldn't want to give the little brat attention. He would like that too much."

"You're kidding. Aren't you?"

"Not at all! Talk it over with your husband, see if he finds the idea as amusing as I do. If so, we can take it from there."

"Enough about that," Tim said, still shaking his head. "We've been out of touch. Tell me how the most recent trip to Japan went."

"A mixture of good and bad. The selfie studio is a roaring success. They have to turn hundreds of people away each day. Already there is talk of opening a second location. I've made sure to patent the idea, naturally."

"What about the new Eric Conroy Gallery?" Tim asked.

"Therein lies the problem," Marcello said. "Everything is going well *except* the new gallery."

Tim swallowed. "I really want this to happen. It would mean a lot to Eric."

"Undoubtedly. I'm sure that, working together, we can overcome any obstacles." Marcello leaned forward. "Here's to our partnership, both as friends and businessmen."

Businessmen! Tim never thought of himself that way, but he supposed it was true. He drummed up business, but for the artists he helped support rather than himself. He took a hearty swig, already knowing that he would need a taxi to get home, because the beer tasted too good to stop at one. "So what's up?"

Marcello's sigh was one of gentle frustration. "The person I placed in charge of establishing the new gallery isn't an artist, despite his claims to be. He selected a space unsuitable for displaying art. The walls, I understand, aren't of a high enough quality to bear much weight. Windows are nonexistent, and proper lighting isn't an option since the entire electrical system needs to be rewired. I also have concerns about the square footage, but none of this troubles me as much as his attitude. He wants to charge each artist a fee for submitting their work, with no guarantee that they'll be accepted."

"Most artists don't have money," Tim said, already shaking his head.

"Precisely! The goal is to make creative work sustainable to the artist, not bleed them dry with monthly fees."

"Monthly?"

"Yes. If their work is accepted, they would be subject to what he calls a listing fee. In order to cover the expenses of running the gallery."

"That's what the annual fundraiser is for!" Tim protested. "Jesus, this is starting to sound worse than a normal commercial gallery!"

"Indeed," Marcello said. "I knew you would be of a like mind, and I remain eager to hear your advice. I've tried reasoning with this person, but to no avail."

"Fire him," Tim said instantly. "Get someone else in there who knows what they're doing." Then he leaned back and groaned, because suddenly it was all painfully obvious.

"What do you think of the beer?" Marcello asked sweetly.

"You probably wish I was on my third already."

"Not really," Marcello said. "I'm confident that we'll reach the same conclusion, once you've been presented with all the facts. Before we get too deep, we'll first address your concerns."

Hell yeah they would! "I have my own gallery to run."

"One that, thanks to your diligence, is a well-oiled machine. I'm sure we can find someone competent to take the reins during your absence."

"How long would that be?"

"Difficult to say," Marcello replied. "You know, I must apologize. Kristallweizen is normally served with a slice of lemon, although I prefer lime. Would you care for either?"

"If you were forced to guess," Tim said, refusing to be sidetracked. "How long?"

"A month at the very least. I really do insist on a citrus slice of some variety. You'll be surprised what a difference it makes." Marcello rose and went to the wet bar on the other side of the room.

He was giving Tim time to think, but he didn't need much. "Sorry," he said when Marcello had returned. "I can't. If this had happened earlier in the year, I would have taken Ben with me and had an awesome adventure. I can't pull him out of school."

Marcello smiled. "That does sound adorable. Like he's your little boy. Do you have any photos of him when he was young? I bet he couldn't leave the house without his cheeks being pinched."

"I mean it," Tim said.

"At least try a sip with the lemon."

"Marcello!" he pleaded, but it was hopeless. He indulged in another swig. The beer really was delicious. Even though Tim was more careful about how much he drank these days, it took more than a few sips to make him sway, literally or figuratively. "I can't."

"You can," Marcello said. "All that remains to be seen is if you will. Are you certain that Ben can't delay his educational pursuits for one semester?"

"He's already a month deep, and it was hard enough to convince him to go back to school at all."

"Still, at least he would be occupied. Young Jason continues to settle into his new life, I trust?"

Tim nodded. "He's doing really good. Entire days go by without us hearing from him."

"A healthy sign if ever there was one," Marcello said, eyes steadily boring into Tim's own.

He nearly gave up then and there, just to save time. "Tell you what, I'll sit down with someone you trust. Someone like Nathaniel. I'll tell them everything that I would do and what to look for. Hell, they can shadow me at the gallery for as long as they need. I'm staying here though."

"Allow me to show you something," Marcello said, setting aside his glass and reaching for a tablet. He didn't have to navigate long before handing it to Tim. Knowing him, the device had been primed and ready to go. "Press play."

Tim did so, confused at first by what he saw. The video revealed a crowded gallery. The attendees were primarily

Japanese, although they weren't evenly distributed throughout the room. Two pieces of art were getting the most attention, clusters of people jostling for a better position from which to see. "What is this?"

"A temporary exhibition to showcase what has been produced by the new selfie studio. Not just photography, but pieces created by artists who were given a space to work in. And do you see what has become, without any exaggeration, an overnight sensation?"

Tim looked closer, pausing the video just as three people were moving away. Then he looked up in disbelief. "That's one of mine."

"Indeed it is. So is the other, although you'll have to take my word for it, since the crowds never seem to part long enough to see it clearly."

"But my paintings weren't created in that studio."

"They were made in the American equivalent. Your work stole the show! I've managed to keep the wolves from the door, but you're in a number of publications now." Marcello gestured to the table, where Japanese newspapers and magazines sat in a small stack.

"Not all of those," Tim said.

"Each and every one. This is just the beginning. But only if you make this trip."

Tim stared. Then he shook his head. "No way. No amount of fame or money is going to tear me away from Benjamin. Not even for a month."

"If I thought such things could tempt you, I would have begun this conversation by appealing to your ego." Marcello laced his fingers together, resting them on his belly. "The new Eric Conroy Gallery will need more than just a suitable space, or someone to get it off the ground. We need publicity. We also require a lucrative method of fundraising. I won't rely on my army of philanthropists with disposable incomes. I could appeal to them, but if we truly want this to be sustainable, then we must cultivate local support and interest."

Tim took a deep breath. When that wasn't enough, he drained his beer. "Tell me your plan."

"You'll travel to Japan—"

"I don't speak the language."

"You'll have a translator at your disposal. Your primary occupation will be seeking out a suitable gallery space. I'll stir the PR pot from over here. When we're ready, you'll host another exhibition of your art, and if you find the idea agreeable, a portion of the proceeds will go to supporting the new gallery."

"All of it," Tim said. "I like the idea of my paintings helping other artists."

"You'll do it?"

Tim opened his mouth, on the verge of agreeing. Then he thought of brown eyes that could be steel-hard with courage at times, and wet with vulnerability at others. "I need to talk to Ben first."

Marcello appeared pleased. "I shall entrust the outcome of this mad scheme to his gentle wisdom."

"Very nice," Tim said. "Maybe you should try writing haikus. We could both be big in Japan."

"Tempting," Marcello said. "I've always been more partial to limericks. I was inspired to write a new one recently. Would you like me to recite it?"

"Crack me open another of those beers," Tim said, "and I'll listen to anything you've got to say."

"You're famous?" Ben asked, clearly struggling to come to terms with the idea.

He wasn't the only one. Tim still found it unbelievable that anyone liked his art. Eric had always been supportive. Ben too, but they loved him. Tim always figured they couldn't separate the art from the man who made it. In other words, they were biased. Maybe they *weren't* just flattering him. He was always enraptured by Ben's singing, and he didn't think love influenced that. Tim had been blown away since the very beginning.

They were still in bed, the day young. Tim had waited a night before broaching the subject so he could sort through his own feelings. He had wanted to be stone-cold sober too. Now he couldn't wait any longer, and for the record, Ben might not be a former super-model, but he also looked damn fine first thing in the morning.

"Mind if I take a photo?" Tim asked, reaching for his phone.

"Of me?" Ben said, recoiling from the idea. "Right now? Why?"

To show Nathaniel, but that sounded weird, so he changed the subject. "Never mind. And no, I'm not famous. These things happen in the art world. It's like Twitter or anything else. An artist will start trending, and for that week or month, they'll be all the rage. Then people will move on to whatever is next. That's why if we do this—I've already said no multiple times—but if we do this, it needs to be soon."

Ben exhaled, no doubt going over the details in his mind just as Tim had done numerous times since meeting with Marcello. "What if you're not just a flash in the pan?"

"Nothing changes," Tim said. "I can paint from here and ship stuff over. I would only go to Japan to get the new gallery set up."

"Which would double the number of artists you can help. And be good exposure for your art." Ben hugged a pillow to himself. "How long would you be gone?"

"Tough to say. Marcello thinks a month at minimum."

Ben was pensive, staring off into space. Then he blinked. "If I put off getting my master's and fly over there with you, what do we do with Chinchilla? Can we take her with us?"

"I wish," Tim said. "Bulldogs are banned from cargo holds, and she's too big to fly in the cabin so… You know what? Don't worry about it. I'm not going."

"I think you should," Ben said. "It's just a month. Even if it's six weeks, it'll still fly by. I'll stay here with Chinchilla and hold down the fort. Between my studies and work, I won't even notice you're gone."

Tim frowned. "Really?"

"No," Ben admitted, grabbing Tim's arm and rolling over so they could spoon. "I'll hate not having you here, and I'll miss you every day."

"Then let's forget about it," he murmured against Ben's neck.

"We can't always be selfish. I really want to be, but think of how many people you could help and where they would be without you. Hitler wanted to be an artist, you know, but he was never given a chance. If you don't go, any future World Wars are basically your fault."

Tim laughed. "When you put it like that… Nah. We should think about this more."

"Maybe," Ben said, rolling over to face him. "I love your art. Even if we didn't take the new gallery into consideration, I'd still urge you to go, just to see what happens. This is what I've always wanted for you. People appreciate your work! Don't turn your back on that. Even if your popularity doesn't last, you'll have touched someone out there." A second later and Ben's eyes grew wide. "I didn't mean physically!"

"Do you want me to stop?" Tim asked, his hand still moving up and down beneath the sheets.

Ben bit a knuckle and shook his head. "Definitely not. I've always wanted to make it with a famous artist."

Tim grinned and ducked beneath the sheets. As soon as he was hidden from view, he let the pain show, because this wouldn't be easy. He didn't want to leave Ben, even for just one day. Still, as he scooted down further, his lips brushing against Ben's hip and making him giggle, he decided to enjoy the time they had left.

Tim sat on the edge of the mattress, fully dressed and ready to go. Occasionally he would look over at the slumbering form next to him and wonder how anyone gathered the strength to say goodbye. Ben's back was to him, the blankets hiding all but his shoulders and head. Tim longed to touch him, to smooth the mussed hair with his hand, or to press his lips against skin while breathing in Ben's scent. Doing so might cause him to stir and wake, so Tim held back. This is what they had agreed on, although to be fair, it was mostly his wish. He wouldn't be able to leave if forced to look into those sad brown eyes, so during the days of planning for this trip, he had begged and pleaded until Ben agreed to treat the morning like any other. Even though it wasn't.

Tim rose and quietly went downstairs. Chinchilla was still outside, where she preferred to stay until the day grew too hot to be comfortable. Only then would she come in, following him around to each room or out to his studio. On days when he knew Ben wouldn't be home, Tim often took her to the gallery with him. They were a team. They had traveled together on many trips, Tim preferring to drive rather than fly, just so they could be together. Not this time though. What nearly broke his heart was how excited Chinchilla had been when he brought the luggage down from the attic. She had walked around it, stubby tail wagging, and he had tried to explain that Japan was simply too far for her to travel.

And speaking of heartbreak... Tim stepped outside to visit her, getting down on his knees so he could caress her fur. After walking circles around him, putting on a show and huffing in a way that seemed like talking as much as her open mouth resembled a grin, Chinchilla plopped down next to him. Tim put an arm around her and rubbed her belly while they stared out at the yard. He was going to miss this place.

"Why does anyone ever leave home?" Tim asked. "Now I see why Jason took so long."

Chinchilla turned her head to look up at him, as if saying he didn't have to go.

"I guess I don't," he replied. "The thing is, I feel like I owe Eric. You never got to meet him, but we wouldn't have such a nice house if it wasn't for him. I don't think I would have gotten Benjamin back either. So I need to repay him, or pay it forward. Same thing, I guess."

Chinchilla didn't appear convinced.

"Okay, we can give all his money to charity, but then we'd have to sell the house and live in an apartment. No more backyard for you to potty in."

Chinchilla considered the green grass, mouth closing in concern.

"That's what I thought," Tim said. "I'll be back. Until then, I need you to take care of Ben. Don't let him get too sad. Give him lots of love. I need you to stay healthy too, you know what I mean? You're not as young as you used to be."

Chinchilla licked her chops and looked away.

"Sorry. I'm not getting any younger either. You're still my baby. Don't worry." He leaned over and kissed her on top of the head. "I gotta go. I love you."

Ugh. He was on the verge of crying. Now he felt good about his decision to let Ben sleep in. This was already too hard. Although he wasn't completely surprised, when reentering the house, to find Ben standing in the living room while wearing a bathrobe, his hair sopping wet.

"That was the quickest shower of my life," he said, chest heaving like he had run straight from the upstairs bathroom.

"Did I wake you?"

Ben shook his head. "I wasn't sleeping. I tried, but I couldn't."

"Then maybe you should give yourself more credit, because that was some damn fine acting."

Ben started to smile before the pressure of the moment forced it away. "How long until the cab gets here?"

Tim swallowed "It might be out front already."

"Oh." Ben nibbled his bottom lip, maybe trying to figure out how to spend these last few seconds together. "I need you to be careful," he said.

"I will."

"Don't drink too much."

"I won't."

"Okay." Ben took a deep breath, eyes already apologetic. "Remember your promise."

Like he could ever forget! Tim always felt the weight of that promise, even though Ben didn't mention it often. Only when he was feeling especially upset or vulnerable. Tim thought of the night he had first taken the oath, when they had reunited after too many years of separation. Ben had recovered from Jace's death as much as anyone losing a spouse could, but he had still been shaken and unable to move on. Not when doing so might subject him to the same pain again, so Tim had sworn that he wouldn't die before Ben did. That promise often made him ease his foot off the gas, or decline another drink, or keep his temper in check during volatile situations.

"I won't forget," Tim said. His phone rumbled, but he couldn't tear his eyes away from Ben to check it.

"Is that your ride?"

"Probably."

"You should go."

Tim stayed where he was. Fuck the gallery and any noble plans because Ben was more important than all of it. Tim would never leave the house again! Why should he, when everything important to him was right here?

That's when Ben said the one thing that could get him moving. "I'm proud of you."

Tim's shoulders sagged. He was willing to stay for Ben, and he was willing to leave for him too. "I'll call," he said. "A bunch. I'll work really hard so I can come home early. How long could it take, right? I'll find someone there, tell them everything I know, and I'll be back as quick as possible. I can't promise when, but I'll try."

Ben's face quivered, a tiny earthquake that threatened to

reveal larger cracks. "There's only one promise I need you to keep."

"I will," Tim said. They heard a honk outside, so he stepped forward, taking Ben's hands into his own. "Study hard but also spoil yourself, okay? At least you won't have to pick up my smelly socks for a while."

"I love your smelly socks," Ben said with the kind of sincerity that only impending separation could induce.

"I love your smelly socks too," Tim said, leaning forward.

They pressed their lips together, holding them there, as if hoping to create a kiss that would remain with them until they could be together again. Then they reluctantly pulled away.

Ben eyes were full of shimmering tears. Then he swallowed and straightened himself up. "My socks don't smell."

Tim managed a laugh. "They do. Like freshly baked cookies."

Ben tilted his head. "I get what you're trying to say, but now I'm picturing cookie dough stuck between my toes, and it's kind of gross."

"I said freshly baked," he complained. "I don't know why you're picturing raw dough."

"Baked cookies aren't much better," Ben countered. "Think of the crumbs!"

"I said they smell *like* cookies. You're the one wanting to shove actual food into your socks." Tim's phone started vibrating. A call, probably from the cab driver, when all he really wanted was to stand here with Ben and keep saying dumb stuff to each other, because even moments like these were the best. He pulled out his phone and answered it. "I'll be right out. Start the meter, I don't mind."

When he pocketed his phone, he looked up to see that they had returned to feeling the same uneasy pain. "I guess this is it."

"No," Ben said, shaking his head. "This isn't even close to being it, so hurry back, okay?"

"Yeah," Tim said, feet unable to move.

"I love you." Ben stepped forward for a quick kiss. Then he moved past him. "I'll check on Chinchilla. She can help me water the flowers. I forgot to yesterday."

Ben was definitely a better actor than he gave himself credit for, because he sounded casual, like nothing was out of the ordinary. He was fulfilling Tim's request, not by sleeping in or pretending to, but by opening the door to the backyard and leaving him in a silent living room. Only then was Tim able to walk to the front door, pick up his luggage, and leave the house. He looked back just before doing so. Through the glass door, he saw Ben standing on the rear patio, arms clutched around himself, but his back remained turned. Chinchilla didn't share his discretion. She waited at the glass door, trying to see past the reflections, and probably wondering where he was. Throat raw with pain, Tim promised not to keep her waiting for long, and stepped outside to face an uncertain future.

Chapter Eight

After travelling for nearly twenty-four hours, Tim was surprised to find his first impression of Japan was subdued. Maybe he had seen too many weird video clips online, because when he stepped out of the plane and into Narita International Airport, he expected to be greeted by hyper teenage girls who were wearing panda hats and speaking rapid-fire Japanese while lobbing gelatin-filled balloons at him. Maybe such antics were reserved for their game shows, because like all airports, this one featured white corridors and people eager to be anywhere but there. He scanned the crowds, having been told that someone would meet him. Mrs. Hashimoto, he reminded himself by checking the notes on his phone. This wasn't the right spot, so he let the flow take him to immigration, where he waited in line and yawned until his passport was stamped.

As soon as he collected his luggage and left the secured area, he noticed people holding up signs with last names on them. Tim spotted his own, but felt less certain when he saw that a man was holding the sign instead of a woman. Then again, how many Wymans could be waiting for a ride from the Tokyo airport? He moved toward the man, who saw him, straightened up, and bowed curtly.

"Wyman-sama! How was your trip?" His English was perfect, with no trace of an accent. "I'm Mr. Tanaka. I'll be taking care of you during your visit."

The man had jet black hair and eyes just as dark. Despite this, he didn't look Japanese. Tim was hard-pressed to say why, and he worried it wasn't a racially sensitive observation, so he quickly moved on to other attributes. Mr. Tanaka was near his own age, his slim figure outfitted in a black suit complete with white shirt and black tie. Not a lot of color, but the low-key look suited him well.

"Hey," Tim said, wondering if he was supposed to bow too. He settled for a nod. "Uh, I was expecting someone by the name of... Sorry, I think it was—"

"Mrs. Hashimoto. She had a family emergency, but I'll work just as hard to make sure you have a pleasant visit."

"Thank you," Tim said, unable to tear his eyes away, because there was something vaguely familiar about this person. He wasn't someone Tim knew well, but they had definitely met before. He just couldn't remember where. "Do you work for Marcello?"

"I had the pleasure of assisting Maltese-sama on one of his recent trips here."

That must be it. Mr. Tanaka was attractive enough, so Marcello had probably included him in some of the photos he brought back.

"We can start the drive to your hotel now, if you are ready."

Tim shook his head. "I still need to get my luggage."

Mr. Tanaka leaned to the right to look behind him. "More than what you already have?"

Tim glanced over and saw his suitcases. Then he laughed and lightly slapped his own cheeks. "Sorry, long flight. I'm a little dazed."

"I understand how you feel," Mr. Tanaka said with a smile. "Let me take one of those for you. Right this way, please."

Tim followed him down more hallways, still trying to place the face. Most of the photos Marcello had shown him were of the new gallery and selfie studio. They weren't his typical vacation photos, which tended to be filled with cabana boys and debonair dandies. He supposed that Mr. Tanaka could have been in some of the work photos by coincidence. Or maybe he merely looked like someone from television. What was the name of that one actor, the cute one who started in the sitcom about aliens? Joseph Gordon-Levitt! Maybe that's who Tim was thinking of.

Or maybe he was just tired. Tim followed his guide in a fog. He had only managed to get a few hours of sleep during the flight, and the time difference had him confused. The local clocks said it was five in the afternoon, but his body insisted he should be in bed. Some mental arithmetic revealed that it was three in the morning back home. Despite feeling like he never wanted to sit again, he was relieved when they reached Mr. Tanaka's vehicle—a black Mazda CX-5—since he could throw his luggage in the back and no longer had to worry about dodging other frenzied travelers. All he needed to do was relax in the passenger seat and let his guide stress about where they were going and how.

"So will Mrs. Hashi... Will the woman I was supposed to meet be back to translate for me?"

"I'll be taking care of your translation needs," Mr. Tanaka said, expression concerned. "I hope that's okay."

"Yeah! Totally. Just trying to get a feel for how everything will work." He looked outside the window, relieved to see that it wasn't so different from home. Most of the signs were written in kanji that he couldn't read. He had tried studying Japanese before leaving, but the trip had been on such short notice, and after a few unsuccessful attempts, Tim had decided he only had enough room in his head for two languages. "How long until we reach Tokyo?"

"About an hour. It's good you didn't arrive on a weekday. Traffic shouldn't be too bad."

"What day is it again?" Tim asked.

Mr. Tanaka laughed pleasantly. "Sunday. I know it's confusing. Give yourself a few days and you'll adjust."

He hoped so. Tim stared out the window a little longer, enjoying how weird it felt to be driving on the wrong side of the road. Then he turned his attention to his phone, wanting to text Ben. He had a signal, but he kept getting a popup message that he couldn't read. "Any trick to using a cell phone here?"

"Did you sign up for an international plan?"

"Yeah, before I left. I don't think it's working."

"I'd be happy to help you with that once we reach the hotel, Wyman-sama."

God that sounded strange, but he had read a little about it. The Japanese had different suffixes, *sama*, *san*, *chan*, and others that indicated respect or affection. If he remembered right, *sama* was way up there in terms of status, but he still didn't understand when to use what. "Should I be calling you Tanaka-sama? I don't really get the rules."

"No, save that for your superiors or customers. If you'd like, you can call me Tanaka-kun."

Great! Another syllable for an unusual name. Practice makes perfect though. "I hope you're patient, Tanaka-kun, because I'm totally lost."

"That's what I'm here for. When we're not together, you'll have my number and can call me for anything. Even if you're just out shopping or need help ordering at a restaurant."

"That's awesome!" Tim said, hoping the offer wasn't a polite one, because he would need frequent help. The first order of business was to get his phone working. He had promised Ben to send a text once he had arrived safely. Despite it being early there, he could imagine Ben staying up just to hear from him, or at the very least, sleeping next to his phone. Tim messed with it a little longer, and when his eyes burned from the effort, he leaned the seat back and closed them. He drifted off briefly, or maybe longer than he thought, because when he sat upright again, the scenery had changed. The street they were driving down was lined with buildings ten stories or higher. With any city came the chaos of trying to keep it running. Trucks struggled to make deliveries, pedestrians swarmed the crosswalks, and an ambulance breezed past them on its way to an emergency. Construction and repairs hampered all of this.

"Nearly there," Mr. Tanaka said.

Tim rubbed his eyes and tried to shake the grogginess. Despite how tired he was, he yearned to get out and explore on foot. The world outside the car window was new and exciting. Aside from a few corporate giants that were impossible to escape, such as McDonald's, he didn't have a clue as to what hid behind the storefronts. He wondered how patient his guide would be about shopping, because Tim was bound to get lost. He couldn't even read street signs!

"Where are we exactly?"

"Shinjuku," Mr. Tanaka said. "That's your hotel ahead."

Tim took note of it, quickly trying to memorize as many landmarks as possible before they pulled into the parking garage. After getting his luggage from the back, they walked to an elevator, but Mr. Tanaka didn't push the button for the lobby.

"I took the liberty of checking you in," he explained. "I hope you don't mind."

"Not at all!" Tim said, glad to be one step closer to relaxation. His room was on the eleventh floor. Mr. Tanaka guided him to a door and handed him a magnetic keycard. Tim wasn't sure how long his guide planned on sticking around, but it seemed rude not to invite him in. "Have you seen the room yet?"

Mr. Tanaka nodded. "It's very nice. I tried to stock it with everything you might need."

"Wow? Really?" Tim pushed his way inside. "Let's see!"

The room was fine. He had stayed in extravagant places before, usually when trying to impress Ben. Tim was also okay with humbler accommodations. This was somewhere in between.

The room was long with a bed at the far end near the windows. A couch and television was next to this, and nearest to the door was a kitchenette. A pair of neatly placed slippers waited before a bathroom separated by a sliding door. His home for the duration of the stay. He was reminded of William and Jason's place, which now felt even farther away than it usually did. Another continent, a different world.

"Something wrong?" Mr. Tanaka asked.

"No," Tim said. "Just a little jolt of homesickness."

"Which is why I stocked the refrigerator with a mixture of comfort foods and new things you might like to try." Mr. Tanaka opened the door to show him.

Tim spotted beer, which was an excellent start. Just about everything in there looked good, which made him realize how hungry he was. A warm meal sounded best, and although the room had a microwave, after eating airline food, he craved quality.

"Is there anything else I can do for you?" Mr. Tanaka asked.

"Does this hotel have a restaurant?"

"They do, and it's highly rated."

Tim hesitated. Would he be able to order there or even read the menu? He supposed he could ask his guide to order for him, but when he tried to imagine the logistics, it seemed a crass request. *Tell the waiter what I want and then leave.* That wouldn't be cool, so he opted for another solution. "Are you hungry? If you've got somewhere you need to be, that's totally fine. If not, we could have breakfast together. My treat."

"Dinner," Mr. Tanaka corrected with a smile. "I have a call I need to make, but why don't you get settled and we'll meet in the lobby. Fifteen minutes?"

"Awesome," Tim said. "Thanks for driving me here and setting everything up."

Mr. Tanaka clearly appreciated the gratitude, even though he tried to hide it. He was handsome, or would be if he loosened up. Tim wasn't used to everything being so formal. Should he put on a suit before eating? Currently he was wearing an old hoodie and his most comfortable jeans. Rather than ask, he saw his guide to the door. Then he checked his phone, trying to figure out how to sign on to the Wi-Fi. When he didn't have any luck, he used the restroom and freshened up, changing into gray slacks and a black dress shirt. Both were more wrinkled than he liked, but he was already out of time.

He went down to the lobby which, as always with hotels, was more lavish than the room. The strategy was to make a good first impression, but to him it always seemed pointless, since few people spent time in the lobby. Who cared about a fireplace or marble bricks with water running over them? Now if those things had been in his room, he'd be taking pics and bragging to anyone who would listen.

Mr. Tanaka saw him and stood up from one of the lush couches, Tim experiencing the same nagging familiarity.

"You look very sharp, Wyman-sama," Mr. Tanaka said.

"Thanks," Tim replied, already sick of hearing his last name so much. "Am I dressed too casually? You look a lot nicer in your suit."

"Between you and me," Mr. Tanaka said, leaning forward to whisper, "most days I can barely wait to get home and switch into sweatpants and a T-shirt."

Tim laughed. "I know the feeling."

"But no, you're dressed fine. The restaurant is just over here."

Down a short hall was a bar and grill. Whatever they were cooking smelled delicious. Tim hung back while his guide took care of the details. Tim was a poor judge, but the Japanese he spoke sounded just as convincing as his English. That had him intrigued, so once they were seated in a booth and had placed their drink orders (a beer for him, a tea for Mr. Tanaka) he decided to ask.

"Are you from Japan? Because your English sounds native."

Mr. Tanaka smiled in a way that was surprisingly playful. "Care to guess where I was born?"

"Oh. Okay. Well your name sounds Japanese—"

"Colder."

They were playing hot/cold? "You're an American."

"Very warm!"

"Or maybe Canadian?"

"Getting cold again."

"*No eres mexicano,*" he tried.

"Colder. Probably. What did you say?"

Tim grinned. "So you're from the States, but which one?"

"It's getting hot in here," Mr. Tanaka said, fanning himself.

That gave Tim pause. His guide had been so stiff and formal at the airport and during the ride here. Maybe now that he was officially off work he was able to be more casual. Tim preferred this, but his brain was going crazy as he tried to figure out why that face, and especially those nearly black irises, were so familiar. Even the mannerisms! They had definitely met before. "Texas."

"Colder."

That left him clueless, so he went with his home state. "Kansas."

"Born and raised."

Tim gawped. Then he grinned. "Same here! Small world."

Mr. Tanaka seemed amused, the dark eyes sparkling. "Smaller than you think, Wyman-sama."

He groaned. "If we're both from Kansas, can we drop the sama-kun-san or whatever? Call me Tim."

"If that's what you prefer."

"It is."

Tim waited. His guide seemed content to stare.

"So uh, do you have a first name too? Or is it Mister, because that would be a really weird name to give a baby."

"I have a name," Mr. Tanaka said, patting his pockets. "I just can't remember what I did with it."

The mischievous grin and those glimmering dark eyes... A memory hit Tim in the gut, one he hadn't considered in years, maybe even decades. He had been in a young man's room, bass thumping from a party downstairs that he had been eager to escape. Not that he had anything against music or underage drinking. Carla had been the reason Tim hadn't wanted to return downstairs, his girlfriend in one of her meaner moods, so Tim had hung out instead with her little brother. They had passed the time by joking around until the big brother/little brother vibe was eradicated with a single sentence. *You can kiss me if you want.*

"Corey?"

Mr. Tanaka leaned back with a satisfied smile. "And now we're on fire!"

"No way!" Tim stared, taking the eyebrows, the cheekbones, the *everything*, and trying to age it all backwards. His memory wasn't perfect. It had been long ago and he never owned a photo of Corey, but it all fit. Almost. "Your last name..."

"I took my husband's name when we got married," Mr.

Tanaka—no, Corey!—explained. "He's Japanese."

Tim shook his head in wonder. "No freaking way!"

"Yes way!" Corey replied with a chuckle.

The waitress returned with their drinks, which was good, because Tim definitely needed help calming his nerves. This was a good surprise. Wasn't it? He and Carla had an ugly history, but that had nothing to do with her little brother.

"Do you know what you want to eat?" Corey asked.

"I'll leave it up to you," Tim said, glancing at the menu. He saw that it was in both English and Japanese, but he might as well take advantage of local knowledge. "You know what we like to eat in Kansas."

"Steak and barbeque," Corey said instantly. He spoke Japanese to the waitress.

Tim could barely wait for her to leave because he had more questions. "Why didn't you say something sooner?"

"You don't think that would have been creepy?" Corey offered his hand, like they had just met. "Hi, I'm your ex-girlfriend's little brother. I shouldn't even remember you, and you probably don't remember me, but I made sure to get this assignment just to see you again."

Tim laughed. "Of course I remember you! You really took this assignment on purpose?"

"God yes," Corey said shamelessly. "Mrs. Hashimoto is fine, by the way. No family emergency. She always double-checks with me about how to pronounce Western names. When she asked me about yours, I couldn't believe it. I searched online, and when I saw a photo..." He shook his head. "Those eyes aren't easy to forget!"

"Neither are yours," Tim said.

"Thanks. I really didn't think you would remember, but when you kept looking at me funny, I figured I might remind you of Carla."

"How's she doing?" Tim asked. Solely out of politeness.

Corey sucked in through his teeth. "She's... still the same."

The same kind of person who would lie and tell people that he had raped her, when in truth, all Tim had done was break up with her. "She's not in Japan, is she?"

Corey laughed. "No. You're safe, don't worry."

Thank goodness for that! "So tell me about this man of yours."

"Kioshi! He's really sweet. He was an exchange student at KU when we met."

"Go Jayhawks," Tim said with a grin. "So you followed him back here to Japan?"

"I was studying Japanese already, which is good, because his English was terrible. It still is. I was one of the few people he could talk to comfortably while he was in Kansas, so I always say that sheer desperation made him fall in love with me."

"Got a photo with you?"

"Of course!" Corey pulled out his phone and didn't take long to pull up an image.

Tim leaned forward to see it better. Kioshi's hair was dark and long enough to cover his ears and run down the back of his neck. Light scruff shaded a kind face. Definitely a good-looking guy. "Handsome couple," he said. "Too bad you guys can't make babies."

"Thanks," Corey said with a laugh. "It's especially funny because lots of people assume I'm Japanese anyway. Our kid would fit right in here."

"Is it legal for two guys to get married in Japan?"

"Not yet. We flew home the same week it was legalized in the States. We had talked about going to New York or wherever before, but I never—*never*—thought it would be legal in Kansas."

"Same with Texas," Tim said. "I still can't believe it."

"I noticed your wedding ring," Corey said. "Who's the lucky gal?"

Tim snorted and got his phone out. "I'll show you."

Corey's face broke out into a gleeful smile when he saw the photo of Ben. "I *knew* it! I even argued about it with my sister once. I told her you were… into guys."

"I'm gay," Tim said. "More or less. Kinsey scale and all that."

"You have no idea how happy this makes me," Corey said. "Wait until I tell her."

"You already did once," Tim said, not looking quite as pleased. "I think you knew before I did."

"Sorry," Corey said. "I've always been too direct."

Tim nodded, putting on an exasperated expression. "I know."

Corey winced. "You remember all of it, don't you? When I made my big move and tried to steal you away from my sister."

"It was fun hanging out with you that night," Tim said,

wanting to spare his feelings. "That's what I remember. Besides, there's nothing wrong with being direct."

"Yeah, well, it didn't get me anywhere."

"You were twelve!"

"I was not! I must have been... Wait, let me think. How old are you?"

They compared notes until their food arrived. As it turned out, Tim was only a couple years older. Corey had been fourteen, Tim sixteen, when they last saw each other, although that age gap had seemed like a big difference back then. While they ate, Tim quizzed Corey about Kansas, asking about places and people he hadn't seen in ages. The food was good, some sort of veggies and meat on skewers. By the time his belly was full and he had polished off two beers, Tim felt so content that he was tempted to sleep right there in the booth.

"I always thought it would be cool to see you again," Corey said. "I just never thought it would be here, of all places."

Tim laughed. "I never honestly considered the possibility. What started your love affair with Japan, anyway?"

"It's embarrassing."

"Why?"

"Because it's such a Westerner answer. Back home we think of Japan and our minds leap to Godzilla, karaoke, manga, and anime. Yes, those things are part of Japanese culture, but there's so much more."

"So which was it?" Tim asked. "Godzilla?"

"Manga," Corey said, shaking his head. "It's all I would read growing up."

"Those are like comics, right?"

Corey sat up straight. "Are you kidding me? You've never read manga?"

Tim shrugged. "I take it I'm missing out."

"Yes! At least, I think so. Especially yaoi. Boys' love!"

"Huh?"

"It's popular with girls. Picture a normal comic except make it all about two guys falling in love."

"And this is what inspired you to learn Japanese and move here?"

Corey smirked. "I guess I've always been boy-crazy. I'll loan you a few books while you're here. Then you'll see."

Tim yawned, but he didn't mean to be rude. "Sounds good."

"You need to crash," Corey observed. "I need to get back to Kioshi. He's a worrier, even when I call to say where I'll be."

"He sounds nice. I want to meet him."

Corey nodded eagerly. "For sure!" Then he straightened his tie and his tone became formal again. "I hope it's acceptable, Wyman-sama, that I arranged a number of appointments for you tomorrow with a real estate agent."

Tim laughed. "You're really good at that."

Corey let himself slump again. "It's crazy formal here. Think you can be ready by nine?"

He nodded. "This is for the gallery space?"

"Right."

"And you'll be there to translate?"

Corey nodded. "That's what they pay me for!"

Tim grinned. "I was nervous about this trip, but you're making it easy."

"I'm not usually this helpful."

"No?"

"Uh-uh. Only my sister's ex-boyfriends get the star treatment."

They laughed, Tim paid the bill, and they said their goodbyes. He was in his room and had just kicked off his shoes when he remembered Ben. They had forgotten to fix his phone during the big reunion, but Tim wasn't about to go to sleep without sending him a message somehow. Even if it meant running out into the street and begging anyone he saw to use their phone. Oh. Right. He turned and saw the old-fashioned kind next to the bed. After some trial and error, he managed to get a call to go through.

"Hello?" Ben said, sounding a little frantic.

Tim felt like melting into the receiver. "Hey, Benjamin."

He heard a sigh of relief. "Was your flight delayed? I looked online and it said— Are you okay?"

"I'm in my room," Tim said, flopping onto the bed. "I'm safe, I'm exhausted, and I love you."

"I love you too," Ben said. "So what do you think? Is everything crazy over there?"

"It's surprisingly normal," Tim said. "And it's also really weird. Just not in the way I expected. The translator they hired for me is from Kansas. I used to date his sister."

"Is he cute?" Ben asked, instantly suspicious.

"Yes. And he's happily married. So am I, in case you've forgotten."

"I haven't," Ben said, tone softer.

"Could you do me a favor?"

"What?"

"Hold on while I take off my clothes and crawl into bed. Then I want you to keep talking so I can fall asleep to the sound of your voice."

"Are you saying I'm boring?"

"I'm saying I miss you already."

"In that case," Ben said. "How about a lullaby?"

Tim breathed out blissfully. He had expected his first night in Japan to be scary and lonely. Instead he felt happy. He would rather have Ben there with him, but for now, this was the next best thing. He hurried to get into bed, placed the phone next to his pillow, and fell asleep while feeling he was already in the midst of a beautiful dream.

Tim's body decided he needed to be wide awake at five in the morning. That was fine. After brewing a coffee in the tiny machine his room provided, he went for a morning jog. This didn't work so well. Even at the early hour, he had to dodge pedestrians and was forced to limit his route to a small radius around his hotel. He didn't want to get lost. If his phone was working, he could have navigated to the nearest park and back. After showering and going downstairs to stuff himself at the hotel breakfast buffet, he still had plenty of time before Corey was due to arrive. He spent this getting unpacked. Tim ironed a charcoal gray dress shirt and slacks a shade darker to wear, but decided against a suit. He would be the client today. He wasn't the one who needed to make an impression.

When Corey arrived in the lobby, Tim had one thing to say.

"Fix this thing!" he said, thrusting out his phone.

Corey laughed and happily complied, Tim sizing him up while he worked. He was wearing the same suit as yesterday, the white shirt swapped for one that was burgundy, the tie still black. His sister had been a real beauty, so it wasn't a complete surprise that Corey was also attractive. Too bad Tim had been a closet-case back then. Instead of a mean girlfriend, he could have had a kickass boyfriend. Then again, the age difference really had seemed like a big deal.

"Here you go, Wyman-sama," Corey said, handing back the phone. "I hope my diligence in this task has exceeded your expectations."

"None of that formal stuff today," Tim said, grinning wryly. When he saw that his phone was functioning normally again, he nearly hugged his guide. "It works! I'm connected to the world again! It's ridiculous how dependent we've become on these."

"No kidding," Corey said. "I put my number in there, just in case you need any help. Or if you want to drunk-text me funny cat photos in the middle of the night."

"I'll do both," he promised. "So, where to first?"

He let Corey worry about the details. As soon as they were in the Mazda again, Tim got comfortable and sent a text to Ben.

I'm online again! Hopefully I'm in your front pocket right now and vibrating. ;)

Yay! Ben responded. *At the hospital. Sorry.*

That just makes it hotter, Tim replied. *Wanna play doctor?*

I'm working! Otherwise, yes.

Tim decided to leave Ben alone and focus on his surroundings because the future gallery's location was just as important as the space itself. He quizzed Corey about the different neighborhoods and struggled to remember the various names that were mentioned.

"This one is close to Roppongi," Corey explained.

"The nightlife area?"

"Very good! It's far enough from the sleazy bars to be quiet and safe, but still close enough that locals and tourists alike won't struggle to find you."

"Sounds ideal," Tim said as they pulled over and parked. "Marcello sent you the list of what I'm looking for?"

"Sure did," Corey said. "There's our real estate agent."

She was an older Japanese woman. Tim forgot her name about two seconds after Corey introduced them. He really needed to work on that. Maybe Corey could help tutor him somehow. For now, Tim turned his attention to the building, which was on a corner. That was its one saving grace. The dingy appearance, and the smell of old cooking oil inside, turned him off.

"This used to be a hibachi grill," Corey translated.

That was obvious from the tables, chairs, and long grills, all still present. The restaurant seemed to have hurriedly closed its doors one day and never opened them again. The only things missing were the dishes and cutlery.

"You can tell from the furnishings that it was a tourist trap," Corey murmured. "Definitely meant to give Westerners an 'authentic' experience."

Interesting, but Tim was puzzled about why they were in a restaurant at all. Then again, the Eric Conroy Gallery in Austin had been a shoe store once. All that really mattered was a large open space, which this place had, and light, which it definitely didn't.

Two pairs of eyes sought his feedback, Tim shrugging in response. "I was hoping for lots of windows."

Corey translated this, the real estate agent pointing to the far wall. Tim wasn't sure what he was seeing until he got nearer. Fish tanks. Lots and lots of fish tanks, built into the wall. Tim tried not to laugh as he turned to Corey. "Are you sure you know how to speak Japanese?"

"It's a difficult language!" his guide protested before trying again.

The woman led them to the opposite side of the restaurant and peeled back brown paper, revealing filthy glass and a distorted view of the street outside.

"Very nice," Tim said, trying to wipe away the dirt. It resisted. If he had to guess, a combination of grease and cigarette smoke was to blame. "Let's keep looking."

The three of them walked a few minutes to a nearby basement. The exposed brick walls appealed to him, but the property was too small, and again, too dark. They left the real estate agent behind and met another on the opposite side of Roppongi. They were shown what was clearly a one-bedroom apartment, a warehouse space that was much too large, and three properties actually suitable to a gallery, none of which excited him. During a brief break for lunch, they compared notes, Corey searching on his phone for better options and making calls. Tim received one of his own.

"How are matters progressing?" Marcello purred.

"Slowly," Tim admitted. "I haven't found anything that I'm happy with."

"I'm not surprised," came the response. "Remember what a struggle it was here?"

Tim did. They had searched high and low for the ideal place, a process that ended up taking six months. More when renovations were added. Tokyo was, by comparison, a much more complex city than Austin. Regardless, he was determined that this search wouldn't be as drawn-out. No way was he staying away from Ben for half a year! "We'll find something soon," he said. "It's still the first day."

"Quite right. And what do you think of Mrs. Hashimoto? She has the wickedest sense of humor, wouldn't you agree?"

"She couldn't make it," Tim said. He raised his gaze to the table where he had left Corey, who was rubbing his head wearily while on a call of his own. "Mr. Tanaka has been helping me instead."

"Corey?" Marcello chuckled warmly. "You sly devil, you!"

"Why do you say that?"

"He's easier on the eyes. His Japanese isn't as fluent, but I can't blame you for making the switch."

"I didn't have anything to do with it. Despite what I've been told, I figured you might be behind this."

The line was quiet. "If there is some conspiracy here, it pains me not to be part of it."

"Oh come on! You always know way more than you should."

"Then I'm sorry to disappoint you. What am I missing?"

Tim grinned. Marcello didn't know! "Never mind," he said. "Looks like Corey has a lead. I have to go."

"Just a moment!" Marcello protested. "I'd like you to clarify what you meant by—"

"Sorry," Tim said. "I'm getting a lot of glares. Cultural thing. I don't want to offend anybody."

"A hint is all I—"

"We'll talk later! Bye!"

He hung up the phone and laughed. He knew something that Marcello didn't? That was a rare occurrence, one that he intended to enjoy. While it lasted. Marcello was probably playing detective already.

When Tim returned to the table, Corey greeted him with good news. He had found two more potential locations and scheduled appointments for the afternoon. This was in addition to three they already had. One of those would surely work out. Then it would only be a matter of getting it set up, and Tim would be back in Austin sooner rather than later.

By the end of the day, he wasn't feeling as optimistic. He was noticing a pattern of real estate agents pretending they had what he wanted, just to get him to a property. He didn't know what they expected to happen then, aside from him deciding what he really needed was a greasy restaurant, or in one case, a glorified chicken coop.

"I'm never eating eggs again," Corey said as they left the former egg battery. "Although maybe putting an art gallery here would make a statement."

"That we were desperate," Tim said, stifling a yawn. "We can do better. We just need to keep looking."

"You're jetlagged," Corey said, looking him over. Then he checked his watch. "We're done for the day. Should we have dinner somewhere?"

"I'd rather grab a drink," Tim admitted. "Besides, don't you need to get back to your man?"

"I'll invite him along. That is, if you don't mind company."

"I need a nap," Tim said. "Once I'm recharged, I'm up for anything. Actually, you know those karaoke rooms you see in movies sometimes where Japanese guys get super-wasted?"

"*Lost in Translation*?" Corey asked.

"Yeah! Exactly. Are those real?"

"Absolutely."

Tim grinned. "Am I a horrible tourist for wanting to do that?"

Corey laughed. "Not at all. I know just the place."

"Good. In that case, forget the nap. Let's just go there now."

"Kioshi isn't off work yet, and I need to pick him up. Besides, I want out of this suit if we're going to get sloppy. A nap will do you good. Then we'll go out."

Tim shrugged, happy they had reached the SUV. "You're the boss."

"I like the sound of that." Corey looked a little concerned as he opened the driver-side door. "Do you and Marcello drink together often?"

"Sometimes," Tim said.

Once they were both seated in the vehicle, Corey asked another question. "Are you able to keep up with him?"

"Why? Worried about how your head is going to feel tomorrow?"

"Yes," Corey admitted, obviously having suffered some past trauma while entertaining a certain client.

"Don't worry," Tim said with a grin. "Nobody can outdrink Marcello. But that doesn't mean we can't try."

Tim was never much for karaoke. Emma had been younger when they bought her a home version, and while it was fun watching her and Ben croon together, this was an entirely different experience. Or maybe the booze was to thank, because Tim was having a good time. He almost felt like he was back home in the living room. The private rented space had a U-shaped couch against three of the walls, a table in the middle, and on the remaining wall, a monitor that allowed them to select songs and also displayed lyrics and even videos.

He was only vaguely interested in the setup. What caught his attention more was the couple seated across from him. Kioshi was easy to get along with. He was soft-spoken and bashful at first, although numerous glasses of saké had loosened him up. Kioshi was a little beefier than Corey, but not by much. They shared the same dark hair and eyes, although Kioshi had stronger cheekbones, and his smile was a lot more innocent. Corey had always seemed a little naughty. Even as a teenager.

They drank and snacked between songs, their needs met by lifting the receiver on the wall and placing an order. None of them possessed true musical talent, although Kioshi sounded cool when singing in his native language. Corey was brave enough to try a song in Japanese too, and somehow it sounded much cuter. Perhaps because Corey kept smiling at Kioshi during this. They were into each other. That much was obvious, especially now. After three hours, they had all abandoned singing for drinking. The television continued to stream videos, which they mostly ignored.

Tim sat alone on his side of the couch, the happy couple across from him cuddling. The lighting was low, LEDs that they could change the color of if they wished, but they had left them on red. Tim watched as Corey snuggled up against Kioshi, whispered something in his ear, and then kissed his cheek. Kioshi reacted, the alcohol making him amorous, or maybe it was just love. He turned his head to kiss Corey, their mouths opening wide, their lips slowly moving against each other. The show they put on was hot as hell, and—whether they intended it or not—Tim was getting aroused.

Ben should be here. This was his arena. Once he started singing, the other rooms would empty out and people would pound on the door to be let inside. They wouldn't be allowed in though, because Tim would be doing the same thing to Ben that Kioshi was to Corey. How many people got it on in these private rooms? A bunch, he'd wager. Maybe he should make himself scarce. He could go elsewhere and call Ben. That would make him feel better. Then again, after checking his phone, he saw that the day was just beginning in Austin. A drunk call home wouldn't earn him any points, but a heartfelt text might.

Before he could stand to leave, the kiss broke off. Corey looked over at him and giggled in embarrassment. Tim raised a glass in salute and drained it. Then he reached for the phone on the wall with a questioning expression. Two heads nodded in unison. What an awesome fucking trip! He had never imagined it playing out like this, that he would find a piece of his past in an uncertain future. He loved it and was looking forward to the days to come. Only one thing kept him from being completely happy. A reoccurring thought that wouldn't go away.

Ben should be here.

Chapter Nine

The next few days were an exercise in repetition. Tim would rise, go for a jog—albeit in a nearby park instead of on the busy sidewalks—and afterwards he would get ready, eat, and meet Corey in the lobby. Then they were off to inspect properties for sale or for rent. None of them suited his needs. Or maybe he was just picky. He reassured Corey that the fault was his own, but that didn't mean he compromised on what he wanted. His guide was infinitely patient, arranging appointment after appointment. At night he dragged Tim out to temples, shopping malls, and restaurants, determined to show all that Japan had to offer. Kioshi joined them for many of these activities, their relationship a bittersweet reminder of what Tim was missing.

Staying in touch with Ben was harder than he'd expected. Tim was busy during the days. The evenings were less hectic, but by then it was early morning in Austin, since Texas was fourteen hours behind Japan, and Ben was usually at work or school. They still managed to send texts back and forth and briefly speak on the phone, but it wasn't satisfying.

Tim felt the most frustration on his fifth morning in Japan. Jogging didn't help, nor did jacking off in the shower or pigging out more than usual at the breakfast buffet. He'd had too many drinks the night before, which hadn't helped either. None of his vices, healthy or otherwise, were doing the trick, so when he met Corey in the lobby again, his spirits were low. He wasn't the only one.

"I only have one appointment lined up today," Corey said. "Sorry. Maybe we could freestyle? Wander around different areas and look for anything advertising or that looks empty?"

Tim exhaled and shook his head. "I need a break. Reschedule the one appointment. Today I want to check out the competition. Show me the successful galleries and museums. I wanna get a feel for what works here and what doesn't."

"Okay," Corey said, the speed of his nod increasing along with his enthusiasm. "That's a good idea. We'll start in Roppongi again."

"Oh excellent," Tim joked. "I know of a fancy restaurant there."

Corey caught on instantly. "Where the only thing on the menu is grease? I'll take you somewhere nicer than that. I promise."

They began at the Mori Art Museum, which was on the fifty-third floor of one of the tallest buildings in the area. The exhibition space was the stuff of dreams: massive white-walled rooms with pale hardwood floors and track lighting above to highlight each piece on display. As for the art itself, the mixture of contemporary paintings and unusual installations helped recharge his creative battery. If that wasn't enough, the roof of the building offered an observation deck. Standing in open air—which seemed crazy—they were presented with a panoramic view of Tokyo.

"I can't believe we're allowed up here!" Tim said. "Look, there's even a helicopter landing pad!"

"The view's not bad either," Corey said pointedly.

"Oh right," Tim said with a chuckle, turning his attention back to the city itself, which was overwhelming in its massiveness. Tokyo was nearly twice the size and population of New York, the United States' largest city. While the Big Apple ranked second among the cities of the world, Tokyo was the undisputed champion. "It's amazing, but I don't know if I could live here."

"I don't think I'll ever leave," Corey countered, looking to the sprawling cityscape with affection normally reserved for Kioshi.

"Really?" Tim said. "You don't think you'll ever go back to Kansas?"

Corey laughed and turned to look at him. "Will you?"

"No," Tim admitted. "Texas is home now. Still, you don't think you'll ever want to return? Maybe not to Olathe, but somewhere else in the States?"

Corey didn't think long before answering. "Nope. It's too exciting here. Everything is different. You know how we spent two hours in that grocery store yesterday?"

"Yeah," Tim said with an embarrassed titter. He had been the one browsing so long. Every single product had been new to him. Even the absolute basics like flour and sugar were brands he didn't recognize, and as for the rest, he hadn't realized that there were vegetables, roots, and other produce that he had never heard of or tried. Tim spent way too much money while there, especially in the candy aisle on what he intended to bring home as gifts. "I get what you're saying, but doesn't the novelty wear off after a while?"

"Not in this city," Corey said, returning his attention to the skyline. "There's always something new to discover. When I get homesick, I fly to Kansas, and before long my family makes sure I want to come back here."

Tim chuckled. "I know the feeling. Next time, come to Texas. We'll take you in. Bring Kioshi too."

"Sounds fun. For now it's back to work."

That meant stopping by more galleries, which was an education in itself. Tim had been seeking neutral spaces, but many that they visited were gimmicky. One used LEDs to an extreme, lighting the sidewalk outside in white while the inside walls changed colors. This in turn altered the viewer's perception of each displayed piece. Tim wasn't sure if that was clever or not. The walls of another gallery were covered in a painted mural of a forest, the art for sale hanging from tree branches. After taking a break for lunch, they visited the next gallery and discovered it was intentionally divided into winding halls, turning it into a labyrinth.

"I think the idea is to give visitors an experience they'll remember," Corey said, picking up on Tim's disapproval.

"It detracts from the art," he countered. "The Mori Museum got it right."

"Then I'm interested to see how you react to our next stop."

The building they arrived at looked nothing like a museum. The roof was pointed, ornate, and curved upward at the edges, placing it in the Edo period of architecture, if his college education was still worth anything. Tim stopped out front to stare.

"It's a bath house," Corey explained.

"I don't do those," Tim said, taking a step back.

"Relax," Corey said. "It's a former bath house, and in Japan they don't have the same connotation." After a sly smile, he added, "Pervert."

"Guilty as charged," Tim said, nodding at the building. "Let's see what they've got."

He was impressed by this one more than any he had seen so far because it combined the two concepts seamlessly. Walking through a centuries-old building was cool. The rooms were laid out in unusual sizes and dimensions, which made exploring fun. While touring the bathhouse itself was a memorable experience, the presentation of the art was right on par. The walls were neutral, the floor dark, and the lights were tastefully mounted on industrial girders.

"Think they'll let us buy this place?" Tim asked.

"I doubt it," Corey said. "You like it?"

"I love it! Maybe we need to think outside the box."

"Speaking of which, I know a little takeout place not far away that does amazing bento boxes. Or are you more in the mood for a restaurant?"

Tim tore his eyes from their surroundings to look at Corey. "What did you say?"

"I'm kind of hungry, so I thought we could grab some street food or—"

"Go to a restaurant," Tim said, a smile developing along with an idea. "That first place we looked at, the greasy grill, can you give them a call?"

"I don't think they're still in business, or that I would want to eat there, even if they were." Corey's mouth dropped open. "Wait, are you saying…"

"That you're a genius?" Tim threw an arm around him and pulled him close. "Yes. Probably. That depends on how it goes. It's worth another look." If a bath house could be turned into a gallery, why not a restaurant? "Set something up for tomorrow. I want to see it again. Then call that handsome husband of yours, because dinner is on me."

"Dinner is always on you," Corey complained. "You haven't let us pay for a thing!"

"Okay, dinner is on you. Drinks are on me."

Corey sighed. "This isn't good for my figure."

"Have you had any complaints?"

"Well… No."

Tim squeezed Corey and released him. "I didn't think so." Then he beamed at his surroundings, imagining a grill that served art instead burgers. Or whatever the Japanese equivalent was.

Another day, the first that felt successful. They revisited the hibachi grill, Tim seeing it in a new light. He took notes, drew a few rough sketches, and had Corey interrogate the real estate agent about prices. The owners were asking a lot, but he thought the agent looked eager enough to close the deal for lower. First he would need to run his idea by Marcello, since that's who would be responsible for ponying up the dough.

"What's next?" Corey asked when they stood outside again. "Should we check out the chicken coop again?"

"I'm happy with this place," Tim said.

"Then we're free! No more appointments or searching."

"We're done," Tim said.

For now. There would still be a lot of work to do.

"I guess I should report to the agency and let them know that I'm available."

"I still need you!" Tim said. As much as he was coming to love Tokyo, he didn't want to be in the city alone. "There's gotta be more you need to show me. This project won't be successful until I understand Japanese culture better. Educate me."

Corey tilted his head back and forth as he considered options. "You haven't seen Marcello's other project yet. Do you need to?"

"The selfie studio? Yeah! Let's go!"

They travelled to Shibuya, a ward known for its trendy youth-driven shopping. What better place for getting pretty and posing for a picture? Tim already knew what to expect because Marcello had shown him plenty of photos. The main entrance was loud, full of flashing lights and high tempo music. An attached shop offered camera equipment and accessories, including a variety of selfie sticks, of course. The noise died away in the main area, which was cluttered with all sorts of things ideal for snapping a quick photo. Painted wooden boards with holes cut out for faces, giant teddy bears, weird mirrors and lights. He was reminded of a carnival. A number of doors led to private booths. These included screens that could be pulled down as backdrops, or used for chroma keying—green screens or whichever color so that different images or even animation could be added later. Costumes and props were available to rent too.

"We have to try this out," Corey insisted. "Let's take some photos together."

Why not? Patronage was still picking up before the evening surge. They didn't have much of a wait. Choosing from the catalog wasn't easy. Should they dress up like pop stars? Or as the Mario Brothers? Or maybe in traditional Japanese yukatas, which were a summer version of kimonos.

"I think I've got it," Corey said, swiping at the touch screen monitor. "Oh definitely."

Fifteen minutes later, Tim was standing in one of the narrow booths, wearing a red and white baseball cap, green gloves, and a blue jacket with white sleeves. "What's my name again?" Tim asked.

"Ash Ketchum," Corey chided. "You should know this."

"Pokémon was after my time."

"We're practically the same age!"

"This is dumb."

"It's not!" It was hard to argue with someone who was dressed head to toe in a yellow jumpsuit, complete with a hood that had two pointed ears at the top, mostly because Corey looked so damn cute wearing it. He made his dark eyes even bigger than usual, stuck out his bottom lip in a pout, and in a high-pitched voice said, "Pika pika! Pikachu?"

Tim shook his head and tossed the ball he was holding into the air, catching it repeatedly. "I'm supposed to throw this at you, huh?"

"Pika?" Corey said, the pout becoming more pronounced.

Tim laughed. "Okay. Let's get this over with."

The experience was a lot more entertaining than he had anticipated. They had chosen to mount their phones on the available tripod rather than rent the expensive camera equipment. The umbrella lights were standard, which was nice. Mostly they argued about the best pose, or laughed while checking the results on their phones. They played with different backgrounds too. In the blink of an eye, nearly an hour had passed. By then even Corey was over it.

"I have to get out of this thing," he complained. "It's making me sweat. I hope they wash these between uses!"

"No kidding," Tim said, not happy that he now had hat hair. "I would do this again though."

"Me too," Corey said, clearly pleased with the experience. "Let's go to the gift shop. I saw a sign that said they offered prints."

Tim knew they did because that was part of Marcello's plan. The man was inspired, although he hoped that Corey was kidding. Or that he chose the photo where Tim had him in a headlock. He bet that had never happened in the cartoon!

Once they returned the costumes, they browsed the gift shop. Corey found the printers, which were automated. While he was distracted, Tim wandered. He had an appreciation for photography, but it wasn't his creative outlet, so most of what was on sale didn't interest him. People in this area seemed really friendly though. He caught more than one person watching him, and when he made eye contact, they would always nod and smile. Tim smiled back. That's all he could do since he didn't speak the language. He wasn't the only American here. As he continued to shop, he heard a voice speaking English. One that sounded oddly familiar. Tim had trouble placing who it was until he looked up. And saw himself.

Tim stared. The monitor played a video, complete with Japanese subtitles. In it he was mixing paint on a palette before applying it to the canvas. He remembered that day. Kelly had come to the new public studio space in the Austin gallery to take photos. At least he thought it was just photos. He didn't realize that Kelly had recorded video too. Surrounding the monitor was a long board covered in text he couldn't read and a few surreal photos of the Eric Conroy Gallery. Two paintings hung to either side of the display—the painting from the video now completed, and another Tim had chosen to send to Japan. Feeling self-conscious and confused, he rushed back to where Corey was.

"I need your help."

"Just a sec," Corey said, tongue sticking out one corner of his mouth. "I'm trying to decide how big I want this print to be. Is a poster too much?"

"I need your help *now*, Mr. Tanaka, and you're on the clock so get your ass in gear!"

That did the trick. Corey let himself be dragged along to where the video played. Then he stared slack-jawed before he turned to Tim. "Did you know about this?"

"No!" Tim gestured up and down the display. "What does it say? Read it to me!"

"Okay. Uh. Art comes in more forms than just photography. In the interest of supporting your creative impulses... It'll be faster if you just let me read it and summarize."

"Fine," Tim said, glancing around and feeling twice as weird about standing there next to himself. Then again, considering that a young woman with green hair had just teetered into the gift shop wearing impossibly high platform shoes—nobody blinking an eye—he was unlikely to draw much attention even if he stood on his head and barked.

"Done," Corey said. "It's for your project! The new gallery.

This talks about the one back in Austin and plans to establish the same thing over here. People can sign up to be notified when it's open. You really painted these?"

Tim looked at the two pieces. The first was of a downtown street in Austin, the same one where the gallery was located. Early on a Sunday morning, he had set up an easel on the sidewalk before getting braver and dragging it out to the middle of the street. The traffic was so minimal that he only had to move twice. Of course he had played with the light, as he often did, transforming it into a prism of colors. Compared to Tokyo, the scene was quaint and caused a pang of homesickness. The other painting was of Kelly, camera held close to his chest as he grinned demonically, the bright red horns nailing down the impression. Tim had given that one to Kelly as a gift and hadn't expected to see it here.

"Not for sale," Corey murmured, reading the label beneath it. He turned his attention to the other. "And this one sold. Wowzers!"

"What?" Tim demanded.

Corey shot him a self-conscious gaze. "I didn't realize that you're so big."

"I hear that a lot," he said, but neither of them laughed. "I'm not famous or anything."

"Do most paintings sell for a million yen?"

"A million! What is that—" He did a quick calculation. "—ten thousand dollars?"

Corey nodded once. "Yup."

"Wowzers is right! And no. Especially not any of mine."

"*Konnichiwa, Wyman-sama!*"

Tim turned. The girl in the platform shoes with the pale green hair gave him a curt bow, then shuffled forward to stand next to him and face in the same direction. She held a selfie stick and started speaking to the camera attached to it while rattling off sentence after sentence in Japanese.

"A little help," he said out of the corner of his mouth.

Corey moved closer, trying to avoid the camera lens. "She's explaining who you are and talking about the project. She loves to paint. Do you?"

Both the girl and Corey went silent and looked at him.

"Oh," Tim said, clearing his throat. He sized up the young lady. Her clothes were skin-tight. Or were they just nylon stockings that she managed to squeeze her entire body into? The insect antenna she wore seemed kind of weird, but all of this came together nicely, meaning she had an artistic eye too. "I love to paint. Yeah. I've been doing it since I was a little boy."

After a pause, Corey translated. The woman squealed happily and spoke to the camera again. Then she angled the stick to show one painting, and then the other, speaking all the while.

"She's talking about the paintings now," Corey said helpfully.

"Never would have guessed," Tim said.

Then it sounded like she was counting down. He didn't know what to make of that, but Corey pulled him aside. This allowed the woman to film the monitor. On it, a much more confident Tim was attacking the canvas with his brush, sending frequent glares in Kelly's direction and occasionally grumbling answers to the questions he was asked. This was silently recorded, the minutes stretching on and making him feel increasingly awkward. Then the girl declared something energetically and turned to face him, still holding the stick and keeping the camera trained on them with expert skill. With an earnest expression, she addressed him with what sounded like a question.

"She uh…" Corey chuckled. "She wants to know if you'll autograph her arm."

"I'd love to," Tim said.

A permanent marker was thrust toward him. Then the woman handed the camera over to Corey, her tone bossy. His job was to record this momentous occasion, it seemed. Tim was presented with the underside of her arm. First he drew a cartoon-cute grasshopper, acting on inspiration from the outfit the woman wore. She made sounds of excitement and surprise during this, which only escalated when he signed his name with a flourish.

Then she was standing at his side again, saying his name and tons of other things, Corey unable to translate without interfering with the video. Finally the woman made a V with her fingers and placed this sideways on her forehead, which just happened to show off the quick sketch and autograph nicely. Acting on inspiration, Tim adopted the same pose and tried to repeat the word she shouted, although he was pretty sure he mangled it. She seemed thrilled regardless. After all the commotion, she kissed Tim on the cheek, thanked him, then took the camera from Corey and ran off.

"What just happened?" Tim asked.

"Are you sure you're not famous?" Corey asked.

"Positive."

"Well you are now. That was Miyû Mitsuishi. She's a YouTube star. I don't know how many subscribers she has, but it's in the millions."

"YouTube," Tim said, laughing with relief. Nothing serious then. Right? Although if millions of subscribers meant that many views, it sounded like a lot. He glanced around. He didn't see any reporters desperate for an interview, but many of the customers were staring. "Can we get out of here?"

"Sure," Corey said. "Although maybe you should hire Kioshi too."

"For what?"

"A bodyguard," Corey said with a grin. "He's tougher than he looks."

Tim shook his head, trying to decide how he felt about all of this. He asked to return to the car so he could make a call. It was past midnight back home, but he knew what sort of hours his best friend kept.

Marcello answered as if expecting his call. "You have good news?" he asked.

"Yeah," Tim said. "They've got me in the studio gift shop. I'm on all the T-shirts and hats. I just need to know what size you wear."

Marcello only needed a split second to catch up. "I would have told you sooner, but you made such a fuss about being on the cover of that newspaper."

"A *gay* newspaper," Tim stressed. "When I was still in the closet!"

Marcello tittered happily. "You're so handsome when you're angry. I'll admit I used to rile you up on purpose, although that particular occurrence didn't play out as expected. You were supposed to march into my office and demand compensation."

"I don't want to hear your depraved fantasies," Tim said, "and I'm not angry. I'm just confused. I didn't sign up to be Bob Ross! And what about the painting of Kelly? That was supposed to be a gift for Nathaniel."

"It shall be, but when I realized how suitable it was for the promotional display... If it's any consolation, Kelly only loaned the painting to me. While charging a sizeable fee for the privilege.

He never misses an opportunity to bleed me dry. I'd hold it against him if I didn't admire his audacity. As for the use of your image, you knew all of this before travelling there. You're trending, as I believe the young people say."

"I'm not trending," Tim said, embarrassed by the whole thing. "But if it helps get the gallery going, then I guess it's fine. Hey! I think I found a space. It's a little weird, but uh, I'll get a rough concept to you soon."

"I wait with bated breath!"

They went over a few quick details before Tim ended the call. Then he looked over at Corey. "Sorry about that. I just had to give him a hard time. It's a thing we do."

"It's fine," Corey said. "Bob Ross was hugely popular in Japan, you know. Kioshi still likes watching him."

"I didn't mean it in a bad way," Tim said quickly. "Bob was the man! I learned all sorts of tricks from watching him."

Corey continued to stare, looking a little star-struck. "I had no idea how talented you are."

"Stop," Tim said. "I'm already weirded out by whatever that was back there. Can we pretend it didn't happen?"

"If you want," Corey said, starting the car, "but only if you do me one favor."

"What's that?"

"Can you sign my arm?"

Tim gently swatted him on the back of the head, and as they pulled away, he couldn't stop grinning. Wait until Benjamin heard about this!

Ben's left hand was pressing the phone to his ear, the right one clicking through his email.

"Did you find it yet?" Tim asked, his voice sounding near, even though he was still far away. Six thousand five hundred and forty miles, to be precise. Ben had looked it up, not that the knowledge had been of much comfort. The opposite, in fact.

"Why didn't you just text me the link?"

"Because you need to see it on a real monitor, not your tiny little phone."

"Give me a second," Ben said with a yawn. "It's still early."

"Oh right. Have you even showered yet?"

"Nope. I'm stinky."

This didn't deter Tim in the slightest. It never did. "Are you in your bathrobe?"

"No."

Tim gasped theatrically. "Are you naked?"

"Nope."

"Then what are you wearing?"

Ben glanced down at black cotton that was tailored a size too large for him. "A bathrobe."

"But you said— Awww! You're in *my* bathrobe?"

"Shut up," Ben said with a laugh. "I miss you."

"I miss you too," Tim said. "You have no idea. Or I guess you do. This sucks for us both."

True, but Ben suspected he had it worse. Tim was in a new country surrounded by all sorts of distractions, and from all accounts, constantly busy. Ben was still in his regular routine. He had traded theater work for school, but it wasn't his first time on that particular campus. After a few weeks of being on edge, college felt routine again. That meant he had plenty of opportunities to mope around and feel sorry for himself, even though he had resisted doing so. Mostly.

"Got it!" he said, opening the email and clicking the link.

A YouTube video loaded and showed a peppy Japanese girl standing outside some kind of business. Ben didn't notice which at first, since he was distracted by her grasshopper getup. At least he thought that's what she was going for. Only when she went inside did he examine her surroundings.

"That's the selfie studio!" he said.

"Pretty cool, huh?"

Getting to see the studio was fun, but Tim had oversold the importance of this email, urging Ben to abandon his breakfast and go upstairs to the office so he could use the full-size computer. Unless there was more to the video. As he continued watching, the girl noticed the gift shop and squealed excitedly. Ben could relate, since he often had the same reaction. Just not quite as openly. The shop offered camera equipment, which she seemed really into. Then she reached some sort of display. A monitor was playing a video, and when she focused in on it…

"Hey! That's you! You're famous!"

"Not quite," Tim chuckled.

Ben watched as the girl put her face next to the monitor

and made kissing noises, like she was smooching Tim. Another reaction they had in common.

"That's really funny," Ben said. "Why is that even there?"

"To promote the new gallery," Tim said. "For the record, I'm totally embarrassed by it."

The Japanese girl wandered away to check out the studio. Ben let the video play, turning the volume down so they could still talk. "How's that going? Have you made much progress?"

"Found a place," Tim said. "A gnarly old restaurant, but I think I can make it work. I've been in my hotel room all day drafting the proposal. I'm lonely as hell, but I work better this way, so I gave Corey the day off. Unofficially. His agency thinks he's still on the clock. Hey, did you get that funny photo I sent? You didn't reply."

"Sure did," Ben said, minimizing the window and double-clicking a file. The image in question opened up. Tim was dressed as the guy from *Pokémon*, his arm cocked back and ready to throw a ball. Next to him was Corey, whose fists were clenched in excitement, like he couldn't wait to be caught. That's how the photo had arrived. Ben had copied and pasted his own face over Corey's last night. "I made a few adjustments. I'll send it back when we're off the phone."

"Oh. Hey, how far along is the video?"

Ben opened that window again. "Looks like a montage of that girl doing selfies. Who is she, anyway?"

"Miyû Mitsuishi," Tim said slowly, like he had been practicing. "Apparently she's a big deal over here."

"Neat," Ben said. Then his heart started beating double quick, because Miyû was back in the gift shop, and this time she had spotted someone familiar. "No way!"

"Crazy, huh?"

"Just a second. I wanna watch." Ben focused on the screen, feeling a strange mixture of elation and sorrow. Tim looked good! It had only been a week, but he still seemed different. His hair was mussed up, his expression panicked as he kept looking to Corey for guidance. Ben felt a stirring of jealousy, but he shoved it back down. He trusted Tim. If he didn't, there was no point in being together. Did this Corey person have to be so handsome though? Couldn't they find a translator who was an old woman or anyone who wouldn't be Tim's type?

Ben watched as Miyû admired the autograph on her arm and saluted, Tim trying to mimic her. After a jump cut, she was back outside again, bringing the video to a close. "That was cute," he said. He was about to click on the like button when a number caught his eye. "That's a lot of views!"

"Two hundred thousand!"

"Double that," Ben said.

"Oh. I haven't looked since this morning. I don't like watching it. She's fine, but I'm so awkward!"

"You're adorable," Ben said. "I'm glad the trip is going well."

"It would be better if you were here," Tim murmured. "What's been going on with you?"

Ben didn't have any exciting news to share. Wanda was being mean to him at work, having discovered his college reenrollment. Like he was trying to rise above his station or something. The classes were going well, even though being there made him feel old. He wasn't the only thirty-and-older person in his classes, but he was definitely in the minority. He talked about Chinchilla a lot, knowing that would make Tim happy, but somehow it didn't seem enough. His life was mundane compared to what Tim was experiencing.

"You won't forget me when you're famous," Ben said. "Will you?"

"Don't worry," Tim said. "I'm only fame-ish. You will be too if Marcello makes his movie."

"Huh?"

Tim laughed. "I didn't tell you about that? I guess not, with all the planning we had to do for this trip. Marcello wants to make a movie about our lives."

"Not a—"

"Not that kind of movie," Tim said. "He said it would be tasteful."

Ben snorted. "I don't think he's ever used that word in his life."

"Maybe you're right," Tim said. "Anyway, there wouldn't be graphic sex. Just us getting romantic."

Ben tried to imagine this and couldn't. "He's not serious."

"I think he is," Tim replied. "It's hard to tell with him, but yeah. What would you think?"

He thought it sounded ludicrous. "Are you messing with me? Why didn't you mention this sooner?"

"Like I said, things have been crazy. Call him yourself and see!"

"Maybe I will," Ben said.

"My point is," Tim said, "we can be fame-ish together. No matter what happens, that's how it's gotta be. You and me. We're a package deal, right?"

"Never doubt it," Ben replied.

They talked a little longer, finding different ways to say that they missed and loved each other. Then they hung up. Tim returned to his adventures. Ben was merely home again.

He consoled himself by rewatching the YouTube video, happy to at least see Tim. They had attempted video conferencing, but the connection at the hotel wasn't great, and their previous attempts had been so frustrating that they hadn't bothered trying again. Ben brought the collar of the bathrobe robe to his nose and breathed in. Then he noticed Jace's photo on the desk staring at him.

"Don't laugh," he said. "I used to do the same thing with yours."

The photo didn't reply. Maybe next time. Ben finished altering the picture Tim had sent, attached it to an email reply, and went back downstairs to finish his cereal.

Chapter Ten

No one enjoyed bureaucracy, probably not even the bureaucrats themselves. Tim tried to remind himself that everyone needed to earn a living, but one delay after another had drained his patience. An entire week had gone by with little progress. He could have easily flown home to see Ben and back again if not for promises that tomorrow would be the day. It always seemed he needed to get one more signature, pay one more fee, pass one more inspection...

Corey was doing his utmost. Tim had no doubt of that. His guide was just as surprised by each unexpected delay and was increasingly apologetic. He and Kioshi did their best to entertain Tim. Often this was welcome. At other times, Tim politely declined because what they had together was a constant reminder of what he missed most. Instead he would stay in his hotel, flipping through the manga books that Corey had loaned him before settling down to read them for real. The plots were hopelessly romantic, the art inspiring. Tim grabbed his sketchbook and tried drawing a few pages of his own. Even then he couldn't get away from the ache in his heart. Trying to appease it, he began illustrating their relationship, starting at the very beginning and focusing on Ben, because drawing him almost felt as intimate as getting to touch him.

Finally the big day arrived. Not the gallery opening or his return flight, but simply the moment when the keys to the restaurant were placed in his hand. Now, no matter what, he could move things forward under his own power.

So that's what he did. Tim pulled the brown paper from the windows, emptied the rocks from the fish tanks, and cleared out a kitchen that Eric definitely wouldn't have approved of because every piece of equipment he shifted or cupboard he opened revealed more filth. He passed a few days this way, happy for the physical exertion, and the visible progress. Today's goal was to get all the tables and chairs moved to the back alley, where they could be picked up. And he had help.

"This wasn't in the job description," Corey said, helping him separate a table in half. The suit was gone. Now wearing an old pair of jeans and a T-shirt, he looked decidedly more American. He seemed equally interested in Tim's outfit, which consisted of shoes, cotton shorts, and nothing else. "The view's not bad though."

"Less flirting, more working," Tim said with a grunt, lifting his half of the table and carrying it toward the rear exit. The air conditioning wasn't fixed yet and the day was hot, or he would be wearing a lot more to shield himself from the grime.

"Are you sure you need me here at all?" Corey said. He sounded impressed, maybe because he had to drag his half of the table.

"You don't have to do this," Tim said, leaning the table piece against the wall with the others. "I know you didn't sign up for it."

"It's fine." Corey nodded his thanks when Tim came to relieve him of his burden and carry it the rest of the way. "Although it strikes me that we have contractors showing up the day after tomorrow. They would do all this for you."

"This saves money, gives me a sense of purpose, and if it gets me home even one day earlier, it's worth it." Tim added the table to the stack next to the door. "Besides, it's not a bad workout."

"I noticed," Corey said. "You need to give me some tips."

Tim turned to face him. "Why's that?"

"I hit the gym pretty regularly," Corey said, "but I'm not getting the same results. Here." He stripped off his T-shirt.

Tim didn't see what Corey was concerned about. He had a nice body. His skin was pale, his build smaller, but he had toned what muscles he possessed. "Looks good to me," he said.

"Really?" Corey said, flexing an arm. "This is impressive? Now you do it."

Tim grinned and curled his right arm, knowing that all the heavy lifting made it appear extra pumped at the moment. "You just gotta eat your spinach."

"I wish it was that easy," Corey said, hands on his hips. "What's your secret?"

"It's mostly genetic," Tim said. "Yeah, I jog and do some lifting, but I inherited the right sort of build. You have a smaller frame, that's all. If I had your body, I'd be happy with how it looks."

"Thanks," Corey said. "I'd still like to work on my pecs. Yours are always pushing against your shirt. Mine are flat. How do you get them so firm?"

"Yours look firm to me!"

"They have the right shape but…" Corey took a step closer, hands raised. "Do you mind?"

Tim snorted. "You want to feel me up?"

"Can I?"

He laughed. "Sure. Knock yourself out."

Tim puffed up his chest, feeling silly. Then those hands touched his pecs and the smile slid off his face. It felt good. His relationship with Ben was just as physically intense as it was emotional. He missed that too. Enough that his body started to react. This was a bad idea.

"Mine aren't near as solid," Corey was saying, cheeks a little red as he looked up.

By accident or design, he brushed one of Tim's nipples, the sensation shooting through his entire body and making him want more.

Boom boom boom!

They both turned toward the noise and froze. A voice, loud and enthusiastic, was chattering from somewhere not far away. The knocking came again, even more insistent.

"Is someone here?" Tim asked.

"Oh!" Corey said, dropping his hands. "You're going to kill me, but uh… Well, you'll see." He grabbed his shirt and put it on. When Tim moved for his own, Corey rushed to snatch it away. "Nope! It'll be better this way. I'll let her in."

"Her?"

"Miyû Mitsuishi!" Corey said. "I told her to come by and check out the new space."

"You *what*?" Tim glanced around in panic. Yeah, he had thrown away a lot of stuff, but that wasn't the same as cleaning. They were still surrounded by dust and grime. "She can't see it like this!"

"She can," Corey said, already at the door. "It'll be okay. You'll see."

Then it was too late. From of a rectangle of daylight stepped a grasshopper in a shredded wedding dress. That was his initial impression. Miyû's hair was still pale green, and she wore the same plastic insect antenna, presumably attached to a headband somewhere. That was about all he could take in, because the camera was out and recording. She ran right over to him.

"*Ohayō gozaimasu, Wyman-sama!*" she cried.

"Ohio," he replied. During all the downtime, he had asked Corey to teach him some basic phrases. Feeling brave, he added, "*Genki.*"

This seemed to thrill Miyû, who stood next to him and launched into rapid-fire Japanese that he couldn't understand while filming every second with her phone on its selfie stick. She pointed to his bare torso with her free hand, commenting on it and making a funny face. He wasn't sure if she was being flattering or not. Then she turned to him more formally and asked a question that Corey translated.

"Mr. Wyman, what does it take to be a painter?"

"Oh," he replied, wishing that Corey had at least briefed him on this. Then he might have had time to think of something clever to say. "You just have to pick up a brush and use it to get paint on the canvas. That's all it takes. It doesn't matter if anyone likes the result or not."

Corey translated this. Miyû addressed the camera again, then asked another question. "Is the goal of this gallery to bring the American dream to Japan?"

"No," he said. "The idea is to help artists living in Japan show you *their* dreams. That's what we do back home. I don't think that's an American ideal exactly. It's just the right thing to do."

Corey translated this while looking proud. Maybe he was doing okay! Tim straightened himself up, ready to take the next question, but instead Miyû chatted to the camera before springing away. To tour the crusty restaurant?

"This isn't good!" Tim whispered, watching as she went to one of the filthy windows, shrieked, and then used a gloved hand to draw a sad face in the muck.

"It's fine," Corey said. "People will think you're crazy for undertaking this, but it'll look even more impressive once the real gallery is finally unveiled."

"Yeah, but... Oh god, she's going into the kitchen!" He followed, which was a terrible idea, because she got footage of him looking mortified. Where was Marcello when you needed him? He understood this public relations stuff. Tim tried to put himself in the older man's mindset. What would Marcello do? Open a bottle of champagne and tell a story that, while dirty, offered a surprising amount of perspective? Tim only had bottled water available, and the sole story he could think of was when Ben had drizzled caramel over his own body and called Tim into the bedroom, but he wasn't sure of the moral. Instead he watched helplessly as Miyû shrieked and recoiled at every mess. Then she returned to him, posing one last question.

"Mr. Wyman," Corey translated. "When will we see you paint again?"

"As soon as I'm done cleaning up this place," Tim said, eyes darting to the chaos around him. Then he made himself focus on Miyû, whose unusual fashion sense inspired him. "Will you come back when the studio is ready so I can paint you? You'll be the first piece of art created here."

Corey started translating, but Miyû cut him off, squealing in excitement and—presumably—explaining it all for her audience. Then she thanked him, and Tim was able to reciprocate, thanks to Corey's tutoring. Like last time, Miyû signed off with a salute, smiling expectantly and waiting for him to do the same. He did.

Then the camera was turned off and the selfie stick compressed. "You really want to paint me?" she asked in heavily accented English.

"I'd love to!" Tim said. "You have amazing style."

"You are very talented artist," Miyû replied. "This isn't my career. I, ahhh—" She reverted to Japanese.

"She graduated from the best art school in Japan," Corey said, looking impressed himself. "With a master's."

"Fashion," Miyû said in English again. "I will launch my own label. First, people must be in love with you."

"Sounds to me like Japan already loves you," Tim replied.

"Japan hasn't met me yet," she said with a wink.

Interesting! They had a short conversation about his plans for the gallery and its opening, Miyû much calmer when the camera was off. He asked about her unusual outfit and learned that everything she wore was of her own creation. He stopped short of asking if she wanted to have an exhibition here herself. Fashion was an art form too, and there was no reason they couldn't incorporate it. Marcello would decide if the offer should be extended or not. No doubt he would have other ideas as well. They made plans to meet again, Miyû shaking his hand and bowing before leaving.

"That went well," Tim said, not hiding his surprise. "Right?"

"Definitely," Corey said. "No need to thank me. The sense

of satisfaction I feel right now is reward enough, although you could take me to dinner tonight."

"I've got a better reward than that," Tim said, grabbing the edge of the largest table. "You want more muscle? Get on the other side of this sucker and lift!"

Corey groaned and dragged his feet, but as they continued working, the grin stayed plastered on his face. Tim found that his own had no intention of leaving either.

"You're a victim of your own success," Marcello said.

The flattery had no effect on Tim. He was too miserable. Another two weeks had gone by. Thanks to unexpected delays—paint running out, equipment not showing up, a holiday that no one had informed him about—they were behind schedule, and although the gallery was nearly done, he couldn't celebrate yet. "I'll take a break and come back to Japan next month," he said.

"When the public eye has moved on?"

That was the other thing that kept eating up his time. A few days ago, he had invited Miyû back to the studio so he could paint her. The gallery wasn't quite ready, but it was still vastly better than before. They recorded a video as she posed and he worked, and after this was posted online, everything went crazy. First websites and blogs wanted to interview him. Then newspapers and magazines. Yesterday he had been on a freaking television show, an early morning one, where they inexplicably had him paint along with an old video of Bob Ross. Now he was getting offers to be on weird game shows, which he kept turning down.

"I don't want this to be about me," Tim complained. "That's not why I'm here."

"No," Marcello replied, "but the attention you are generating will help launch the gallery and cement its importance. Fundraising is never easy. I worked hard to cultivate the group of supporters you've mingled with here, and believe me when I say that stunts were required, some public, others private."

"I was supposed to fly home tomorrow."

"I sympathize," Marcello said. "An extra week, that is all. Or perhaps slightly longer so the media can reach you in the aftermath. Ten days would allow time for the gallery opening, your exhibition, and the fundraising gala."

"Yeah, but—"

"I'll be joining you at the gala and will take over from there. Your toils are nearly at an end. A few more sacrifices, and you'll leave Japan secure in the knowledge that you've established a lasting legacy not only for yourself, but for Eric as well. A mere ten days of your time will benefit others for years to come."

He couldn't argue with that. Logically, anyway. Emotionally was a different matter.

"If I stay here, I'll miss Ben's birthday."

"Ah. At the risk of sounding callous, I dare say he'll have plenty more birthdays. An opportunity like this comes once in a lifetime or not at all."

He was right. Tim had no reason to believe that he could prolong his fifteen minutes of fame. If he left and came back later, it might be too late. Hell, he might find it too hard to return, the pain of separation too fresh. "I'll need to ask Ben."

"Of course," Marcello said. "There are two minds in every marriage and they must share each decision. That is how it should be. I only ask that you present him with all the facts."

In other words, appeal to his better nature. For once, Tim wished Ben's resolve was as weak as his own.

"Are you happy?"

Tim considered the question carefully. Currently he was sitting on a hibachi grill, one that was sparkling clean. They had kept three, two for displaying objects on—be it sculpture or otherwise. The counters and chairs that used to surround them had been removed. The third grill still had its seats, since it would be used as a desk. That was in a far corner. The grill where he and Corey sat now—shoulder to shoulder—was toward the end of the room. Ahead of them was his favorite space: three solid white walls lit to perfection from above. The rest of the gallery was nice too, although not as traditional. The fish tanks had turned out well, having been repurposed as display cases. Only one was still filled with water. It would be populated with robotic fish designed by a local artist, which would hopefully encourage word-of-mouth advertising.

The wall he now faced was his favorite, and the ideal place for a featured piece of art. He would need something big to fill it for this exhibition—a challenge because he normally stuck to a more manageable size of canvas.

"Still thinking about it?" Corey said, leaning against him briefly to get his attention.

The physical contact felt good. Tim missed it a little too much. He and Corey had started hugging hello and goodbye, and sometimes they held on longer than was wise. "I'm happy," Tim said, not sounding certain even to his own ears. "Ben should be here though."

Corey groaned. "I think I've heard you say that before. Today. Multiple times."

Tim laughed. "I'm not just saying it because I miss him. I'm about to hang my paintings on these walls. That's something I never would have done if not for him. I used to hide my art from everyone. It was too personal, and I thought if people really knew how I felt, they wouldn't love me anymore."

"Are you talking about coming out?"

"All of it, man. I was a mess. Being gay was just one of the things I hid. No one really knew me back then.

Corey frowned. "Not even me?"

"We didn't know each other that well."

"I guess not." Corey started kicking his feet back and forth, a smile slowly building. "Do you remember the petting zoo?"

"Huh?"

"It was my birthday. I had just turned thirteen and my mom made a big deal out of it, so the whole family had to be there. Including my sister. She dragged you along."

"Yeah!" Tim said. "The details are hazy, but I think I remember. Seems weird though. Why take a teenager to a petting zoo?"

"Because that's what I asked for." Corey laughed and shook his head. "So lame! I was going through a phase where I wanted to be a veterinarian, and I thought some hands-on experience would help."

"Corey Tanaka, Petting Zoo M.D.!"

"Shut up! My sister teased me enough about it. She hated being there. Do you remember? She was in such a bad mood that it was bringing me down, but you were cool. You bought a ton of those pellets to feed the animals. Your pockets were stuffed. The rest of my family didn't go into the pen with me. Mom tried until the llama scared her off." Corey grinned at the memory, before looking over at him. "Don't laugh at this next part. Or go ahead, because it is pretty dumb, but I remember watching a goat eat out of your hand and thinking how I would be willing to do the same."

"Sorry," Tim said, trying to hold back a smile and failing. "Could you repeat that last part? I didn't quite hear you."

"I wanted to be your goat!" Corey said, laughing at himself. "I know how crazy that sounds, but you *do* have really nice hands."

"Well, thanks."

"No problem. I was just figuring myself out at the time. You weren't the only thing that helped me realize that I'm gay, but it was a big piece of the puzzle."

"You helped me too," Tim admitted.

Corey perked up. "Really? How?"

"I'd never had a guy try to kiss me before."

"I didn't try!" Corey protested.

"No, but you offered, and those words haunted me. Do you remember them?" When Corey shook his head, Tim spoke the words aloud. "You can kiss me if you want."

"I said that?"

"Those exact words. Yes."

Corey thought about it and nodded. "Sounds like my style. No tact at all. 'Hey, if you want me, come and get it!' How did that help you?"

"Like you said, it was another piece of the puzzle. When Ben showed up in my life, I started wishing he would say the same thing."

"And did he?"

Tim smiled. "We didn't do a lot of talking. We pretty much went from zero to a hundred and twenty."

"Details?"

"I'm saving those for my next interview," Tim joked, but his expression grew serious. "Hey, do you mind if I ask you something? Why'd you tell your sister about me? Just before I moved to Texas, she showed up at my place to make peace or give me hell. I'm not sure there's a difference in her mind. One of the last things she said was that you were right about me, like you had told her that I'm gay."

Corey grimaced. "You mentioned that your first night here. Did I cause trouble?"

"Kind of. You had to know that would mess with me."

"Not really! I didn't struggle with coming out. Believe it or not, I was trying to help. You guys had broken up, and she was ranting about all her dumb plans for revenge. I liked you. A lot. I didn't want her to mess with you, so I thought if she knew the real reason you dumped her, that she wouldn't take it so personally. I wanted her to leave you alone."

"I didn't break up with her because of my sexuality," Tim said. "I hadn't figured it out by then."

"Oh. In that case, I'm sorry."

"Forget about it. Like you said, you were trying to help."

"My heart was in the right place," Corey said, leaning against him again. "You were my first crush."

"Really?"

"Yeah." Dark eyes bored into his, just as they had two decades ago, except they were softer this time. More emotional. Their faces were dangerously close. "You really can kiss me if you want."

Tim waited for a laugh, but neither of them were joking around. Not anymore. Corey moved closer, bringing his lips near.

Tim slid farther down the grill, putting distance between them. He nearly fell off in his haste to stand. "What about Kioshi?"

"He knows," Corey said, shaking his head in confusion. Then he seemed to understand. "Oh! We're not... I wouldn't call it an open relationship, but we're allowed to sleep around."

"What?"

"We don't date other people, but sex isn't a big deal." Corey stared. "You and Ben don't have that?"

"No! We're married!"

"So are we! Kioshi and me. We're just not monogamous. Most gay couples I know aren't, so I just assumed... Sorry, I should have asked, but I thought that you were out of my league anyway and um..." Corey covered his hands with his face. "I knew this would happen. One way or another."

"I'm not out of your league," Tim said, looking him over. Corey was wearing his black suit, except the tie had been loosened and the shirt was untucked. The style suited him, but so did the old T-shirt and jeans he had worn when clearing out the gallery, or less than that, because Tim had stolen plenty of glances at Corey's bare torso the other day. What he'd seen was sexy, and no doubt the rest of him was too, but it was too late for that. Wasn't it? "I wish I had kissed you back then."

"What about now?"

"I don't want to answer that," Tim said.

"Why not? Worried the truth will hurt me?"

"I'm worried it'll hurt Ben."

Corey hopped off the grill. "So you do want to kiss me?"

"Yeah," Tim admitted. He needed to be intimate with someone. He was tired of feeling lonely and longing for someone he couldn't have.

Corey took a few steps closer. "And have you thought of us doing more than that?"

Tim swallowed. Then he nodded.

Corey flashed a smile. "Then maybe you could talk to Ben, ask permission."

Or he could keep it a secret. He was far from home, and hungrier than he wanted to acknowledge. Tim had always needed love. He had gotten by on what little attention his parents gave him, and when he'd met Ben, he finally discovered what it was like to be truly loved. The intensity of that feeling had haunted them after they went their separate ways, Tim getting by on scraps from Travis and Ryan. And then there was Eric... Those had been good days, but aside from him and Ben, Tim had always been forced to make do with less than he wanted. And now, after six weeks of fasting, nothing sounded better than letting go and basking in the affection of another person.

"Might be worth a shot," Corey said, looking vulnerable as he approached again. "I'd even say it's long overdue."

"Come here," Tim said.

Corey slid into his arms, and Tim kissed him at last... but only on the top of his head. That's all he would allow himself, aside from clutching him closer.

"We really can't do this," Tim said, throat constricting. "I mean it. I like you, but I'd rather die than hurt Ben. I wouldn't put him through that. Even just asking would upset him, I know it, especially when we've been apart for so long. And yeah, I still look at other guys and have all sorts of fantasies, but when I'm with him, I'm not like this. He gives me everything I need. Without him I feel like I'm starving."

Corey pulled away. "He must really be something."

"He is," Tim said. "That's why we're monogamous. He's all I need. I don't think it's wrong what you and Kioshi have agreed to. It's just..."

"Not for you," Corey said, nodding his understanding. Then

he sighed. "You're always going to be the one who got away. I can't tell you how often I fantasized about you when I was younger. Or more recently. You want to know what else you did for me? I saw how my sister treated you and it made me sick to my stomach. I swore I would never do the same, and that became a promise I made in every relationship. I wouldn't be like her. I wouldn't take anyone for granted or treat them like dirt. Especially if I was ever lucky enough to have a guy like you."

"Kioshi is amazing," Tim said.

"He is!" Corey enthused. "I love him with all my heart. And for the record, it's not just me who likes wandering. Kioshi may be soft-spoken, but he's got a wild side. We're a good match that way."

"Ben and I are too," Tim said. "We're both lucky."

"Yeah," Corey said, eyes still filled with longing. Then he tore his gaze away. "Did I ruin everything? I loved the past month! I want to come see you in Austin, and for Kioshi to meet Ben. Please don't let this ruin our friendship. I promise to keep my dumb ideas to myself."

"One more hug," Tim said with a laugh. "Just to prove things are all right. You didn't ruin anything. I promise."

After embracing, they separated and made polite conversation, mostly about the plans for the gallery and the work that remained. The vibe between them was a little awkward, but he had no doubt that given time, things would return to normal.

"I should probably head home," Corey said.

"Okay. Tell Kioshi to take care of you for me."

Corey smirked. "Do you mean that the way I think you do?"

"Absolutely," Tim said. "Now get out of here. I'm busy."

Corey took his time walking to the door, turning around halfway. "At least one of my fantasies came true."

"What's that?"

Corey's smile was wistful. "You've got me eating out of your hand."

"Good night, Mr. Tanaka."

"*Shitsurei shimasu, Wyman-sama.*"

Sweet guy. Just not his own. Tim watched him go, thinking of the past and what could have been. Then he focused on the present because he still had one big wall to fill. Ben should be here. Tim decided it was time to finally make that happen.

Chapter Eleven

Loneliness was a familiar companion to Ben, and to his surprise, he didn't mind getting reacquainted with it. Not at first. Yes, he missed Tim. Saying goodbye to him, even temporarily, had hurt. Past that, he recognized how long it had been since he had privacy. He used to have more of it since Jace's work often took him out of town for days and days. After he died, Ben had more time alone than he ever wanted, all those empty nights a gentle sort of hell. Now his life was happy again, filled with an unexpected second chance, old friends, and his own little family. So when Tim left for Japan, Ben treated it like a vacation of his own.

Food was a big part of that. Frozen pizzas, takeout Thai, and cartons of ice cream. He watched the kinds of shows Tim didn't enjoy, ignored his appearance, and let the house get messier than usual. Allison dropped by for a sleepover, complete with bad movies and a late-night gossip session. He did the same things a teenager did when their parents went out of town, short of throwing a party. During the second week he indulged in drinking, once the novelty of privacy had worn off.

He loved Tim. Cohabitating meant getting on each other's nerves, but it made him happy more than it ever irritated. Ben missed the comfort of Tim's presence, how just having him there in bed, even sound asleep, made him feel safer and more secure. And he missed the way he could be himself more than with any other person. Even Allison. With his friends, Ben felt he had to at least make the effort of being interesting. With Tim he never worried if a topic was entertaining or not. They told each other everything, no matter how pointless.

By the third week he had stopped his occasional drinking, recognizing that it didn't help. If anything, it brought the pain to the surface. Ben threw himself into his work instead and focused on his studies. That carried him to the fourth week, when he felt high from anticipation because Tim was coming home! Except he didn't. Since getting the news that Tim needed to stay longer in Japan, things had turned sour. Ben allowed himself to be unapologetically despondent, except when he worked with patients at the hospital. For them he put on a brave face. For everyone else, he was a miserable fifteen-year-old all over again.

That should have been the worst of it, but week six—one day in particular—really brought him down. October twenty-seventh. His birthday. Those were *always* good. Ben struggled to remember one that hadn't been the highlight of his year, or at least a serious contender. This birthday was cursed. He wasn't normally superstitious, but too many bad things had happened to ignore, starting with the obvious. Tim was gone and had been for far too long. No problem, because his best friend would be there to lift him up on his special day. Right? Not so. Brian's father had suffered a mild stroke, and while he was doing okay, Brian's mother had fallen and fractured her hip earlier in the month. Allison and her family left for Utah to help take care of them both. Real problems, Ben tried to remind himself, but emotionally, he wished his friend could be there to help him celebrate.

He had other friends, and a big family. They would reach out to remind him he was loved. If only he hadn't misplaced his backpack the day before and his phone along with it. Ben had powered off the device before class, and because of that, he couldn't use the GPS to find where it was. He could only keep visiting the university's lost and found in the hope that someone had turned it in. Ben felt cut off from the world. He supposed he could drive to Houston after his shift at the hospital, but a round trip of six hours didn't sound like fun.

Nothing left but to accept his fate with dignity. Life had given him a lot. It had also taken away someone precious to him. This was better than that. A temporary separation instead of a permanent one. So when his birthday came, Ben started his morning by putting on his favorite music and making himself french toast. Chinchilla joined him, getting her own plate, because he figured she was suffering just as much heartbreak. Next he opened a package Tim had sent from Japan, which was full of gifts. Exotic grocery items, miniature versions of everyday objects, clever toys, and bizarre knickknacks. The box was packed with seemingly everything he had come across while there. Tim had written little notes for each item, his comments funny or just an explanation of why he had included it. *Have you ever seen such a tiny tape dispenser? What would anyone use it for? Reattaching eyelashes, maybe?*

Ben savored the experience, sitting on the floor while unpacking and handing each item to Chinchilla to sniff. Once finished, he longed to call Tim and thank him. With his phone still missing, he tried Skyping on his laptop, but neither he nor Tim used it much and didn't stay signed in. When that failed, he settled for writing an email. Then it was time for work, where the staff surprised him with cake. That was good. The day might not be ideal, but he had to admit it wasn't a complete disaster. After working his shift, he hurried home to let Chinchilla out to potty. He had just enough time for a quick sandwich before he left for class. Still no missing backpack at the lost and found, and the day's lectures didn't hold his attention like they usually did. Ben returned home feeling tired, his spirits slowly sinking. That's when he heard the front door open.

"It's only me!" declared a husky voice. "I'm not usually in the habit of announcing myself, but I'd hate for you to mistake this as a different sort of surprise."

In other words, his guest didn't want to be mistaken for Tim coming home early. Ben had entertained such fantasies, but with the exhibition opening tomorrow in Tokyo, he knew it wasn't likely. Still, as he turned around from the kitchen counter to face the doorway, Ben didn't have to fake a smile, because he genuinely liked this person.

"Oh, I'm so sorry!" Marcello said, stopping and pressing a hand to his chest. "I seem to be in the wrong house! I'm here to congratulate someone on his thirty-sixth birthday, but you don't look a day over twenty-one. I do apologize! Shall I see myself out?"

"It just so happens to be my birthday too," Ben said, moving forward for a hug, "so you might as well stick around."

"I would be honored," Marcello said, squeezing him affectionately and stepping back. "Now then, what are you up to?"

"Celebrating," Ben said lamely.

Marcello looked past him to the mug of tea that was still steeping. "I see. If you don't mind me making a suggestion?" He moved past Ben to the refrigerator and opened the door, but the shelf he looked to was empty. "Ah."

"Sorry," Ben said. "Tim's the one who always restocks the champagne."

"His absence continues to take a toll on us both, doesn't it?"

"Yes," Ben admitted. "It does. I think a bottle might be in the cupboard."

"Room temperature?" Marcello asked. Then he shook his jowls. "No, we're left with little choice but to seek our fortunes elsewhere. It just so happens that I have a table reserved at one of my favorite restaurants. Comfortable despite the exquisite offerings. I do so hate dining alone. Won't you join me?"

Ben smiled. Birthday saved! Marcello was good company, so of course he agreed. Ben didn't even have to drive. He rode in absolute comfort in some sort of fancy car that Tim had drooled over previously. Multiple times. That made Ben feel closer to him, as did spending time with Tim's best friend. They arrived at a parking lot with plenty of empty spaces. There didn't seem to be much worth parking for.

"This was one of Eric's favorite restaurants," Marcello explained once they were out of the car. He walked them toward a glass door tinted so dark that the interior of the building was obscured. Only a stencil of a garlic bulb hinted at anything beyond. "I don't suppose Tim ever brought you here?"

"Never," Ben said. "I don't know if he even mentioned it to me." He stopped just as they reached the curb. "Maybe for a reason. Do you think it's too private? If this was their special place…"

"What's more likely," Marcello said, urging him forward with a hand on his lower back, "is that Tim worried he wouldn't be able to secure a reservation. This restaurant *is* rather exclusive. I have a feeling he would want you to experience it on such a grandiose occasion."

"Is that more than an educated guess?"

Marcello's smile was just enigmatic enough to confirm his suspicions. He hadn't shown up at Ben's house by coincidence. Tim had probably asked Marcello to check in on him. Especially if he had gotten Ben's email, which did include whining about everything that had gone wrong.

"He loves you very much," Marcello said, reading him like a book. "But for the record, I didn't need any coaxing to spend this evening with you. I've always cherished your company."

"Smooth talker," Ben said, offering his arm. "Let's stuff our faces."

Marcello looped an arm through his. "And quench our thirsts."

Beyond the door, a host welcomed them by name. Then they were guided into what resembled a cozy sitting room. The lights were low, relying on brass lamps with colorful glass shades. Tiffany style, or maybe even the real deal. The rest of the furnishings appeared comfortable despite being antique. Ben counted six tables, each separated by thriving potted plants, dressing screens, or fully-loaded bookshelves. To him it looked as though someone had attempted to rearrange a nineteenth-century living room into an intimate banquet hall.

"New theory," Ben said as they were seated. "Tim never brought me here because he knew I'd always want to come back. I'm guessing it's not cheap!"

"At this establishment, people eat for free on their birthdays. Their companions do too. We're in luck!"

Ben didn't believe that for a second. Champagne was brought without them ordering. In fact, they were never shown a menu. Marcello assured him that all they needed to focus on was "maintaining a lively conversation" and that the rest would be taken care of, so Ben relaxed and decided to enjoy himself, which wasn't difficult. He loved being spoiled. Not always, but definitely today. They toasted, they drank, and they chitchatted, but not for long, because Marcello clearly had something important to say.

"I feel the need to explain myself," he said, swirling a near-empty flute before draining it. The waiter swept in with impressive speed to provide refills. "I hope it doesn't appear opportunistic that I sent Tim on this mission. Nor do I intend to sound vain when I point out that I already have more success than any one man truly deserves. Had the matter been so clear-cut—a choice between increasing my material wealth and separating you from your husband for an extended period—I would have refrained from mentioning the idea to him. In fact, my motivations are twofold, both borne out of love."

"Eric," Ben said. "You loved him and want to keep his memory alive. I wish I could have met him, because from the way Tim talks, he must have been an amazing man."

"Death has a funny way of changing the way we think of people," Marcello said. "Too easily we forget faults in favor of singling out positive attributes, but I assure you, everything good you've heard about Eric is true. So yes, the idea of keeping his memory alive, of finding a way for him to help other artists as he once did Tim, proved much too tempting for me."

"I understand completely," Ben said. "I feel the same way about Jace sometimes. I want people to know how amazing he was, but it's frustrating because they can't meet him and see for themselves. This must be the next best thing."

"Yes, although when it comes to Jace, I can think of one way of sharing his legacy with the world."

Ben stared. "Tim wasn't kidding, was he?"

"Your life would make an excellent movie," Marcello said, "and that story wouldn't be complete without Jace. We could only strive to capture the merest glimmer of his noble soul, but this would still greatly benefit the audience, I feel. And what are your thoughts? Do you like the idea?"

Ben hesitated. "Yes, but I don't want people paying money to watch him die. That feels wrong."

"You would prefer, in the movie version, that Jace lives."

Ben struggled with himself. "I wish he hadn't died at all, but it's part of his story, and I really do want people to know what an amazing man he was, and how much we're losing without him here. Some of the details are too personal. Our last moments together… Those are private."

"Say no more," Marcello said, holding up a hand. "The plot doesn't need to strictly adhere to real-life events. It's only the essence I wish to capture. Think on it, and we can discuss it again at a later date. I can tell when a man is teetering on his tiptoes and could fall in either direction. I know when not to push my luck."

"No matter what," Ben said, "it's very flattering. Thank you."

"I am in your debt!" Marcelo said. "You might have wondered, during these long weeks, why I did not send someone else to Japan in Tim's place. Nathaniel possesses more than enough competence for such a task, and his husband, Kelly, has the artistic vision he sometimes lacks. They could have gone together, and I have no doubt they would have enjoyed the experience."

"Okay, now I'm starting to like you less," Ben joked. He did wonder though. "How come you chose Tim?"

"It all comes back to Eric. I wanted to continue the work that he began. No, that's not accurate, is it? You were the one to start it all, the first to recognize Tim's talent and to coax it out into the open."

"He's really gifted," Ben said. "Isn't he?"

"I believe so. Ever since his reunion with you, his work has flourished, which is unusual because the quality of art is often proportional to how much the creator suffers. Somehow he has managed to channel his happiness into truly compelling pieces, but you and I are biased, aren't we? Our affection for Tim blinds us to some degree—"

"Or helps us see him clearer."

"Ha! You may be right. Either way, Tim is aware of our bias, and I don't think he takes our words of encouragement to heart. Not as much as he should."

"My mom still insists I have the best voice in the world," Ben said. "Literally. Name any famous singer you can think of and she'll say I'm better without blinking an eye."

"Are you certain that she's wrong?" Marcello said generously. "It's an apt example, one that I suspect encapsulates Tim's own viewpoint. We love his art because we love him. So when the opportunity arose to prove to him that others appreciate it just as much, if not more… What's most crucial is just how divorced from him these new admirers are. Had it been a friend of mine praising his art, he would assume it was done so out of politeness."

"Yup! Tim has gotten compliments from people you know, and he always makes some comment about how they're more into his body than his art. I know that sounds like him being vain, but he's dismissive when people are nice to him, thinking they're only interested in the superficial."

"Exactly!" Marcello leaned forward. "Now he's on a completely different continent in a culture alien to him. One that, like all powerful nations, tends to ignore the creative efforts of other countries. The odds are stacked against him there, and yet, his art is succeeding."

"Do you think he really believes that? He told me a lot of foreigners are on game shows over there, like it's a novelty."

"He'll find out the truth tomorrow," Marcello said. "His exhibition will be well-attended, but it's money that speaks loudest. People don't pay four million yen for a painting by an amusing imbecile."

"Four million?" Ben asked incredulously.

"Yen," Marcello stressed. "That's only forty thousand in our currency."

"*Only* forty thousand," Ben repeated, chuckling madly. "For all of them combined?"

"For the central piece of the exhibition, the crown jewel."

"Which one is that?" Ben asked.

"You know, I can't seem to recall, but I hope Tim's reaction to the price is as equally awed as your own. He has talent, and his paintings have value. Monetarily, yes, but also true value as artistic pieces. If he returns from Japan having learned that lesson, his confidence buoyed enough to encourage his continued efforts, well then… I suppose it's not up to me to decide if his absence is worth a paradigm shift. Only the two of you can decide that, but if you don't mind humoring me, if we'd had this conversation before his departure—if you had known then that he would be gone even beyond the estimated four weeks—would you have agreed?"

"Yes," Ben said. "Part of me always wants him here, no matter how good a cause, but I'd like to think that the selfless part of me would have won out."

Marcello smiled. "Considering what a large piece of you that is, I have no doubt that we still would have ended up here on your birthday. Speaking of which, the first course is about to arrive!"

The food couldn't be described as good or even great. Those words weren't sufficient. This cuisine was on an entirely different level! Ben felt like he had been eating fast-food his entire life and this was his first home-cooked meal. The difference was that great, leading him to a new theory. The reason Tim never brought him here was because it ruined normal food by comparison. After three courses, Ben was certain he didn't have room for more. That's when the birthday cake arrived. A single layer and perfectly round, it looked as though someone had scaled down a normal cake until it was the ideal size for two people to share with nothing left over. The surface was covered in rainbow sprinkles, which Ben loved, mostly for the burst of color normally absent on a white cake with buttercream frosting. Boringly basic, but that's what he preferred. These weren't sprinkles, as it turned out. He sampled a few and discovered they were shavings of white chocolate in six different hues.

His only complaint was the presentation, since the candles weren't even lit, and while the waiter wished him a happy birthday, he disappeared again without singing. Marcello wasn't very interested either, attention on his phone instead.

"Ah!" he said. "Here we go. If you'll be so kind as to excuse me."

Marcello stood and handed him the phone before leaving. Any questions Ben had were silenced when he saw the screen. A video call was open, Tim grinning at him. "Happy birthday, Benjamin!"

Ben opened his mouth to respond, but emotion got to his throat first, leaving him unable to speak.

"Are the candles lit?" Tim asked.

Ben spotted long matches next to the cake. He set down the phone to pick one up, his hands shaking slightly as he focused on lighting the candles. Luckily he only had ten to light instead of thirty-six. Once his task was completed, he picked up the phone again and smiled, having recovered somewhat. "Okay."

"You might want to plug your ears," Tim said. Then he broke into song. Just the usual birthday one, and yes, he had a terrible singing voice, but right now Ben could have put on headphones and cranked the volume to the max, just to hear it better.

"I miss you," he croaked when Tim was finished.

"I miss you too," Tim replied. "Now make a wish."

At the start of the day, he would have wished for Tim to come home as soon as possible, or even right away. Having spoken with Marcello, he felt a lot better about the reason they couldn't be together. He decided to give his wish to the new gallery, hoping it would be even more successful than the one in Austin.

"I heard that wish," Tim said, leaning the phone against something and standing up. Soon the camera was focused on the belt of his jeans, which was being undone. "Time for me to make it come true."

"Stop!" Ben said, giggling while looking around. Normally he wouldn't allow himself to talk on the phone while at a restaurant, but he had ample privacy here.

Tim was only kidding, having already sat back down. "I wish I could be there. This is killing me."

"You'll be here for the next one," Ben said. "And the next. And the next."

"I like the sound of that." Tim sighed. "I thought about flying Jason down to be there, but—"

"They're moving into the new apartment," Ben said. "I'm glad you didn't. Besides, I don't want Jason to feel like I'm not okay on my own."

"Are you?"

Ben looked around again to confirm his privacy. "No! Of course not. I need you." He looked at the screen more carefully. Tim appeared a little haggard, like he hadn't been sleeping enough, but it couldn't be too late or early there, because the room behind him was filled with sunlight. "What about you? Are you okay?"

"Great!" Tim said. "Just a little exhausted. I was up all night and didn't sleep much the one before."

"Why not?"

"Because of this." Tim picked up the phone and stood, the picture unstable and bouncing before it focused on a white wall and a single piece of art. This was the new gallery, but Ben didn't recognize the painting he saw. The subject was exceedingly familiar though, even if he wasn't used to seeing his own profile. He only hoped it was that flattering in real life!

The painting depicted him dressed in a traditional silk robe. A kimono? He wasn't sure if that was the right word, but the crimson fabric spoke of passion, and this combined with the pink and white cherry blossoms in the upper left and bottom right corner made him think of Valentine's Day. Or love. Both of Ben's hands in the painting were occupied, one gripping a stand, the other a microphone, his lips close to touching the round tip. That made him think of something else. His hair was wilder than normal, brown waves that wrapped around his ears and down his neck. His eyes were closed in concentration. It all had a decidedly Eastern feel. Tim's trademark prism highlights came this time from the golden pattern painted into the robe, which caught the light and reflected it again in different directions.

"What do you think?" Tim asked. "I know it's weird to see yourself like this. Kind of like when people hear a recording of their own voice and don't like it, so if you don't—"

"I love it!" Ben said. "It's gorgeous! Wait, I'm not saying that *I'm* gorgeous, only that you did a good job considering how flawed the subject is."

"You're too beautiful to ever capture on canvas, but this is close. You really like it?"

"It's amazing how you've grown," Ben said, shaking his head in disbelief. "I've always known you were talented, but you continue to surprise me. Again, it feels a little weird to talk up a painting of myself, but I'm sure that people will love it even though they don't know who I am. You could have put anyone else there and it would have been just as good."

"I disagree," Tim said, "but I'm glad you like it, because this is the featured piece of my exhibition."

"The four million yen one?"

Tim narrowed silver eyes. "Did Marcello ruin the surprise?"

"No! He just told me the price of the most expensive painting without saying what it was."

"That's a lot higher than I was expecting," Tim said. "Size has a lot to do with it. You need some sense of scale. Here."

After some shuffling noises, the phone was set down again. Tim moved to stand next to the painting, the bottom of it near his knees, the top well above his head.

"Wow," Ben breathed. "How big is that thing?"

"You've forgotten already?" Tim said with a grin. Then he stretched an arm above himself, the tips of his fingers lining up with the top of the painting. "About seven feet."

"Have you ever painted anything that large before?"

"Nope! That's why I've barely slept in two days. It was way more work than I was expecting, and I needed to get it done before the grand opening tonight." Tim returned to pick up the phone. "It's my birthday present to you. I wanted you here with me in Japan. Now you are."

"You're so sweet," Ben said, "although I'm not sure I can afford the price tag."

"That's the awkward part," Tim said sheepishly. "I made this for you, and if it doesn't sell, I'm bringing it back with me. If it does—"

"The money should go to the new Eric Conroy Gallery," Ben said. "That's how it should be, and it *will* sell, so make sure you take plenty of photos so I can see all the details."

They talked a while longer, Tim making Ben eat a piece of cake so he could watch. He looked happy, but he did have circles under his eyes.

"Is everything ready for tonight?" Ben asked, adjusting for the time difference. His tonight was Tim's morning, which was Ben's tomorrow and, well, best not to dwell on it.

"Yeah," Tim said. "We're all set and ready to go."

"How much longer until then?"

"I don't know. Six or seven hours?"

"Then go back to your hotel room and sleep."

"I will," Tim said, stifling a yawn. "I just need to double-check a few—"

"Right now," Ben said. "Take a taxi or whatever is fastest and get straight into bed. You can't meet your legions of fans when you're this tired, and you *know* not to argue with the birthday boy."

"All right," Tim said with a smile. "I'm going. Right now. See? I'm heading out the door."

"Good," Ben said. "Hey, do you have a return flight yet?"

"Not yet," Tim said with a guilty expression. "We're not real sure how much media attention this will get and if I'll have to do interviews afterwards."

"That's fine," Ben said bravely. "I'll take care of things here. You do what you need to do."

Tim stopped walking and sighed. "I love you so freaking much!"

"I love you too. Get some sleep."

They stared longingly at each other before hanging up. Ben's heart ached, but he knew this pain was temporary. As soon as they were together again, everything would be fine.

Chapter Twelve

"I forgot to give you your birthday present," Marcello said.

The car was idling in front of the house, Ben just about to step out the passenger-side door, when he was handed an envelope. "What's this? Dinner was enough!"

"Please. You'll be doing me a favor by accepting it. Help an old man clear his conscience."

Ben accepted the envelope and opened it, pulling out papers with more details than he could take in, but they all seemed to list different international destinations.

"A thirty-day cruise," Marcello said, "to make up for the month I've stolen. You may choose which route and the time of your departure at your leisure. Just promise that you'll accept this gift. A couple is meant to discover the world together, not apart. This is the only way I could think to set things right."

"You've never done us wrong," Ben said, leaning over to give him a hug. "Thank you. For everything."

"The pleasure was mine," Marcello replied. "Be careful, next year I might find some other excuse to send Tim away, just so I can have you all to myself."

Ben laughed, hugged him again, and got out of the car. He was wearing a smile as he entered the house. Chinchilla was thrilled to see him, even more so when she saw that he'd brought leftovers. Ben grabbed a plate and took it out back with them, waiting until she went potty before she got her treat. Then he reclined in his favorite deck chair, enjoying the solitude. Crickets chirped and he sighed, at first in contentment, and later with a heavy heart, because as nice as the day had turned out, he still missed Tim.

"I'm not the only one, am I?" he asked, stroking Chinchilla's head.

She looked up at him with a woeful expression.

"He'll be back soon, I promise. We're almost there. Just a little longer."

Something caught her eye and she hopped to her feet, racing off to the corner of the yard where Samson was buried. Probably a moth. Ben smiled, wishing he could be so easily distracted. Then he remembered that he could. He went back inside, put on some music, and sang along while looking again at all the things Tim had sent him. He straightened up the house a little, made sure Chinchilla was back inside and that the doors were locked. Then he went upstairs to get ready for bed. He was walking down the hall and had just passed the office when he skidded to a halt. Flipping on the light switch, he went inside.

"It's my birthday," he said to Jace's photo. "You at least have to sing to me."

No reply.

"Not in the mood to talk, huh? We could cuddle instead." Ben grabbed the picture frame and took it to the bedroom. He set it next to the sink while he brushed his teeth, then brought it with him to bed, placing it on the side table. "Just for tonight," Ben said sternly. "I don't want Tim showing up unexpectedly and catching us in bed together."

In truth, he could fill the room with photos of Jace, and Tim wouldn't complain. He was too generous about the situation, always taking Ben's feelings into consideration. That's exactly why Ben didn't keep the photo there, to pay him the same courtesy.

He got into bed and made sure the photo was angled toward him. Ben stared at it for a solid minute, absorbing every detail of the smiling face and using memory to animate it in his mind. His hand touched the glass affectionately before reaching to turn out the light. Scooting deeper into the blankets, he closed his eyes, drifting off to sleep.

When he woke again, the sun was on his face, warming it and making it all too easy to keep his eyes closed.

"Happy birthday to you."

Ben's eyes shot open. He was still facing a window, but the view had changed. He was on the first floor now instead of the second.

"Happy birthday to you. Happy birthday, my dearest Ben…"

The voice was soft, and while the owner still wasn't much of a singer, it was leagues better than Tim's. He rolled over, a tall figure standing next to the bed, still in his bathrobe. In his hands was a tray, but Ben ignored it to focus on the face.

"Happy birthday," Jace continued, singing the final line, "to you."

Ben stared. Then his lips trembled and he started crying, all while shoving the sheets away and stumbling out of bed, just to reach him.

"Whoa, whoa, whoa!" Jace said, quickly setting down the tray of food on the side table. "You always get like this. Come here."

Ben threw himself into those arms, unable to get any words out or to stop sobbing, because he had fantasized about moments like these countless times, little daydreams where he would turn around from whatever he was doing to find Jace standing behind him. Oh. Of course. Ben got himself under control and pulled away. "This is a dream. Isn't it?"

"No," Jace said, using a thumb to wipe away the tears. "Not exactly."

Ben's eyes went wide. "Oh god! I'm dead, aren't I? Really good food must mean extremely bad food poisoning."

"No," Jace said, chuckling warmly. "Although the meat did look a little raw."

"I think it was supposed to be that way," Ben said. He sat on the edge of the bed and glanced around. He was home. Just not the home he had been living in the past seven years. This little house belonged to the past. To him and Jace. "I was going to ask how you're here, but I guess the right question is how *I'm* here. Is this Heaven?"

"A reflection of it," Jace said. "All I can do is meet you halfway."

"So you're still…"

"I'm afraid so."

Ben looked him over. Jace hadn't aged a day. Everything was just as he remembered, even the slightly frayed sleeve of Jace's robe. He could smell the eggs on the serving tray and hear the sound of a car driving down the street outside. Only the light was different. Purer, somehow. Warmer.

"I wanted this to be possible," Ben said. "I didn't think I'd ever see you again, but I hoped."

Jace smiled. "Someday we'll be together again. Not too soon, I hope, but eventually."

"So it's all true? The afterlife? Heaven? Hell?"

"The good stuff is true," Jace replied. "The bad stuff is just people trying to scare others into doing what they want. There's nothing to fear. For anyone."

Ben barely heard his words, emotion rising in him again.

"Why did you wait so long? If I could have just seen that you're all right and known that we'd be together again someday..."

Jace sat next to him and took his hand. "I will always be there when you need me. I promise."

Ben squeezed the long fingers, missing the comfort they had always brought. If Jace could have visited him sooner, he would have. It was silly to doubt that. So why now? Why not shortly after he had died? Unless... "When I first woke up," Ben said, mind racing, "you said that I always get this way. Didn't you?"

Jace nodded. "I did."

"This isn't the first time."

"No, it's not." Jace sighed. "There are rules. I don't make them, believe me. You have to understand that we're not supposed to interfere too much. We can try to nudge people in the right direction, but we're not allowed to appear and tell people who they should vote for. Unfortunately. You can imagine how much trouble it would cause if the dead were allowed to meddle with the living, so there are systems in place. Even if some of us choose to cheat and—oh, I don't know—contact the person they are supposed to be watching over, even when it's not an emergency." Jace cleared his throat. "If that were to happen, theoretically of course, the living still won't remember. A person might wake up with hazy memories of having dreamed about the dead, but the important details are lost. By design."

"So we've done this before?"

"We have. Yes."

Ben looked up at him, on the verge of tears again. "How many times have we had this exact conversation?"

"It doesn't matter," Jace said with a chuckle. "I'll never tire of hearing your voice."

"How many times?"

"Hundreds. We must be getting close to breaking into the thousands."

Ben squeezed his hand. "You've been gone for ten years. Is it every single night?"

"No," Jace said firmly. "That wouldn't be healthy for you. At the beginning, I visited too often. I think that made it harder for you to move on."

"So what?" Ben said, his laughter hollow.

"I don't want you waiting for me," Jace said. "That's my

burden. I'll wait for you. And before you ask, yes, I know about Tim, and yes, I'm fine with it. I'm happy in fact. And since you won't remember this anyway, I'm not exactly alone here. Do you remember Victor?"

Ben stared at him. Then he made sure his expression was believably angry. "You swine! You've got some nerve! You show up—*on my birthday*—to tell me that you're fine with Tim, when really, you just wanted to clear your own conscience because you're screwing around?"

"I'm not screwing around on you!" Jace protested.

"Oh really? Last time I checked, you're still married to me. Unless you got remarried? Is that what happened? You and Victor had some sort of afterlife wedding?"

"You're one to talk!" Jace said. Then he peered at him and laughed. "You almost had me. Almost."

Ben grinned. "I miss you."

"I miss you too," Jace said, putting an arm around him and pulling him closer.

"You know the best thing about this? You're my dream guy now. Literally."

Jace laughed. "I suppose I am!"

"Isn't this tedious for you?" Ben asked. "The same conversation over and over again?"

"It's only the beginning that stays the same; your reaction and me having to explain things. The joke you just made, that was new. So was you teasing me about Victor." Jace rubbed a hand up and down his arm. "I've got it easy, to be honest. I'm still allowed to look in on you when I want, although it's hard when I want to say things to you, or reply when you speak to me."

"You hear me when I talk to you?" Ben said.

"I'm going to say no this time, but only so I don't have to see you cry anymore. It's your birthday! I want you to be happy."

"This is me happy," Ben said, wiping away tears. "Trust me. This is just about the best present ever."

"Just about?"" Jace teased. "I'll have to try harder next year."

"Maybe bring Samson with you," Ben said, intending it as a joke, but then he looked over hopefully. "Can you?"

"One visitor at a time," Jace said, shaking his head. "Sorry. He's busy making his own rounds."

"How long do we have?" Ben asked.

"Not very," Jace said. "I bend the rules as much as I can. If I ever find a way to break them, I will. For you."

Ben nodded, feeling tremendous pressure. There was so much he wanted to say to Jace, a list so long that he found it impossible to choose. "Have I told you before? All the things I feel about you, and all the little regrets. The things I wished I had said, or what I could have done better while you were still alive."

"You have," Jace said. "And I've told you all of mine. If you want, we can do that again. I don't mind."

Ben shook his head. "I want this time to be as different for you as possible."

"Then try the eggs," Jace said, releasing him. "I always go to all that effort, and you always say—"

"I'm too emotional to eat right now," Ben said. Then he grabbed the tray, which had a little of everything. Pancakes, toast, eggs, sausage, and fruit. Jace always made a good omelet, so he started there.

"What do you think?"

"The eggs are heavenly," Ben said. Then he snorted.

Jace rolled his eyes. "Keep in mind that I have to remember these conversations, no matter how bad the jokes get. Did you notice how the eggs are still warm even though they've been sitting there? Neat trick, huh?"

Ben nodded eagerly. Stuffing more and more food in his mouth until he could barely chew. He did this just to make Jace laugh, the sound like a drug to his ears. He had missed it so much. This place too. Their home. Ben managed to swallow eventually and set aside the tray so he could stand. "Is the rest of the house here? I miss it."

"You always complained about it being too small," Jace said.

"I know, but I loved it anyway. Expect for the bathroom, which was literally smaller than some of our closets."

"It was fine," Jace said, standing to follow him into the hall.

"Anything seems spacious when you spend too much time on an airplane." Ben spun around to face him. "Hey! What do you do all day? Besides stalk me. Do you have a job? Does Heaven have an airline?"

"There's plenty to do. Anything you can imagine and more."

Ben swayed, enough that he had to reach for the wall to stabilize himself. "I'm dizzy."

"Already?" Jace said. "We don't have much time. Come back to bed with me."

Ben felt like someone had slipped a drug into his drink. The hallway seemed slanted as he walked down it to the bedroom. Only when Jace put him to bed and slid in next to him did the room stop spinning.

"Better?" Jace asked.

"Yeah," Ben said, scooting backward so they could be as close as possible. "Can we stay like this?"

"Of course!"

"I'm on my way out, aren't I?

"Afraid so. It's like drifting off to sleep, and when you wake up, you'll be home again."

"You're my home." Ben pulled the arm tighter around him. "Can we keep spooning while I sleep? Even if I'm not aware that you're with me?"

"I usually don't do that," Jace said.

"Because of Tim?"

"Because it breaks my heart, but I won't let that stop me. Not tonight."

The light had gone from the room and Ben found it hard to see, but he didn't feel afraid. "I love you," he said, putting all of his emotion into the words.

"I love you too," Jace replied. "There's something else I need to tell you."

"What?" Ben struggled to hear, but he was as good as blind now. Maybe even deaf, because he didn't hear a thing. Just a whisper. Two words, but he must have heard them wrong, because they didn't make sense. No matter how he rearranged them, he couldn't figure out how they were significant to his relationship with Jace.

Trunk.

Car.

Ben shot awake, blinking against the morning light. He groaned, trying to remember how much champagne he had guzzled with Marcello. Enough that he had slept rough. His body was stiff, like he had been in the same position all night, but at least his head didn't hurt. He rolled over so he was no longer on his side. Then he rose, used the restroom, and let Chinchilla out back. Afterwards he went to the kitchen to make himself a tea. While standing there, he decided eggs sounded good for breakfast, even though he normally didn't go to the effort. Especially not omelets, which he wasn't skilled at making, but why the hell not? He could learn! He decided to watch a video on his phone first, just to get some guidance. Then he remembered it was still lost, along with his backpack. So annoying! He struggled to remember the last time he had seen it. He knew which class it had been, but he had already checked there. He didn't have it with him when he got home that night, because his hands had been full of groceries and—

No! He couldn't be that stupid. Could he? Laughing at himself, Ben grabbed the car keys and went outside to the garage. He looked to the left and right of the car, wondering if he had set down the backpack while unloading groceries and forgotten about it. Nothing. Then he popped the trunk where the groceries had been. Sure enough, the backpack was right there. He had been driving around with his missing stuff this whole time! Lucky thing he thought to check there. He supposed he would have found it eventually, but maybe not before buying a new phone. Laughing at himself, Ben slung the pack over one shoulder and went back inside, ready to face another day on his own.

Tim stood in the Narita International Airport. Ahead of him was the security checkpoint. He was so eager to get through it that he would willingly abandon his possessions and strip off all his clothes if it helped get him home any sooner. He was returning on a high. The grand opening of the New Eric Conroy Gallery had gone better than he dared hope. Miyû Mitsuishi had much to do with that, since she live-streamed the unveiling of her portrait. Tim had presented the painting to her as a gift in thanks for all the exposure she had given him. More traditional media had attended too. Newspapers, magazines, and even a television reporter showed up to cover the opening. Tim's art had sold well, but all that really mattered to him was the fundraising. The gallery had been swarming with visitors since opening night, and already enough capital had been raised to keep it running for the next year, with the first scholarships likely to follow. His business in Japan wasn't quite concluded though. One small thing remained.

He turned, Corey not far behind him.

"I guess this is it," Tim said.

"I'm never going to see you again," Corey said, voice raw. "Am I?"

"Are you kidding?" Tim said, jostling him to keep the mood light. "We said goodbye—what, twenty years ago? Then we met again on the other side of the globe. Seems like we're meant to be in each other's lives, and at least this time we've got phone numbers. We know where to find each other."

"I wish you were my older brother." Corey rubbed the back of his head sheepishly, and even though the words were already out, he mumbled, "Never mind."

"No!" Tim said enthusiastically. "I like it! Are you kidding me? I'm an only child. I've always wanted siblings."

"And I've always wanted someone I could look up to. I love my sister, but... you know."

"Yeah," Tim said, not hiding his exasperation. "I do." Then he smiled. "I like this. I'm running with it. When people ask, I'll tell them I have a little brother. In Tokyo, of all places."

"I guess this means I can't put the moves on you anymore. Not if we're going to be brothers." Corey narrowed his eyes thoughtfully. "Although..."

"Don't even go there!" Tim said. "You've made it to second base with me. That's already far enough."

"When I felt you up?" Corey laughed. "Yeah, I guess so. It's just too bad we skipped over first base completely. I'll stop now, don't worry. I'm just glad you're in my life."

"Someone needs to run the new gallery," Tim said. "Think about it. Your language skills would be useful when tourists come by. And we would have an excuse to stay in contact."

"I don't know a lot about art," Corey said.

"You'd have all day to study. Besides, if you can learn a language like Japanese, you can learn to tell the difference between Cimabue and Giotto."

"Translation?" Corey teased, since Tim had been forced to ask that countless times during his stay, but he shook his head to show it wasn't important. "I'll think about it. Even if I don't take the job, promise me we'll stay in touch."

Tim nodded. "Easiest promise I've ever made. I better get going now or—"

Corey slammed into him. The kid sure had a way of hugging! Tim rubbed his back and stroked the head buried against his chest. Then he squeezed and let go, Corey doing the same. He hated goodbyes. Part of him wanted to remain, but the rest… Tim looked back at the security checkpoint longingly.

"Ben must be an amazing man," Corey said.

"He is." Tim reached out and ruffled the dark hair. "But so are you. Give Kioshi my thanks again. As for you, I'm not sure how I can repay you for all that you've done."

"The agency will send you a bill," Corey said, pulling himself together. "Now get out of here before I really get emotional!"

"Okay." Tim refused to say goodbye, so instead he opted for, "See you later."

Corey's eyes filled with tears. "Can you upgrade that to a soon?"

Tim grinned. "I'll see you soon. I promise."

He gripped Corey's shoulder. Then he let go, picked up his bag, and turned around, taking his first steps toward home.

Ben closed his textbook and stood up from the table. As he gathered his things and returned them to his backpack, the other students around him spoke of their plans. Halloween might be tomorrow, but plenty of parties were happening tonight, from the sound of it. Ben would be doing his own celebrating soon enough. First he needed to return home and get the house in order. He was happy for the distraction, since it would make the hours pass faster and help him get to sleep, because tomorrow they would be together again. Finally.

He was walking down the hallway, working on a mental to-do list when a voice stopped him in his tracks.

"Well well well. If it isn't Bendover Bentley."

He hadn't heard that hateful nickname since he was in high school and was forced to be around idiots like Bryce Hunter and Darryl Briscott. Neither of them could be here. Could they? Then again, he had never expected to return to school in his thirties. Ben spun around. He saw one of the popular kids leaning against the wall. How did he know? Because the guy was too good-looking to be low on the food chain, and if he remembered right, he also had a bitching black sports car.

"Who are you?" he asked, struggling to keep up the act when

what he really wanted was to run straight into the arms of his husband.

"Wyman," Tim said, checking his nails like the conversation didn't interest him. "Tim Wyman. I'm new in school, but I've already heard some crazy rumors about you."

Ben jutted out his jaw. "They're all true."

"All of them?" Tim said, looking up. "Even the dirty ones?"

"Especially the dirty ones," Ben said, spinning around and walking away.

"Hey! Where are you going?"

"I've seen the jerks you hang out with," he called over his shoulder. "Whatever you're looking for, I'm not interested!"

"They're not really my friends," Tim said, his voice not far behind. "I don't want to hang out with them at all. I thought maybe you and I… "

"You and I what?" Ben said, turning around. They were close now, enough that he could smell Tim's cologne and see that his hair was still damp from a shower.

Tim pointed to a poster on the wall. "I thought we could go to the dance together."

Ben glanced over. "That's a poster about breast cancer screening. Never mind. Close enough. I'll be your date!"

Tim picked him up and spun him around. Then he slowly brought his face close to Ben's, smiling until their lips met. Ben felt the wall against his back, heard someone whistle in appreciation, and proceeded to melt from head to foot. Then he wrapped his legs around Tim's waist and hugged his neck.

"Your flight wasn't supposed to arrive until tomorrow."

"It's that whole time change thing," Tim said. "I flew fourteen hours and landed the same day that I left, but an hour earlier. Don't ask me how that works. Do you want to hop down?"

"Nope!" Ben said. "I'm never letting you go. Carry me home."

Tim laughed and turned, walking them down the hall.

"The house is a mess," Ben warned.

"I've already been there. It's fine. Chinchilla nearly had a heart attack when she saw me." Tim hoisted him, shifting his weight to a more comfortable position. "She's in the car. I couldn't stand leaving her again. The windows are cracked, but we should hurry anyway."

He broke into a jog, Ben laughing as he bounced up and

down. "Okay, okay," he said, once they had burst outside into the sunshine. "Put me down."

Tim placed him gently on the ground, silver eyes sparkling. "I missed you," he murmured.

"Being without you was a living hell," Ben admitted. "Are you done now? No more going to Tokyo?"

"I'd like to go back someday," Tim said. "See how things are going, check in on my little brother."

"Your what?"

Tim grinned, clearly enjoying being mysterious. "My little brother. I told you about him."

"You mean Corey? The guy who couldn't keep his hands off you?"

"Happens all the time," Tim said wistfully. "People can't control themselves around me."

"Then we'll see how long I can go without touching you!" Ben crossed his arms over his chest. Then he dropped them again and grabbed Tim's pecs. "I made it five seconds. New record. You do have the nicest boobies!"

"Thanks," Tim said, laughing and brushing away his hands. "Whenever I go back to Japan, I'm taking you with me. I swear."

"So that's it?" Ben said. He put on his best doe eyes. "We never have to be apart again?"

"Never. I mean it. I don't know how we're getting your car home, because from now on, you're stuck with me. Sound good?"

"Like a dream come true." Ben grinned and took hold of his arm. Together they walked toward the car, a gentle breeze making him shiver, but this time he had a warm body to press up against, and not just any! "Wait until Allison hears about this."

Tim furrowed his brow. "About what?"

"That the coolest guy in school asked me to the dance!"

"You always did get that backwards. Even at the very beginning."

Ben looked over in confusion. "What do you mean?"

Tim slung an arm around his shoulders. "I'm the one dating the coolest guy in school. Can't say it's always been that way, since I messed it up a few times, but from here on out, with any luck…"

Ben slipped an arm behind Tim's back, holding on to his hip. "You and me. Always."

Part Two:
Austin, 2018

Chapter Thirteen

Ben opened the door to a room that didn't get much use these days. The most recent visitors had been from Japan, and while that had been a delightful week, he couldn't think of any other guests he would be more excited about than the current ones. His parents? They would have to stay elsewhere. Tyler Hoechlin? Take your handsome self to the nearest hotel! Dione Warwick? Okay, that would be pretty cool, but he knew someone even cooler.

"And this is the guest room where you'll be staying," Ben said, standing aside and unable to stop grinning. "Bring back any memories?"

"One or two," Jason said, strolling into the room. "I remember it being cleaner when I lived here."

"Ha ha," Ben deadpanned, following him into the room. "I'm sure at the end of two weeks, it'll be exactly as clean as back then."

"Not with William here," Jason said, fingertips tracing the wall as he walked around the room. "He's actually got me picking up after myself these days, because I know if I leave a mess, that he'll be the one cleaning. So I actually try."

"But do you succeed?"

"Sometimes," Jason said, turning to flash him a smile. "I like that my old dressers are still in here. I know they were yours originally—"

"I think of them as yours too," Ben said, sitting on the edge of the bed, "and that's exactly why they're still in here. Two weeks! I can't believe I've got you for that long!"

"You might not be so happy when you find out why I'm really here." Jason plopped down on the bed next to him. "Wait, that sounds wrong. Of course we're here to see you. William's family too. But there's another reason, and it might cause a little stress. Or a lot of stress. Guaranteed."

"You're getting married!" Ben said, hopping to his feet in excitement. "This is wonderful news! Forget about the stress. We'll make it work. Do you have—"

"Quiet!" Jason hissed. He hurried to the door and shut it. "I haven't asked him yet."

Ben forced himself to calm down. He sat again and patted the mattress so Jason would do the same. "Tell me everything."

"Our four years are up," Jason said, sounding a little overwhelmed. "Remember? After you and Tim got married, William proposed to me—"

"Which is why I'm confused. One proposal is usually enough."

"True," Jason said, laughing at himself. "I guess what really needs to happen is for me to finally give him my answer. Assuming the offer still stands."

Ben was about to reassure him of the obvious: Of course William wanted to marry him! The anticipation and uncertainty was all part of the magic though, so he kept his opinion to himself. "When is this going to happen exactly? Do you know?"

"Tonight," Jason said. "I'm going into town for some wine, and you said you wanted to cook, so…"

"I'll try not to burn anything," Ben said. "And I'll make sure to go easy on the onions and garlic. Do you plan on asking him during dinner?"

"After," Jason said. "That way he's too sluggish to resist. I'll ask him to go on a walk with me in the backyard, since that's where he proposed. Um. That sounds stupid, doesn't it?"

"Maybe ask him to have a drink with you out there instead. So you can enjoy the evening weather together. That sounds more natural."

"Good idea!" Jason said. "Do you think we could have some privacy? I don't want any witnesses if I bomb."

"Of course! You'll do fine." Ben looked him over. Jason wasn't a boy anymore, even though the father and son dynamic of their relationship made it feel that way. Jason was nearing the end of his twenties and had come into his own. He carried himself with confidence these days and was handsomer than ever. William's active lifestyle suited him well too. Jason didn't have the same muscles as William did, but he wasn't struggling with love handles either. "I noticed the new hairstyle. Now I know why. It looks good!"

"You think so?" Jason reached up to hair that was still medium-length and messy on top, but closely trimmed on the sides.

"Very handsome. Brings out your cheekbones nicely."

"Thanks." Jason chewed his bottom lip. "Do you think I should put on a suit for tonight?"

"Do you even own one? I can't imagine it being very useful for wildlife rehabilitation."

"Definitely not," Jason said with a laugh. "Did I tell you that someone brought in a skunk last week? Cutest thing in the world. Just a baby. We're not sure what happened to the mother."

"Can they spray when that young?"

Jason sniffed one of his hands. "If you had asked me that yesterday, I'd have let you smell for yourself. After nearly a week, I think it's finally faded completely."

Ben was immensely proud of all his son had accomplished. Jason was thriving in Oregon. The coffee shop job had lasted the better part of a year. While trying to find another animal shelter to volunteer at, he had discovered a wildlife rehabilitation clinic instead, and despite his lack of formal training, he was eventually offered a paid position. Now he was taking classes while juggling work, but this was good too, since William was often busy or unavailable. Couples were happiest when they ran at the same pace, Ben felt. Figuratively. He had no intention of joining Tim on one of his nightly jogs.

"Just wear what you feel comfortable in," Ben said. "If all goes well tonight, it won't be your outfit that William remembers."

They heard voices in the hallway. Jason leapt to his feet and opened the door so nothing appeared suspicious. Just before he did, he whispered. "Wish me luck!"

Ben did so, even though he knew Jason wouldn't need it.

"Move over!" Ben complained, shoving at Tim ineffectually.

"You move over," Tim retorted, except when he shoved back, Ben toppled over.

"No fair," he whimpered, laughing as he grabbed the windowsill to pull himself back up to his knees again.

They were in the guest room and tipsy from the wine that had accompanied dinner. Outside the sun had already set, but just enough light remained that they could see two figures in the backyard below. Jason and William had sat on the patio, sipping from their glasses and talking. Then they had stood and toured the yard, not that there was much to see. A grill, some trees, the patch of flowers where Samson was buried, and on the opposite side, Ben's failed attempt at a water feature. That's what he liked to call it, anyway. In truth it was a pile of jagged stones covering a faucet that, when turned on, sprayed water in multiple directions, none of them intentional.

"It's getting dark," Tim said. "If they don't hurry up we won't be able to see them anymore."

"We could turn on the patio light," Ben said. "Think that will kill the mood?"

Tim grimaced. "What if we turn it on right when they're getting serious?"

"Yeah, you're right." Ben ducked when the two figures turned to walk toward the house. The light was off in the guest room, so they probably couldn't be seen, but he wasn't taking any risks. "Think it's happened already?"

"No," Tim said. "Look!"

Jason and William had stopped halfway across the yard. The exact spot where Ben and Tim had taken their vows and adopted Jason, and where William had popped the question four years ago. "We should erect a statue there," Ben said. "Or maybe a plaque."

"Erecting things sounds good," Tim said. "Uh oh!"

"What?" Ben said. Then he saw for himself. William was shaking his head and backing up. Ben's stomach dropped. Jason's probably did too! Then William went down on one knee. "He's asking again!"

"Smooth move!" Tim said. "He must not have wanted to hear Jason's answer before getting to ask again."

"Quiet," Ben said, tongue poking out one corner of his mouth as he slowly—and very carefully—lifted the window so they had a better chance of hearing. Jason was talking, a hand extended that he used to pull William to his feet, which must have taken some effort. Ben still couldn't hear anything so he tried opening the window wider. It squeaked. Loudly.

The two heads below turned at the noise. Tim fell backward to escape their sight. As for Ben, he lowered himself slowly, like they wouldn't be able to detect the slower motion.

"Busted!" Tim said, hissing laughter as he pulled Ben back with him. "I hope we didn't ruin anything."

"Then we might want to get out of this room," Ben said. "What if they want to—you know."

"You're right," Tim said. "Let's go."

Together they crawled on hands and knees to the door, Ben having to backtrack to shut the window. Chinchilla thought this was a game, which it sometimes was since Tim would often crawl around to be on her level. The dog took turns moving between them to lick their faces, Ben's covered in slobber by the time he reached the hallway and could stand again.

"Yuck," he said, hurrying to the master bathroom so he could wash off at the sink.

"It's just kisses," Tim said, following behind and showing no intention of washing his face. "I think that went well."

"Our spying or the proposal?"

"Definitely not the spying," Tim said. "The rest, yeah. Looks like we have a wedding to plan! Or at least to help arrange."

He sounded excited. Ben turned off the water and grabbed the hand towel. "Romantic, isn't it? Especially when it's not your own."

"Yeah," Tim said with a chuckle. "Although that doesn't have to be true."

"Hm?" Ben asked, folding the edges of the towel inward before hanging it again.

"We could get married," Tim said. "For real this time."

"We are married for real," Ben said dismissively. He walked to the bedroom area so he could close the door. The boys deserved their privacy. And he wanted an excuse to escape the conversation. His eyes darted to the nightstand, the spot where Jace's photo had once sat.

"Why not?" Tim said, standing in the middle of the room. "I keep asking, and you— I'm doing it wrong. You need something big and romantic, like those crazy proposal videos on YouTube. I could have all the kids at your work ask you in unison. Or maybe—never mind. You want to be surprised."

"I don't!" Ben said, trying to imagine how he would react if every person in the grocery store started dancing and Tim popped out of one of the freezers with a ring. "Please. No surprises."

Tim frowned and crossed his arms over his chest. "Okay, then why not after Jason and William's wedding? If we're going to set up everything anyway—"

"This is about them!" Ben said, moving past him to the bed. "Not us."

"They're part of us," Tim said. "We're about to become one family. We didn't mind when William wanted to propose on our wedding day. We adopted Jason then too! They'll be fine with it. We can get married the day after."

Ben grabbed his side of the blankets and yanked them down. "We're already married!"

"Not according to Uncle Sam, we're not."

"I don't care."

"I do!" Tim walked around the bed to reach him, taking hold of his arm and gently urging Ben to face him. "I agree that we're married. All I want to do is make it official, so nobody can say we're not. Yeah, we've got legal documents that make sure of visitation rights and stuff, but a marriage doesn't have to be explained. A hospital lawyer won't have to examine the papers before I can get to you or vice versa. You know all this, so why not? You must have a reason. Just tell me."

Ben sighed. "I don't want to hurt your feelings."

"Too late," Tim said. "At least help me understand. It's better than being hurt *and* clueless."

"I'm sorry." Ben hugged his arms to himself. "I didn't mean to hurt you. And you're right, you deserve an explanation. The way I see it, I had a private ceremony to marry you, and I also had one to marry—"

"Jace," Tim said. "You would only want to make it official with him."

"No!" Ben said, grabbing Tim's hands. "It's not like that! I want to be married to you both! I mean, I am already but..." He shook his head. "I'm trying to keep things fair. I'm proud to call you my husband, and I want to spend the rest of my life with you. It's just—"

Tim pulled his hands free and held one up. "Let me ask you a question."

Ben nodded. "Okay."

"If marriage equality existed back when you and Jace got married, would you have done it officially?"

"Yes."

Tim's expression became strained. "And if everything else had played out the same—if you and I still ended up together like we are now, would you have married me officially?"

"Yes!" Ben said without hesitation. "Absolutely!"

"Okay," Tim said, his features relaxing. "That makes sense."

"It does?" Ben asked. "Because it sounds crazy to my own ears."

"No, I get it." Tim sat on the bed. "You want things to stay equal between me and Jace."

"I guess I do." Ben sat next to him. "It doesn't mean I love you less than him—"

Tim shook his head. "I promised myself to never ask that. It doesn't matter who you love more. That you love me at all is enough. Now that I know where you're coming from, I'm okay with the way things are. We're married. We're together. That's all I need." Except his forehead was crinkled, his eyes darting around the carpet beneath his feet as he tried to reconcile his feelings with what he probably felt was the right thing to say.

"I don't deserve you," Ben said. "It's funny when I look back at everything I had to put up with from you. Now it's all reversed, isn't it? I'm the one who's hard to pin down."

"Butterflies aren't meant to be pinned down," Tim said.

Ben over looked at him, recognizing his own foolishness. Of course he wanted to marry Tim and make it official! He just wasn't sure if he could live with the guilt. "I'm sorry," he said.

"Don't be. I've already got so much. Anything more is just greedy."

"It's not," Ben said. He flopped backwards into the bed, head turned toward Tim. "You know, some butterflies like to be pinned down. Just temporarily, mind you. And not with pins."

Tim shuffled sideways like he was leaving the bed. "I'll go get the glue."

"Is that code for lube?" Ben asked.

"Nope!" Tim said, still scooting away. "I'm getting the superglue. Then I'm going to sniff it to get high, because you've driven me to it."

"No!" Ben cried, relieved by the humorous tone. "Stay here. If you really want to go down on one knee, I'll let you. Just make it both knees instead."

Tim shook his head but he was smiling. "I should probably go check on the boys. Maybe I can talk them out of getting married before it's too late."

"Or maybe I can talk you into staying," Ben said, grabbing his arm and pulling.

Tim let himself be dragged into bed. He was smiling now, and that was good, but Ben wanted to make sure he really understood. He climbed on top of Tim, hands pressing down on his chest. "I love you," he said. "With all my heart. You probably think that there's a part of me you'll never have, but that's not true. I can't explain how it works. All I know is that all of me, every single atom and molecule, loves you. Okay?"

Tim's silver eyes were emotional as they stared into Ben's own. Then he nodded. "Okay."

William surprised no one by saying yes. Or to be more accurate, he had asked again, and this time Jason gave an answer both clear and concise. They were getting married! This meant there was much to plan.

Ben sat down with the newly engaged lovebirds the next day, to figure out the details. Weddings weren't a piece of cake, despite involving one. The guest list was a good starting point. Jason and William agreed that they wanted a small and intimate ceremony. People often said that, and yet, when they started tallying the guests... William had his parents and his two brothers, each person mostly likely wanting to bring a date. Eight people. He wanted Lily and Daisy there, and two of his closest friends from the Coast Guard, bringing it to an even dozen. Jason's side of the family wasn't any smaller. Aside from Tim and himself, Ben also pointed out that Michelle and Greg should be there, since they were his aunt and uncle. Allison played a similar role. Ben's own parents would want to attend, and they were obligated to invite the Wymans, in case they wanted to see their grandson get married. Ben wasn't sure how that would be received. Mrs. Wyman seemed to become more accepting as the years went by while her husband only grew worse. Emma would be there too, and William wanted to invite Kelly, who would no doubt bring Nathaniel... So two dozen easily.

"Is it too late to elope?" Jason asked at one point.

"Now you know why it took us so long," Ben replied. "Change of strategy. Forget small. Make a list of everyone you would like there, regardless of inconvenience or expense. I bet it's not far from the number we've already reached."

He was right. Once other names were added, they were closer to thirty-six, which Ben felt was still reasonable. Especially since the wedding would take place at their home. Not needing a venue would save money. The guest list and location decided, they were still left with a tremendous amount to do. Ben helped where he could, secretly relieved that some matters were out of his hands. Like finding the right outfits.

Jason and William left early in the day to go shopping, giving him downtime to relax and recharge. Ben's work schedule often allowed him slow mornings. He was officially a speech-language pathologist now. After earning his master's, he had found a position at a grade school, which Ben loved, since he felt children could benefit most from what he had to teach. He also freelanced, visiting private homes or community centers to help people regain a skill they had once possessed. With children, he had the potential to give them a better start to their life, so that's where he preferred to focus.

His schedule was clear this morning until eleven, so Ben spent much of it yawning himself awake and drawing out breakfast as long as he could. Even once he was showered and dressed, he made himself another cup of tea and retreated to the back patio. Chinchilla kept him company, sitting next to him and surveying the yard.

"Better enjoy it while we can," Ben said. "This time next week we'll be up to our knees in decorations. You can help me plant some flowers. That should be fun, right? Digging around in the dirt. You always like that. Maybe this time we can keep the flowers alive longer." Just the thought of so much work made him yawn again.

Chinchilla's mouth was open too as she panted. She got down on her belly, probably hoping the stone patio would help her cool off.

"Or maybe we can hire someone to do the work for us. We'll still take credit though. I can keep a secret if you can."

Chinchilla spread her legs wide, stretched out her neck, and coughed. Then she licked her nose and continued panting, except this time, it sounded ragged.

"Are you okay?" Ben asked.

He got down and sat on his knees, which was normally enough to excite Chinchilla. Instead of standing, she remained flat on her belly, her breathing labored.

"Are you too hot?" Ben asked.

Occasionally she was stubborn and stayed out too long, or in rarer instances, they would forget to bring her in when the temperature started to rise. In such cases, Tim would hose her off, or put ice in her water bowl and encourage her to drink. No matter what, she was always brought back inside to cool down and rest. *"You need to chill out!"* Tim would joke each and every time. Except it wasn't very hot out at the moment, and Chinchilla never made such a gravelly noise when breathing.

"Okay," Ben said, trying not to panic. "Let's go inside. Come!"

He stood. Chinchilla remained where she was.

"Do you want a treat? Let's go! Come get a treat!"

That did the trick. She got to her feet and hobbled toward the door, but she didn't sound any better. Once she was inside, she sat down again, when normally she would have led the way to the kitchen to get what she'd been promised. Instead she coughed.

"I'll turn up the air," Ben said, his heart racing as he moved to lower the temperature. Should he call Tim? Or load Chinchilla in the car and take her to the vet? Once cool air was blowing through the vents, he went to the kitchen, deciding to see if she still had an appetite. He returned with one of the soft meaty sticks she was so fond of and nearly cried out in relief when she trapped it between two paws and started chewing. She took breaks to rasp in between bites, but she seemed more lively. Maybe she just swallowed a bug or something. Or perhaps her age was finally catching up with her.

Ben swallowed, then checked the time. If he didn't head out soon, he would be late for work. He couldn't leave her here. At the very least, he could drop her off at the vet on his way to the school. While there, he could ask how serious it was and decide if he should call in or not.

First he pulled his car out of the garage and parked it as close to the front door as he could manage. Then he went back inside, grabbed the leash from next to the door, and followed the ragged sound to where Chinchilla sat. She had finished eating and now seemed focused on breathing.

"Come on," he said. "Wanna go for a walk?"

This made her perk up. Chinchilla strained to get to her feet, which wasn't so unusual. She was an old lady now. The hip dysplasia had begun a few years back, but nothing too serious.

Not compared to what he had read about online. She was stiff when first waking up and needed more time to get around. Once she warmed up, it was just like old times.

"Good girl," Ben said, encouraging her to follow him to the front door. He didn't bother with the leash. Chinchilla wasn't likely to sprint away from him in her condition. She understood that they were going for a ride when she saw the car. Tim drove her around often enough. The only struggle was lifting her rump to help her into the passenger seat. Once she was settled, Ben got behind the wheel and cranked up the air conditioning to the max. She had a body like a packed sausage. Maybe the day felt hotter to her.

Ben kept looking over at her during the drive to Austin. Perhaps it was wishful thinking, but her breathing seemed to steady and sounded less forced. By the time he needed to decide which way to turn—toward the school or the vet's office—she appeared perfectly fine.

"Don't scare me like that!" he scolded.

Now his biggest concern became what he was going to do with her while he worked. Luckily his job allowed him to make use of a variety of tools. Not just tablet computers or his singing, but anything to get the students excited about learning. Chinchilla would have to be his assistant. He arrived at the school with time to spare, so he parked and debated calling Tim again. His husband didn't do well with things like this. If anyone asked Chinchilla's age, Tim always found some way of avoiding the question. When her hips had been particularly bad one winter, necessitating medicine, Tim had only referred to the pills as vitamins and came up with a lot of theories about why the veterinarian was wrong, especially when the treatment had worked. "Couldn't have been a hip problem. She's fine now!"

Ben decided to call someone else who knew a thing or two about animals.

"Can't we just wear normal clothes?" Jason said when answering the phone.

"Up to you," Ben said, managing a smile. "Shopping isn't going well?"

"I blame William. He looks good in everything. He's like the mannequins they have on display. Most people don't have all his curves and bulges though. By that I mean muscles, not uh…"

"I get it," Ben said. "And I know exactly how you feel. Whatever you choose, make sure it's comfortable and that you actually like it. Who cares what anyone else thinks?"

"Besides William, of course," Jason said. "I want him to think I look—stop smiling like that!"

"You're cute no matter what you wear," William said in the background.

"I don't want to be cute. I want to be hot!"

Ben laughed, his troubles far away, but it didn't take long for them to come rushing back. "I'm having a rough day myself. Or Chinchilla is."

"What's going on?" Jason asked, his tone instantly serious.

Ben described what had happened as best he could, not sparing a single detail, just in case it helped. "Any idea what that might be?"

"It's not unusual for bulldogs to have breathing problems," Jason said. "They have narrow tracheas anyway, and if something is blocking it even a little bit... Ever had her soft palate checked?"

"That could be it," Ben said. "She seems fine now, so crisis averted?"

He could hear Jason's hesitation. "I'm not a vet. I'd still take her in, when you can. How old is she again?"

"Fourteen," Ben said. He only knew the answer because he had done the math himself. He had a better chance of learning Marcello's true age than getting Tim to tell him Chinchilla's.

"That's old for a bulldog," Jason said. "Most live around ten years if you're lucky."

"What are you saying?"

"Nothing," Jason said quickly. "Just that it's probably not unusual for her to have trouble at this age. Better get it checked."

"I will. Think it can wait until my lunch break?"

"If she seems okay, it can wait until you're off work. Just keep an eye on her. If the coughing starts again, I would take her right in."

"I'll send her to the school nurse," Ben joked, mostly for Jason's benefit. He didn't want his son to worry too much when he should be focusing on his big day instead. "I need to clock in now. Thanks for your advice. I love you!"

"I love you too. Keep me posted."

"I will."

They said goodbye, Ben looking over at his passenger. "Ready for your first day of school?"

Chinchilla raised her head. She seemed stable and alert, so together they made their way inside the building. Ben hurried down the halls, wanting to avoid unwanted attention because he didn't have permission to do this. He was fortunate to have his own teaching space, even though it was half the size of a normal classroom. He didn't mind, since he had fewer students. Just seven at the moment, but that number often fluctuated as issues were resolved in some students and identified in others.

Already his mind was working overtime, trying to figure out how to incorporate a dog into his lesson. He supposed words like 'veterinarian' would be challenge enough, so that might work. He didn't plan on introducing terms like trachea and soft palate though. His job was first and foremost to get his students talking in general, and what better topic than pets? Especially for the younger age group he dealt with, none of them older than nine.

After some encouragement, he managed to get Chinchilla hidden beneath his desk. He hoped that she would settle down there, but as soon as students started filing into the room, Chinchilla ventured out to see what the commotion was. She instantly became the star. School was boring enough for most children, and a dog was the antithesis of humdrum textbooks.

"Okay everyone!" Ben said, trying to get the classroom under control. "Today we're going to talk about animals, and if we do well, you'll each have a chance to pet Chinchilla before you go to lunch. Let's start there. Can anyone repeat the name I just said?"

"Do we get sticker?"

"Yes," Ben said. "Everyone who works hard will get a sticker *and* time with Chinchilla. This is the only day she'll be here. If you don't try your best, you won't have another chance tomorrow."

That did the trick. The children attempted to focus on him and respond to his questions, even though their eyes often returned longingly to the corner where Chinchilla had settled down to sleep. Ben kept looking at her too, wanting to check that she was still okay and breathing normally. Or at all. He hadn't considered that possibility when bringing her here. He could already imagine having to meet with the parents and explain why mortality had become a subject in his classroom.

At the end of the hour, the children lined up with impressive self-discipline to pet Chinchilla. She remained on all fours, but she clearly loved the attention. Ben wished he had thought to bring her sooner. Stickers simply didn't command the same respect, but they would have to do, because he had already decided she couldn't stay.

He waited just long enough for the hallways to clear out, calling to cancel an appointment with the school psychologist and trying not to think of the evaluation forms he needed to fill out. Right now, all that mattered was getting Chinchilla to the vet.

"You're such a good girl," he said while loading her into the car. "Yes you are! You've definitely earned your sticker. Or how about I make you a burger tonight?" When this failed to impress her, he added, "Or we'll have Tim grill you a burger."

Now she looked excited. Treacherous mutt. Ben loved her regardless. He wanted her to be okay. Not just for Tim's benefit, but his own. She was as much a part of their family as Jason. Maybe they should hold another adoption ceremony during the wedding.

When he reached the veterinarian, Ben explained the situation, including that he needed to get back to work. He felt bad leaving her there. If the worst happened, he wanted to be present to comfort her, but he was trying hard not to think in such terms. No matter what was wrong, she was in the safest hands imaginable.

Once back in the classroom, he couldn't concentrate. Ben did his best, singing any song about animals that he could think of in between drills. He definitely didn't earn a sticker. His heart just wasn't in the job today. He even broke his own rule and pulled out his cell phone, needing to tell Tim what had happened.

Chinchilla was coughing and panting this morning. I took her to the vet, just to be safe.

He braced himself, waiting for Tim to panic, but he should have known better.

It's the new rawhides we bought. They're too dry. She probably got dog treat shrapnel stuck in her throat.

He even included a cute dog emoji. Tim might not be worried, but Ben was fighting off dread after school as he drove back to the veterinarian's office. When he was shown to an exam room and Chinchilla was brought out, she was excited to see him and seemed at full power again, her little butt wagging in excitement.

"Who's my baby?" Ben enthused. "We've had a busy day, haven't we?" He kissed the dog's wrinkly face, happy that her breathing sounded normal. Then he turned his attention to the vet when she entered, certain he was about to receive good news.

Ben kept walking to the front door to look outside the windows there, which was dumb because he could track Tim using his phone. Ben knew how far away he was, but sitting and relaxing was unthinkable at the moment. He would rather pace, which he did, back to the living room where Jason and William were snuggled up and watching television. Then he returned to the front door again. This march continued until he finally heard an engine approaching. Chinchilla did too, rising and joining him at the door. She looked perfectly fine, which wouldn't make this conversation any easier.

"Let's go see your dad," Ben said to her, waiting until the car was parked before he opened the door.

They walked outside together. Chinchilla's butt might have wagged for him earlier, but her whole body shook as she made her way over to Tim as fast as those stubby legs could carry her. Tim dropped to the ground as he often did, rubbed the scruff around her neck, and allowed his face to be licked. Then he looked up with smiling eyes. "What's the verdict? Bad rawhides?"

Ben started easy. "The vet said there's fluid in her lungs."

"Did you catch a cold?" Tim said to her in his baby voice.

No choice now but to put it all out there. "She said that this is probably the beginning of heart failure."

"What?" Tim said, sounding like he had just heard something silly. "Why does she think that?"

"It's common in bulldogs, and at her age—"

"She's fine!" Tim said. "Bulldogs can live to be eighteen, and that's a record we're going to break. Aren't we, my little princess?"

Chinchilla licked her chops and fixed Ben with a gaze like she too thought he was being silly.

"Most bulldogs don't make it past ten."

"She isn't most bulldogs," Tim said dismissively. "What did they say we should do?"

"Make her comfortable," Ben said, his throat aching. He had

already cried on the way home, even needing to pull over briefly. "We have some pills we can give her too, which might help."

"There you go," Tim said, sounding unconcerned. "More vitamins."

"This is serious," Ben stressed.

"I'll make sure she takes her pills. Listen, vets aren't always right. Nathaniel's dog had that stroke, remember? The first vet was all doom and gloom, but when he got a second opinion… You've seen Zero. He's like a puppy on crack! And the first guy wanted to put him down!"

"I trust this vet. Don't you?"

Tim shrugged. "Sure, but that doesn't mean she knows everything." He rubbed Chinchilla's fur some more, serious this time as he looked her over. "She seems fine to me."

"Right now she is," Ben conceded.

"So we'll keep a close eye on her. She'll take her vitamins, and just like last time, it won't be as bad as everyone says. Remember when she was supposed to get hip surgery?"

The vet had only mentioned it as an option, but Ben saw no sense in arguing. He could stand there and shout that Chinchilla was going to die, but Tim must know that already. He had witnessed death before at Eric's bedside, and Tim had nearly lost his own life once, thanks to a psychotic ex-boyfriend. Pet deaths were different though. As they went inside, Ben thought of Samson, and how painful that loss had been. Partly because it felt like another piece of Jace had died, but also because pets were similar to children: innocent and in need of constant care. The love they returned was special too. Purer.

"Are the boys back yet?" Tim asked. "We could all go out to dinner."

"I think they're tired of running around town," Ben said. "Besides, I promised Chinchilla you would grill. You owe her a burger."

"A burger tonight," Tim said. "A nice juicy steak tomorrow. I'll pick some up on the way home."

That fell under the heading of making her comfortable, so Ben nodded. At least they had managed to agree on something.

Chapter Fourteen

The gazebo was made of cast iron, three pillars of looping metal curls that rose ten feet in the air to join in an ornate knot. Vines climbed two of these pillars, the very ones Jason and William would step through to take their vows, purple blossoms already in bloom. All around the gazebo were lush ferns and a variety of exotic flowers, transforming a small area of the backyard into a garden paradise.

"You guys are insane," Jason said. He was seated on the patio next to Ben, shaking his head at what he saw before him. "How'd you manage this?"

"I was up all night," Ben lied. "Bending the iron was the hardest part. Once I had the gazebo built, it was just a matter of planting the seeds and speeding up time so they would grow."

Jason laughed. "This must have cost a fortune!"

"It's no more than what you did for us."

"Your wedding?" Jason said. "We tried our best, but it didn't look this nice."

"It did," Ben said. "And don't thank me yet. We went overboard on the flowers. Try to get through your vows before you get stung."

"A swarm of angry bees won't stop me," Jason said. "I'm so ready. Emotionally, anyway."

"That's the easy part," Ben chuckled. "Do you have everything figured out?"

"I think so," Jason said, not sounding certain.

"Let's go over it then. Vows."

"Got them up here," Jason said, tapping the side of his head.

"You might want to write them down anyway. I blanked when marrying Jace. I literally didn't say a thing."

Jason laughed again. "Okay. Uh, what else? I asked Emma to be my best man."

Ben nodded his approval. "What about William? Bridesmaids?"

"We considered it! But no, he'll have a best man too. Christie Patel is flying down to be his."

"Who's she again?"

"The mechanic from his Cape Cod days. The one who came to see us last year."

"Oh right. If you need a place for anyone to stay—"

"We're good," Jason said. "His mom's house has extra space, so Christie and her family will stay there. Lily and Daisy too. Guess who else?"

Ben shook his head.

"William. Only on the night before."

Ben grinned. "So you don't see each other before the wedding? I didn't realize he's that superstitious."

"He says it's to make sure everyone settles in, but yeah, I think that's the real reason. Back to the list."

"Catering is taken care of," Ben said, forcing a serious expression. "Did I tell you I decided to cook?"

"Really?" Jason said, doing a commendable job of hiding the strain in his voice.

"No, not really. What else?" Ben squinted into the horizon. "Oh! You still needed to choose an officiant!"

"Taken care of," Jason said with a smirk. "We didn't tell you who?"

"No." He hazarded a guess anyway. "Allison? Michelle? They would have to get ordained."

"We found someone who already is. He's a close family friend."

"Marcello?" Ben said disbelievingly. Then he laughed. "He certainly knows how to give a speech!"

"Exactly. That just leaves the cake, which William's mother is making. Kelly is our photographer. Outfits, done. Guest list, done. We're all set!"

Hardly, but Ben already tackled other arrangements, such as the DJ. Jason had insisted they could use a playlist from his phone, but as with other corners he kept trying to cut, Ben stepped in and spent the extra money to make the occasion even more extraordinary. Jason never asked him to. He even fought against it a few times.

"I'm really proud of you," Ben said.

"For getting married?"

"For turning out so well. You had to raise yourself, to a large extent. For much of your childhood, you didn't have parents to guide you, and look who you've become! You have a good heart. You aren't greedy or cold. You aren't lazy. You work hard and don't expect much in return."

Jason grinned sheepishly. "Gee, I wonder where I got all that from?"

"I can't take credit for it. I tried to be a good role model. I wasn't always, but I tried. At the age you came to us, so much about your personality had already been defined. You're special, Jason. You deserve all the good things that have come your way."

"Thanks," Jason said. "I try to make you proud. I know we don't see each other as much anymore, but you're still with me every single day."

"You're with me too," Ben said, pressing a hand to his heart. "And I couldn't be prouder."

From between them, Chinchilla raised her head and grumbled. She was doing well. The pills seemed to be helping. She still coughed on occasion, but he hoped that the vet's advice had bought them more time.

"I think she's jealous," Jason said. "She says it's not easy being the youngest child."

Ben laughed. "Especially considering that she was around before you."

"Tough break, little sister," Jason said. "But if you want, you can have my old room."

Chinchilla cocked her head, seemed to consider the offer, and settled back down.

"I think that's a yes," Ben said. Then he was struck by another thought. "Rings?"

Jason looked smug. "I'm pretty sure William has taken care of that."

"Not the best thing to leave to chance," Ben advised. "If he bought rings, he hasn't mentioned them to me."

The smile slid off of Jason's face. "Oh god." He pulled out his phone and started texting. He watched the screen, read the response, and turned paler. Then he fired out a reply and waited again.

The back door slid open, William hurrying out. "I thought you wanted to surprise me! You asked what my ring size is."

Jason twisted around in his seat. "I only asked so you would know mine! You told me not to stress about it."

William rubbed his forehead. "Meaning you didn't have to go crazy when buying them. I'm not picky, but I'd like to have a ring of some sort!"

"Okay," Ben said with a sigh. He pushed himself up and stood. "Into the car everyone. We've got shopping to do!"

Ben was straightening up the living room, brushing off the couch and fluffing pillows, when he heard coughing. The morning was still young, the windows open so the house could air out. The back door was open too, and that's where the sound was coming from. Ben went to investigate and saw Chinchilla stretched out on the patio, legs to each side of her and neck extended as she continued coughing. She had taken her pill an hour ago. Maybe this was part of that. He went outside to check on her, noticing the bloody froth around her mouth.

"Okay," he said, trying to reassure himself as he got to his knees. "The vet said this might happen. We can get through this!"

Chinchilla strained to get to her feet. Then she moved away from him and plopped down in the grass. He could understand that. Sometimes feeling bad meant not wanting to be around anyone else. He watched her continue to cough and retch, his stomach sinking further with each ragged breath.

"Just take it easy," Ben said, moving toward her again.

Chinchilla saw him coming, forced herself up, and limped away. She didn't stop until she reached the corner of the yard where Samson was buried. Ben's mouth went dry. With a trembling hand, he felt for his phone. When he didn't find it in his pocket, he hurried inside. What a terrible time to be alone! Jason was with William at his mother's house, and Tim was at the gallery. Ben could try to get Chinchilla in the car, but she was heavy, and he wasn't sure he could lift or drag her without causing harm. Besides, he was certain what the vet would recommend.

Tim needed to be here. Such a decision couldn't be made without him. Ben wouldn't do that. He forced himself to calm down long enough to send a text.

Could you please come home. Right away.

He was scared to say more, worried that Tim would panic and get in an accident along the way.

Can it wait until lunch? Tim replied.

Please. Right now. I need you here.

What's wrong?

I just need you. Drive safe. Please.

He paced back and forth, waiting for a response. When it was clear none would come, he returned to the backyard, already talking to Chinchilla as he made his way across the grass.

"It's okay," Ben said. "I'm not going to make you go anywhere, if that's what you're scared of."

He could see Chinchilla's torso rising and falling with the effort to breathe. She was still aware of her surroundings, because when he got near, she started to stand again. Like she wanted to get away. That was a sign. A bad one. Ben was sure he had read somewhere that animals sometimes wanted to be alone when it was time.

He turned around, not wanting Chinchilla to see him crying. Whenever she saw him weep, she always got upset, doing everything in her power to lick away his tears. It usually worked too. No matter how sad he was, he couldn't help but laugh when a dog was slobbering all over his face. He wiped at his cheeks, composed himself, and turned around again.

"Tim's on his way home. Your daddy is coming, okay? Just hang in there."

Chinchilla had been watching him out of the corner of her eye, and these words seemed to soothe her, because she looked forward again, eyes closing. She was still breathing. Poor thing must be exhausted. Ben stood there, wanting to do something for her. *Make her comfortable.* What the hell was that supposed to mean? He went back inside to get her bowl of water, putting ice cubes in it like Tim did to spoil her. It's all he could think of. All that coughing couldn't feel good. When he brought out the bowl, he was barely able to get close enough to set it next to her. He didn't understand why she kept pulling away from him. Maybe she just didn't want to go to the vet. Maybe she hurt too bad to be touched. He hoped that wasn't true. Ben kept his distance, still standing near enough to keep an eye on her. When he heard a voice call his name from the house, he ran toward it, unable to hold back. Tim had just come out the back door when he caught Ben in his arms, clearly puzzled by the tears.

"Chinchilla," Ben said with a sob. He pointed to where she was. "She won't let me near her. I think it's—" He couldn't get the words out, but he had to say it. "I think this is it."

Tim pushed past him and ran, Ben wanting to follow, but he didn't want to upset her again. He watched as Tim hit the ground, skidding to a halt next to the dog. She raised her head, stubby tail wagging, and Ben felt a mad sort of hope that he was being dramatic. She was sick, but maybe Tim would pick her up, carry her to the car, and the vet would do something to give her more time. Except that didn't happen. Tim leaned over the dog and kissed her, saying words that Ben couldn't hear. He slowly walked closer, hearing coughs that sounded even worse than before. Tim was hunched over, hugging her, and that seemed to help because the ragged sound of her breathing slowed. Then it stopped.

"Tim?" Ben asked, his voice a broken squeak.

Tim didn't respond. He pulled the dog closer to him, but her tail wasn't wagging anymore. She wasn't moving at all. Ben tried keeping himself together, but he couldn't stop shaking. He finally got close enough to put a hand on Tim's shoulder, causing a reaction that he didn't expect. Tim shot to his feet, grabbed Ben's arm, and walked him away. Ben stumbled along with him until he reached the patio. Tim let go of him, eyes red and wet, but his expression was stony.

"Wait here."

That's all he said before walking into the house. Ben looked back to the corner of the yard. In spite of Tim's words, he ran over there, needing to touch her fur again and kiss her wrinkled face. He stopped halfway, painful memories of his own rising. He knew how bad grief could be, and while he was suffering with his own, Tim's had to be even worse. Chinchilla was gone. Ben would ache over that later. For now, he was too worried about what Tim might do, because this sort of pain could make a person want to die rather than continue suffering. Ben rushed back to the house and went inside, relieved when he saw his husband approaching. Tim was crossing the living room, the handle of a shovel clenched in one fist.

"How can I help?" Ben asked.

Tim held up a hand, palm flat, like he was asking Ben to stay where he was. "I need to do this."

"Do you want me there?"

Tim's expression was strained. He wouldn't let himself say the words, but Ben heard them anyway. Tim needed to be alone.

"I'll be right here," Ben said. "Just let me know if you need me, okay? I'm right here if you do."

Tim's mouth trembled. Then he steeled himself again before he went outside to the backyard. All Ben could do was stand at the door and watch. When he cried, he tried to do so quietly. He was devastated over losing Chinchilla, but he ached more for Tim, because he knew this sorrow. Didn't he? As much as Samson's death had hurt, Ben hadn't known him since he was a kitten. Tim had been with Chinchilla ever since she was born, more or less. Ben had found her up for adoption outside a grocery store, the last of her litter to be given away, her scrunched-up puppy face puzzled as he drove her across town to someone he had needed to say goodbye to. And he did. Ben had parted ways with Tim that day, never expecting to see him again. That had hurt them both. Ben had returned to his life with Jace. Tim only had Chinchilla, both of them on their own, and no doubt missing those they had once turned to for comfort.

He watched as Tim finished digging, lifted Chinchilla, and cradled her in his arms. Ben could hear him murmuring soothing words, as if still assuring her that she would be okay. Then Tim fell to his knees, shoulders shaking and head bowed, before he gently lowered her into the ground. Ben was on the verge of going to him—despite his request for privacy—when Tim stood again and began shoveling dirt into her grave. That was enough. Ben couldn't stay away any longer. He walked across the yard, reached Tim, and placed a hand on his back. The patch of flowers had a hole now, brown dirt where pink and yellow petals should have been. Chinchilla was buried close to Samson's grave, the pain of that loss a renewed ache in Ben's chest.

"I'll be okay," Tim said once her grave was filled and patted down. When he turned, he kept his back to Ben. Shovel in hand, he marched across the yard.

Ben took the opportunity to say his goodbyes, which consisted of more tears, spluttered words, and all the love leaking from his broken heart. Then he forced himself to walk away, needing to check on Tim. He didn't find him in the house, so he went out to the garage, where the shovel was kept when not in use. The door was still open and the shovel was there, but Tim wasn't. Neither was his car.

"Shit," Ben hissed.

Then he broke into a run, sprinting down the long drive and hoping to catch the Dodge Challenger before it drove away.

Too late. The car was gone and so was Tim. Ben pulled out his phone. He didn't want to call or text. Not while Tim was driving and upset. That would only make an accident more likely. Ben opened the GPS tracker app instead, impatiently waiting while it promised to update the last known location. When it finally did, Tim wasn't far away. He was in West Lake Hills. Eric's old house? Is that where he was going? Ben continued to watch before it clicked. Another possibility was in the same area. It was the weekend, meaning Marcello should be at home instead of at the studio. Acting on impulse, Ben called him, the voice that answered jovial.

"You know," Marcello said, "whenever I see your name on the display, I swear the sun comes out and the birds start to sing."

"We lost Chinchilla," Ben said, not capable of pleasantries because it took all his effort to speak without crying. "Tim took off. I think he's headed your way."

"I see." Marcello's tone was serious now. "I'll meet him at the front gate and keep you informed. Try not to worry. I'll make sure he's taken care of."

"Thanks," Ben said, emotion overwhelming his resolve. "Whatever he needs, okay?"

"Whatever you need as well," Marcello replied. "Please don't hesitate to contact me."

"Okay. Thank you." That's all Ben could manage. He too needed to grieve, so he hung up, went back inside, and lost himself in memories of a goofy dog who had been the light of their lives.

"He doesn't deal well with death."

Marcello stopped by the next afternoon. No quips, no champagne, and no amusing anecdotes. He was grim and appeared exhausted. He accepted Ben's offer of tea, and once the two mugs were steeping, they sat down together at the kitchen table.

"When Eric died," Marcello continued, "Tim was... stoic. I know some people felt he was cold, but I had seen enough of him to know that wasn't true. Tim didn't cry at the funeral, at least not where anyone could see him. He insisted on handling every tedious detail involved in laying Eric to rest, but between you and me, he was incapable. I believe it took all of his willpower to hold his emotions in check. I helped where I could, and quickly learned not to ask how he was feeling. If I did so, Tim would react with anger. It's easier to grind our teeth at how unfair this world is and rage against invisible injustices rather than let the pain flow to our eyes. A reluctance to cry is the curse of every man. We are fools, only delaying the inevitable. Once Eric was buried and the funeral over, Tim retreated into the house they shared and didn't come back out again. I checked in on him once and found him passed out next to a bottle of morphine."

"Morphine!" Ben repeated. He knew Tim had experimented with drugs while dating Ryan but imagined him pressured into doing so, not because he sought relief.

"Tim is no junkie," Marcello said, picking up on his thoughts. "I believe he would have risked anything to stave off the pain he felt, and Eric's leftover medicine—well, they *are* called painkillers. Who could blame him for trying? Morphine wasn't the only bottle he turned to. After enough of this indulgence, I stepped in and forced him to face the world again. I'm afraid this pattern is repeating itself now. Without the drugs, mind you."

"He's been drinking," Ben said, neither surprised nor judgmental. He was glad for the update, since Tim hadn't responded to any texts or attempts to call. "How is he now?"

Marcello grimaced. "Last night he drank himself unconscious. When he woke again, he was sick and then started drinking again. He's sleeping it off now. Don't worry. Nathaniel is in the next room, just in case Tim should wake. I know this sort of behavior isn't favored by spouses but—"

"Just make sure he doesn't kill himself," Ben said. "Or poison himself too much. And definitely no drugs! Try to make him eat something and drink water occasionally. I know it won't be easy, but please try."

Marcello's smile was weary. "You are a testament to love. I've been told many times just how selfless it can be, although I'm not sure I believed it until this moment."

"I understand what he's going through. It's hard to deal with the pain, so he's doing so through a filter until he's strong enough to face it sober." Ben swallowed. "I just... Please don't tell him I said this, but why can't he do that here? With me? Because he thinks I wouldn't let him drink that much?"

"Would you?"

Ben hesitated. He probably wouldn't, only because he would worry for Tim's wellbeing. Or maybe Ben would have joined him. He wasn't sure.

"The issue, I believe," Marcello continued, "is that Tim feels the need to be strong for you. Something he is entirely incapable of at the moment. I'm sure he is also aware of the migratory nature of pain, how love can be a pathway for hurt to travel along and reach others. I have ached deeply while watching him suffer. The effect would be tenfold for you. I suspect Tim would spare you such unpleasantness."

Ben wanted to argue that he was willing to hurt for him—that it was a promise of their marriage—but he knew it wouldn't be fair. Tim already had enough to deal with without feeling guilty. "Tell him that I love him and that I understand."

"You have my word that I will convey your message, and that I will return him safely to you."

Ben felt a surge of gratitude. "Whenever someone dies, it always makes me want to tell the other people in my life how I feel about them. I love you, Marcello. Tim does too. You're part of our family."

Marcello smiled. "And both of you are not only a part of my family, but also pieces of my heart. I can see in your eyes where you would rather have me be. If you don't mind, I too feel the urge to check in on him."

Ben nodded. He wished he could be there instead, but there were few people he would entrust Tim's welfare to more than Marcello.

Tim woke up feeling like Hell had moved into his body and wasn't concerned about the security deposit. His stomach was empty and acidic, his head throbbed, and his mouth was so dry that he expected to cough dust. What came next was worse. His mind caught up with his body, reminding him what real pain felt like. A hangover was nothing compared to irrevocable loss. His little princess was gone.

As dehydrated as his body was, it still managed to produce more tears. Tim let them wrack his body. Then he forced himself out of bed. The room was unfamiliar to him. He had chosen a different guest room last night, or maybe Marcello had moved him for some reason. The past few days were too much of a blur to piece together. He had fallen asleep in his clothes again, the outfit not the same one he had been wearing the day she died, but the T-shirt and jeans belonged to him. Ben had probably sent them. He'd been thoughtful enough to make sure the clothes were black. Guilt intermingled with the pain. Tim was incapable of facing either, so he stumbled from the room.

Marcello's house was too damn big. Reaching the kitchen took an eternity. He winced against the natural daylight streaming through the windows and glared at speakers that were playing gentle classical music. He saw Marcello at the far end of the room, loading fruit into a juicer. Were they having cocktails? He wouldn't wait to find out. Tim needed to start with something cold. Beer. Wine. Champagne. Anything.

"It's ten in the morning," Marcello said pleasantly.

Tim paused. "And?"

"Let's begin with breakfast."

"That's what I'm doing." Tim opened the refrigerator, annoyed when he didn't find what he was looking for. "You forgot to restock," he grumbled.

Booze was never in short supply at Marcello's house. Tim walked into the pantry and switched on the light. The bottom shelves were bare. He had been drinking a lot, but not that much! He checked the other shelves too, but the conspicuously empty patches confirmed that all alcohol had been removed.

Tim returned to the kitchen, where Marcello had just finished running the juicer. "What's going on?" he demanded.

"What's going on?" Marcello repeated, albeit in kinder tones. "Well, for starters, your son is getting married tomorrow."

Tim stared. Then he worked his jaw. "How many days have I been here?"

"Five."

"You're serious?"

"Aren't I always?"

"I'm missing a couple days."

"A common occurrence in this home," Marcello said, pouring two glasses of juice. "Someday I suspect we'll find a room stuffed full of missing days. For now, let's focus on the present, shall we? Begin with this, slowly, and I'll whip up something more substantial for us to enjoy. I must warn you. I don't possess Eric's level of culinary talent." He looked over. "Does it bother you when I mention his name? Should I avoid doing so?"

"No," Tim said, taking a tentative sip of the juice. "It makes me happy that we still talk about him."

"You'll find the same is true for anyone you lose. Not at first, of course. The process is gradual, but eventually, she'll return to being a source of joy."

"Okay," Tim said, his throat tight. "I'm going to go sit down."

"I won't be long," Marcello promised.

The kitchen was, like the rest of the house, huge. At the far end, away from the stove and counters, were two small couches that faced a table. These were next to a tall window, so Tim forced himself to sit in the sunlight even though it made his head hurt worse. Marcello was right. It was time to pull himself together. Tim had hidden himself away for selfish reasons. Oh sure, he had wanted to spare Ben seeing him like this and the burden of taking care of him, but mostly he had needed somewhere to curl up and ache. Marcello had been as accommodating as ever and infinitely patient. Funny how, past the initial drink or two together, he couldn't remember Marcello getting wasted with him, or drinking anything at all in the last few days—or however long it had been. When the large man walked over to the couch carrying two plates of hash browns and eggs, Tim rose to help arrange the table.

"Thank you," he said with enough emphasis to mean more than just the food.

Marcello nodded and sat down across from him. "Despite the unjust nature of this world, there is still much to celebrate, and perhaps even an opportunity to help spread happiness. Let's find out, shall we?"

Tim nodded, ready to face reality. His mind was. His body still wasn't pleased with him. After breakfast he took a long shower and found another fresh outfit that had come from his home. He longed to return there, even though he knew it wouldn't be the same. How could it be? Once clean and shaven, he really wanted a nap, but he had imposed on Marcello long enough. After saying goodbye to his friend and hugging him tight, he got into his car and drove home.

He approached the front door with a lump in his throat. Chinchilla would always greet him at the door when he came home, except when she was in the backyard. In such circumstances, Tim would walk through the house and make the yard his first stop, just so he could see her. He supposed that's how it always would be from now on. He would still go to the backyard to greet her, but no longer would he expect a response.

The front door was unlocked. Tim opened it, tears escaping from his eyes as he did so. He looked to the floor out of habit, knowing his little girl wouldn't be there. Except a little girl *was* there, four years old, and sitting in the entryway. A woven basket was between her legs as she took out a flower and tossed it away. Plenty more littered the floor. The little girl looked up, brushing the blonde hair away from her brown eyes to see. Then she froze.

Tim did too. "Hi," he said, sniffing and wiping the tears from his cheeks.

"Hi," Daisy replied. She sized him up. "Are you sad?"

"I guess so," he admitted, shutting the door behind him. "What are you doing?"

"Practicing," Daisy said, taking out another flower and tossing it aside. "You're going to be my new grandpa."

"That's right," Tim said with a laugh. Then he stiffened, his body not knowing how to react anymore. He didn't want to feel happy. Not without Chinchilla.

"I've already got two grandpas," Daisy said, her tone disapproving. "Now I'm supposed to get two more."

Tim sat down next to her. "Then maybe I could be something else. Instead of Grandpa, you could call me Lito."

"Lito?" Daisy said, face scrunching up. "What's that?"

"It's Spanish. Lito is short for *abuelito*."

Daisy nodded. "I like that better."

"Lito?"

"No, the other one."

"Abuelito," Tim said. "Okay. That's what you can call me. And you can call Ben—"

Footsteps made him turn his head. Ben himself had just walked into the entryway, face creased with concern. Tim stood, an apology on his lips, when Ben rushed over to hug him.

"Are you okay?" they asked at the same time.

Ben pulled back, his smile fading. "I'm glad you're home. If there's anything you need, or anything I can do…"

"I'm tired," Tim admitted.

Ben nodded his understanding. "Go take a nap."

"But I haven't been around and—"

Ben put a hand over his mouth to stop him. "We're fine. We've all missed you, but we're better now just knowing that you're here. Go rest."

"Okay," Tim said, looking toward the living room and the back door. Part of him wanted to go out there, lay down on Chinchilla's grave, and never get up again. But he couldn't. Not when other people were depending on him. He kissed Ben and thanked him. As he left the room, Tim looked back, locked eyes with a little girl, and promised himself to get better. If not for his own sake, then for the people he loved.

Chapter Fifteen

Tim felt like a butler, constantly opening the front door, greeting the guests, and directing them to where they should be. He didn't mind so much, since for the most part he was happy to see each person as they arrived. If only his stupid mind would let go of old habits. He kept worrying about Chinchilla slipping out the front door or getting underfoot before remembering with a jolt that she was no longer with them. Staying busy helped him work through this, as did all the smiling faces, which reminded him of what a special occasion this was.

One face in particular made him feel better. Tim ducked into the kitchen for a drink and noticed Jason standing at the sink, gulping down water. He spun around when hearing Tim's approach, resembling a skittish animal. Jason looked handsome despite his transparent panic. His suit jacket, vest, and pants were slate gray, the dress shirt white. The only splashes of color came from the tie around his neck and the handkerchief stuffed into one pocket, both pale blue.

"Everything all right?" Tim asked.

"Yeah," Jason said, glancing around the room, which wasn't empty, so he leaned forward and whispered, "I might be freaking out."

"Cold feet?" Tim asked, grabbing a glass for himself and filling it with water.

"No way!" Jason said. "I'm ready to marry William. One hundred percent! I just wish we could go up to my old room, shut the door, and do it there."

Tim snorted. "I bet!"

"Poor choice of words," Jason said, chuckling himself. "I wish we could get married there."

"I get it," Tim said with a nod. "Right now it doesn't feel too romantic, does it?"

"No," Jason said. "I haven't seen William since yesterday. Not for more than a few seconds. He keeps running away and saying it's bad luck and uh…" He glanced around again. "There are so many people here!"

"Give it a little more time," Tim said. "Once the ceremony is over, you'll feel relieved and will be able to relax and have fun.

You'll have William at your side then too, which will make facing the masses easier. Just remember that we're all here because we love you. Me especially. I'm proud of you, Jason! You didn't have an easy road. Relationships are hard enough to figure out without having issues. I had plenty and they tripped me up bad. You—"

"I'm no saint!" Jason said. "I've made mistakes."

"You stayed true to your heart. Everything you did was in the name of love. I've only known one other guy like that, and I made sure to marry him. William is smart to do the same. Ben was the best thing to ever happen to me. At least until you came along. Remember what a jerk I was the day you showed up?"

"You weren't a jerk," Jason tittered. "You were just nervous. Right?"

Tim nodded. "I was scared I would ruin it all. Had I known then how much better our lives would be because of you, I would have been the first one hugging you when you stepped out of that car. Hell, I would have forced you guys to pull over while still on my riding lawnmower, just to get at you."

Jason laughed. "Stop!"

"Nope!" Tim said. "This day is the perfect excuse to tell you how I feel. I love you, Jason, and I'll always be there if you or William need anything. I promise. Now come here."

He opened his arms, and Jason clung to him, stifling a sob. Tim didn't want to let him go. He wanted to be selfish and insist that yes, Jason and William could get married, but they would have to spend the rest of their lives in this house with him and Ben. Funny how that worked. At one time Tim had wanted nothing more than to be alone with Ben, but Jason had snuck into his heart and found a place there. William had too. So had Marcello, Corey, Eric, Chinchilla... Tim had a strange little family, some of the members lost to him or too far away, but he felt blessed by how much fuller his life was now. He had come a long way from the dark days when he only had Chinchilla for company, but he would be forever grateful to her, and he would now look back on those times as precious. They hadn't been empty. Not with her around.

"Jason," Emma said, strutting into the room in a black tuxedo. "Can I borrow you for a second?"

Jason finally pulled away from Tim and casually rubbed at his eyes. "Sure. What's up?"

"Marcello wants to go over the ceremony with you and William."

"Really?" Jason said, clearly excited by the prospect. "But he says it's bad luck to—"

"See each other? That's why I'm supposed to blindfold you before we go in the room. No kidding."

Jason groaned in exasperation and dragged his feet while leaving. He looked back once, eyes full of emotion. Tim just grinned and gave him a thumbs-up. Then he turned that smile on the room, expecting to share it with the other people there. He found only one other person, who was seated at the kitchen table and looking uncomfortable. Thomas Wyman. His father. Their relationship had never been great. These days it consisted of pompous lectures about how things should be, his own life included among all the other problems of the world. His father only had criticism for him, but then that's how it had always been. Tim's normal strategy was to minimize contact with Thomas and ignore any personal slights, but he was still emotionally raw from all he had been through recently.

Tim nodded to the door Jason had left through. "That's how it's done," he said. "That's how a man is supposed to treat his son." He pushed away from the counter, not expecting a response.

"That might be how your kind do it," Thomas murmured.

"What's that supposed to mean?" Tim said, rounding on him.

"Just an observation," Thomas said coolly.

"Fine." Tim marched over to the table. He pulled out a chair and sat across from his father. "Let's hear it."

Thomas regarded him with a hint of disapproval, probably because he always kept his emotions in check. If he had any at all. "The man who gave you all the money. What was his name?"

"Eric," Tim said, irritated that his father didn't know. His place of employment, the gallery he worked in, was named after the man! He should at least know it for that reason!

"I never understood your relationship with him. Your mother promises me that it wasn't... inappropriate. Watching you and Jason together made me wonder if that's what it was like."

Was that a question? Not technically, but Thomas never asked him about anything personal. Not about his relationship with Ben, what it was like to be gay, or even how his own grandson was doing. All he wanted to discuss was work, sports, and politics. Tim was too jaded to expect this to be a heartfelt conversation, but he supposed he should at least encourage an open dialog. "Eric was like a father to me. I guess that's why my relationship with Jason is similar."

"But he doesn't have a father. You do."

"Not one who's proud of me."

"I was proud of you!" Thomas said, showing some passion. "How many of your games did I attend?"

"Baseball?" Tim laughed. "Sure, you were proud when my team won a game or I scored enough points, but come on, Dad, that's ancient history! Have I done anything since senior year to make you proud? Can you name one thing that you've bragged to a client about? I bet you don't talk about me at all."

His father was silent.

"Really? I've had two art exhibitions. One in Japan! I was on television! That's not worth mentioning to anyone?"

"I supported your art," Thomas shot back. "I provided you with a space to work in. I gave you a studio!"

"Only after Mom complained about me making a mess at home. You didn't do that for me. You did it for her. I'm glad you love her so much. It's just too bad that you didn't have anything left for me. And I don't care what it is—baseball, painting, or hell, even if I had stayed home all summer to learn the freaking accordion—as long as I wasn't hurting anyone, as long as I was doing something to better myself, you should have told me you were proud. You never even came to look!"

"What do you mean?"

"The studio was in your office building. You must have walked by it every day, but did you ever ask to see inside? Did you show any interest in my art?"

"You were very private about that room."

"Yeah, but you could have tried." Tim felt like kicking himself for letting the conversation get this far because he knew it wouldn't be productive. He had tried speaking calmly to his father before, and he had also tried shouting. Nothing seemed to work. He pushed away from the table and stood. "If you'll excuse me, I need to focus on my son's wedding."

He didn't have to listen just in case his father made a heartfelt plea for forgiveness, or at the very least, understanding. That never happened. Instead he went to the living room where adults talked and watched the younger generation play together. Allison's son was nearly six now, William's daughter was four. Tim loved having children around. He wasn't alone. His grandmother, Nana, always made them laugh with her broken English and was currently thrilling them with exotic candy and toys from Mexico. His mother participated too, beaming with joy as she helped Daisy unwrap a treat. Moments like these were bittersweet for Tim. Unlike his father, he could talk to his mom, and Ella had apologized long ago for not giving him what he needed when he was growing up. He didn't harbor any resentment toward her because she at least had tried. She might not have done a great job, but he never felt like his mother didn't want him. His father would trade him in for a heterosexual twin without blinking an eye, preferably one who had never put down the baseball bat in favor of a paint brush.

The doorbell rang, drawing Tim away before he could get settled. When he opened the door, he found Nathaniel standing a few steps back, his trademark scowl absent in favor of concern. His legs were close together, blocking something from view.

"If this is a bad idea," Nathaniel said, "just say the word and I'll take him home again. No hard feelings." From behind his legs, a dog peeked at him, wearing an expression similar to that of his owner.

"You brought Zero!" Tim said happily, squatting down and patting his lap in invitation.

That's all it took. Zero burst forth from behind Nathaniel, nearly knocking over his owner and succeeding with Tim, who fell onto his rump and laughed, face already wet with dog kisses. That felt good. The Siberian husky was nothing like Chinchilla. Sure, he was a dog, but his girl had a different temperament, and they didn't resemble each other in the slightest. Zero being here didn't dredge up painful memories, but that same canine love—perfect and pure—was like a salve on his scorched heart.

"That's enough," Nathaniel said eventually. "Zero! Come!"

The dog backed off, Tim still laughing. "It's never enough!"

"No," Nathaniel said, holding out a hand. "I guess it isn't. Not for people like us. I'm sorry."

"Thanks," Tim said, letting himself be pulled to his feet and straight into a hug. He wasn't expecting that!

"If there's anything I can do," Nathaniel said, squeezing him like a python. "Anything at all. If you want to spend time with Zero or just need someone to talk to, don't hesitate. I mean it!"

"Thanks," Tim managed, ribs sore when he was finally released. He didn't know how Kelly survived those hugs! "It's been rough, but I've been trying to focus on the good memories, you know? She never liked it when I was sad."

"Zero's the same way," Nathaniel said, nodding his understanding. "Or maybe he just likes the taste of my tears. I wouldn't put it past him."

Tim laughed, reaching down to pet the dog again. "I'm glad he's here. It sounds cheesy, but it kept bugging me that Chinchilla can't be. This is an important day! There's supposed to be a dog greeting people, getting in the way—"

"—knocking down waiters for their trays," Nathaniel said with a twinkle in his eye. "Zero would be honored to represent her. Just for this day."

"I think she'd like that," Tim said, emotion rising as it so often did as of late. "It's good you're here. It helps to be around someone who gets it."

Nathaniel shook his head. "It's a day I dread. I know there's a price to be paid. I just don't like to think about it."

"Cherish every moment," Tim said. "That's all you can do. Come on in. Your handsome husband will be glad to see you too."

"Speaking of ill-behaved creatures," Nathaniel said. He held out the leash. "Would you care to do the honor?"

"I'd love to," he said, accepting it.

"Just don't let him rip your arm out of its socket," Nathaniel warned.

A little too late, because Tim was yanked forward, but he didn't mind. He laughed as Zero dragged him into the house. The dog raced for the nearest crowd, in this case the people gathered in the living room, where he dived right in. The kids shouted with delight, eager to pet him.

"Maybe we should take him out back," Nathaniel said, watching with unease how Zero stomped over everything and nearly head-butted Nana in attempt to kiss her.

"Can we go with him?" Davis asked.

"Okay," Tim said, raising his voice to make an announcement.

"Everyone who is ten or younger, outside, right now!"

The kids led the way with a cheer, Zero close behind. Tim and Nathaniel followed, the dog set free from his leash once he was safely in the fenced yard.

"Maybe I should have had you sign a waiver first," Nathaniel said, eyeing the setup. "This is really nice!"

"Thanks," Tim said.

The wedding wasn't so different than his own had been, although they had learned from experience. Catering was inside this time, the food safe from the Texas heat and sun. Tables had been set up on one side of the yard beneath white umbrellas so people could enjoy their food in the shade. No seats had been assigned or anything complicated. There weren't any chairs at all! Those were currently in rows in front of the gazebo. They would be moved to the tables after the ceremony instead of having to be cleared away to make room for dancing. God, he hoped he wouldn't have to dance this time! People in mourning shouldn't dance. That's what he would claim, anyway. On each side of the patio were two more tables, one set up with sound equipment for the DJ, the other already filled with gifts. Everything was white: tablecloths, flowers, and all the lacey gauze that popped up at weddings like weeds in a garden.

"Do you have to work today, or can you just relax?"

"Officially?" Nathaniel asked. "I'm off duty, but those two waiters over there looking at their phones instead of refilling their trays are going to be sorry."

"Yell at them in a second," Tim said, noticing where Kelly sat. He wasn't alone. Next to him was Caesar, who was a shameless flirt. Hopefully that wouldn't be an issue. Marcello had told him that Nathaniel sometimes struggled with jealousy.

"What's going on here?" Nathaniel said as they approached. "You came early to take photos, not associate with... whoever this is."

"Oh very nice," Caesar said, grinning at him. "Sorry, but you guys can't sit in this section."

"That's right," Kelly said. "It's reserved solely for ex-boyfriends of the grooms. Although... Tim, you used to date Jason. I was there. Bonnie's recital?"

"That wasn't a date!" he protested.

"No," Kelly said. "It was a double date! Come to think of it, you also went on a date with Nathaniel once, didn't you?"

Caesar tsked and shook his head. "And people accuse me of getting around!"

Nathaniel crossed his arms over his chest. "You've left through more windows than Superman!"

"Superman is hot," Caesar said. "Does anyone have his number?"

"No," Kelly said, "but you've given me the perfect costume idea for Nathaniel this Halloween."

"In that case," Nathaniel retorted, "how about you do your job, Jimmy Olsen, and start taking photos?"

Caesar sighed wistfully. "He used to boss me around in the same way. So hot."

"It is," Kelly agreed, standing and adjusting the camera strap around his neck. "I already got some nice shots of Jason. Any idea where William is hiding?"

"Probably still upstairs," Tim said.

"Can you show me where?"

He looked to Nathaniel, who nodded that they should go on without him. That decision might be regretted, because Caesar patted the empty seat next to him. Nathaniel looked with hope to where the slacking waiters had been, but now they were mingling and offering drinks, just as they should be. Left without an excuse, he grudgingly sat next to Caesar.

"They used to date, right?" Tim asked when they were a respectable distance away.

"Ages ago," Kelly said, not sounding concerned.

"I wish I was as secure as you! You left your husband alone with his ex, and you're about to see *your* ex get married. That's not weird for you?"

Kelly shrugged as they entered the house. "I love William. I want to see him happy. Nathaniel loves Caesar too. Somewhere deep down, anyway. I'm hoping he'll let go of any residual anger. There's no point in holding on to it. Otherwise part of you is still tied up in that relationship, which can't feel good."

"Very mature of you," Tim said.

"Thanks," Kelly replied. "Of course, I'm also eager to take photos of William while he's stressed out before the ceremony. If I know him, he's a hot mess right now, and I do plan on enjoying that. Just a little bit. Please don't tell him I said so."

Tim laughed. "Your secret is safe with me."

"Good. I'll atone for my sins by reminding him what a catch he is, which is true. Jason is too. They're both amazing men, aren't they?"

Tim nodded, his chest swelling with affection. "Yeah. They are."

"Do I click here? Oops! The window is gone. Does that mean we need to start over? Don't tell me! I know what to do. Oh. That's not right!"

Ben watched his mother click icons on the laptop screen, seemingly at random, and wondered when the carnage would end. So far she had managed to create three new shortcuts (all leading to the recycle bin) and had agreed to an update of iTunes before losing patience and cancelling it halfway through. Now she had opened the file explorer and would probably manage to format the hard drive before somehow causing the machine to burst into flames.

"Mom!" Ben said. "You said you wanted my help!"

"You *are* helping me," June said innocently. "Do you think we should reboot?"

Ben looked around the office in exasperation. Why didn't they stash booze up here? Or chloroform, so he could dab some on a cloth and use it to stop his mother before she did any more damage. "Can I take over? Please? It's my machine."

"There's no need to be snippy," his mother said, rolling away from the desk.

Ben hunched over the laptop, closing everything before making sure his mother's phone was connected. That was the irony. She did just fine on her phone, surfing the web, posting on social media, and contacting him via texts and video conferencing. But place her in front of a computer and the madness began.

"I just need you to get the photos off my phone," she said for the fourth or fifth time. "I can't believe I didn't think of it sooner. If I can't take photos during the wedding—"

"They're downloading now," Ben said, turning around and shielding his laptop protectively by standing in front of it. "Five minutes."

"Thank you, darling!" His mother beamed at him. "I bet you're just dying of excitement!"

"Because of the wedding?" Ben grinned. "Yeah. It's silly, because they're already together. Technically this isn't going to change their lives. They'll still live at the same place and work the same jobs. I know their routines aren't going to change, but them being married... I'll worry less."

"I know exactly what you mean," June said pointedly.

Ben covered his face. "Not this again!"

"When are you finally going to get married?"

Ben dropped his hands. "We *are* married."

His mother pursed her lips. "Yes, but not really."

"You were at the wedding!"

The facts were ignored. "Does Tim not want to?"

"He does," Ben said in exasperation. "There's just no point. We're married. Today is supposed to be Jason's big day. Can we focus on that?"

June nodded and was quiet. He was just starting to relax when she decided to change topics.

"When are you going to give me grandbabies?"

"If you even suggest that Jason isn't—"

"He's my grandson!" June said, head held high. "I love Jason. But there's nothing like a newborn baby. Jason might enjoy having a little brother or sister. Have you asked him?"

"Has anyone asked me what I want?" Ben grumbled, turning around to check the status bar.

"I've just about given up on you and your sister," his mother complained. "Neither one of you is married—"

"Karen was. And I am!"

"—and I'm always the only one in my book club without baby photos to show off. Your old ones just aren't getting the attention they used to."

Ben shook his head and laughed. "I'll have Allison give you a bunch of photos of Davis. You can tell your friends that he's your grandchild."

"Can Allison have more babies? If so, you and she could—"

Ben spun around. "Mom!"

June shrugged. "It was just an idea. I have a better one. What if Karen had Tim's baby?"

Ben stared, aghast. "I want that image wiped from my mind. Forever."

"I'm serious! That would be the closest way you could have a biological child together. It would be half Tim, and half your sister. Don't look at me like that! When you first came out of the closet, I was scared you wouldn't have a relationship or anything normal. Do you remember Marcy? I worked with her for years. She always gave you gum when she came to visit. Very into dental health. Anyway, her son is gay, and along with his husband, they just had twins from a surrogate. Now they're going to try again, but with sperm from whoever didn't get to go first. So all you need to do is have Tim—"

"All done!" Ben said, unplugging her phone and handing it back. "You have plenty of room now to take photos. Better get started!"

"Think about it!" his mother said. "I can help babysit. Of course it would help if you moved back to The Woodlands so we could be closer."

Ben laughed and shook his head. "I need to finish getting dressed. Go check on Dad. Please. Last time I saw him, he was trying to sell a cable package to Tim's mother."

"He better keep his package away from her!" June said, heading for the hallway.

Ben watched her go, shaking his head. Then he looked over at Jace's photo. "I invited your parents too. They declined, for some reason. I can't imagine why." He stared at the photo longingly, then went to the master bedroom, where he found another little piece of Jace. Two of them, actually.

"We're not doing it in your bed," Michelle said. "I swear. We're just lying low."

"Until they start serving drinks," Greg added.

Jace's sister and her husband, Jace's best friend. Ben loved having them around, since it made him feel more complete. Greg was stretched out on the bed, Michelle lying sideways to him and using Greg's thighs as a pillow.

"The waiters are making the rounds," Ben said. "I saw booze on my way up."

Greg tried to rise but Michelle shoved him back down. "Stay. I'm not ready to face the masses yet. Besides, your penis pillow is too comfortable."

Ben grimaced. "Unless he's unnaturally gifted, you aren't actually touching his— Never mind. I don't want to know."

"There's that blush!" Greg said with a cackle. "I haven't seen it in ages."

"I came in here to hide from family," Ben said. "You're

contaminating my sanctuary. This is a relative-free zone, and you guys count."

"We were trying to figure that out," Greg said. "You're our brother-in-law, so Jason is our nephew-in-law, right?"

"We don't normally think of either of you as in-laws," Michelle said. "That's too technical and cold. We're family."

"Right," Greg said, "but just for the sake of argument, after the wedding, does that make William our in-law in-law? You know what I mean?"

Ben sat on the edge of the bed and thought about it. "Maybe it's like a second cousin. A second nephew-in-law?"

"I'm just going to call him William," Michelle said wisely. "I'm also going to encourage our children to elope, because weddings are a circus. How are you holding up?"

"Fine," Ben admitted. "I like having everyone here. When I was little, the holidays used to be stuffed full of people. Now everyone has grown up, moved away, or died. It's not the same anymore, but this reminds me of how it used to be."

"Spoken like someone who still knows what privacy feels like," Greg teased. "Try raising three kids and then tell me about the good ol' days."

"You'll change your tune," Michelle said. "Sylvester's off to college next year, and I think Preston is finally serious about moving out. Pretty soon we'll be on our own." They considered this in silence, neither one looking too eager. "You promised me ten kids."

"I did!" Greg said with a smile. "That was part of our wedding vows."

"I wish I could have been there," Ben said. "Couldn't you have waited until Jace and I met?"

"Very thoughtless of us," Michelle said. Then she sat upright. "I took a bunch of old photos and videos in to be digitized recently. I have a few on my phone."

"Of the wedding?" Ben asked, already leaning near.

"Yup!"

"I'm going to rejoin the current wedding," Greg said, sighing theatrically. "They could probably use my help."

"Don't drink too much," Michelle said as he went. She focused on her phone, swiping through images. "It's more than just Greg and me in these photos," she said, her tone casual, but he understood the warning.

"I figured," Ben said in equally cool tones. Rarely did he stumble upon an unexpected photo of Jace, or find anything significant that he had left behind. The gut-wrenching surprises had dried up years ago, so these days, even seeing an image from a slightly different angle was exciting rather than upsetting. "Was his hair still long?"

"No!" Michelle said. "No power mullet, don't worry. Here."

Ben leaned near and laughed. The image was of Jace and Greg, standing at the altar together, Jace pretending to be a bashful bride. "Is that your veil?"

"Yes," Michelle said, shaking her head. "They thought it was so funny."

"It is, kind of," Ben said. Then he fawned over the next photo, which was the proper couple, Michelle and Greg as they took their vows. "Where was this?"

"A church in downtown Warrensburg. I wanted an old-fashioned wedding." She glanced up. "I like this better, having it here, where the memory will always be part of your home. Are you excited?"

"About Jason and William?" Ben sighed contentedly. "Yes. You were dead-set on him finding parents, and I was obsessed with him finding a partner to spend the rest of his life with. We did it!"

"We did!" Michelle said, laughing happily. "Now what are we going to do with our free time?"

"Find someone else's life to meddle with?" He noticed the clock on her phone. "I really have to finish getting ready."

"I'll go mingle like a civilized person. Help me up?"

Ben stood so he could offer her a hand.

"He's here with us," Michelle said once on her feet. "Especially on days like today. I know Jace is here watching us."

Ben nodded. He liked the idea. If only he could feel as certain as she did. "I still talk to him."

Michelle grinned. "I do too. All the time! He's probably sick of listening to me."

They shared a moment of grieving as they sometimes did, just a few seconds where they both stood and thought of him. Then it was back to the world that had continued in his absence. "I better check on my husband," she said. "I don't want him drinking alone."

"I bet you don't!" Ben said. "Have fun."

Once she left the room, he moved to the walk-in closet, taking out the suit jacket and struggling with his tie until it looked right. While doing so, he couldn't help thinking about how many weddings there had been in history, how each had felt like the most important moment in that couple's life, and also in the minds of their friends and families. Eventually though, all those weddings were lost to the past. Very few people were remembered after a century went by. He didn't want those he loved to fade away, but he supposed there was little choice. If they had to disappear into history, at least they would take that journey together, but he was still tempted to write their stories down. Just on the off chance that someone would find and appreciate them.

Tired of contemplating endings, he checked himself in the mirror and went to witness a new beginning. When he entered the hallway, he saw people filing out of the guest room and heading for the stairs. Marcello, Emma, and Jason. He hurried to catch up, then noticed someone still lingering in the room. William was standing by the window, having just pulled a blindfold from his eyes. He tensed up when he saw Ben, but then breathed out again.

"For a second, I thought you were Jason."

"Better not make that mistake at the altar," Ben teased, "or it'll be awkward for us all. Did I just miss a game of pin the tail on the donkey?"

William looked down at the blindfold and laughed. "I know it's crazy. I don't think it'll really jinx us if we see each other before the wedding. I just like the romance behind it. I'm going to be excited to see him no matter what, but if I deprive myself for even a day…"

"Haven't you two spent enough time apart?"

William was silent.

"That was supposed to be a joke," Ben said. "Although I have to admit, it wasn't very funny."

"It was!" William said generously. "You hit a little close to home, that's all. Jason got cold feet once before."

"When he was supposed to move to Oregon."

"Yeah," William said. "Since then, I try not to take things—" He laughed. "I don't take Jason Grant for granted. I work harder at our relationship. It's not healthy to assume he'll always be there."

"No, Ben said, "but there are times when you should take comfort in the thought regardless. Are you worried he'll leave you waiting at the altar?"

William's expression became vulnerable. "Anything is possible. Right?"

Ben was tempted to tell him the obvious truth that Jason would be marrying him today. Nothing short of nuclear war would stop his son from taking those vows, and even then he would probably just insist they skip to the important part. Still, those wedding day jitters were part of the experience, and he didn't want to deprive William of the overwhelming cocktail of emotions. "Those boys who keep you guessing…" He shook his head ruefully. "They're hard to resist!"

"God yes!" William guffawed. "I've always wanted Jason, but not always being able to have him made me want him more."

"Forbidden love," Ben said knowingly. "It's like a drug. I was a junkie for it when I was younger. I also know what it's like to be with someone like you. Someone who is honest and open. You have a good heart. You're generous and kind. Don't feel like you need to walk on eggshells around Jason. Just be yourself. That's enough. There's a reason why he loves you. Tim and I do too."

"Thank you," William said, cheeks red as he grinned down at the blindfold in his hands and toyed with it absentmindedly. "I also love you guys."

"So when do you get to see your beautiful bride?" Ben asked. Unlike his own wedding, it wasn't immediately obvious who wore the lighter shade. Jason's suit was gray, while William's was beige, his tie and hanky pale green. "Or are you playing that role? Is someone giving you away?"

William shook his head. "What do you mean?"

Ben fought down a smile. "Well, traditionally when the bride and groom aren't allowed to see each other, the big reveal happens while the groom is waiting at the altar. Here comes the bride? When that song plays, usually the bride's father walks her down the aisle and gives her away."

"Like she's an object?" William said.

"I always thought it was weird too. So what's your plan?"

William opened his mouth. Then he closed it again.

Ben laughed. He couldn't help himself. "This is why people have rehearsals."

A knock caused them both to turn. Tim stood in the doorway.

"Hey, you two," he said, walking inside. "Mind if I interrupt?"

He wasn't alone. Kelly was behind him, looking over his shoulder and grinning when he spotted William. "There you are! I need to borrow you for some photos."

"Right now?" William asked. "Can't it wait until after?"

"When you're all sweaty from nerves? No no. It's better this way." Kelly moved forward and took William's arm. "Come out front with me. I want photos of you next to the pool, looking sad in your suit because you can't go swimming."

"Who are these photos for exactly?" William asked.

"Jason will love them. I promise. Come along! There's something deliciously ironic about you spending your last moments of freedom with the man who chained you down for so long."

Ben shrugged helplessly as William looked to him for help before he was dragged from the room.

"Alone at last," Tim said, moving near and placing his hands on Ben's hips.

"Don't you look handsome?" Ben said, straightening the bowtie for him. Then his attention moved up to Tim's face. "Doing all right?"

"Yeah," Tim said, breaking eye contact. "Of course."

Ben stared until Tim met his gaze again. "You know you can cry around me, right?"

Tim furrowed his brow. "I want to be strong for you."

"Crying is one of the strongest things a man can do. Letting yourself feel that much pain takes more strength than holding it in. If you needed to cry in front of me, I'd be just as impressed as when you flex."

"Oh yeah?" Tim asked, making sure to do just that.

"Yup! Just keep in mind that either is fine with me."

"I will," Tim said solemnly. He leaned forward and nuzzled his nose against Ben's. "Are you ready for today?"

"Almost," Ben said. "I can see why parents struggle with this. Just imagine if we'd had him since he was a baby. I wouldn't mind turning back the clock."

"How far?" Tim asked.

"To when he first settled down here. When it was just us and we finally felt comfortable around each other."

"Before he met William?"

Ben nodded. "Just for another week. I know it's selfish. I wouldn't keep them from meeting or anything else that happened in their lives. I've wanted this day for him, but now that it's finally here, I can't help grieving for a time that we'll never have again."

"Samson was still alive then," Tim said. "Chinchilla too, so I'd like another week of that. I wouldn't waste a single minute of it, I swear. I wouldn't even sleep. Not unless it was another nap on the couch with her." Tears began to stream down his cheeks.

"Very strong," Ben said. "Sweet too. Come here."

He opened his arms, holding Tim against him as best he could. They stood embracing each other until they heard someone calling for them downstairs.

"I guess it's time," Ben said.

Tim rubbed at his eyes with the back of his hand, then put on a smile. "Let's go watch our son get married."

Chapter Sixteen

The humidity was building, the sky on the horizon dark and threatening rain. Outdoor weddings were more romantic than they were practical. Ben felt grateful that he and Tim had lucked out during their big day, but he was worried that Jason and William might be wiping away sweat instead of emotional tears when taking their vows. Everyone was seated, most guests cooling themselves with the foldable fans that had been placed on each table as decorations. Another lesson learned from his own wedding, although if they were really smart, they would have found somewhere sheltered and air-conditioned to stage this event.

Then again, Ben adored the idea of his son getting married in the same spot where he and Tim had. The very same place Ben was proposed to! This yard held a lot of memories. The corner where Samson and Chinchilla were buried, the patio where he sometimes shared drinks with Tim at night, or sat and talked with Jason and Emma. In all of their discussions, had they ever imagined this day?

Ben turned in his seat, looking down the aisle. Daisy was hopping along the carpet, tossing flowers around and giggling at all the complements she received along the way. Behind her were two people. Emma sauntered along in her tuxedo. The woman next to her had russet skin and straight black hair that touched her shoulders. Christie Patel, the mechanic William had worked with so closely during his Cape Cod days, and who he had remained friends with ever since. The white dress she wore gripped her figure and shimmered in the sunlight. Together with Emma, they resembled a bride and groom, except they were actually the two best men. Or best women, who kept laughing and turning to look behind them.

He soon saw why. Emma and Christie were guiding a pair of blindfolded grooms down the aisle. Jason and William were walking with outstretched hands. They grinned and sometimes grimaced when accidentally kicking chairs or tripping over the carpet. The music they had chosen to accompany them wasn't the traditional bridal march. Jason had chosen Led Zeppelin, of all bands, but Ben's initial concerns had disappeared when Jason first played the song for him. *Thank You* was a tune both wistful and passionate. Ben found himself singing it recently while getting teary. He had expected to cry now, since the walk to the altar was when many people started to weep, but amusement reigned instead, helping to combat the heaviness caused by humidity.

When the group finally reached the gazebo where Marcello stood behind a podium, the two best women attended to their respective grooms, turning the men to face each other before they loosened the blindfolds and slipped them free. Jason and William blinked against the light. Then they focused on each other. William smiled bashfully, Jason stared longingly. They must have felt irresistibly drawn to each other, because they leaned forward and started kissing.

"Gentlemen!" Marcello boomed. "You are getting ahead of yourselves!"

"Sorry," Jason said after pulling away. "I'm pretty sure I heard you say we should kiss."

"Me too!" William said, backing him up.

"Then I suggest you pay closer attention." Marcello scowled with the authority of his position. "No more outbursts! This is a sacred institution you are entering into. Let us show proper reverence! I find it is always advisable to exercise self-control before entering into anything or anyone."

Ben exchanged a glance with Tim. Whose idea was it to let Marcello preside over the wedding?

"Now then," Marcello said, clearing his throat. "I find myself in an unusual position, for I wish to impart advice, and yet I have never been married. I have, however, been in love, which I consider an experience as common as the days are long. But ah, not all days are created equally! Some days you venture out into, only to be burned by the sun. Others leave you chilled and wondering if you'll ever find warmth again. The best days, in my experience, are blessed by summer. Slow hours filled with sunshine that stretches from the moment you wake up until the last dwindling light of the evening. Such days are best spent with someone special. Jason and William, you have this kind of love. Despite the years of history you have already accumulated, you are still in the early morning of your relationship. Imagine yourselves, if you will, standing side by side at the kitchen counter and yawning. Well, gentlemen, this is the moment of your awakening! This is when the coffee kicks in and you discover all the potential of the day together. This is the moment your love becomes one."

Ben felt like applauding, or maybe blubbering, and he wasn't alone. He looked across the aisle to see William's mother dabbing at her eyes with a tissue. William's father beamed proudly. Closer to him, Tim slid an arm around his and took Ben's hand.

"Fear not," Marcello continued. "I won't let you begin this journey unprepared. Poetic words might move the heart, but the mind requires more pragmatic instruction. How fortunate then, that we have an expert in our midst, someone with more than forty years of experience in this arena. I would like to step back momentarily so that you may benefit from her knowledge. Esmeralda, if you please."

Ben was confused. The name was vaguely familiar. He believed he had seen it recently on a travel reservation, but he certainly hadn't greeted anyone by that name today. A chair creaked from the other side of Tim and a short woman stood up, her bouffant hair compensating for her lack of height. Nana, Tim's grandmother, took her time walking to the gazebo, moving around the grooms and not looking in the audience's direction. Not until she was behind the podium. Marcello placed a box behind it first, taking her hand and helping her step onto it. Nana gripped the podium with both hands and squinted at everyone gathered there.

"Marcello, he help me with the translation," Nana said. "Whatever I get wrong, it his mistake."

"I accept no responsibility!" Marcello declared. "I suggested we hire a professional translator!"

Nana shook her head. "No one fills my mouth with words. I prefer cake. Or a nice drink."

"You'll get no argument from me," Marcello replied. "On that note, I set aside a bottle for us that— Sorry, time enough for that later. Go ahead."

Nana sniffed and considered the two people in front of her. Her expression was stern, although it nearly wavered when she focused on Jason. "Marriage is serious. Too many people put it on like a hat they can take off again. I say you try it on at the store. You like it? Leave it and come back the next day. And the next. Don't buy the hat unless you are certain." She peered at them both critically. "You had enough of the shopping?"

"Yes," William said.

"Absolutely!" Jason said, nodding eagerly.

Nana nodded too, seeming satisfied. "Now I tell you what to do. Remember these words, because marriage is no easy." She closed her eyes briefly, as if concentrating, then opened them again. "Admit when you are wrong. And if you are right, don't goat!"

"Gloat," Marcello chimed in helpfully.

"Yes," Nana agreed. "Never demand forgiveness or hold it back. Always give it freely and learn to wait for it too. Understand?"

Jason and William nodded in unison.

"Good. Spend time apart every year. That way you see what life is like alone. Then you will remember how good it is to be with your husband. Always take a step back so you can see your own luck, and also find new ways to make the other person happy. Stay healthy for you and for him. Have sex one time every week, maybe more if you want. This help you stay connected. Let the other person have bad moods and good moods. Don't let anger make you act too fastly. Walk away until anger gets bored and leaves. Then you can talk again." Nana unfolded a piece of paper. "This next part is hard," she said. "I need to cheat." She took her time putting on a pair of reading glasses. "The only rules in marriage are those that you both agree to. None of them are permanent. Reassess and renegotiate as the years go by. You will change. So will he. The marriage must change with you or it will no longer fit as it once did. Keep love at the center of it all. That is the one constant. As long as you nurture that love and allow it to grow, you will be fine."

Nana took off her glasses. Then she considered everyone. "Are we done?"

The audience burst into applause.

"One more thing!" Nana said over the noise. "Remember to visit your great-grandma. That's very important. Or come live with me. That's fine too. Okay. Bye bye."

Marcello helped her step down from the box. Jason and William each hugged Nana before Tim rose to guide her back to her seat. Then they all took their places again.

"You've heard from your elders," Marcello said, "and now you should hear from each other. Just pretend you are alone together. We promise not to listen, don't we, everyone?"

Murmured laughter and nodding heads preceded a perfect silence, one especially surprising given how many people were present. Only chairs creaked as everyone leaned forward to listen.

William took Jason's hand, body angled toward their friends and families. "I met this troublemaker once," he said. "I swear I was minding my own business when he barged into my life, and I did my best to ignore him, but Jason kept showing up. At my work, at the gay youth group I attended, and during my morning swims. He was always around. But there was one place in particular, no matter how late it was, or even if I was behind locked doors, that Jason kept appearing. In my thoughts. Even when I tried forcing him out, because I had these dreams... I wanted more than anything to rescue people. What I didn't realize is that I needed rescuing from myself. I had forgotten that love doesn't mean giving until you've got nothing left. It also means opening your heart and letting others give back, and Jason has given me so much! Confidence in myself especially. It's hard not to feel that when you're loved by someone who is so amazing. He also gave me time when I needed it, and freedom, and a reason to come back home again." William turned toward Jason fully, taking his other hand. "Do you remember what you said at the very beginning? I think it might have been the first words you spoke to me. You said 'Have we met before?' You know what? I think we did. Maybe in another life. But after that, you said you felt like you knew me already, and that was true too. From the very beginning, you knew exactly what I needed and you gave it to me, but I also knew you, well enough to understand the sacrifices you made so I could be happy. Today I'm promising to give it all back. Whatever I can do to make you feel happy and loved, I will. I'll never lie. I'll never betray you. I'll never abandon you, no matter the circumstances. I'll let you go whenever you need it and welcome you back whenever you're ready again, but this will go on forever. You and I started a long time ago, and now it's going to continue, through this life and whatever follows. My love for you is eternal, Jason Grant. Our hearts belong together."

They kissed again, Ben laughing when Marcello wagged a finger sternly. The speech was moving, but more than that, Ben found it reassuring. William let his sense of duty define him, so it made sense that he loved in a similar fashion. Jason would be cared for. Even if something should happen to Tim and himself, Ben knew that William would always be at Jason's side, stalwart and protective.

"I never felt like I belonged anywhere," Jason said, still holding William's hands as they faced each other. "Maybe when I was little, but we all start that way. That's what the Garden of Eden is really about, I think. We get to be with our creator and feel loved unconditionally. We're protected and everything is perfect. Or so it seems. Eventually, one way or another, we're all cast out and told that what we had is lost. There's no going back. I wasted a lot of time learning that lesson. There were places I wanted to stay and people I wanted to be with, but none of them were for me, so I pressed on. I kept looking forward, and that's what made it possible to see you. Maybe that's what I recognized when we first met. I saw that same garden, my home, but this one really was perfect. I wouldn't be cast out this time, because there's no separating us. We've spent years apart, but that's just the physical. You've always found a way to reach me. Even when we didn't see each other. Even when we didn't talk, you were still right there with me. I hear your voice in my thoughts and feel your presence when I'm scared. You've even made it possible for me to let go of the anger and hurt, because I'm glad now. Had I stayed in that first garden, I never would have found you, so maybe it's an act of love when we are cast out. Or maybe life is just random and it was pure luck that brought us together. Either way, I've found my way to paradise. I know marriages are supposed to be beginnings, but this feels more like an ending to me. The hard times are over, no matter what we have to face, because now you're with me. Nothing can take that away. Not even death. You'll always be in my heart, and I'll always be in yours. I love you."

"I love you too!" William said, moving in for another kiss.

"The rings, gentlemen!" Marcello interrupted. "First the rings, then the fireworks. Now then, after hearing what you've both had to say, making you take any sort of vows would be tedious if not insulting. You both seem determined to make this arrangement permanent, am I right? You wouldn't like to play the field just a little longer to be sure?"

"I'm sure!" William said while laughing.

"I'm pretty sure," Jason teased. "Close enough, anyway."

Marcello nodded as if satisfied. "That's all anyone could ask for. Who has the rings?"

"Right here," Emma said, passing one to Jason.

"I'm tempted to keep this for myself," Christie said as she handed hers to William. "So beautiful! Can we trade?"

"Maybe later," William stage whispered. "To be honest, I was hoping for a tiara."

The audience laughed, then grew somber again.

"Jason Grant," Marcello boomed. "William Townson. Before you place the rings on each other's fingers, recognize that the circular shape represents an infinite loop, a promise of forever. Search your body, mind, and soul for any doubt, and only proceed if—well, that was quick!" The rings had already been exchanged, the grooms looking to Marcello for confirmation. Marcello opened his mouth, his chins trembling. Then he placed a hand to his chest. "My goodness. You'll have to pardon me. I didn't realize how moving it would be to speak these words." He cleared his throat. "By the power vested in me, I now declare you husband and husband. You may now—well, I think you know what to do!"

Jason and William kissed. People clapped, blew noses, and whistled. Then the laughter started, because the kiss *still* hadn't ended.

"I think we might need to give them privacy," Marcello said. "Perhaps someone could set up a curtain around them? Or a dressing screen?"

Jason finally pulled away while wearing a giant grin. "Or how about some champagne?"

"I thought you'd never ask!" Marcello said, signaling the waiters, who sprang into action.

Ben also hopped to his feet but was stopped from moving forward when an arm grabbed his.

"I wouldn't mind one of those myself," Tim said.

Ben turned around. "A glass of champagne?"

"I was thinking of something sweeter."

Ben grinned, the wedding and everything else forgotten as he was pulled into Tim's arms and reminded just how good the gardens of paradise could be.

* * * * *

The rain broke halfway through the wedding banquet. Texans knew their weather. Most of the guests were indoors before the first drops hit, but not everyone ran for shelter. The umbrellas over each table were large enough to provide cover. Mostly. Rain splashed all around them and their shoes and cuffs were slowly getting soaked, but Ben was enjoying himself too much to seek drier surroundings. Instead he scooted closer to the table and the people he loved.

"At least it didn't happen during the ceremony," William said.

"I wouldn't have let that stop me," Jason said from beside him, their shoulders pressed together.

"Still, it's kind of a bummer," Tim said, his arm around Ben's waist. "We won't be able to dance if this weather keeps up. There's no room inside."

"Yeah, that is tragic," Jason said, trying to hide a smirk and failing. Then he exchanged a fist bump with Tim.

"Don't worry," Ben said. "We'll all go out to a nightclub later so we can dance. Right, William?"

"Sure!" his new son-in-law said, grinning bashfully back at him. "And if they don't want to dance…"

"You're married now," Jason said. "No more boogying with other boys. And if you really want to dance, I won't let the rain stop me there either."

"Or we could do presents!" Tim said, sounding anxious. "That's *way* more important than dancing! Be right back."

They watched Tim dart through the rain to the patio. Most of the gifts had been rescued during the rush inside, but a transparent plastic tarp shielded the others, Marcello's waiters covering anything that needed saving. Tim returned with an armful of wrapped boxes. He chose a simple envelope first, handing it to Jason. "That's from us," he said.

"You guys have already given us so much," Jason said, shaking his head.

"Then give it back," Tim said, lunging at the envelope.

Jason dodged backward. "No way! It's already got my name on it. Too late."

"That just means the envelope is yours," Tim shot back.

Ben sighed and looked at William. "Welcome to my life."

"Could be worse," William replied. When the table wobbled and a bottle of beer toppled over the edge, he managed to catch it just before it hit the ground. "Probably," he added when setting it back on the table.

"Okay, you two," Ben said. "Let's pretend to be civilized, at least until there aren't any witnesses around."

"We're just having fun," Tim said, ruffling Jason's hair. "Go on, open it."

Jason did, his smile replaced by a scrunched-up nose. "I can't read this. Hey, is this your gallery? The one in Japan?"

"Yup!" Tim said, nodding at the brochure. "I thought you would like to see it in person."

"Is this our honeymoon?" Jason asked, holding back his reaction until he was certain.

"We said we'd take care of it," Tim said. "You'll love Tokyo. I know a great tour guide too. I'm sure you'll want to be alone for most of the trip but—" He was cut off when Jason hugged him around the neck. "Okay, no need for a sales pitch then."

"I love it!" Jason said. "Thank you!" Then he looked to William with longing. "Do you think we could? Somehow?"

"Could what?" Ben asked.

"You were nice enough to share your honeymoon with us," William explained. "We want to do the same." He addressed Jason. "And yes, of course we can. We've gotten more than enough cash from my side of the family alone."

"You aren't paying for our tickets," Ben protested.

"We don't mind!" William insisted. "It's only fair."

"It's a waste of money," Tim said. "I booked two extra flights when I made your reservations. They're for the next day, just in case you didn't want us tagging along, but I bet I can still get us on the same flight."

Jason was laughing. "You were going to stalk us if we didn't invite you along?"

"It's not stalking," Tim said. "It's chaperoning. From a distance." He looked at Ben. "What do you think?"

"That I'll need to call work and get time off!" he said, because all of this was news to him. It was a good surprise though. "I finally get to see Japan?"

Tim grinned. "Yup! And I get to see it without missing you this time, so it'll be a new experience for us all."

"This is how it's supposed to be," Jason said, looking emotional. "We're meant to be together like this. I know it's not practical right now, but maybe when we all retire?"

"I could imagine a little cabin somewhere in Oregon," Tim said.

"A big cabin," Ben corrected, "so there's room for everybody."

"And we'll spend our final days there together," William said, tone warm. "We could agree on it now."

"Like a pact," Tim said. He stretched out his arm so his hand was above the table. "Who's in?"

"I am." Ben placed his on top of Tim's. "It's an easy promise to make."

"I agree," William said, adding his hand to the pile.

"One big happy family," Jason said, eyes watery as he looked to each of them. Then he placed his hand on top of William's. "Together until the very end."

Ben stood outside on the patio, his back pressed against the house so he wouldn't get wet. The rain had reduced to a drizzle. Many of the guests had left, but there were still plenty in the house, the vibe getting rowdy. Spirits were high as more and more spirits were consumed. He liked that, but it felt good to slip outside for a break. He wanted to remember the details of this day, so he went over each, committing them to memory.

The solitude didn't last. Ben heard the gate open and slam shut again. Seconds later, a dog darted across the grass. A Siberian husky. The dog noticed him, skidded to a halt, then sprinted over, tail wagging and nose sniffing.

"Zero!" a voice called out. "Leave him alone!"

The dog looked over at its owner, then took off for the far yard.

Ben laughed and watched him run before facing the owner. Nathaniel was one of Marcello's crew, and one of Tim's friends, he supposed. The two didn't hang out all that often, but when they did, they got along well.

"How's it going?" Nathaniel said, joining him on the patio. "Sorry about that."

"It's fine," Ben said. "It's always good to have animals around. They're sort of like children. You can get away with more when they're in the room. If adult conversation is boring you, go play with the kids. When you're done, people will act like you performed some sacrifice by having fun with them."

"And dogs?"

"They're a good excuse to step outside for some fresh air. It's either that, or start smoking. I know which I prefer."

"I like the way you think," Nathaniel said. "Just don't let him jump on you when he comes back. Muddy paws. I came prepared, but there's only so much a towel can do." He held it up.

Ben glanced at it and away again. Then he did a double take. The towel was red and black with the head of a braying mule in the center. He only recognized it because Jace had owned a T-shirt with the same design. Jace never wore the shirt, but he also hadn't wanted to throw it away, since it had been a gift. After enough years of it hanging in the closet, Ben had tossed it in a bag destined for Goodwill. "Is that from CMSU?" he asked.

"UCM these days," Nathaniel said. "No idea why they changed the name. You into college sports?"

Ben shook his head, watching as Zero ran back and forth across the lawn in an impressive display of stamina. "My husband grew up in Missouri. My first husband, I mean. Widowed, not divorced." He felt the need to add that sometimes, just so people understood that he and Jace hadn't called it quits.

"Sorry to hear that," Nathaniel said.

"That he passed away, or that he grew up in Warrensburg?"

Nathaniel eyed him, hopefully taking note of the lofty tone. "Both, if I'm honest."

Ben laughed. "Small towns can be boring, but they also have their charm."

"Ever been there?"

"Just a few times. To meet the parents. Stuff like that. I take it you went to school there?"

"Because of this?" Nathaniel held up the towel, then draped it over one shoulder. "A present from my grandma. She had her heart set on me going there. Doesn't matter that I got my degree years ago. Now she wants me to get my doctorate, but not from just anywhere."

Ben smiled. "Were you born in Warrensburg?"

"Close by," Nathaniel answered. "I lived there when I was really little, until we moved. I don't suppose you know my mom? Star Courtney? Back then she was Star Denton."

Ben shook his head. "Doesn't ring a bell. Sorry."

"Oh. Maybe my dad then. Victor Hemmingway?"

Ben was already shaking his head because he could count the people he knew in Warrensburg on one hand. Then he paused. Victor wasn't an uncommon name, so it seemed unlikely, but just in case... "Punky guy?"

"That's right!" Nathaniel said, sounding excited. "You knew him?"

Ben shook his head again. "Sorry. I don't think it's the same one. He didn't have a kid. I think my husband would have mentioned that."

Nathaniel's brow knotted up. "Jace?"

Ben was surprised until he remembered that Nathaniel and Tim knew each other. "That's right. Jace used to date a guy named Victor, but I really don't think it's the same one." He knew an easy way of disqualifying this other person. "Is your father still alive?"

"No," Nathaniel said.

That wasn't the answer he was expecting, but it still wasn't definitive proof. "Did he have mismatched eyes?"

"One brown, the other green," Nathaniel said.

Ben didn't know which colors Victor's eyes had been exactly, but it was a small town, and no way were they still dealing in coincidences. "Holy shit," he breathed.

"You knew him?" Nathaniel asked, clearly eager for confirmation.

"I think it's probably the same person," Ben said, "but he died before I knew Jace. I never had a chance to meet him."

"That makes two of us," Nathaniel said, sounding deflated. He leaned against the house, head resting on it as he watched Zero explore the yard. "Technically I met him when I was really little, but I don't have any memories. Just a couple of photos. That's it. Makes you wonder why we start out that way. Entire years are lost to us. You would think our brains would hold on to more of our pasts. All that stuff at the beginning has to be useful, right? It's when we learn to be little people, so why can't we remember?"

"I don't know," Ben said, "but I can imagine how frustrating that would be for you. He must have died when you were young."

Nathaniel didn't answer, choosing to switch topics. "It was a beautiful wedding. Almost as good as the one four years ago."

"Thanks," Ben said with a smile. "You were here with Marcello's crew, right? You were in charge of the waiters?"

"Only way to get in without an invite," Nathaniel confirmed. "This time I'm a plus one."

"You're with Kelly," Ben said. "I can't tell you how happy I am that he found someone."

"He told me that you feel guilty," Nathaniel said. "The shut-in?"

Ben hid his face in his hands briefly. "Exactly."

"No complaints from my side. Whatever got us to meet."

"I did that on purpose," Ben said. "I'm highly psychic. Did I fail to mention that? I saw all of this coming."

"Your powers failed you," Nathaniel said. "Otherwise you would have realized that you're— Let me make sure I've got this right. Okay. You would have realized sooner that I'm the son of your first husband's ex-boyfriend."

"I can beat that!" Ben said after thinking it over. "My second husband went on a date with my first husband's ex-boyfriend's son. Right?"

Nathaniel digested these words. Then he laughed, the sound a deep rumble. "Yeah. That's right!"

Ben shook his head. "This is one weird little world we live in."

"It is," Nathaniel said. He pushed away from the house and whistled.

Zero raced over, and after a few false starts, sat obediently as Nathaniel dried him off. Ben watched him work, wishing that Jace could be here because he would have stories about Victor to share. Maybe even photos and other souvenirs from the past too.

"Hey!" Ben said, an idea occurring to him. "Would you mind coming upstairs with me for a second? There's something I'd like to show you."

Nathaniel shrugged and agreed. After making sure Zero's paws wouldn't track mud on the carpet, they went inside. The dog was distracted by children on the way, so when they reached the upstairs hallway, he and Nathaniel were alone.

"It's in the attic," Ben said, hopping in an attempt to reach the rope that hung from the ceiling door. "Do you mind? I'm too short."

Nathaniel didn't share this problem. He easily grabbed the

rope and pulled, revealing a ladder of wooden steps that reached the floor.

"After you," Ben said. "I'm pretty sure I have a photo or two of Victor. If you want to see."

"Yeah!" Nathaniel said.

He might have more than that, but he didn't want to make promises he couldn't keep. Ben climbed up the ladder, grateful that Tim had organized it all a couple of years back. All of Jace's things were in a neat stack of boxes, and he didn't have to dig far to find what he wanted. An old shoe box, worn down and droopy around the edges. The contents were still pristine. He found the stack of photos, feeling a little strange when flipping through them because many were of Jace. Just not *his* Jace. This person was younger, a teenager with shoulder-length hair and features that weren't yet as masculine as Ben remembered.

"Jace looked a lot different back then," Ben said, handing over a photo. "I'll show you a newer one of him when we're downstairs again. Anyway, that's my man! One of them."

Nathaniel was more interested than he expected, staring at the photo intently before looking hungrily at the stack. "Are some of them private? Because I wouldn't mind seeing them all."

"Go right ahead," Ben said, handing him the photos and moving closer so he could see them too.

Nathaniel skipped past many, but any with Jace interested him. He paused at a photo of a girl who shared a strong family resemblance. "I know her. I think."

"Michelle?" Ben said. "That's Jace's sister."

"The same Michelle who was here earlier? The social worker?"

Ben nodded. "Yeah."

Nathaniel looked up in shock. "I knew she went to school with Victor. She helped me before when my brother... I never made the connection. Had I known that she was Jace's sister, I would have pestered her for details."

"Maybe that can still be arranged."

"I'd appreciate that." Nathaniel resumed digging through the box and struck gold, because a sequence of photos—possibly an entire roll—were of Victor. Many were similar. Victor smoking, the angle changing only slightly as Jace must have captured image after image with infatuation-fueled obsession. Then he reached an image of Jace and Victor together, side by side, their arms draped over each other's shoulders. He paused the longest on this one, considering it in silence. Then Nathaniel looked over at him.

"I need these. Name your price."

"You can have most of them," Ben said. "Jace would want you to have the ones of Victor. I'm sure of it. The others we can make copies of." He moved back to the shoe box. "There's more here. Not much, but…"

He pulled out an old Zippo lighter, handing it to Nathaniel, who took it with reverence. Then he looked at Ben for confirmation.

He nodded. "I know that's not Jace's. He didn't smoke. I think you can see it in one of the photos where Victor is lighting up. There's also this." He took the wooden lion from the box. The carving was primitive, but not without talent. "I wish I remembered the details better. I know this was special to Jace. We had it sitting on the mantle of our house. Before then, it was in this box for the longest time. When Jace died, it seemed right to return it to the box." He stopped talking long enough to hand it over.

Nathaniel took the lion, fingers moving along the rough edges. "This looks homemade."

"Victor made it," Ben confirmed. "I don't know if he was into carving things, just that it was a gift for Jace."

Nathaniel continued caressing it with awe, like he hoped it would reveal its secrets. Ben understood how he felt. At times he would discover something Jace had left behind, a special Christmas ornament or a forgotten video recording, and it always felt like Jace had reached across the void to communicate with him. Nathaniel seemed to remember he was there and tried handing it back.

"Keep it," Ben said, but not without hesitation. "Actually, hold on." He pulled out his phone and took photos of the lion from different angles. "Just in case I miss it. Or maybe, if I ever needed to see it in person again…"

"Of course!" Nathaniel said. "Just call. We'll have you and Tim over for dinner. We meant to ages ago."

"That would be nice." Ben put away his phone and dug through the box. There was more, but much of it related only to Jace. The rest he simply wasn't sure about. "Sorry," he said.

"Are you kidding?" Nathaniel breathed in and exhaled again, expression overwhelmed. "I literally have nothing of his. Mom didn't keep anything besides some photos, so an old lighter and a carving he made? Give me a choice between those things and a chest full of gold, and I wouldn't think twice. This is more valuable to me. Thank you."

"You're welcome!" Ben said. "It's a shame you didn't have a chance to talk to Michelle when she was still here. She's going to flip when she finds out! Maybe she'll have some memories to share. I wish I had a few so I could do more for you."

"You've done enough," Nathaniel said, still clutching his treasures as he turned toward the stairs. "This is more than I ever expected. I can't think of anything that would mean more to me. Not unless you know where he's buried."

He said it like a joke, but Ben stopped in his tracks. "Victor doesn't have a grave. Not exactly."

Nathaniel turned around, wearing guarded hope. "If that's a joke, I'm not angry, but please *please* don't mess with me on this."

"I'm not," Ben said. "Victor was cremated. Jace scattered his ashes."

"Did he say where?"

"Yes." His throat ached, but he forced the words out anyway. "The same place where I left Jace. I've never told anyone where. Not even Michelle."

Nathaniel swallowed. "So you can't tell me."

"No," Ben said, weighing the pain in his heart and realizing that, on the other side of the scale, sat Nathaniel's own. He couldn't say what Victor would have wanted, but it wasn't hard to guess what Jace would have done. The same thing he always did: whatever was most generous and kind. "I can't tell you, but I can show you."

Chapter Seventeen

Tim pushed aside the hotel curtain, all of Tokyo spread out before him. That wasn't right. The thought was poetic, and even though the buildings and streets stretched on as far as the eye could see, the view revealed just a fraction of the massive city. He struggled to comprehend how so many lives could be out there—over thirteen million—all occurring alongside each other, each with their own dramas, failures, and victories. He turned as Ben stirred. His husband was still in bed, scanning him with weary eyes before they shut again.

"Going?" Ben mumbled. Perhaps realizing this wasn't a complete sentence, he tacked on, "Jogging?"

"Yeah." Tim stooped to kiss him on the forehead. "Get up and take a shower so we can have breakfast together. Wake up the boys too."

"Nnnkay," Ben said.

Had he agreed? Or was that supposed to be a 'not okay'? Tim supposed he would find out when he returned. He just hoped this outing wasn't as brief as the previous. He rode the elevator down, feeling apprehensive. Usually he looked forward to his runs like a junkie about to get a fix. That had changed yesterday, when after five minutes of jogging, he was forced to stop and gulp in oxygen. He wasn't sure why. His best guess was the sea level, since he knew high altitudes meant thinner air. Except when he had looked up the sea level, he discovered that Tokyo was a good three hundred feet *lower* than Austin. So that couldn't be the cause.

Today he was determined to offset the previous day's failure with a longer run. Last night he avoided alcohol and even sex, wanting to be as fully charged as possible. He felt good. As he walked toward the park, he paid close attention to his body. No aches or pains. He might be turning forty next year, but he still felt like he was eighteen.

Tim took a long route to the park. Twenty minutes of warmup was too much, but he needed the odds in his favor. After stretching next to a park bench, he slowly began his jog. The first few minutes were fine. As were the ones after that, so he allowed himself to pick up the pace. No problem! He was on the verge of grinning triumphantly when his lungs felt tight again. Just like yesterday. He pressed on, wondering if he needed to break through a wall. But why? He wasn't an amateur just starting out. Tim had been running since he was a teenager! There had to be another explanation. Pollution? Maybe. Living outside of Austin had spoiled him in that regard. And yet, he had no trouble running during his initial visit a few years back. Tokyo hadn't changed that much. Was it the time of day? Tim had always been a night jogger, and it *was* nighttime back in Austin, so his internal clock shouldn't be upset with him.

He forced himself to press on, despite his need to gasp for breath. He could do this! When the tightness in his lungs became a sharp pain, he slowed long enough to cough. It could be a cold or some other bug. And yet his nose wasn't running and he felt fine when not exercising. Nothing added up. Glaring at the world in general, he stopped and allowed himself to catch his breath. Then he kept going, starting slow again and building up to a moderate speed. The shortness of breath came quicker this time, as did the pain. He wouldn't let it stop him. Maybe he hadn't been taking good enough care of himself, or working out as often as he should, or—

Tim stumbled off the path, a coughing fit forcing him to hunch over, his hands on his knees as he struggled to breathe. He spit, trying to clear his airways, not once but twice and a third time. Then he stared. The saliva on the grass was tinged with red. Blood? Was he spitting up blood? He spit again, more carefully this time. Red. He even moved back to the pavement, wanting to see his spit on the neutral gray. Lord only knew what the locals thought! He was a Westerner, huffing and spitting and making a scene like some sort of savage. The spit came out of his mouth in a long string of dark mucus. Then it pooled on the slab of concrete, undeniably red.

Okay, no more running! Panic mixed with the adrenaline he was already feeling. Tim sought out the nearest bench, walking at a controlled pace and sitting. Then he waited for the pain to subside and for his lungs to start functioning normally. He wasn't sure how long he sat there, just that it took more time than it should. He had spit blood on previous jogs. Especially when younger and pushing himself too hard. But this hadn't been a long run! He hadn't sprinted at top speed. Not even close! He should be fine. He wasn't though. By the time he finally rose, he had decided to seek help.

Tim returned to the hotel, walking slowly. He went upstairs and discovered the room empty. That meant Ben was probably downstairs eating. Grabbing his phone, he sent a text to Corey.

Can you meet us as soon as possible?

We just walked into the lobby, came the reply. *Should I come up?*

No, Tim wrote back. *Grab some breakfast or something to drink. I'll be down soon.*

He took a shower, developing a plan as he stood under the hot spray. Then he threw on a comfortable T-shirt and jeans and went downstairs to the breakfast buffet. He spotted a table of five people, conversation becoming more animated as coffees were sipped and sugar entered bloodstreams. Ben, Jason, William, Corey, and Kioshi. His concerns receded as he filled a plate for himself and sat among people he cared for, but his worries didn't disappear completely. As the meal wound down, he still felt the need to face his fears.

"What's on the agenda for today?" Ben asked.

"I'd like to visit the Meiji Shrine," William said.

Jason looked confused. "I thought we were going to that yoyo park?"

"Yoyogi Park," Kioshi said quietly. "It's very near the shrine."

"Perfect!" Ben said. "Let's do that."

Tim cleared his throat. "You guys should. Corey and I have to work, but we could meet you later."

"We have to work?" Corey asked.

Tim probably should have texted him about his plan first, but he was rusty when it came to lying. "Yeah! I told you there was some gallery stuff we needed to go over."

"Now I see why you chose Tokyo," Ben said. "You're supposed to be on vacation!"

"Hey," he shot back, "this way I can write off most of the trip as a business expense."

Ben blinked. "I do like it when you're frugal."

Tim smiled at him. "There you go. We won't be long. A few hours. You guys see the sights, and we'll meet back for dinner. Do you mind playing tour guide, Kioshi?"

Corey's husband nodded. "I'd be happy to."

They finished their meal. Tim was braced for probing questions or suspicious glances, but he was in the clear. Soon he and Corey were walking down the sidewalk, aiming for the nearest metro station.

"So what's on the agenda?" Corey asked.

Tim was silent. He wished this was only business. Corey still worked for the same agency as he had before. He didn't man the Tokyo gallery full-time like Tim did in Austin. Corey only worked there part-time, his language skills useful in communicating between the two galleries, for answering foreign correspondence, preparing promo materials, and more. Tim figured if he kept pushing enough work Corey's way, that he'd eventually realize it was more practical to take on the entire position.

"We aren't going to the gallery," Tim said. "Or maybe we should and do a little work. That way it isn't a lie."

Corey pulled him away from the stream of pedestrian traffic and into the doorway of a shop. "What's going on?"

"Don't freak, but I need a doctor."

Corey's dark eyes were concerned. "Why?"

"I spit up blood earlier when jogging. It's like I can't get enough air. It's probably asthma or an allergic reaction of some kind."

"You've had this happen before?"

"No. It started yesterday. I wanna have it checked out. Do you have a doctor you like?"

"Yes," Corey said, "but this sounds like a hospital trip to me."

"It's not an emergency!"

"Yeah, but they'll have all the equipment there that you need. My doctor has a tiny office. I don't know if he even has an X-ray machine."

"Is the hospital closer?" Tim asked.

"Much."

"Okay. Whatever gets us done the soonest."

Corey kept asking questions on the way. How much blood? Did he feel sick? What if he spit now? Tim kept his answers short, not wanting to discuss it, but he understood. He would do the same if the situation were reversed, but right now, he didn't want to think about his health until forced to.

Eventually they reached a hospital. Corey was a godsend, which is exactly why Tim wanted him along. Ben would have provided emotional comfort, but he also would have worried. Not to mention that filling out forms and answering questions in another language was downright impossible for them. Corey translated everything, making the process much smoother. Then, like with most hospitals, they sat down to wait.

"I really like them," Corey said, head leaning against the wall. It rolled to consider him. "Jason and William. They're so sweet!"

"They are," Tim said, happy for the change of topic. "William especially."

Corey laughed. "Not Jason?"

"God no!" Tim said. "I know him too well. He's trouble. Has been since day one. Only makes me love him more."

"William sure keeps himself in shape," Corey said innocently.

"You've got to in his line of work. He told me once that he—" Tim looked over sharply. "You know they're married, right?"

"So am I," Corey said patiently. "Do you need me to explain how that works again?"

"No," Tim spluttered, "but they're on their honeymoon!"

"I just want to make it a memorable one. Any idea if they're boringly monogamous like you?"

"Afraid so," Tim said. "I don't think they'd be open to making an exception either."

Corey sighed. "What's wrong with you Texans? Get with the times! Live a little!"

"Hey, I'm from Kansas, just like you!"

"Then you've forgotten your roots." Corey smiled deviously. "It's so hot down there in the South. I pictured half-naked cowboys having to lick the sweat off each other, just to stay cool. Instead you keep your shirts buttoned all the way to the top, just in case anyone catches a glimpse of skin."

"So not true!" Tim said. "I'll make you a list of all the times I've been naked in public—"

"Please do!"

"—and you met Marcello. He makes you look like a saint."

"I like him," Corey said, smile widening. "A lot."

"I don't want to know."

"I'm not saying we did anything with him!"

"Are you saying you didn't? Because I know he's got a thing for Asian guys. Kioshi definitely caught his eye!" A nurse appeared at the end of the hall and spoke his name. "Saved by the bell. Let's get this over with." Tim rose so they could follow her.

Japan was vastly different from the United States in many ways, but this experience was reminiscent of when his ankle had been severely sprained when he was younger. The nurse took his vitals. Then the doctor came in, Corey explaining the situation and acting as mediator. A stethoscope was pressed to Tim's chest as he breathed in and out. Then he was handed over to a technician so his chest could be X-rayed. He started feeling silly in the middle of this, because surely he had overreacted. A little blood in his spit after a run? So what! By the time he was in the exam room again and facing his results, he no longer felt as concerned. The doctor put the X-ray on the screen, and to his eye, it looked fine. The doctor pointed at different things as he spoke, but he didn't sound upset. Then he pointed at one area in particular with his pen.

"Do you see..." Corey swallowed and started over. "There's a lighter area in your right lung. Toward the bottom."

Tim shrugged. "Okay. What's that mean?"

Corey addressed the doctor again, but not just to translate his question because their conversation went back and forth, Corey looking paler the longer this continued. Then he faced Tim.

"That spot in your lung isn't normal. He refuses to give a diagnosis without further tests. He wants to know if you want to continue that here, or wait until you're home again."

"It can wait," Tim said. "Can't it?"

Corey pulled out his phone. "I need to make sure of something."

"What?"

"Medical vocabulary is very specific. I don't want to tell you the wrong thing."

Tim waited impatiently, the calmness he had found slipping away. "Well?"

Corey looked up. "That spot in your lung, it's a tumor."

"A tumor?" Tim nearly shouted. "Like cancer?"

"That's what he can't tell me. He won't even say definitively that it's a tumor, but he admitted that's what he thinks it is."

"Ask him if he thinks it's safe for me to wait."

Corey remained focused on him. "Do you think that's a good idea? What if it's serious?"

"Ask him!" Tim said, nodding at the doctor.

Corey did so, Tim frustrated as the conversation went on. If his life wasn't in immediate danger, he wanted to do this at home.

"He says you can wait, but that you should have a scan done as soon as you're back. He wants to know where he can forward the X-ray."

Tim got the address from his phone, focusing on the task rather than the implications. Corey helped him communicate the right information. Then they were set free.

"Are you hungry?" Tim asked as they were walking down the sidewalk again. They still had time for a late lunch.

"Yeah," Corey said, phone in hand. "I'll text Kioshi and see if they've eaten already. Maybe we can meet them."

"No," Tim said firmly, putting his hand over the screen to block it. "I'm hungry now. How about this place?" He didn't wait for an answer. The door he pushed through belonged to a bar, but they probably had food too. Not that he was interested.

He hung back so Corey could lead the way. His friend didn't ask for an explanation. Not until they were seated at a table in a secluded corner and both sipping beers.

"Aren't you worried?"

"I'm shitting myself," Tim said. "Not literally, but the day isn't over yet. Listen, you can't tell anyone. Not even Kioshi."

Corey took a swig of beer while studying him. Then he shook his head. "Why? When I get bad news—even if I just have a rough day—Kioshi is the first person I tell about it. Talking to him always makes me feel better. Isn't it that way with you and Ben?"

"Yes, but not during this trip. It's Jason and William's honeymoon. I don't want to ruin that."

"Okay, but Ben—"

"Wears his heart on his sleeve," Tim said. "Usually that's a good thing, but with situations like these… Jason would be able to tell. Even if I swear Ben to secrecy, he would figure out that something's wrong. And we don't even know if it is! Why worry everyone before I know more? I realize it's asking a lot, but if you can hold off telling Kioshi until we're on the flight home…"

Corey took another sip. Then he nodded. "It's probably nothing," he said.

"Yeah," Tim replied, already knowing he would need another drink. "Everything's going to be fine."

* * * * *

Tim was hunched over his laptop, his hope dwindling with every link he clicked. He had started out with completely neutral keywords. Lung. Tumor. Almost every result contained the word *cancer*. After reading a few of those articles and scaring himself silly, he decided to try again. Tumor was too loaded. Most people associated that word with cancer, so he changed it to *mass*. He had an unidentified mass in his lungs. That was a little better, since there were a variety of potential explanations. The number one cause though, was cancer.

"Already back from your jog?"

Tim looked over his shoulder at the bed. He had risen early, unable to sleep well, and had already showered and dressed. "I'm not running today. Probably not for the rest of the trip either. This is supposed to be a vacation, right?"

"My feet hurt just from walking," Ben said, getting out of bed and padding to the restroom.

Tim hurried to read more, listening to make sure Ben wasn't on his way back. He heard the toilet flush and an electric toothbrush start to whir. When the bathroom door opened again, he slammed the laptop closed.

Ben wore a white bathrobe. And a knowing smile. "Were you looking at porn?"

"No," Tim said. He regretted his honesty, because porn was a decent cover story.

"Are you sure?" Ben said, coming nearer. "I can guess what kind of guys you're looking at."

Tim turned to face him. "What's that supposed to mean?"

"I've seen the way Corey looks at you," Ben said, not sounding upset. "And the way you sometimes look at him."

Tim shrugged. "He's cute, but he's more like a little brother to me."

"Are you sure?" Ben leaned against the desk. "You're allowed to fantasize about anyone you want. There's nothing wrong with that. Maybe I could help. Should I dye my hair black?"

"No," Tim said with a chuckle. "I'm perfectly happy with the guy I married."

"That doesn't mean we can't roleplay." Ben walked over to the bed and threw himself onto his back. Propping himself up on his elbows, he put on a seductive expression worthy of the stage. Then he said, "You can kiss me if you want."

Tim laughed. Then he rose, because he did want to kiss Ben. More than anything. He didn't know what the future held. Right now it was terrifying as hell, but it also made him appreciate the present and all the good things in it. None were more precious to him than the man stretched out in bed, whose lips were puckered and making exaggerated kissing noises. Tim rose and turned his back to the laptop and questions that couldn't be answered yet. Then he leapt onto the bed, tickling ribs and grinning at the resulting giggles, not stopping even when Ben begged for mercy.

"Thanks for the ride," Tim said, reaching for the door. "I'll text when I need to be picked up again."

"A moment, if you please," Marcello said, looking from him to the building they had stopped in front of. "What precisely are we doing here?"

Tim was back in Texas. The honeymoon had gone great, despite the scare. He hadn't ceased worrying during the remainder of the trip, but the heightened awareness of just how much he loved his family helped make the good times that much better. As soon as he was back in Texas, he had gone through a series of medical appointments and tests. The first had been a consultation, his doctor also concerned by what the X-ray revealed. Then he was sent for a CAT scan, which required *another* appointment with an oncologist, who was paid way too much to tell him the obvious. He needed to have the tumor checked to find out if it was malignant or not. That brought him to today, where he would be sedated and have a camera shoved down his throat. Kind of. He kept imagining the huge kind of camera used to film television shows, equipped with a robot arm and a little pair of scissors to take a tissue sample. This cartoonish vision helped take the edge off his fear, but not by much. Even the idea of a small tube being inserted into his lungs was disturbing.

"Just some routine tests," Tim said, answering the question at last.

"Allow me to make an observation," Marcello replied. "That you didn't drive yourself here indicates that these tests are not routine, or at the very least, are more invasive than usual. It also strikes me that you could have hired a taxi instead." He put the car in gear and pulled forward.

"What are you doing?" Tim demanded.

"Finding a place to park. Then I shall accompany you. That's what you want, isn't it?"

Tim opened his mouth to protest, but as usual, Marcello was right. He needed emotional support. Ben should be here, but Tim was still determined not to worry him without reason. "It'll take hours," he warned.

"I always have time for you," Marcello replied. After he pulled the car into a spot and shut it off, he looked over at him. "Now then, what are we facing?"

"A bronchoscopy."

Marcello was silent. Then he nodded. "Let's not keep the hospital staff waiting."

Tim felt a surge of affection for the man, and as they walked across the parking lot together, a little less afraid. Twenty minutes later, he wasn't feeling so grateful. "Would you stop?" he snarled. "Put the phone down!"

"I do so love a hospital gown," Marcello said, trying to get behind him to take a photo. "They can be more revealing than a slumber party game of Truth or Dare."

"You're the worst!" Tim said, clutching the gown shut and backing up against a wall.

"Will anesthetic be involved today?"

"Yes!"

Marcello lowered the camera. "In that case, I shall bide my time. What you don't know can't hurt you."

Tim breathed out and hopped up on the gurney that would wheel him to the procedure. "If that was true, I wouldn't be here."

"Yes." Marcello grew somber. "You're quite right. My apologies. When can we expect the results?"

"I have an appointment the day after tomorrow."

"With?"

Tim swallowed. "The oncologist. I hate waiting."

"As do I," Marcello said, patting his hand and leaving it there.

The nurse walked in then. She had clearly seen stranger sights than an older man with his hand on that of a younger man because she barely blinked. Instead she inserted an IV into Tim's arm and had him gargle with liquids to numb his mouth and throat. This concerned him because he didn't want to be awake to feel anything at all.

"Maybe you should give me two of those," Tim said as she injected him with anesthetic. "Name your price!"

"One for me as well," Marcello said. "To help the time pass swiftly."

"No way! He's my ride home!" Tim raised his head. Then he looked around, because he was no longer on the gurney. Marcello and the nurse had disappeared. The examination room was gone too! He was somewhere else entirely. His throat ached with thirst. No surprise since in preparation he hadn't been allowed to eat or drink anything after midnight. The room he was in now had windows next to each bed, allowing sunlight to filter through the blinds. He wasn't alone. He couldn't see much to his left and right due to the privacy curtains, but he could see the end of other beds and hear other patients. Directly across from him was medical equipment and wall-mounted televisions. Off to one side, toward the door, was a nurses' station, currently attended by a heavy-set man with dark hair and darker skin. He noticed Tim trying to push himself up and hurried over, pressing a button so the back of the bed raised for him.

"How are you feeling?" the nurse asked.

"Nervous," he admitted. "When do we start?"

"You're already finished," the nurse said. "Nice, isn't it? I wish I could have gotten through school that way."

Tim wanted to laugh, but his throat felt like the doctor had left the tube in there, along with his car keys, wrist watch, and maybe some LEGO bricks. "Thirsty," he managed.

"I know, but you can't have anything to drink until you've been awake for ninety minutes."

"I woke up ages ago," Tim rasped. "Eighty-nine minutes ago, actually."

The nurse grinned at this ruse. "I'll start the clock."

Tim made his peace with having to wait, but he wished he had been more prepared. He didn't care for daytime television and didn't have access to his cell phone. After half an hour dragged by, he got the nurse's attention and asked for pen and paper, so he could at least draw. He preferred paint and canvas, but this made the next hour pass more quickly, even if he was tempted to break the pen in half and drink the ink. Instead he used it to sketch out more of his story with Ben, trying very hard not to think about how it might end.

When the nurse returned with a tiny cup of apple juice, Tim felt like giving him a high five. He downed the juice like a shot, despite warnings to be cautious, and then begged for another. He got it five minutes later, along with a miniature muffin. More time went by. He suspected they were waiting to see if he would puke. Not a chance! He was too grateful for the sustenance. He would keep it down by willpower alone, if need be. His stomach was a champ, not giving him any trouble. The IV was removed and he was given his clothes. Tim felt like he was getting out of prison. Then he was escorted to the waiting room, where Marcello greeted him warmly.

"There he is, the man of the hour!" He peered at Tim critically. "I've seen better facelifts, but it's not bad. You can hardly tell any work was done. The breast implants, on the other hand, are phenomenal!"

"Stop," Tim said. "Or at least wait until we're out of here. If they find out a crazy person is driving me home, they might make me stay longer."

"My lips are sealed," Marcello promised. Together they walked to the parking lot. "Lunch is in order, if you're feeling up to it. They made you skip breakfast, didn't they?"

"Yeah," Tim said, "and I can definitely eat!"

"Excellent. We'll take our time, have a leisurely meal, and then we'll see what the doctors have to say."

"Not until Thursday," Tim said. He noticed Marcello's enigmatic expression. "Right?"

"You'll have your results this afternoon. But first, we shall feast!"

The oncologist Marcello brought him to was nothing like the one Tim had visited previously, but he wasn't surprised. With Marcello, everything in life was a first-class upgrade. The scented candles and gentle music playing in the front office was nice, as were the beverages and snacks the staff offered them while they waited in the examination room, but all that really mattered were the results. If this doctor was even more qualified to give him an accurate assessment, then great.

"Do you have any experience with this guy?" Tim asked.

"Woman," Marcello corrected, "and yes, she worked closely with Eric."

A name that had been on his mind of late, even more so than usual. Still, it wasn't the most sterling of recommendations because Eric hadn't survived his cancer.

"If I had any doubt about the physician's abilities," Marcello said, reading him with ease, "you wouldn't be here. Do keep in mind that Eric had mesothelioma, which sadly, is always terminal. The progress we made in staving off his disease came from following Pat's recommendations."

She might have been Pat to Marcello, but when a short, white-haired woman entered the room, she introduced herself as Dr. Staples. Tim shook her hand and was polite, when really he wanted to grab her by the shoulders and throttle an answer out of her. Did he have it or not?

"Before we begin," Dr. Staples said, "I want you to know that there have been tremendous advances in the fight against cancer in recent years."

Her lecture continued, but he didn't need to hear more. She was softening the blow. Otherwise she would have told him it was good news and been on her way. He felt dizzy with the revelation, his hope dwindling down to the diagnosis being on the better side of bad, but either way, Tim couldn't deny it any longer. He had cancer.

Fuck.

He tried to be a big boy and listen to what the doctor had to say, but Tim felt like he was falling backward into a bottomless pit of despair and anxiety. He was scared for himself, and he worried for Ben. This would change everything, whether he came through it or not.

"If you have any other questions, you can call me," Dr. Staples said.

Tim nodded numbly. Marcello had done most of the talking, but he thanked the doctor for her help, scheduled another appointment at the front desk, and was led outside. Marcello's hand remained on Tim's back to guide him. As soon as they were on the sidewalk, the hand moved up to his shoulder and was joined by another, the grip firm as Tim faced the man.

"You won't fight this alone," Marcello said, gaze intent. "No expense shall be spared! Whatever you need, you shall have. You're my best friend. I won't lose you!"

"You're my best friend too," Tim said, chin trembling. Then

he was pulled into an embrace, the shoulder he cried against soft. The worst was yet to come. As much as he was freaking out, what he really dreaded was having to tell Ben.

The house was dark when Ben arrived home. He set down his things, switching on lights until he noticed a candle burning on the patio. Funny how fire could be either romantic or ruinous, depending on the amount. A little went a long way, because he loved when they would leave the lights off and snuggle up in a cozy setting together. The patio was one such place, especially lately, with the memory of the wedding still so recent.

Ben turned off the lights again and went outside. Tim was seated in one of the deck chairs. A bottle of wine sat on the small table next to him, an unused glass awaiting Ben. Near this were three bottles of beer, all but one of them open already.

"Sorry," Tim said, twisting around to look at him. "I got a head start."

Ben hesitated. No smile. That was unusual. "Is everything okay?"

"Have a drink with me," Tim said, taking the bottle to pour a glass. "Sit down. Tell me how rehearsals went."

Ben noticed it was his favorite wine. Of the reds, at least. He ignored the empty chair, plopping down on Tim's lap instead. This earned him a smile and helped put him at ease. He was still worried, but if Tim had something he needed to say, he would in his own time. "I like the new play. It's a sung-through!"

Tim chuckled. "A what?"

"That means it's all singing. No dialog. I'm not sure about some of the people Brian cast, since one definitely doesn't have vocal training, but— Oh!" He was handed a glass of wine. "Cheers, baby!"

"Cheers," Tim said, clinking his bottle against Ben's glass. A swig finished it off, so the third bottle was opened. "Keep going. I love listening to you talk."

"I'm probably hurting your legs," he said, starting to rise.

Tim grabbed his arm. "You're fine. Keep going. Please."

That gave Ben pause, but it hadn't been long since Chinchilla's death. The wedding and trip to Tokyo made it seem more distant than it actually was. Now they had time to pause and reflect again. Deciding that's why Tim was feeling down, Ben talked more about his night, focusing on the funny parts to make him laugh. Ben's glass was soon empty. "Tell me about your day," he said, watching Tim carefully tilt the bottle to pour him a refill.

"I saw the doctor this morning," Tim said.

"Really? Did you have an appointment? I must have forgotten."

"You didn't," Tim said. "And it was more like a procedure. And a series of doctors."

Ben stood. "What? Are you okay?"

"I didn't want you to worry," Tim said, shaking his head. "I stopped running when we were in Tokyo because it was hard to breathe, and while I was there, I had Corey take me to the hospital so—"

"Tim!" Ben pleaded.

Silver eyes met his, an apology reflected in them. "I have cancer, Benjamin."

"No," Ben said firmly, as if this was something irresponsible that he could talk his spouse out of doing, like drinking too much or sky diving. "Who told you? Some doctor in Japan? You probably didn't even understand them right!"

Tim rose and seemed completely lost. His bottom lip was trapped beneath his teeth, his hands came up and fell to his sides again. Then he spun away, tears in his eyes, and Ben knew it was serious. Tim didn't cry. Not if he could help it. Ben moved toward him and placed a palm on Tim's back. This caused him to whip around and clutch Ben with so much desperation that it hurt, but the pain was nothing compared to the fear filling his stomach.

"What kind of cancer? How serious?"

Tim let go, forcing a neutral expression. "I'm going to be okay. I'll fight."

"You said it had something to do with your breathing. Lung cancer?"

Tim nodded. "There's a tumor in my lower right lobe."

"Okay, but that doesn't mean—"

"They took a biopsy today," Tim said. "The tumor is cancerous."

Ben's legs felt weak, so he sat in a deck chair. Tim sat too. The yard was quiet, especially without Chinchilla. They lived far enough away from the city that they rarely heard sirens or any other noise. Tonight even the insects weren't singing. Ben couldn't help thinking how quiet it would be if he ended up living here alone. That was possible. He knew that no one was guaranteed a long life or a happy ending. "What stage," he asked, his voice coming out as a whisper.

"Two."

Ben pulled out his phone, determined to find every possible solution.

"What do you want to know?" Tim asked. "Trust me, I've looked it all up."

Ben wanted to know the survival rate, but he couldn't bring himself to ask directly. "Are you going to be okay?"

"Yeah. Of course. I start chemo in a couple days and—" Tim's voice faltered. He drained more of his beer so he could continue. "If we're lucky, the tumor disappears. If not, they have to remove that part of my lung."

"Jesus," Ben breathed. "How risky is that?"

"I don't know," Tim said. "It doesn't scare me nearly as much as cancer does!"

"I'll be there," Ben said. "For all of it. I won't leave your side!"

Tim opened his arms. "Come here."

"No, you come here!" Ben said, patting his lap.

"I'm too heavy," Tim protested.

"I don't care."

Tim rose, and even though Ben had intended to provide a place to sit, he was too upset to remain stationary. He stood and hugged Tim. The embrace didn't end. Ben lost track of time. All he could think about was how there might come a day when he could no longer enjoy the simple pleasure of holding his husband. He already knew he wouldn't be able to cope. Thoughts of suicide weren't necessary, because he wouldn't survive that kind of pain again. He couldn't. That was the worse-case scenario. For now, he should stay optimistic.

"You're strong," Ben said. "You've already got this beat!"

"Of course," Tim said, managing a cocky smile. "I made a promise, didn't I?"

He had. Ben sometimes felt bad about that. He had been emotional at the time, still raw from losing Jace and uncertain if he could handle loving again. Not when it came with so many risks, so Tim had promised that there was nothing to fear, that he wouldn't die first. Ben knew such a promise wasn't possible to keep, but he had hoped they might be lucky.

"Enough feeling sorry for myself," Tim said. "I'm not the first person to get cancer, and I won't be the first person to beat it. And I will. You'll see."

"I already know you will!" Ben said, following his lead. That had to help their chances. If they could face this with a positive outlook—well, they needed every advantage they could get.

"I gotta pee," Tim said.

The announcement was refreshingly mundane. "Okay," Ben said. "Are you coming back out?"

"Yeah. It's a nice night." Tim started to move toward the house and then hesitated. "Don't look stuff up while I'm gone. You'll just scare yourself. You know how the internet is. It's worse than that medical book your mom has. All doom and gloom."

"Okay," Ben said, but he didn't promise, because there was one thing he needed to know. A simple statistic. He resisted anyway, having enough concerns to make his brain buzz with nightmarish visions of the future. Then he swore and took out his phone, because maybe he was wrong and this would be the easiest way to reassure himself.

stage two lung cancer survival rate

His fingers were a blur as they typed out these words, the results popping up immediately.

Thirty percent. Five years. He tried to calm himself enough to understand the answer properly. After diagnosis, the number of people still expected to be alive after five years was thirty percent. He imagined a room filled with ten people. Then he removed seven of them. Those weren't good odds.

"God damn it, Benjamin! What did I tell you?"

"You can't keep this a secret!" Ben said, turning on him and wanting to be angry because that would be easier, but he couldn't. He was too scared. "Please." His voice was a whimper. "From now on, tell me everything. Don't push me away, because if this really is all the time we have left—"

He couldn't finish the sentence. He started crying, which he hated, because one of them had to be strong, and he knew Tim would make that burden his own. He brushed away the tears, not that it stopped more from falling.

"I won't let you down," Tim said, pulling Ben's hands away to look him in the eye. "I've got this. You'll see."

"Okay," he said, trying his hardest to be brave. "We'll face it together, right?"

"That's right," Tim said, hugging him and murmuring his next words like a promise. "You and me. Always."

Chapter Eighteen

"We're going to be late." Ben stood at the front door, car keys in hand. He felt as though someone had opened him up, coated his insides with anxiety, and sealed him up again. Today would hopefully change that, since they were about to start actively fighting against the cancer. When he didn't hear a response, he went to investigate. He found Tim sitting on the couch, shoes dangling from the tips of his fingers. "What's the hold up?"

"I'm not ready yet," Tim said, not moving to resolve that.

"It's your first chemo appointment!"

"So?" Tim shot back.

Ben made sure his response was patient. "You don't want to be late."

"Who cares if I am? What are they going to do, give me detention?"

Ben walked over and sat next to him. "Are you afraid?"

"Kind of," Tim admitted. "I just can't help wondering if this is as good as it gets."

"What do you mean?"

Tim shrugged glumly. "Like maybe it's all downhill from here. I start the chemo, feel like crap, have surgery, and then…" Die. He wouldn't say it.

Nor did he need to. Ben had imagined the same scenario. "Or maybe you'll kick this thing in the ass and life will be even better."

Tim looked at him, silver eyes vulnerable. "But if it's not?"

Ben took a deep breath and exhaled. "I'm not sure. You still need to go today."

"I know."

"We can call and tell them we'll be there an hour later."

Tim perked up, looking hopeful. "Or two."

Ben laughed. "What would we do?" He had already prepared a huge breakfast of scrambled eggs and pancakes, and for once, everything had turned out perfectly.

"I don't know," Tim admitted.

"Well, pretend there's a meteor hurtling toward Earth and we only have an hour left."

They stared at each other. Then they started kissing and

tearing at each other's clothes. Ben had a knee to either side of Tim's hips, facing him while they pressed their lips together, but he pulled back and slowed once their shirts were off. Tim had always seemed so healthy, the tan skin vibrant, the dark hair silky. Tim had grown it out a couple of years back, just for him, to a length similar to when they were teenagers. His body had always been a constant reminder that Ben should take better care of his own. Of all the struggles Tim had gone through, emotional and philosophical, the physical had never been a problem. Ben caressed the muscles lovingly, recognizing that they might fade along with everything else before this battle was over, but he didn't care. He simply didn't want to see his husband suffer. When it came to the love he felt… Ben couldn't imagine that ever stopping, no matter how withered Tim might become. For now, he was determined to enjoy his body while he still could, because Tim was right. Maybe this would be their last chance to do so.

Ben kissed his neck and moved down to his pecs, licking the nipples even though Tim always ended up laughing and jerking away. Ben smiled up at him when he did, intending to go south, when reality interjected itself into his fantasies. Sometimes he hated being an adult.

"The appointment," Ben said. "Let me call real quick."

"Go right ahead," Tim said, but when Ben tried to move away, his hips were held firm. "Stay here."

"Okay." Ben rose only to get at the phone in his pocket. He remained in this position when finding the right number, and when he pressed the phone to his ear… "Hey!"

"You worry about the call," Tim said, tugging on the zipper of Ben's jeans, "and I'll worry about this."

His shorts and underwear were yanked down, exposing him. One of Tim's palms rubbed up and down and felt much too good. Ben was stifling a moan when a voice spoke in his ear. "Oh!" Ben said. "Hi! Ummm."

"How can I help you," the voice repeated.

"We have an appointment today for Timothy Wyman and uh—" Ben sucked in air, because Tim was busy sucking something else. "Stop!"

"Is everything okay, sir?"

"Car troubles!" Ben said. "One of our tires exploded. Popped! It went flat."

"Not yet, it didn't," Tim murmured. He moved Ben aside and rose, walking across the living room to the stairs.

"So you'll be late?"

"Yeah," Ben said. "But I think we can still make it. If we're an hour or two late, is that an issue?"

"Just a moment." He was put on hold, which was annoying, because Tim was no longer there to entertain him. He sat on the couch and waited. Then the phone clicked.

"That should be okay. I can reschedule you for eleven, if you think that'll work. Where are you now?"

Tim reappeared, completely naked and carrying a bottle of lubricant.

"Jiffy Lube," Ben said. "They're about to inspect the hole in the tire now."

"Oh. Well, maybe just an hour instead?"

"No! Better safe than sorry."

"I don't think we have condoms," Tim whispered.

Ben held back a laugh. "Eleven o'clock?"

"I've got you down for then. I hope the repairs aren't too expensive."

"Thank you. Goodbye." Ben ended the call and set the phone aside. "How much *do* you charge?"

"What?" Tim asked, shaking his head.

"You're a mechanic."

"Am I?" Tim sauntered over to him. Ben was still seated, which meant he was at the perfect height for something fat and hard to wag in front of his face. "Tell you what, polish this piston for me, and I'll fill you up free of charge."

"Sounds like a bargain!" Ben said, opening wide.

This was good. His mind had been plagued by worries the past few days, but now with his body asserting control, his brain was doing less and less thinking. This was as effective as popping a Xanax or getting drunk, but much healthier and a lot more fun. Tim was lost in lust too. Ben could always tell because that's when Tim stopped being gentle. He didn't mind though. He just sucked like his life depended on it and nearly cheered when Tim repositioned him, encouraging Ben to roll over onto his stomach.

Tim moved further down the couch, getting on his stomach too and shoving his face between cheeks. Ben really started moaning then, because having a tongue loll against his ass felt better than it had any right to. He was ready and rearing to go when Tim shuffled upward, but he didn't feel anything hard slide between his buns. Instead strong arms wrapped around him, holding him tight. Tim rested his full weight on Ben, which was comforting, or would have been if he wasn't so worried.

"You okay?" he asked.

"Call them back," Tim said, his voice hoarse. "Tell them we need all day."

Ben wanted to. If that didn't come with consequences, he would lock all the doors, lower the blinds, and keep the world from them both. "I need you to do this for me."

"Okay," Tim whispered. When he spoke again, he sounded more like his old self. "Do you mean the chemo or the sex?"

"Both," Ben said. "Just not in that order."

"I'll see what I can do."

Ben knew exactly what he could do. He had experienced it more times than he could count, but he never tired of it. Ever.

Twenty minutes later he was beginning to regret those words, because Tim was making it count. Ben was still on his stomach. Tim's arms still gripped him, sliding occasionally to change positions: an arm tight around his neck, the other beneath his waist. Both beneath his armpits, hands gripping his shoulders. Both coiled around his stomach, lifting him up for a better angle. Tim kept pumping and Ben continued moaning, wondering if he should have asked for three hours more instead.

"Are you close?" Tim asked.

"Very," Ben said. "Not like this though."

"Huh?"

"Let me roll over."

Tim slipped out, letting Ben roll onto his back. As Tim eased back inside, Ben raised a hand to his face, pressing his palm against it and staring into his eyes. Tim stared back, the love unmistakable, his motions gentler now like he was determined to savor what time remained. That was their relationship. Too many false starts and years apart had ingrained this instinct in them both. They treated each touch, each kiss, like it was their last.

Tim's expression became yearning. Ben nodded. The pace didn't increase. Tim remained disciplined, each motion of his hips rocking them back and forth, but he no longer held back. Neither of them did. When Tim collapsed onto him, Ben clung tight, kissing his shoulder, smelling his skin, and sending out a silent prayer.

Please don't let this kind of love be taken from him. Not again.

Tim was in the shower when he pulled his hands away from his head and saw clumps of hair mixed in with the shampoo suds. He wasn't shocked. Not like he had been yesterday. He knew that chemotherapy might make his hair fall out, but after two weeks of minimal negative side effects, he thought he had lucked out. He rinsed for longer than usual. Better it go down the drain than get stuck in the towel. His parents could deal with any clogged pipes, since that's where he was, back in Houston and facing yet another appointment.

He longed for the days when he was able to wake up, go to the gallery, and deal with starving artists and skittish customers. Normal days, like those he had known before, and not this never-ending parade of physicians, medication, and waiting rooms. Dr. Staples wanted him to consult with a specialist at MD Anderson. Tim supposed he was lucky to live within driving distance of one of the nation's leading cancer centers. Unlucky to need to, but still fortunate to have that option. His appointment wasn't until later today, but to avoid a six-hour roundtrip drive, he had decided to travel the day before and stay the night with his parents.

He looked at himself in the mirror after drying off. So far so good. He had lost a little weight, since his appetite wasn't the same, and he looked tired. He blamed anxiety more than the treatment. Thoughts of cancer tended to keep him up late. Despite his hair starting to fall out, it mostly still looked okay, just not as thick. He didn't think anyone could tell he was sick by appearance alone.

After getting dressed, he went downstairs and found his mother straightening the kitchen. "I need a haircut."

"Do you?" Ella said, turning to consider him. "You look very handsome."

"Thanks," he grunted, "but it's falling out."

"Your hair?"

He nodded.

"Oh my poor baby!" Ella pressed her hands to his cheeks, oblivious to the fact that it made his face look fat and pooched out his lips. "¡Mi pobre Gordito!"

Okay, maybe she did realize since she still insisted on calling him her little fatty. "Mom!" he said, pulling away, but he secretively loved the attention. She had taken the day off, and as always, he enjoyed being the center of her world.

"It's all my fault," she said. "I made you! I should have tried harder."

"You did fine," Tim said. "Actually, I wouldn't have minded being a little taller."

"We'll get you new shoes today," she said, patting his cheek and turning back to the kitchen sink. "Ones that make you taller."

"I was kidding!"

"So was I."

"Not about shopping though," Tim said. They didn't need to buy anything. He just liked going out with her.

"I never joke about shopping," Ella said. "Put on your shoes. I'll call my stylist."

All he needed was a barber, but he knew she would insist on the very best for him. Once at the salon, his mother sat in the waiting area and read magazines, giving him privacy while his hair was cut. That was good, because it allowed him to pretend that genetics were catching up with him instead of a disease.

"Might as well say goodbye to my hair now," he said. "My dad was bald as a cue ball by the time he was forty."

Not true. His father still had a head full of thick white hair, but Tim enjoyed taking that away from him, if only in his own imagination. Instead of buzzing his hair down to one uniform length, the stylist left the top slightly longer. This looked nicer, and he supposed when it did fall out, it wouldn't make as much of a mess. Still… "Just a little shorter on top," he said.

When he was finished and went to the front, his mother could barely look at him. She paid—even though he insisted she didn't need to—and they were in the parking lot before she turned to him wearing a forced smile. "You look very handsome," she said.

"I'll be fine," he said for her benefit. "Trust me. We've got the best doctors on this. Now tell me what you really think of my hair. I still want to look good for Benjamin."

"It's very masculine," his mother said. "Ben will love it. I do too."

He hugged her before they returned to the car. The subject of cancer didn't come up again as they strolled through the mall and had lunch together. She made it easy to pretend that everything was normal. Sometimes having parents who shielded their emotions was an advantage. There was no avoiding the subject after they drove to the hospital. They parked and were making a beeline for the entrance when someone called their names.

"Ella! Tim!"

He turned and saw his father waving, standing next to his own vehicle. Tim was too surprised to wave back. It was a weekday and he didn't remember his father ever taking off work. Not for his benefit, at least.

"You told him to meet us here," Tim said accusingly.

"I did not!" Ella said, sounding equally surprised.

Tim had mixed feelings. Whenever his father was around, his mother tended to focus on her husband, leaving Tim on the sidelines. He didn't like their day together being sabotaged like this. The rest of him was curious. What did his father want?

"Let's not be late," Thomas said when close enough, nodding toward the building.

Nice to see you too, Tim thought. *No no, stop hugging me! There will be time for that later!*

His father didn't hug him, of course. Instead he kissed his wife and led the way. Not only was their day interrupted, but now Thomas was in charge of it. Great. It only got worse in the waiting room.

"Why don't I get us all some coffee?" Ella said, smiling at them both.

"I'll do that," Tim said. He stood, glancing at the vending machines and patting his pockets.

"I saw a sign for Starbucks when we pulled in," Ella said. "Much better. Be right back!"

Short of tackling his mother, Tim wasn't left with any options to stop her. He sat again next to his father and braced himself for a long awkward silence, because Tim wasn't going to talk sports or make conversation. Those days were finished. He was done trying.

"My father, your grandfather, died of lung cancer," Thomas said.

Tim kept his attention forward. "Is that supposed to make me feel better?"

"My father asked God to heal him. He didn't do any of this. You have a better chance."

Tim leaned back in his chair to see him better. "Did he at least go to a doctor?"

"Only for the diagnosis," Thomas said. "That shows how serious it was."

Tim didn't hide his confusion. "Isn't it the Christian Scientists who don't go to doctors?"

"I don't know," Thomas admitted. "We didn't go to church. I'm not sure what denomination he practiced. Religion didn't make much sense to me until I met your mother."

This was news to him. "I thought you were both raised Catholic?"

Thomas shook his head. "My father's idea of religion was consulting the Bible. For everything. He used it as a guide for how we should live our lives. Not just morally, but what we ate and how we dressed. When one of us kids got into trouble, he would look up our punishment. Sometimes we would have to wait overnight, or even days, while he read. Those times were the worst. I hated the anticipation more than the actual punishment. Usually."

"Sounds rough," Tim said.

Thomas nodded grimly. Then he was quiet. Long enough that Tim thought the conversation was over. He nearly jumped when his father spoke again.

"I tried to give you a better upbringing. We were watched constantly. None of us had our or own room, or any privacy. I had an eight o'clock curfew until I was eighteen and moved out of the house. I wasn't allowed to drive except for work, and television was forbidden. I used to sneak over to Ralph's house to watch *The Tonight Show*. I thought Johnny Carson was the devil, but gosh was he funny! I didn't want you to have to do that. I gave you your space and your freedom. I tried to be a better father."

Tim wanted to argue that all Thomas had to do was basic little things like acknowledge his accomplishments and remind him that he was loved. Then he forced himself to think it over, wondering if his father already had. Maybe that's what the Mitsubishi 3000 GT had been about. It was a luxurious car to give a teenager as a present, especially brand new. Tim still thought the studio space was for his mother's benefit instead of his own, but when he compared that to the life of his father... Tim had been given privacy. His own room, and his own place to paint, which he could lock. He'd had his freedom too, a curfew that was never enforced, and past a certain age, the liberty to stay home when his parents were out of town. If anything, they had given him too much space, making him feel unwanted or unimportant. Maybe his father had overshot in his effort to do better. Maybe this had been his inept way of loving Tim. Then again...

"I never felt that you liked me," Tim said. "After a game, yeah, and as long as my grades were good, but not me as a person. We never spent much time together, and when Benjamin came into my life—" He shook his head instead of travelling down that tired old road.

"I used to feel sorry for you," Thomas said. "When it became clear that this wasn't just a phase or some sort of experimentation, I thought you were setting yourself up for an unhappy life. The only joy I had ever known—true happiness—came from meeting your mother. I wanted that for you too, so I tried to convince you that you were wrong. Now, with every year that goes by, more of the world seems to agree with you, and fewer people agree with me."

Tim braced himself for a lecture about the world going to hell, but it never came. He looked into eyes the same color as his own, but despite the similarity, couldn't decipher their intent. "So who do you think is right these days?"

"I want you to be happy," Thomas repeated.

"Ben makes me happy," Tim said.

"Good."

Tim stiffened in shock. Good? For his father, this was practically like him leaping up and marching around the waiting room while waving a rainbow flag.

"I also want you to get better. Your mother and I will help you however we can. I thought I could explain what I remember of my father's battle with cancer, just in case it helps. I've seen what it can do to a person."

"So have I," Tim said.

"Because of Eric." His father nodded musingly. "Then neither one of us wants to see you go through that."

"Definitely not." Tim shot a glance over at his father, who looked exceedingly uncomfortable. Somehow he didn't think a hug would improve the situation. His own mind was racing.

This wasn't an apology. It was almost better, because it was an explanation. He hadn't realized how messed up his father's upbringing had been, or how much easier his own was by comparison. Thomas had wanted to do better, and for what it was worth, he had.

They sat in silence, Tim wondering how far away that Starbucks was, because his mother was taking her sweet time. Thomas probably wasn't feeling too relaxed either. Tim noticed the television in one corner, a sports anchor reporting on the game from the night before, and realized the easiest way to make peace. "The Astros sure fucked up last night."

"Language," Thomas scolded. Then he visibly relaxed. "And yes, they did. The Royals stand a real chance this year. They were smart to bring in Martinez. Have you ever seen anyone pitch like that?"

"He's got arms like Popeye," Tim agreed. "If he was standing on the pitcher's mound, I'd drop the bat and run."

Thomas grinned. "Me too. First I'd get his autograph. There's a game coming up, you know. In three weeks at Minute Maid Park."

"Oh yeah?" Tim asked, not daring to read into this.

"We could go. If you're feeling well enough."

"Okay," Tim said. "Yeah. For sure! We need to cheer the Royals on, let them know they've got fans here, even on enemy turf."

His father nodded, launching into a lecture about a game he saw when he was younger, and how great teams could still falter even when at home. They kept talking sports once Ella returned with coffee and after the appointment on the ride home. Tim wasn't foolish enough to think he would have the warm sort of relationship with his father that he'd had with Eric. The love hadn't grown between them, but something was now there that had been missing before. Respect.

Chemo fucking sucked. The first round had been so different. Maybe they had messed up and given him an incomplete dose, because round two was kicking his ass. Tim glared at his reflection in the bathroom mirror of the doctor's office. Despite buying clippers and buzzing his hair to its shortest length, entire patches were missing. Tim put the blue baseball cap back on (Go,

Royals!) to hide his scalp, which helped somewhat. He looked more gaunt than before, thanks to his continued lack of appetite and chemo making food taste bad. He was on protein shakes to keep his weight up, and following Dr. Staples' advice, was still exercising as best he could. Maybe he needed to rethink the hat and buy clothes that fit better. Tim felt he looked creepy, like the kind of guy who would loiter around a cruise park at night, hoping to appear twenty instead of fifty.

He needed good news. Today could be the turning point. He washed his hands and returned to a seating area lined with chairs and dotted with outdated magazines. All the world's a stage, Shakespeare had claimed. These days, Tim's world was a waiting room. He walked over to where Ben was sitting and joined him.

"Please tell me you didn't stink up the bathroom," Ben whispered.

"Why? Do you need to use it?"

"Nope, but a lady went that way as soon as you came back, and I'm worried she'll get in there and lose consciousness."

"Then it's a good thing we're in a doctor's office," he retorted. "Should we send in a bomb disposal robot to check on her?"

A nurse entered the waiting room. "Mr. Wyman?"

"The moment of truth," Tim muttered as he stood.

"It'll be good news," Ben said. "I just know it."

He sure hoped so. If the tumor had shrunk or—better yet—disappeared, then this nightmare would be over. Dr. Staples didn't keep them waiting. She met them in the hall, gesturing to an exam room where scans of his lungs were already hanging up and backlit. His eyes moved to his lower right lobe, easily spotting the tumor, now that he knew what to look for. Nothing seemed to have changed, so he assumed these were the original results, and that she would reveal what two grueling rounds of chemo had achieved.

"Everyone has a different physiology," she began. "While we can predict with some accuracy how most patients will react to treatment, there are always outliers, exceptions to the rule."

That sounded good! Maybe his body had pummeled cancer into submission. Soon he would be a poster boy testifying to the wonders of modern medicine.

"These latest scans—" Dr. Staples said, turning to the images hanging up. That's all he heard. He swayed, his brain wanting to deny the evidence of his eyes. If he hadn't been sitting down, he would have fallen. Those couldn't be his latest scans, because he had studied the old ones and had them memorized. The scans hanging up were identical. Nothing had changed.

"Mistake," Tim mumbled.

"Are you okay?" Ben asked, eyes wide with concern.

"Sorry," Tim said, shaking his head. "Those aren't the new scans."

"They are," Dr. Staples said patiently. "Take a deep breath. I know it's a lot to digest, but we can go over it slowly. If you have any questions, we can start there."

"Why does it look the same? The tumor. You said it would shrink."

"Not all tumors respond to chemo in the same manner. Some even start to grow faster, but that's exceptionally rare. In your case, the tumor appears to be the same size, which—"

"So I was on chemo for nothing?" Tim demanded. "I feel like shit and my hair is falling out! I can barely eat!"

Dr. Staples held up her hands. "I understand your frustration, but we agreed to try this instead of an invasive surgery. Remember?"

"Yeah," he admitted.

"Keep in mind too that the tumor might have grown over the previous weeks or even metastasized, but it hasn't. The cancer is controlled! You're still at the same clinical stage. While we haven't made progress, we haven't lost any ground either. It also gave us time to explore other solutions."

Like the genetic test to see if he had the EGFR mutation. If so, he could have popped some miracle pill that might wipe out the cancer. He hadn't looked into that much, not wanting to get his hopes up, and he was glad because it turned out he didn't qualify.

Dr. Staples sighed. "I really expected better results, but we aren't out of options."

"The lobectomy," Tim said, mouth dry.

"Yes," Dr. Staples replied. "There is a surgeon at MD Anderson I'd like you to meet."

Tim nodded. "And if I go through with the lobectomy, after we remove that part of the lung, the cancer can't come back? I'll never have it again?"

"You'll be in remission," Dr. Staples said carefully. "That

means we won't be able to detect cancer in your cells with any of our tests. But there is always a chance of recurrence, or even a secondary cancer elsewhere, so I can't make that promise. No physician can, but considering your age and excellent general health, I feel very confident of your chances."

Tim checked out mentally for the rest of the appointment. Ben had plenty of questions to compensate for his silence. Afterwards, when Ben suggested they go out to eat or do something fun, Tim declined. All he wanted was to be home, so that's where they went. Currently he was in the kitchen, looking in the refrigerator for a beer. A single bottle sat there, chilled and ready to go. At least one thing had gone right today!

"It's a little early," Ben said when noticing him opening it, opting instead for a glass of water. Then he shook his head at himself. "Go ahead. You've earned it. I'm sorry the results weren't what we were hoping for."

"It's fine," Tim said, taking a swig. Then he clenched his jaw, because nothing was fine. "I don't know if I can keep my promise."

"What?" Ben set his drink on the counter and marched over to him. "What's that supposed to mean?"

"You heard what she said!" Tim was on the verge of shouting. He didn't mean to, but all the anxiety and doubt he had been holding back finally engulfed him. "Do you know what a lobectomy is?"

"They'll remove part of your lung. I know it's scary but—"

"Scary?" Tim spluttered. "It's fucking terrifying!" He set down the beer and lifted up his shirt, pointing beneath his right pec. "They're going to cut me open starting here, and all the way around to my back!" He let the shirt drop. "Then they're going to spread my ribs open. That's what they call it, but if you haven't noticed, our ribs aren't too flexible, so what they really mean is a fracture. I'll have a tube shoved down my throat so I can breathe and one shoved up my dick so I can pee. That's just the beginning! How about one in my spine for the pain meds, or another in my chest to drain puss and air? Don't forget that they're doing all this to rip out a chunk of my lungs and—" He couldn't breathe. He felt too winded and his hands were shaking, but he forced himself to continue. "After all that, they can't even promise I'll be better. Assuming the procedure doesn't kill me, I've got a—" He braced himself against the counter, still huffing.

"I think it's a one in twenty chance of being in chronic pain the rest of my life. No wonder Eric didn't want to fight! Sometimes I think I'd rather…" He shook his head, unwilling to say the words, but only because he knew they would hurt Ben.

"Breathe," Ben said, coming closer and putting a hand on his arm. "You have every right to be upset. I would be too. I am! Just take a few deep breaths for a second. Okay?"

Tim nodded, but he wasn't finished. "I'm freaking out. I've always tried to be brave for you, but I'm a coward, Benjamin. I'd be running away right now if I thought it would do any good. I don't want to let you down. I really don't, but I might. If that happens… I guess I should apologize now, just in case."

"You don't have to apologize," Ben said, chin trembling. "You don't have to keep that promise. We'll strike it from the record. You only made it to cheer me up. You were being romantic, and I took it too seriously. So no more promise."

Tim felt relieved. He was surprised how much of a burden was lifted from his shoulders. Part of him would miss it, but right now, he was too weak to shoulder anything. "Thanks."

"I love you," Ben said, moving closer. "No matter what happens."

"Don't kiss me right now," Tim said, trying to back away but he was up against the counter. "It's not the right time."

"It is," Ben disagreed, "because you're much braver than you think."

He came near, and as much as Tim loved that face and the person attached to it, he was forced to shove Ben away. Then he was running for the guest bathroom at the front of the house, skidding painfully on his knees just to make it on time. Tim threw up into the toilet, which wasn't even surprising because the chemo or the cancer or maybe just the constant emotional strain had him puking a lot these days. He couldn't even enjoy a beer or a kiss from his husband. Fighting for your life wasn't easy when all the joy had been sucked out of it.

Ben came to check on him. Tim waved him away, not wanting to be seen like this. Once he was finished retching, he brushed his teeth and used mouthwash. An extra set was kept in the downstairs bathroom lately. When he felt stable again, he went to the living room. Ben stood there with a determined expression on his face and a phone in his hand.

"I'm canceling my trip," he said.

Ben had planned on going to Warrensburg with Nathaniel, and had looked forward to it since the wedding when the idea first came up. Together they were going to revisit old haunts. Tim had encouraged him to make solid plans, not wanting his illness to limit Ben as it did him. The flight left tomorrow, but they had expected to be buoyed by good news by then.

"You're going," Tim said. "I know how much this means to you."

"Not as much as—"

"I could use some space. Seriously. You're home way too much."

Ben looked stung. "If that's what you want."

"No, it's what I need!" Tim snapped. Then he exhaled. "Sorry. Sometimes you've gotta wallow in your own misery. I'll be fine. I'll feel sorry for myself a few days, and by the time you come back, I'll be over it and we'll face whatever's next. Okay?"

Ben shook his head. "You're sure?"

"Yeah."

It might be the only thing he was sure of. As Tim went about his day, trying to pretend that everything was normal, he couldn't help thinking of the huge black wave looming over everything, threatening to crash down on all he loved and leave only wreckage in its wake. Cancer was a monster, one harder to face than coming out and years of living alone, but not worse than losing Eric and Chinchilla. The only comfort Tim could find is that he might be seeing them sooner than he had anticipated.

Chapter Nineteen

The weather was not cooperating. Ben stood beneath a large umbrella held by an even larger man. He was used to feeling small because Tim was so much brawnier than him, but Nathaniel was ever bigger. Both in height and muscle. He wasn't as toned—from what Ben could see, anyway—but it wasn't hard to understand how he had landed a smoking-hot husband like Kelly.

Romance was the furthest thing from both their minds at the moment. They were standing on the sidewalk outside a small house, the rain pouring down. As inconvenient as the weather was, it fit the somber mood.

"This is where he grew up?" Nathaniel asked.

"Yes," Ben said after double-checking the address on his phone. Before making the trip to Warrensburg, he had grilled Michelle and Greg for every detail about Victor they could remember. They promised to meet with Nathaniel the next time they were in Austin, so they could share personal stories. For now, the information they provided had helped greatly when planning this trip. "Victor was born here. Or at least, we think this is where his mother brought him after they left the hospital. We know for sure that he grew up here, although from the sound of things, by the time Jace met him, Victor didn't stay here often. Not until he was older. Um."

Nathaniel looked over at him questioningly.

Ben supposed there was no easy way of saying it. "This is also where he took his own life."

Nathaniel returned his gaze to the house, considering it in silence. Ben left him to his thoughts for as long as he could, but they were supposed to meet someone soon, and the time they had left was dwindling. "Do you want to go inside? We could knock and see if anyone is home."

"Would there be any point?"

Ben didn't take offense. Nathaniel could be gruff, but he was a good guy. More direct than most people, but not with the intent of being rude. He simply didn't sugarcoat things.

"Sometimes I still drive by the house where Jace and I lived together," Ben said. "I'm never tempted to knock because I know it'll be different inside. It's not the house itself that's important, or that he died there. The memories we made together, that's what matters most to me. I wish I had memories of Victor I could share with you. Sorry."

"You're doing fine," Nathaniel said. "All of this helps. I know Warrensburg, but not in the same way Victor did. Now I feel like I'm starting to. I wouldn't have gotten that by coming here alone. Thank you. Jace's parents have been generous too. If there's anything I can do for them, let me know. Hearing their stories last night was amazing."

"I'm glad." After flying into Kansas City yesterday and driving to Warrensburg, they had gone to see the Holdens. They treated Ben like a surrogate son and extended that same courtesy to Nathaniel, welcoming him into their home and sharing whatever memories they could. This was a treat for Ben too, since most of them involved Jace. "There's someone else I want you to meet. Ready?"

"Yeah," Nathaniel said, still holding the umbrella above them as they walked back to the car. "Bernard, right? Who was he again?"

"Victor's boss at the local gas station. I know that sounds lame, like he wouldn't know much, but he was a sort of mentor to Jace. They were close."

They drove to the edge of town to a large house tucked deep within the wooded lot of a cul-de-sac. An older woman opened the door, her hair long and dark except for graying temples, her skin baked from a lifetime of enjoying the sun. She introduced herself as Alani, Bernard's wife.

"Don't get him too excited," she said as she showed them in. "He has a weak heart, and he thinks he's still twenty-three."

She led them to the living room, where a hospital bed had been set up. The back was upright, Bernard already smiling at them both. He greeted Ben first, his hand feeling like soft old leather as he was pulled in for a hug. Nathaniel was given the same treatment, despite being a perfect stranger.

"So good to see you again!" Bernard said, eyes twinkling at Ben. "You'll pardon me if I don't rise. My ninetieth birthday is coming up, and my doctor assures me that if I stay in bed until then, I'll be able to dance."

"He said no such thing!" Alani interjected. "Can I get either of you coffee? Or tea?"

"Coffee would be nice," Nathaniel said.

"I'll help," Ben offered. "You guys are okay?"

He was barely heard. Bernard's attention was on Nathaniel instead. "So you're Victor's boy? Will wonders never cease!"

They were definitely okay. He couldn't imagine not feeling comfortable around Bernard. Ben helped Alani in the kitchen and made polite conversation. By the time he returned, the living room was full of laughter.

"At this stage, Victor was just messing with me," Bernard was saying. "He could hear that old truck of mine coming down the road and knew I was checking in to see if he had shown up for his shift. As soon as I got close, Victor would duck behind the counter. Didn't matter if customers were in the shop. Oh no, his top priority was making me look like a fool! I ran in there once, apologizing and offering everyone a free fountain drink for having to wait. Then he pops up, walks over to grab a cup, and pours himself a soda. I definitely didn't mean to include Victor in the deal!"

"Did you take it out of his paycheck?" Nathaniel asked, clearly amused.

"I threatened to! On that occasion and others. Never did. I was too much of a softy, and I knew he needed the money. I can see him in you."

Nathaniel grew somber. "You can?"

"Yep. Something in the mouth. He didn't smile or laugh easily either. It always took work, but it was a welcome sight when it happened. Do you like to read? Your father was a real thinker. A modern day philosopher."

Ben interrupted just long enough to deliver the coffee. Then he hung back and enjoyed listening to the rest of the conversation. He tried to imagine what it would be like not to have known one of his parents, and to slowly build a mental picture of that person from the impressions of others. Jason was in a similar situation, never having known his biological father, but for whatever reason, he didn't seem to need to. If ever he did, Ben would try to help him in a similar fashion.

When it was time to go, Nathaniel excused himself to use the restroom, leaving them alone.

"How are you holding up?" Bernard asked, patting the mattress next to him.

Ben went and sat there, feeling like he was about to tell Santa what he wanted for Christmas. "I'm fine," he said. "What makes you think that I'm not?"

"I can see your worries from across the room! That, along with it being a small town. Believe it or not, I do still manage to get out on occasion, and I happened to run into the Holdens the other day."

Ben swallowed. "So you've heard."

"I have," Bernard said grimly, "and I know how you must be feeling. Alani had a touch of cancer ten years back. Scared the bejesus out of me! Worst year of my life, aside from when I lost my son. She fought hard though, and just look at her now."

She wasn't in the room, but Ben had already noted her pep, hoping he would be as energetic when her age. Bernard too. They both were full of life, despite being toward the end of their own. "If things don't work out," Ben said, shaking his head, "I don't know what I'll do."

"Do you have any reason to expect the worst? From what I hear, the doctors caught it early."

Ben nodded. "They did. I just don't want to go through losing someone again. I can't."

"Jace was one of the finest men I ever met," Bernard said. "A shining light. You'd be surprised what a person can survive. Are you a religious man?"

"Not really," he admitted

"Well, even if you don't think you'll ever see Jace again, I bet you still feel like he's with you. You'll remember things he used to say, and you knew him well enough to know his advice, even if he's not around to give it. Am I right?"

"Yeah," Ben said hoarsely.

"There you go. None of us truly lose the people we love. They stay with us, one way or another. I'm afraid this is just part of life, especially as you get older. You'll keep facing down death until the day he comes for you. It's a hefty price to pay for getting to experience this world, but I think it's worth it."

"So do I."

"I'm glad to hear it! You say hello to the Holdens for me, would you? Tell them they're welcome by anytime. Bob's not getting any younger either. If need be, they can roll their beds over here and park them next to mine."

Ben laughed. He had only met Bernard a handful of times,

but he walked away from each encounter reminded that life was pretty damn awesome, no matter what it threw at you.

Ben awoke early the next morning with the nagging sensation that he had already woken up that day. To use the restroom? Still unsure, he took in his surroundings. Currently he was on an inflatable mattress in a home office. At least, the mattress had been inflated when he went to bed. Now it was mostly flat. The office hadn't begun as one either. Once upon a time this had been Jace's childhood bedroom. Ben had insisted on sleeping there, the notion romantic. This allowed Nathaniel to take the guest room, which seemed fair, since there was so much more of him. Nathaniel's grandparents lived in town, and he could have stayed with them, but Ben understood why he declined to. Being at Jace's old house was one step closer to Victor and his final resting spot. If the weather was clear today, as the app on his phone had promised, they could finally go there. With their flight leaving in the afternoon, this was their last opportunity.

Ben stood, his back aching from sleeping rough, and was struck by the same sense of déjà vu. He had already gotten up. No, he had sprung from bed, because Jace had walked into the room, which had looked nothing like it did now. The bed had been on the far wall, a dresser directly across from it. As for Jace, his hair was long like in those old photos. Ben blinked, laughed, and shook his head. A dream. He wished he could remember more of it, because it must have been a nice one.

You never would have let me get away with that.

He heard the words in Jace's voice but struggled to remember when he might have said them.

A promise is a promise.

Again, when had Jace ever said that to him? The mind was a funny thing, and so were dreams. Ben took a shower, got dressed, and went downstairs for breakfast. By the time he had finished eating, he could barely remember the dream at all. He had seen Jace somewhere. That was all he could recall, aside from those two snippets of conversation, which continued to nag him.

"What are your plans today?" Serena asked as Ben helped her clear the table after breakfast. Her hands were shaky, and there was talk of her and Bob moving to Houston to be closer to Michelle and her family. Eventually. Jace's parents were still doing okay. Bob was a little rough around the edges and kept falling asleep in his old recliner, but he still had the same ornery personality. Serena seemed plenty capable of taking care of them both.

"I thought I'd show Nathaniel around the neighborhood," Ben said.

"There isn't much to see."

"No, but there's the lake. And the woods."

Serena nodded her understanding. She might not know everything that he did, but she remembered a time when Victor had camped there.

"Thank you for everything," Ben said. "For letting me come here and bring company."

"You're our son," Serena said, matter-of-factly. "You are always welcome here."

He smiled his gratitude, eyes lingering for a moment, because he sometimes caught glimpses of Jace in her and Bob. Ben wondered what Jace would have looked like when older. More like his mother probably, elegant in age, since Jace shared the most traits with her.

Nathaniel took longer in the mornings. He had been too bleary to talk much during breakfast and needed a lot of time to get ready. This worked to their advantage. The sun was higher, the rain of the past few days burning off in the summer heat. They walked down to the lake together, Ben pausing there and trying to remember the stories Jace had told him.

"Jace taught Victor how to swim here," he said. Then he thought about it. "Or fish? I think that's right. Or maybe they were supposed to be fishing and went for a swim instead." He shrugged apologetically, Nathaniel taking it in stride. Ben led them next into the woods. "I hope I can find the right place."

"If you can't, it's fine," Nathaniel said, but his voice had an edge of desperation.

Ben was determined not to fail him. If he could have drawn Nathaniel a map, or simply told him where to look, he would have. Forcing them to travel together would have been ridiculous if that were possible. This was only Ben's third time looking for the spot, and a gap of years separated each visit. At the very least, he could make sure Nathaniel understood the reason they were here.

"As you've heard, Victor spent a lot of time living off the grid. I'm not sure there was even a term for it back then. He was in these woods when he and Jace hit it off. A lot of their relationship took place here. The first kiss, for sure. Other things too. It was an important spot for them both. After they broke up and just before Jace left for college, Victor was here every night. I guess that was unusual. He liked to move around."

"Sounds like Jace broke up with him," Nathaniel said. "Otherwise, he wouldn't have stuck around."

"That's right. I know Jace was touched by the gesture, but he still didn't feel like they could be together."

"My father had some unusual ideas about relationships," Nathaniel grumbled. "If he put Jace through the same things he did my mom, then I'm not surprised."

"It's probably worth remembering how young they all were. You can't expect teenagers to know how to maintain a healthy relationship." He thought of Tim. Then he smirked and thought of himself. "Although some people are naturals. I was pretty awesome. Others need to break a few hearts before they figure out how not to."

"I was the same as you," Nathaniel said. "Ready to get married at age fifteen. Still, those heartbreakers get in deep, don't they?"

"Yes," Ben said. "They certainly do."

His foot kicked something. They were on the edge of a clearing, which meant it might be the right spot. Ben squatted, brushed away dry leaves, and saw broken tree branches clustered together. He shifted them until he found two still joined by frazzled twine. Then he stood.

"This is the place."

Nathaniel looked around, eyes wide. "Here?"

"Yeah," Ben said, throat already feeling tight. "Jace wasn't very forthcoming about Victor when we first started dating. He would mention him, but in a way that made him sound alive. He told me later that Bernard did the same thing with his son on occasion. I guess that's where he got the idea. Jace let it go on a little too long, because when I met his family and friends, they all knew the truth. I didn't." He gestured to the clearing. "This was his apology to me. A secret he gave to me that no one else knew. He scattered Victor's ashes here. In their special place. Jace must have loved him very much, because he asked me to scatter his ashes here too."

"Did you?"

Ben nodded, unable to speak more.

Nathaniel put an arm around him, hand clamped on his shoulder. They stood there in silence, Ben trying to collect himself, because he wasn't here for his own needs. He nudged the branches on the ground with his foot. "This was a lean-to. Greg told me how he helped Victor rebuild it. He was a Boy Scout. Greg, not your father. He used to visit Victor after Jace left town and tried to help him as much as he could. He says the original one was over here." They walked across the clearing together. It wasn't very big and there wasn't much to see. The silence, broken only by the wind in the trees, made his skin prickle. This was a special place. He hoped Nathaniel thought so too.

"Some old cans here," Nathaniel said.

"Yeah. I'm not sure about those. I doubt either of them cooked much, so that might have been dinner. Greg will be able to tell you more. Speaking of which, I know it's silly, but if you could keep the secret… I don't know why Jace never told anyone but me. Maybe it was only to make me feel special. If so, it worked. I think he would like the idea of giving you the same thing—a piece of your father that no one else has. Just me and you."

Nathaniel's head was bowed. "It means a lot to me. Thank you."

"You're very welcome." He had another request, one he felt bad asking for.

To his surprise, Nathaniel got there ahead of him. "Do you think I could be alone? There are some things I need to say."

"Only if I get to go first," Ben said.

"Yeah! No problem. That fallen tree we climbed over—"

"I'll meet you there," Ben said.

He waited until the sound of footsteps faded away. Then he went to the spot where he had left Jace's ashes, clutching at himself as he looked around. "I really need you right now," he said. "I'm scared. Tim is sick. Cancer. If he doesn't pull through then I'm as good as dead, because I can't handle going through that again. I'd rather come back here and curl up into a ball until I'm ashes too. Or dust. I know you must think that I'm being dramatic, but it's not just cancer. That's bad enough. What worse is that it feels like he's already given up."

You never would have let me get away with that.

The words popped into his head, but then, they had been there all morning as he continued puzzling over where exactly they fit into his life. He had assumed they belonged to the past, but maybe...

"You're freaking kidding me," Ben whispered, wiping at his eyes. "Jace?"

He waited for a response. Nothing came.

"Okay," he said, shaking his head. "Get a hold of yourself, Ben." Whether it was coincidence or not, he still had worries to exorcise. "I keep thinking of you, toward the end. You needed me to let you go, and I can't help wondering if this is the same. Maybe it's just the beginning, but if it keeps getting worse, if Tim comes out of the surgery with complications like you did, then maybe... I don't know. Maybe this is what life is all about. Loving is only the beginning of the lesson. Letting go is the rest."

A promise is a promise.

Ben froze. His thoughts had been elsewhere. A small house in the heart of Austin, and a larger one on the outskirts. He hadn't been trying to remember the dream or make sense of it, but the words fit perfectly. Tim had promised. Expecting him to fulfill that wish was ridiculous, but then so was seeking answers from the dead.

Ben laughed at himself, shaking his head at his own foolishness, but just in case he wasn't crazy... "I love you," he murmured. "Like Bernard said, one way or another you're still with me, and I want you to know that I think of you every single day. You're a part of me. Thank you for—" He shook his head, overwhelmed by the countless happy memories they had made together. "—everything. Thank you for all of it."

He let himself cry over the past and his worries of the future. When he was finished, he walked through the woods until he found Nathaniel.

"All done," Ben said. "Do you know the way back?"

Nathaniel nodded. "To both the clearing and the house, yeah."

"Okay. I'll meet you by the lake. Take your time. All you need. I mean it."

"Thanks," Nathaniel said.

Ben patted him on the arm, then gave him his privacy. When he reached the lake, he walked along an old rickety dock, unsure if it would hold his weight. He thought of Jace, and how nice growing up here must have been, even though he had felt the need to seek his destiny elsewhere. Astounding what some people were willing to do for love. Not just Jace, but himself, and even Tim, who had strived to become the sort of man Ben needed. Maybe he would be willing to grow a little more. After all, a promise was a promise.

Tim was painting in his studio, the private one on their property, separate from the house. He stood in front of a canvas that continued to frustrate him with its emptiness, so he dragged two thick vertical streaks down it in contrasting colors, one orange, the other blue. He was hoping this would jumpstart his creativity, but an hour later, he was still staring at the same two lines.

Strange, because the hardest times in his life—missing Ben or grieving Eric—had fueled some of his best art. Why not now? He had lost his little princess and was facing his own death. He had been separated from the love of his life for three days! Usually just one night was enough to send angsty emotions racing from his heart and down his arm to the paint brush. Instead, he felt like one more joy in life had been stolen from him.

Tim glanced at his phone, which sat on the small table in front of the sofa. His appointment with the surgeon was tomorrow. Twice he had picked up the phone and nearly called MD Anderson to cancel. He knew he didn't want to go through with the surgery. He just wasn't sure what his backup plan would be. Letting the cancer slowly kill him? That scared him too. More chemo perhaps. Dr. Staples had said that they could try a higher dose. That meant even worse side effects, but he would rather have a super-powered flu from Hell than let someone cut him open. Those horror movies Jason liked so much were nothing compared to the photos Tim had discovered when researching lobectomies. The procedure might not be as gory, but seeing an open maw in the side of someone's torso…

Tim winced against the mental imagery and wondered if he should try painting something surgery-related to purge that fear from his system. He had hoped for catharsis when coming out here to paint, but he had also hoped to escape the constant nightmare, not delve deeper into it. Tim sighed, set down the paintbrush, and sat on the sofa. Then he grabbed his phone. He would call and reschedule the surgery for a few weeks later. That was fair! He needed the time to think.

Before he could, he heard the sound of a car outside. He rose and went to the door, opening it in time to see Ben pulling a suitcase along behind him.

Tim leaned against the doorway, hoping he looked cool despite feeling like shit, and gave his best, "Hey."

Ben leapt in surprise, not having noticed him. Then he abandoned the suitcase, rushing over to give him a hug and a kiss. "How are you?" Ben asked, but not casually. Whenever people spoke these words to Tim lately, each syllable was soaked with concern.

"Fine," Tim said. "Just getting some painting done."

Ben brightened up, well aware of his limited output since the diagnosis. "Oh! That's great! Can I see?"

"Uh," Tim said, wanting to say no. But he couldn't. His art was too synonymous with his feelings, and denying Ben either would hurt him, especially now. "Okay. There's nothing to show. I just got started." Two hours ago.

He led Ben inside the studio and gestured at the pathetic attempt. Ben considered it, struggling to find anything complimentary to say. "Well, I look forward to seeing how it turns out."

"Assuming I finish it before I croak," Tim said. It was meant to be a joke. One of poor taste and timing, because it did more than bomb. It made Ben explode.

"What's that supposed to mean?"

Tim blinked, surprised by the anger. "I was just—"

"Do you want to marry me?" Ben was scowling, arms crossed over his chest. Had he meant to say divorce instead? Because he didn't look happy.

"Um... We're already married?" he tried, hoping it was the right answer.

It wasn't. "No, we're not. Not legally. According to the law, I've never been married. Ever." Ben took off the ring Tim had given him, and even more shockingly, did the same with Jace's ring. Then he slammed them down on the table. "If you want to be the first man—the *only* man—to have married me, then you need to keep your promise."

"Benjamin, you know I want to, but—"

"I don't need words from you," Ben growled. "I need you to get better! Fight this. Beat it or die trying! When the doctor says you're in remission, *then* I'll marry you. And when I do, I'll only put one of those rings back on, and it won't be Jace's." Ben stared right into his eyes, no doubt wanting Tim to know how serious he was, before he turned and stomped out of the studio.

Tim watched him go. Then he looked back at the canvas, and instead of seeing two lines, he saw two people who couldn't be more different, and yet, still belonged to each other. Tim walked over to the easel, picked up his paintbrush, and started working.

The surgeon's name was Dr. Jacob Bishop-Sanchez. That's how he introduced himself. He looked like he was fresh out of college. His black hair was slicked back, and perhaps wanting to appear older, he wore smart dark-framed glasses that Tim was sure weren't prescription. He was a good-looking guy. Or maybe he was really hot, because Ben kept giggling, even when the doctor hadn't made a joke.

Tim glared at his husband, then turned back to the doctor, who, for his own sanity and to save time, he had decided to think of as Dr. Sanchez. "I'm going to need help before the surgery," Tim told him. "Anxiety meds would be good. I didn't take any for the chemo because I still wanted to feel stuff, but for this, I don't. I need to be completely numb emotionally or I'll chicken out and won't show up. Wait, can I get drunk? I'd prefer that instead."

"You want to be drunk in the days leading up to surgery," Dr. Sanchez repeated carefully. For whatever reason, Ben giggled. "It's normal for patients to have concerns before a procedure like this. Why don't you tell me yours?"

"The rib fracturing thing," Tim said instantly. "Aside from how painful that sounds, I don't want a giant hole in me, even if I won't be conscious for it."

"Do you mean rib spreading?" Dr. Sanchez smiled, causing Ben to gasp. "That isn't part of a video-assisted thoracotomy."

Tim shook his head. "A what?"

"It's a less intrusive way of performing a lobectomy. We make three small incisions instead of a large one, as with a posterolateral thoracotomy. Rather than relying on direct visual contact, we utilize a camera to locate the offending lobe instead."

"I understood half of that," Tim said, "but it sounded positive."

"It is," Dr. Sanchez said. "Take off your shirt for me."

Ben giggled again.

This time the doctor turned to him. "Are you all right?"

Ben's face flushed. "I get nervous when I laugh. I mean, I laugh when I'm nervous."

He didn't, but Tim was too excited to worry about that now. His shirt was already off. "How big would the incisions be?"

"Relatively small," Dr. Sanchez said. "A posterolateral thoracotomy would run from here to here." He traced a long line from Tim's back to beneath one of his pecs. "With a VATS, we make a small incision here beneath your armpit, and two smaller ones here and here on your back."

"No cracking my ribs open?"

Dr. Sanchez struggled with his choice of words, but he nodded. "No spreading your ribs."

"That sounds so much better!" Tim enthused.

"In my opinion, it is. One advantage of this method is that it greatly reduces the risk of chronic postoperative pain."

"Even better!" Tim said. "Can I still get drunk?"

Dr. Sanchez chuckled. "No. If you could refrain until you've recovered, that would be preferable."

They discussed the procedure in greater detail, and while Tim still wasn't thrilled to be losing part of his lung, or to have anyone poking around inside of him, this whole VATS thing sounded a lot more hopeful. Enough that he was grinning as they walked across the parking lot.

"We finally got some good news," Tim said.

"We did!" Ben said, smiling back at him. "I have faith in your surgeon. I like him. A lot."

Tim scowled. "I noticed!"

"Oh stop," Ben said. "You know I have a soft spot for Latino guys. You have to admit that he's handsome. I love the name too. Dr. Jacob Bishop-Sanchez. So regal! And all those big words he uses? Hold me down, lube me up, and whisper in my ear until morning!"

"Benjamin!"

"What? I'm not a married man. I have every right to play the field."

"Oh I'm going to marry you," Tim said. "I'm going to marry you so fucking hard!"

They both looked at each other. Then they laughed.

"Wanna grab lunch somewhere?" Ben asked. "I feel like celebrating."

The thought of food made his stomach clench and refuse, but Tim didn't care. Just getting to sit across a table from Ben and watch him eat would be reward enough.

"Okay, class!" Ben clapped his hands to get the attention of his students. "Today we're working on a special project, but don't worry, because it's going to be *fun!*" Stressing the last word hadn't helped convince the children. If anything, they seemed even more wary. No doubt other teachers had promised them fun before breaking out a math workbook, so he tried again. "Who likes drawing pictures and making things?"

Most of the hands shot up.

"Good," Ben said, walking around to the front of his desk, which was loaded up with construction paper, crayons, markers, glue, glitter, and other art supplies, because he wanted the end results to be stellar. "Today we're going to make get-well cards for a very brave man who—" He checked the clock on the wall. "—will be going into surgery soon."

He hated that he couldn't be there. Tim was about to have his lobectomy, and Ben should be at his side, or at least in the waiting room. He had taken too many personal days since the cancer was discovered, and would need more during the initial recovery, so Tim had insisted that he shouldn't waste this one. It wasn't as simple as Ben taking off for a few hours. Tim was at MD Anderson in Houston, a three-hour drive away. This meant they hadn't even been together the night before the surgery. Ben hated that.

They had little to worry about, just a seven percent chance of a major complication and a refreshingly miniscule point three percent chance of death. Ben worried regardless that Dr. Jacob Bishop-Sanchez (so yummy!) might discover something the scans hadn't yet revealed. What if the cancer had spread to other organs since then? Ben really should be there. Just in case.

He walked around to the marker board, writing Tim's name in three huge letters with a lump in his throat. "This is who we are making cards for. He has a hard day ahead of him, but you can make him feel better. Any words you write should be in pencil. Before you use anything permanent, we'll go over them together, but when it comes to the actual art, let your imagination run wild. Now then, one at a time, each of you please come up here and choose—"

And so it went. Soon he was seated behind the desk again and hunched over his phone. Ben counted down the minutes, sending texts that used an excessive amount of emojis—any that were even remotely romantic—along with declarations of love and encouraging words. Tim didn't respond to the most recent round. He was either drugged or no longer had access to his phone. The final text Tim had sent simply read, *Don't worry. I've got this.*

A knock on the door made Ben jerk upright. "Keep working," he said to his class as he went to answer it. He expected another teacher. Not his best friend.

"You have me worried sick!" Allison hissed. Then she angled her head to address to the class. "Hi, everyone!"

A few kids answered. The rest stared into space before they resumed scribbling. Ben noticed one face covered in glitter and pretended not to have seen. "What are you doing here?" he said, stepping aside so she could enter.

"You aren't answering your phone!"

"I have to keep the line free in case Tim calls. Or my mom or anyone else at the hospital."

Allison wasn't satisfied. "So why didn't you answer my texts?"

"I was just writing you back!" He led her to his phone and held it up so she could see.

She stroked the screen so it scrolled upwards. "This looks like the first chapter of a book."

"It was a long reply."

"Can you summarize?"

Ben glanced over his shoulder, but thankfully, most kids found adult conversations boring. "It says that I'm freaking out."

"Understandably." She perched on the edge of his desk as he sat again. "You should be there."

"I know! I would be too, if not for..." He tilted his head toward the students. "You know."

Allison's expression was sympathetic, but she wasn't done yet. "Who's taking care of Tim?"

"My parents. His parents too. His dad drove out yesterday to pick him up. That's who gave him a ride to Houston."

"His father," Allison deadpanned. "The man with no heart."

"Yup."

"I guess that wife of his tore into him again. Was she there too?"

"No. It's crazy. I'm not getting my hopes up that this will continue if—*when*—Tim pulls through. But for now, I can tell it makes him happy."

Allison exhaled. "I'll be damned. When does Tim go into surgery?"

Ben checked the clock again, his stomach sinking. "Right now."

"Right now, right now?"

"Yeah."

"And how long will the procedure take?"

"Two or three hours," Ben said, not able to imagine the courage needed to operate on another person, nonetheless for hours at a time. "Then we should hear something."

Allison raised her eyebrows. Uh oh. "Or you could leave now, drive *very* safely to Houston, and be there just in time for him to come out of surgery."

God he would love that! "You're forgetting the room full of children who have been entrusted to my care."

"No, I haven't," Allison said. "I work with children all the time, when I'm not busy making them, so I could stand in for you. If someone came into the room while you're gone... Does that happen often?"

"Not really."

"Good. But if it did, I'll tell them there was a family emergency and that you'll be right back. Unless they show up the second you leave, your class will probably be close enough to ending that they let it slide. I'll be sure to tell them that you *just* left, no matter when they arrive."

"I love you," Ben said, already on his feet.

Allison smiled. "Who could blame you?"

"Class," he said, making his voice loud. "I have a small emergency I need to take care of. The lovely person here, who I am eternally indebted to, is my best friend. She'll be taking care of you. Her name is Ms. Cross, and until I come back, she's your teacher, so be good and do what she says. Do you have any questions?"

"Yeah," said a boy named Donny who raised his hand but didn't wait for permission to speak. He addressed Allison instead of Ben. "Why are you so fat?"

"That's not nice—" Ben began, but Allison waved away his concerns.

"The reason I'm so fat," she said, "is that there's a baby in my belly. Until it's ready to come out, I need to eat twice as much, so it has food too."

"Babies comes from storks," said another boy.

"They do not!" a girl next to him scolded.

"I'm just keeping the baby safe," Allison said. "When the time comes, the stork—his name is Dr. Stork by the way—will deliver the baby to the hospital." She turned to him with a reassuring smile. "Go! I mean it! Drive safe."

"I will," he promised.

And he did. As much as Ben wanted to floor it all the way to the hospital, he had never been a great driver, and ending up as a pizza on the highway wouldn't help Tim's recovery. Ben even used the cruise control, not trusting his own foot. The journey seemed tediously long, but he arrived in one piece. When he reached the correct waiting area, he saw Tim's mother first. She stood and rushed over to him, tears in her eyes, and after one heart-stopping second of dread, he saw that they were of the happy variety.

"He's out and doing fine," Ella said, giving him a hug.

"No complications? No unpleasant surprises?"

She took a step back and shook her head. "He's fine. God took care of my baby today."

More like Dr. Jacob Bishop-Sanchez had, but the way Ben was feeling right now, he would gladly grant the man divine status. He would worship anyone who got Tim through this! When they were allowed into the recovery room, Ben had to exercise patience, even though he didn't want to. Only two people were allowed in at a time. He was willing to negotiate. He understood that Ella would want in there right away. He could go with her! One look from his own mother showed that she expected him to do the right thing, so Mr. and Mrs. Wyman went first. Ben's reward came when he was walking with his mother to the recovery room.

"I'm suddenly feeling peckish," June said. "I think I'll wander the halls and try to find a vending machine. I'll probably be twenty minutes or so. Is that enough time, do you think?"

"Yes!" Ben said, kissing her on the cheek.

This was even better. While he didn't feel any shame, fawning over his man would be easier without an audience. He really shouldn't have been surprised to find Tim flirting shamelessly with a nurse. Not after all these years. Ben casually pushed his way between them, pretending to stumble. "Sorry," he told the nurse. "I'm just so excited to see my husband!"

"Still got it," Tim croaked when she had gone. "And I'm not—" He grimaced, unable to continue.

"Not married?" Ben said, kissing him on the forehead. "I'm sure it's just a matter of time before you find that special someone."

Tim was sitting upright. He looked haggard, and more tubes were snaking from him than Ben wanted to acknowledge, but considering what he had just been through, Tim was surprisingly lucid.

"Is it late?" he asked. "Or early?"

Okay, so maybe he wasn't exactly sober, but Ben understood what he meant. "I got a substitute teacher. Don't worry, it won't count against my time off. I hired a private one."

"Sounds expensive."

He thought about it. "She'll make me pay. Babysitting, most likely. How do you feel?"

"Great. Wanna go out dancing tonight?"

Ben laughed. "I don't think so!"

"You always complain that I don't take you dancing." Tim's face contorted with discomfort, but he pressed on. "I finally offer and you say no? This totally counts. Remember that the next time. You had your chance."

"No fair!" Ben said with a laugh. He had expected to find Tim unconscious and on a ventilator, not sitting up and dishing out jokes. "I'm so proud of you."

Tim stuck out his tongue, as if grossed out. "You sound like my mom and dad."

"Okay," Ben said, leaning over to stroke his cheek. "In that case, I think that guys who are brave enough to face surgery are super-hot."

This pleased Tim more. "Yeah?"

"Yeah. So hot that I need to change my underwear because I just blew a load. Maybe two."

Tim started to laugh. Then he groaned. "Don't do that!"

"Hurts too much? I'll try not to be witty. Just for today. You really are the man. I can't wait to get you home."

Tim grinned, and despite all he had been through, he still had a winner's smile. "I can't wait until you uphold your end of the bargain."

"Complete remission," Ben said. "No more, no less. Although right now, when it comes to my many suitors, you're in the lead."

"Ahead of Dr. Sanchez?"

"Dr. Jacob Bishop-Sanchez," he corrected, "although he lets me call him JBS. And please don't tell him this because it would break his heart, but yes, you're way ahead of him. Although I am a little jealous that you've had him inside you."

"You're terrible," Tim said, offering his hand.

"And you're the greatest." Ben brought the hand to his lips to kiss it. "The absolute best."

Chapter Twenty

Tim was starting to feel more like his old self. He was home again after just a few days in the hospital. Over the two weeks that followed, his appetite had returned and his hair was starting to fill in. Aside from the occasional twinge of pain, his body felt okay too. The shortness of breath persisted, although that was expected, because he had less lung to work with. He did the assigned breathing exercises and went on morning walks. He was just about to leave for one when Ben stopped him in the entryway.

"Why don't you put on your jogging outfit and try a short run?"

Tim shook his head. They had been over this before. "I'm not going to risk messing up my lungs."

"But the doctors want you to stay active."

True. They had him up and walking around the ward the day after his surgery. Staying active was part of his recovery but... "Maybe that's what caused the tumor in the first place. You read about that sometimes, guys like me who always make sure to stay fit and eat right. I'm not perfect. I drink beer too much, but there are athletes who don't even do that and boom! They get cancer and everyone is shocked. Maybe I was putting too much wear and tear on my lungs and that's what caused the tumor to grow."

"Maybe." Ben was clearly humoring him. "We can ask the doctor about that next time, but today, I think you should try. Or we can call Dr. Staples and ask right now."

Tim shook his head again. "There's so much about cancer that we still don't know. She might not think that running is the cause, but what if I'm right? You think I'm crazy, don't you?"

"I think you're being silly," Ben said. "You *love* running! Are you saying you're never going to do it again?"

Tim shrugged. "It's not worth the risk."

"All right," Ben said, clearly not happy with this decision.

Tim gave him a peck on the lips to show there were no hard feelings and left the house. He was tempted. Of course he wanted to jog. Tim hadn't done so since his failed attempts in Japan. He let himself walk faster than he usually did, not struggling to breathe. He might be capable now. That was possible, and maybe the cause of his cancer was a crackpot theory, but he felt it was safer to err on the side of caution. Tim could still swim. It wasn't his first choice, but it might be enough to keep him in shape. He returned to the house forty minutes later, not even winded, and sadly without the rush of endorphins that he was used to. He could get those from the painkillers he had used sparingly. Or better yet, why not celebrate life with a beer?

He resisted, but the temptation grew stronger as the day wore on. Tim hadn't resumed working, and Ben had made sure to clean the house so he wouldn't need to strain himself. Tim was bored, and he knew that drinking would help pass the time. Ben returned home before this happened. They ate dinner together, talked, and settled down to watch TV. At least Tim did. Ben was hovering around the entryway.

"What's up?" Tim asked.

Ben was about to reply when something outside the window caught his attention. "Just keep an open mind," he said before answering the door.

Tim rose to see what was going on, confused by who walked over the threshold.

"Well well, if it isn't my new running partner," Kelly said with half-lidded eyes.

"I talked to Dr. Staples about your concerns," Ben said quickly. "She told me— Well, she said a bunch of sciencey stuff, but I understood enough to feel confident that exercise doesn't give anyone cancer."

"Just think how many Olympians would have it," Kelly chimed in. "It would be an epidemic."

"I guess so," Tim said. "But I still think I should take it easy from now on."

Ben exhaled, looked to Kelly in frustration, and left the room.

Were they supposed to follow? Tim turned to Kelly. "Whelp... This is awkward."

"He's worried about you," Kelly said with a smile. "It's adorable."

"It is," Tim agreed, "but I'm starting to wish—"

"That he would treat you like he did before? Less pity? More normality?"

Tim nodded in surprise.

"I've been there," Kelly said, walking closer to him. "When I was recovering from the car accident, people drove me crazy with their concern. I wanted them to act like I was the same person as before. What I didn't figure out until later was the obvious. They were treating me differently because I wasn't behaving like the same person. That makes the solution easy."

"I'm not the same person," Tim argued. "I'm missing a part."

Kelly wasn't impressed. "You have one and a half lungs. I have one and a half legs."

"Sorry," Tim said quickly. "I shouldn't have—"

Kelly held up his hand and smiled. "Less pity, more normality."

Tim laughed. "Right."

"Part of my problem back then," Kelly continued, "is that I convinced myself that running would never be the same. Does that concern you? Are you worried you won't be able to run as far as before, no matter how much you practice and heal? Would that make you feel like less of a man?"

Tim had considered the possibility, but until now, he hadn't said it out loud. "Yeah. That would suck."

"I was the same way. I wanted to be the fastest, and if I couldn't be, I decided not to try at all. I'll be honest with you. I *still* can't run as fast as I once did, but now I feel good about what I can accomplish, and this is why." Kelly hiked up his shorts, revealing an artificial limb that went halfway up his thigh. "I lost my leg. I don't just mean my foot, or some of the calf. I lost my knee. I'm working with a serious deficit, and I still kick ass on the track. That's why I'm prouder now than ever before."

"And it looks cool too," Tim said, nodding at the prosthetic, "but I don't know if I can be that brave."

"If I can hit the pavement with only one leg instead of two, then you'll do fine. But only if you let yourself."

"Please," a voice said. "Just try."

He turned to find Ben standing in the doorway between the entryway and the living room. In his hands were jogging shorts and an old shirt. Tim wanted to put them on and feel good about himself again, so he nodded.

Ten minutes later, he was standing out front with Kelly, the sun setting on the horizon. Thank goodness Ben had given them privacy, because failing in front of him would have been harder.

"Do you need to warm up?" Tim asked.

"No," Kelly said. "This furnace goes from ice cold to a blazing inferno in three seconds flat."

"Okay," Tim said with a grin. "Let's see what you've got!"

Despite all their bravado, they started slow, the sort of jog that was the right motion but without the speed. They stopped at the end of the drive, Kelly assessing him. "And?"

"I'm doing okay," Tim said, puffing a little, but not feeling any discomfort. "There's a path just down the road. It winds through the woods and back behind the house."

"Sounds nice," Kelly said. "Lead the way."

Tim did so, still going slow. When they reached the path and one of the few straight stretches, he took a break and asked Kelly to show him what he was really capable of. Kelly was happy to demonstrate. He took off down the path, disappeared around a curve, and returned again with impressive speed. Tim watched with fascination, the artificial leg working seamlessly with the rest of Kelly's body, but it was the graceful movement and liberating speed that had him longing to catch the wind again.

"Shall we keep going?" Kelly asked.

"Yeah," Tim said. "And I won't make you go as slow this time."

He took off in a controlled run, and when that proved sustainable, Tim let go of his fears, letting them fall behind and tumble to the wayside, soon forgotten as he rediscovered one of his greatest joys.

Tim was shirtless and holding one arm over his head. He remained perfectly still. Not for the doctor's benefit. He was simply too cautious at this point to celebrate. The news sounded positive, but the last time he jumped the gun, he had learned that he needed surgery.

"You're healing nicely," Dr. Staples said, sounding pleased.

"Will there be any scars added to my collection?" Tim asked. "If so, I need to choose names."

"Sorry?" Dr. Staples said, pushing gently on his arm so he would lower it again.

"He names his scars," Ben explained from a nearby chair. "So far he has a Ryan and a Travis."

"And if the three incisions become scars," Tim said, shooting him a wink, "I'm going to name them Joseph, Bishop, and Sanchez."

Dr. Staples smiled. "I see. Well, if these keep healing the way they are, there might not be much to see. What's your secret?"

"Cocoa butter," Ben said.

He had been rubbing it nightly on Tim's wounds and—on one occasion—other places too.

"Keep it up," Dr. Staples said. "I'm very pleased. Not only are you healing quickly, but the results of the surgery are promising."

"About that," Tim said, returning to what she had revealed earlier. "When you say I'm in remission... I know that's good news, but I read all sorts of stuff online that says not to get happy because it's no guarantee."

Dr. Staples sighed. "There is always a chance that the cancer could return. In fact, you're twice as likely to have a recurrence when compared to someone who never had it. You're also slightly more likely to develop a second cancer somewhere else, but in my professional opinion, I think you should feel optimistic. You beat cancer! Take pride in that. We'll keep monitoring your health. Regular checkups will be part of your life from now on, so we'll detect anything before it gets far. Just try to stay active, eat healthy, and don't worry so much. Let us do that for you."

Tim looked at Ben and grinned. The gesture was returned.

"So I'm good to go?" Tim asked, turning back to the doctor.

"Yes, although I would like you to consider adjuvant chemotherapy."

More chemo? Tim put his shirt back on, grimacing while his face was hidden behind the cotton. "Why?"

"If any cancer remains on a level we can't detect, the chemo might wipe it out. I know you didn't have the best results with it before, but we could try different agents. We would wait another month to give you more time to recover. I do need to stress that this would only make it slightly less likely that you would have a recurrence, but it would increase the odds in your favor."

Chemotherapy had been a terrible experience, but all he needed to do was look at Ben to find his answer. "Okay. We can try that."

"Good. You can still change your mind. Think about it, read some studies, and then we can—"

"I'm doing it," Tim said. "It's a promise, and I tend to keep those."

The word choice wasn't lost on Ben, who sniffed emotionally. The doctor went over a plan of action, Tim already acting on one piece of advice: He could be happy now. He had faced a lot of fears and overcome many obstacles, but he didn't have just medical professionals to thank. He looked again at Ben, and when they walked outside together, Tim knew he couldn't wait. Their surroundings weren't the most romantic—the parking lot of an office building—but it would have to do.

"You heard what she said," Tim said, stopping them before they left the sidewalk. "I beat cancer."

"Yes you did!" Ben said. "Let's go celebrate."

"Hold up." Tim took a deep breath. Then he took Ben's hands. "I don't know if I could have survived this without you, but I made a promise and so did you. That made the difference. Now I'd like to ask if you would—"

"Stop," Ben said, his tone full of good humor, but he was trying to pull away.

"I won't," Tim said, getting down on one knee. "It was the dream of this moment that kept me going, so please, will you—"

"Stop!" Ben said, yanking away his hands. "Get up. Please."

Tim stared, mouth going dry. What now? Ben still didn't want to marry him? He didn't want to admit defeat, but he also didn't understand. Maybe the location was the problem. Tim stood, feeling uncertain. "I thought—"

Ben pressed fingers to his lips. "I've been married twice, and I've never gotten to propose before. Considering that I've been wanting to do this since the first time I laid eyes on you…" He took one of Tim's hands, then it was Ben who went down on one knee. "Timothy Wyman, survivor of cancer and my knight in tarnished armor, would you do me the honor of spending the rest of your very *very* long life with me as your husband?"

Tim was trying to hold back tears, but it was hopeless. "Yeah," he croaked, using his free hand to wipe at his eyes. Then he grinned and nodded. "Hell yeah!"

He pulled Ben to his feet and kissed him. Even once they had finished—and it took quite some time—Tim continued to hold him, never wanting to let go. Sure, a few people walked by during this demonstration, no doubt on the way to medical appointments of their own, but when faced with things like illness and mortality, it was good to be reminded of love.

Summer was officially over. The double-wide trailer had been converted into a classroom, and despite the calendar's promise that this was the first day of autumn, the day was too hot to conjure up visions of falling leaves and carved pumpkins. Especially in this stuffy trailer. One window air conditioner unit wasn't enough. All it did was make noise, forcing the teacher to nearly shout every word. Luckily they weren't seated too near the front. Their chair and desk combos were in the third row, and might have belonged normally to young children. Ben fit comfortably into his, but he wasn't nearly as big as his current and future husband. Tim caught him looking, grimaced while trying to shift into a more comfortable position, and returned his attention to the front.

Ben allowed himself a smirk. They were in the middle of a pre-marital education course, an eight-hour lesson on how to maintain a successful relationship. He had signed them up for it, thinking it would be fun, but three hours in and the novelty had worn off.

"What are some of the healthiest ways to resolve a disagreement?" asked the teacher who—ironically—didn't have a wedding band on her finger.

A teenage girl raised her hand. "By talking about it?"

"Very good!" The teacher trilled.

"Who else?"

Tim raised his hand. "By having sex?"

Ben snorted.

The teacher wasn't so amused. "Sex should *never* be used to address underlying issues. That's not a permanent solution."

"But it helps blow off steam," Ben chimed in. "Which makes it easier to have a levelheaded discussion."

"And it's really hot," Tim added helpfully.

The teacher narrowed her eyes in their direction. Then she addressed the half-dozen couples around them. "What else can you think of?"

"Ask someone to mediate," said an older man.

"Very good!"

Ben rolled his eyes and raised his hand. It was ignored until he said, "Sorry, quick question."

The teacher's nostrils flared. "Yes?"

"If someone keeps leaving their dirty socks around the house—like on the couch—what do you think the best strategy is? To yell at them until they finally change, or to silently throw the socks away each time so that person is forced to buy new ones?"

"More like forced to dig socks out of the trash can each morning," Tim said, his hand shooting up. "I have a question too! If you're with someone who always squeezes the toothpaste from the front of the tube instead of the end, don't you think it's perfectly reasonable to buy your own tube and hide it so that you don't have to deal with their sloppiness?"

"That's perfectly fine," Ben said, "but when the other person runs out of toothpaste, surely any good spouse would, after being asked if there was more somewhere, fess up and share."

"I did share! Eventually."

"Only when you wanted to kiss me, and even then, you wouldn't let me touch the tube of toothpaste. I had to hold my brush out like Oliver Twist and beg." Ben put on his best Cockney accent. "Please sir, I want some more!"

"Let's get back on-topic," the teacher said. "What are other ways we can—"

"What do you think about calling your partner's mother to complain about perfectly harmless issues," Ben said, "knowing full well that she'll badger her son about it for months afterwards?"

"That's not why I called her!" Tim shot back. "It came up in conversation, that's all."

Ben shook his head. "First of all, I only snore when I've been drinking, and she's *still* sending me crazy cures that I don't actually need." He whipped out his phone, pulled up a text he had gotten earlier in the day and held it up. "Look at this chin strap she expects me to wear!"

"It's supposed to keep your mouth shut," Tim grumbled. "Doesn't seem to be working."

A girl sitting across the aisle from Ben leaned over to look. "Oh hell no! I wouldn't be caught dead wearing that!"

"Even while sleeping, am I right?" Ben asked her.

She pursed her lips and nodded. "Mm-hm!"

"Okay!" the teacher said, sounding desperate. "Let's take our lunch break early. Everyone meet back here in thirty—no, let's make it an hour. And when we reconvene, let's try to focus, shall we?"

"Too bad," Ben murmured as he and everyone else stood to collect their things. "I was just starting to have fun."

"Yeah," Tim agreed. "I thought we were making real progress."

Together they walked outside. The class was being held on a church property, and after agreeing that neither of them were hungry, they instead strolled through a neighboring park.

"I can't believe we have four more hours of this," Tim grumped. "Some things are worse than chemo."

Ben laughed. "I *was* starting to feel nauseous in there. I might pull my hair out too. Still, what can you do? This course is required if we want to get our marriage license."

"That's so dumb," Tim said. "And weird, because I asked Jason if we would have a test at the end, and he had no idea what I was talking about."

"Really?" Ben said innocently.

"Yeah! Must be a new law."

"Could be," Ben said. They sat on a bench together, facing a playground full of kids gleefully using their outdoor voices. "What kind of wedding should we have?"

"I've been wondering about that too," Tim replied.

"Well, we could do it like before, have all of our friends and family at the house. We have a few new ones we could invite. Corey and Kioshi. Daisy would be there this time. Lily too."

"Yeah," Tim said, not sounding thrilled.

"Or," Ben said, scooting nearer, "this one can be private. We'll apply for our marriage license, make our vows without any witnesses, and have Marcello sign off on it later."

"Just you and me?" Tim asked, putting an arm around him.

Ben nodded. "Sounds nice, doesn't it?"

Tim nuzzled his nose against Ben's cheek. "Sounds like Heaven."

"We should probably eat something before going back to class."

"And that sounds like Hell. The class part, not the eating."

Ben sighed. "Yeah. If I'd known what a drag this would be, I wouldn't have signed us up."

"But then we wouldn't be allowed to get married."

"Hm? Oh."

Tim pulled back. "Is that right? Or is there another way?"

Ben tried hiding a smile and failed. "Strictly speaking, we don't *have* to take this course."

Tim looked more hopeful than angry. "We don't?"

"But if we complete it, the County Clerk will waive the marriage license fee."

"Oh. How much is that?"

"Sixty dollars."

"Sixty dollars?" Tim repeated incredulously. "Are you kidding me? I was ready to bail after the first thirty minutes when she made us all write our names on the board and say one thing that we're grateful for."

"Electric body groomers was a good answer," Ben said before laughing.

"I panicked! It's all I could think of! We have sixty dollars to spare, you know. I don't like throwing away money, but wasting time is even worse!"

"I thought it would be funny," Ben said with a shrug.

Tim shook his head ruefully. "What am I going to do with you?"

"I'm sure you'll think of something."

"Do we have to go back?"

Ben basked in a gentle breeze that cooled his face, then thought of the muggy trailer. "It would be rude if we bailed now. Wouldn't it?"

"Honestly? I think she'll be relieved if we don't show up."

"You're probably right. Remember what I said I was thankful for?"

"Pasta?"

Ben nodded, his stomach rumbling at the idea. "I shouldn't or I'll never fit into my wedding dress."

"You're perfect just the way you are. Even when you pull shit like this."

"I adore all of your faults too," Ben said. Then he patted Tim's leg and stood. "I think that's all the marriage counselling we need. Let's go eat."

"No. First we go to the county clerk and get our license. I don't want to wait any longer."

Ben smiled. "Neither do I."

They treated the day like any other. They woke up and had breakfast, although they smiled at each other over the table more than normal. They took a shower together, washing each other affectionately but not allowing themselves to go further. Not yet. Then they got dressed in the casual clothing they usually wore. They both had fresh haircuts, and Ben spent more time in front of the mirror than he would have otherwise. After making sure their phones were turned off, they went together to the backyard, and even though Ben had told himself over and over that this was a mere formality, he couldn't help but feel excited.

"We have to find the exact spot," Tim said, walking into the yard. "I think it was riiiight... here."

"You're thinking of Jason and William's wedding," Ben said, crouching to inspect the ground. Then he stood again. "This is where the gazebo was set up. You can tell because the grass still hasn't grown back as thick."

"Yeah, but they took their vows in the same spot we did."

"That was closer to the patio. Remember how we made the rows of chairs wider instead of deeper?"

"No. Well... Maybe. Why do weddings have to be so stressful?"

Ben laughed. "It doesn't have to be. I think we were about..." He strode forward, then turned around. "This is it. Right here. I can feel the good vibes."

Tim laughed but stayed where he was. "Sounds like something I would say. And I can feel good vibes here too."

"Didn't we learn something in our marriage course about meeting halfway?"

Tim grinned. "You know, I think we did!" He took a step forward. "Maybe we should have stuck around for the rest of it."

Ben also took a step forward. "Eh. We'll figure it out as we go along."

"We did fine for all those years already, didn't we?" Another step forward.

"Yes, we did." And another.

Tim raised a foot, letting it hover before he put it down nearer to him. "So our first wedding, does it still count? Do we still say we were married back then?"

"It counts," Ben said, following suit. "Of course it does! That was our public wedding. This is our secret one. Sting had a song about that, you know."

"I don't," Tim said. "Sing it to me."

Ben did, or he started to, anyway. Tim picked up the pace,

and when reaching him, swept Ben up into his arms.

"This must be the spot," Tim said, gently setting him down again.

"Feels right to me," Ben agreed, smiling sheepishly. "So I guess we just go for it. I didn't write any vows. I figure we did that already, and what's left to be said besides—"

"Wait," Tim took a step back and patted his pockets. Then he pulled out a ring and held it up.

Just the sight of it made Ben's heart leap and his stomach sink. "That's not the right ring."

"It's the one Jace gave you, I know." Tim held it out to him. "You never should have taken it off. I don't need you to. I also won't be the only man to have married you. I know you were trying to motivate me, and it worked, but now that we've made it through, it's time to invite Jace back into our lives."

Our lives. That he included himself in this was enough to make Ben want to skip to the part where they kissed. But first he held out his hand. Tim respectfully placed the ring in his palm. Ben eyed the golden band, having missed it, and looked up. Tim smiled and nodded encouragingly, so Ben returned the ring to its rightful place on his left hand.

"Feel better?" Tim asked.

"Yeah," Ben admitted, his throat tight. "I still get to wear your ring too, right?"

"I sure hope so! I also miss mine. It doesn't feel right not wearing it. Are you ready to keep going?"

"Not yet," Ben said.

"I understand. We can take a break, and when you're ready—"

"You're just as good as him," Ben said, emotions rising. "You told me once that Jace was the better man and always would be, but you're both equally wonderful. I'm so ridiculously lucky to have had you both in my life. I just needed you to know that before we continue."

"Thanks," Tim said. Then a smile tugged at his lips. "But you have to admit, even with the chemo hair, that I'm a *little* bit hotter than him."

Ben laughed. "Yes, and Jace was a little bit classier! He never would have said such a thing."

Tim shrugged. "So I've still got a lot to learn. I'll get there eventually. Depending on how much time you're willing to give me."

Ben thought about it carefully. "How about all of it? Every single day we have left on this earth. I want to spend them all with you."

"I thought we agreed not to do vows," Tim said, "but for what it's worth, there's nobody better than you. Jace and I, we were the lucky ones." His silver eyes were shining. "I still can't believe that I get to stand at your side. So even though there isn't anyone here to ask us if we're sure, my answer is yes, I want more than anything to continue being your husband."

"And I swear with all of my heart to continue loving you from now until forever."

The power vested in them came from the love they shared, and as they exchanged rings and their lips touched, Ben swore he could feel that power growing. Enough to ensure that this fairytale-come-true would never end. They would always have each other.

From now until forever.

Epilogue

The world had moved on. Politically, culturally, and technologically. Especially that last one. Ben was reminded of that today as he stood in his living room and consulted with a New York cardiologist via his television screen. Or data streamer, as they called them these days, but to him it looked like a television screen and they could watch shows on it, so that's what he called it. Like most people his age, he had opted for a unit with medical enhancements, which is what allowed the doctor to scan him. All he had to do was stand still for a whopping twenty seconds. What amused him was just how old-fashioned even this was. He could have met the doctor in a virtual environment that for all intents and purposes perfectly recreated an office in Manhattan, but he was old-fashioned. No, he was old.

Life definitely didn't begin at eighty. Nor did it get any better at eighty-eight. Still, it wasn't all bad, and he felt fortunate to live far away from a world he found increasingly exhausting. Austin had grown, like all cities tend to do. By the time the area around them began to be developed, Tim had the foresight to buy up as much connecting land as they could. Their little house was still padded by trees, giving them solitude and maintaining the illusion that nothing had changed after all these years. Just two gay guys living out the rest of their years together. Ben had a feeling he was about to discover just how many years they had left.

"I have your results," the doctor told him. "Are you ready?"

"Just try and surprise me," Ben said. "I dare you."

The doctor smiled. He looked like he was twenty. Maybe he was. Or maybe he was forty. Aging could be slowed these days, at least externally, but by the time that technology had been developed... Well, there was little point in preserving a wrinkled old fruit like himself.

"The shortness of breath you've been experiencing, paired with the chest pain, led me to believe you might be experiencing heart failure."

"Uh huh," Ben said dutifully. Computers might be capable of providing a flawless diagnosis in mere seconds, but the human ego still demanded the right to go first.

"I'm afraid the scans confirm my findings. Your heart failure is categorized in the advanced stages, but please don't panic. In the past, this condition would have left you with mere months to live. The good news is that modern medicine is able to nearly halt the deterioration. I can't promise that you'll reach your hundredth birthday, but another five years isn't unrealistic, perhaps even ten."

No, the doctor was definitely as young as he looked. Otherwise he wouldn't consider another ten years as a feeble old man to be good news. "And the symptoms? The breathing problems?"

"I'm prescribing a medication to help ease the discomfort, although the symptoms won't abate completely. You'll just have to learn to slow down and not stay out so late partying. You're not exactly young anymore!"

"Ha ha ha," Ben said dutifully, trying to make it sound convincing, while inside, he comforted himself with the knowledge that one day the doctor too would be old. No matter how good he looked, he would still experience creaking bones, memory loss, and tiredness despite how often he fell asleep in his chair.

"I've transmitted the details to your pharmacy. Expect the prescription to be drone-dropped within the hour."

Ben thanked the doctor for his help before his memory nudged him. "Just a moment. My husband has a cough that won't go away. If you don't mind?"

He didn't wait for permission. Ben shuffled to the kitchen, then peered out at the backyard. When this didn't turn up anything, he went to the stairs and shouted. His hearing was still sharp, as was Tim's, and there definitely wasn't a response. When he returned to the television screen, the doctor was wearing an expression of forced patience. Ben recognized it from when he was young and had to deal with old people who no longer cared who they inconvenienced.

"Sorry," Ben said. "He must be out partying. I'll have him call you back."

He ended the transmission. Then he thought about the prognosis. He didn't need long to decide how he felt about it. His memory nudged him again, this time a little too late. "Oh right." He cleared his throat, because he might not be hard of hearing, but he swore their computer was. "Locate Tim," he said. Then, under his breath he added, "You infernal thing."

"Tim is currently in the studio," said a pleasantly neutral voice. Ben grunted and headed for the front door.

"I'm sorry, I did not understand your request."

"I bet you didn't." Then louder he said, "Contact the store and have them deliver whatever groceries we need with my prescription." That should keep it busy.

He went outside, blinking against the light. Then he stood on the front stoop, letting the sun warm his skin. He closed his eyes, which made it easier to remember being young, when things like moving and breathing were done without effort or discomfort. Another ten years. Ben tried to imagine them. Then he decided to see if Tim felt the same way as he did.

Ben went to the shed, the same one that William had helped repurpose as a studio. That made him smile. William was still such a kind man, infinitely patient with Jason and catering to his every need. As always, that reminded Ben of someone else he had once known. Sometimes his relationship with Jace felt like ancient history, but more often than not, he could have sworn it had taken place just the other day. All the feelings were still there. Even age couldn't touch them.

He knocked gently on the studio door, understanding how delicate the creative process could be. When he heard a voice say his name, his heart reacted as if eager to prove it wasn't failing. Ben opened the door and found Tim standing before a canvas. Lord he was handsome! His hair was stark white, which instead of contrasting with his eyes, now complemented them perfectly. Tim's hair was still thick, which Ben envied. Maybe he should have talked to the doctor about that instead. Then again, what point was there in being vain at his age? Attraction transcended the physical. For them both. He tried to consider Tim more harshly, seeing how his body was stooped, the once-firm arms sagging with gravity, the face lined and worn, like paper that had been crumpled and smoothed out over and over again until it was soft, which made it so much nicer to kiss. Nope, no sense in trying to be critical. Any time Ben looked at Tim, all he saw was a beautiful man whom he still found just as attractive now as he had in decades past. Even more so, in fact.

"I know that look," Tim said, setting down his paintbrush. "Although I have to say, I was expecting a glare instead of bedroom eyes."

"Because you skipped another doctor's appointment?" Ben

shook his head, closed the door behind him, and ambled forward to the sofa. He sat, Tim joining him, and for a moment they both basked in how good it felt to be off their feet.

Ben nodded at the large painting on the easel, which was still in its earliest stages. If he had to guess, it would be some sort of building. "What are you working on?"

"You'll see when I'm finished," Tim said. "How'd it go with the doctor?"

"Heart failure," Ben said, seeing no need to soften the blow. Death wasn't nearly as frightening or as distant anymore.

"How serious?"

"Very, but only if left untended. With the right medicine, you'll get another decade out of me."

"Good," Tim said, but he appeared pale, and when he coughed, it went on for longer than normal.

"Is it a good thing?" Ben asked. "I can't help asking myself that lately. We've had long lives."

"What are you saying?"

Ben chose his answer carefully. "That I miss my parents. I know it's been a long time now, but it still hurts. I'm tired of people disappearing from this world. It makes everything feel so…"

"Unfamiliar," Tim finished for him. Then he pointed to the wall, at a painting of a dog bounding through a field of rainbow light. "I still miss Chinchilla. Sven too. And Pierre and Boris."

"You and your dogs," Ben chided.

"Yeah. Me and my dogs. It feels strange not having one now. It's more than just them." Tim took a shuddering breath, either due to the cough or maybe emotion. "I miss Marcello."

Ben patted Tim's hand and left his own on top of it. "Yes. So do I. Life just isn't the same without him. Still, Nathaniel and Kelly have done a good job of keeping it all afloat."

Tim nodded. "Noah and Harold too. They've all preserved his legacy, but it's not the same. None of us could replace his personality. I'd give just about anything for one of his weird gropey hugs."

"He was always a gentleman with me," Ben said. "Never put a hand where he shouldn't."

"With me he was *all* hands," Tim said, shoulders shaking with laughter. And maybe a little sorrow. "I loved him. Just about more than anyone. Except you. And Jason, of course."

They sat together in silence, lost in memory.

Tim was the first to speak. "I'm not avoiding the doctors. I've already been."

"In person?" Ben looked over at him. When he saw a nod of confirmation, his stomach sank. "Then it's serious?"

Tim put on a brave smile. "Nothing I haven't faced before."

"The cancer is back!" Ben forced himself to calm down. Hardly anyone died of cancer these days. Not when medical screenings were so effective at early detection. "Did they catch it soon enough?"

"No," Tim said. "I only have myself to blame, but there are options. Best case scenario, they keep it in check. The cancer won't spread further. It won't kill me."

Ben took in his reassuring expression and shook his head. "Why didn't you tell me sooner?"

"Because I wanted to see what the cardiologist had to say. If the news was bad and you weren't going to be okay… Once you go, I don't plan on sticking around. Don't worry though. I'll keep my promise."

Ben intertwined their fingers and leaned against him. "We've had good lives," he said.

"Definitely," Tim agreed.

"And everything has its time."

"That it does," Tim said.

"What if we let nature take its course?" In the silence that followed this question, he listened to Tim's breaths, which sounded more labored than even just a month ago.

"I can't make that decision for you," Tim said. "I don't believe death is the end. I know you're not so certain. Maybe we should face this question with the assumption that you're right and I'm wrong. If there's nothing after this world, would you still want to go?"

"One life is more than enough for me," Ben said. "Especially as good as mine has been. Clinging to it at this point seems ungrateful."

"We can still think about it," Tim said, nudging him playfully. "We're not facing the executioner just yet."

"I suppose not," Ben said, laughing at his own melodrama. Maybe it was the theater he missed instead of his youth!

"I would worry about Jason," Tim said.

"When our time comes, he'll hurt just like we did when losing our parents. We can't keep him from that experience indefinitely. Not unless he goes first, and frankly, that's a day I don't want to live long enough to see." Ben nearly shuddered at the thought. "No, he'll find his way past the pain. If not for his own sake, then for his children."

"I'm so proud of him," Tim said. "I know we didn't make him, but still."

Ben nodded, thinking of all the foster children Jason had given a home to. And how many grandchildren and joyful memories that had resulted in. "I'm proud of him too."

The fingers interwoven with his own squeezed. "So where do we stand?"

Ben took as deep a breath as he could manage. "The pharmacy is sending my new medicine. You?"

"I have an appointment at MD Anderson next week."

"How nostalgic," Ben joked. "I've been wanting to revisit the past lately. I guess I should have been more specific."

"I guess so," Tim said with a chuckle. "Still, it's not so bad, is it? Being old men together?"

Ben looked into eyes that were still as bright as the day they met. Then he leaned closer for a kiss. After their lips parted, he smiled and said, "No. Not bad at all."

Tim picked up the paintbrush with a shaking hand, but as soon as it neared the canvas, it grew steady again. He wasn't sure why. He couldn't will it to stop shaking normally, but something about this activity calmed his mind. Or maybe it was the decades of practice. He would ask the doctors about it at MD Anderson tomorrow. One of them might know. For now, he was much more interested in putting the finishing touches on this piece. He was just about to coax out a particularly delicate line when someone knocked on the door, nearly causing him to mess up. After pulling back carefully, he looked over and said, "It better be important!"

The door opened. Ben stuck in his head, the brown eyes surrounded by crinkles, the hair wispy and thin. Tim had planned on staying crabby, but that was impossible when faced with the greatest love of his life. Especially when he had been revisiting so many memories as of late, it was nice to be reminded of the good things that were still a part of his present.

"Can I see it yet?" Ben asked.

"No!" Tim said, bracing himself to turn the easel if need be.

"So it's a gift for me?" Ben asked with a knowing smile.

"Yes," Tim said. To commemorate their seventieth anniversary, which they had already celebrated, but inspiration couldn't be rushed. "If you don't stop bothering me, I'll never finish it and you'll never see it."

"Just a peek?" Ben put on a pouty expression that was intentionally adorable. It almost worked.

"I should be finished soon. Not much longer, I swear."

"Okay. I'm making sandwiches for lunch. Do you want me to bring them out here? We could eat together."

"That would be nice," Tim said, already knowing it was a ruse to see the painting, but he didn't truly mind. He would probably be done by then because he really was close. He just needed a little more privacy. "Go easy on the mustard this time. And try not to burn them."

"They're sandwiches!" Ben said. "How am I going to burn them? I wasn't even planning on using the toaster."

"You'll find a way," Tim said. "You always do."

Ben glared, but it was soon replaced by a gleeful expression, his eyes moving to the canvas again. "Am I going to like it?"

"I hope you'll love it."

"Okay." Ben still didn't leave. "Do you like me?"

Tim laughed. "I love you, Benjamin."

That did the trick. Ben smiled as if it was the first time Tim had ever said that to him. "I love you too," he replied, finally leaving and closing the door behind him.

Tim turned his attention back to the canvas, creating one line and another, bringing it all together. The finishing touches. He liked, when it came to painting at least, how literal that was. Another dab of green, a touch of yellow, and then... Finished.

Tim took a step back to look at the canvas. If he walked to the door and opened it, he would see a similar scene. An old house, every inch cared for and covered in memories. Tim had delved deep into the past for the painting. Parked outside of it was a slightly battered car, the one Jason had inherited from Ben shortly after he first came to live with them. Inside the nearby open garage was a Bentley. The vehicles made him nostalgic, but not nearly as much as the front stoop, where a bike leaned against the house and two men stood next to each other. One of them, muscular and blond, had his arm around the shoulders of a smaller guy with messy brown hair. Jason and William had helped fill their house with love, but they weren't the only ones to do so.

Tim went to the corner of the studio where he had hidden another canvas. A single painting wasn't enough to surprise Ben anymore, so Tim had completed two. A pair, one not complete without the other. Once they were side by side, he took a step back, pleased with the result. He hoped it would make a good present. The longer they were together, the more impossible it seemed that Tim would ever find a way of truly communicating what he felt. His love for Ben was too colossal to be expressed in words or any other artistic medium, but he had to keep trying.

Tim moved to the sofa and sat, still studying his work. His eyes closed of their own accord a few times. One of the perks of being an artist was getting to take plenty of naps. He liked to think they refueled his creativity. With his lungs so tight, as they had been of late, he felt especially tired. Tim tried the old breathing exercises he had been taught during his recovery, and when they failed to help, decided to stretch out on the couch, knowing that Ben would let himself in even without permission. What better way of being roused from sleep than with food? Aside from sex. Maybe they would manage that too. Before he drifted off, Tim's attention shifted to a different painting, one that never failed to make his heart swell with affection. Chinchilla, his little princess. He stared at it as long as he could, and as his eyes shut, he swore he could hear her barking in excitement, as if she was happy to finally see him again.

Ben set the serving tray down on a small table outside the studio. A chair was to each side of it. Tim would sometimes sit there on the cooler nights to drink a beer, Ben joining him occasionally, but he wasn't willing to sit now. Not when getting up again took so much effort. Instead he leaned against the shed to catch his breath. He was tempted to knock on the door and have Tim carry everything inside, but that would give him the opportunity to cover the painting. And besides, Ben might be hopelessly old, but he still tried to hide that. He wanted Tim to see him as energetic and self-sufficient, to make him proud and keep him falling in love over and over again. He supposed another ten years together wouldn't be so bad. A lot of work, but their love had always been worth the effort.

Ben pushed away from the shed, picked up the tray again, and held it against himself with one arm so he could use his free hand to open the door. He tried to do so quietly, but a butter knife slid off the tray and clattered to the ground.

"Can you grab that?" he said, hoping to distract Tim long enough that he could slip inside and see the painting.

As it turned out, he could have barged right in. Tim was on the couch, stretched out on his side, taking a nap. Ben smiled, shuffled inside, and set the tray on the table. Then he turned around to consider the painting, concerned he was seeing double. Two paintings, not one! At first he was disappointed. The work was beautiful. That came as no surprise, but the subject seemed so commonplace, since they spent most of their time at this house. Then he noticed the pair standing outside the home. Jason and William when they were still young, but best of all, they were home again. This filled Ben with so much emotion that he was tempted to rush outside to see if this wish had come true. Instead he turned his attention to the other painting. The first had shown their house from the front. The second was the same house from the back, where they had made more memories. When he noticed the bulldog sitting on the back patio, a little gray cat not far away, Ben covered his mouth with his hand to stop himself from crying out. Seeing them again felt too good. Then he noticed the two figures in the yard, facing each other while holding hands. He grinned at Tim's dark hair, his upright posture, and those irresistible muscles. As for Ben, he seemed impossibly young. He often felt that way when not dealing with aches and pains or looking in the mirror, but it was still nice to see himself that way again. Those had been such rich times, so new and full of turmoil, but even through the worst of it, they'd still had so much.

Ben spun around, his cheeks wet. He needed to wake Tim up. This was always his favorite part, when his art managed to move Ben to tears. He wouldn't want to miss it.

"They're both such gorgeous paintings," Ben said, walking toward him. "No, *you're* gorgeous!"

Tim didn't wake up. He didn't even stir. Ben felt a jolt of panic. Then he stopped, watched for that strong chest to rise and fall, or for the old gnarled fingers to twitch in a dream. Tim was perfectly still.

Ben wasn't completely surprised. At their age, they had both imagined countless scenarios of how death might come. This was one of the better ones. Peaceful. His heart still ached as he went to the couch and got down on his knees to kiss those lips one final time. When his tears landed on Tim's cheeks, they looked like they could have belonged to him instead.

"Don't cry," Ben said. "I never wanted you to keep your promise. Not really, because I didn't want you to know how this feels. I've been through it before. I can handle it again. It's okay, Tim. You did good."

Ben pressed their foreheads together and wept. He kissed Tim's cheek, then sat next to him and held his hand. He knew he needed to let Tim go, but it was hard knowing that they would never touch again. After allowing himself enough time, Ben sang one last song to his husband. Then he forced himself to pull away, because one way or another, Tim was no longer there. Ben rose on unsteady legs and turned to the two paintings that depicted an impossible dream full of endless happiness, laughter, and love. More than any one man could wish for.

"We're just two old widows," Allison said. "Aren't we?"

"Yeah," Ben said, nose stuffed up from crying so much. His throat hurt, his eyes were sore, and most of all, he was tired. The funeral had gone well enough. Tim had long ago bought a plot next to Eric's. He had offered to do the same for Ben, but that's not what he wanted. Cemeteries weren't places that Ben cared to visit, and he didn't want anyone else to feel obligated to do so. He'd rather be cremated, and while he didn't care what happened to him after that, a delicate inquiry had revealed that Jason wanted to keep his ashes.

Ben swallowed. Saying goodbye to Tim had been hard enough, but seeing how inconsolable Jason had been, holding him during the funeral and trying to shield him from the pain... Ben's arms simply weren't big enough to do what was supposed to be Tim's job. William was there for them both. Two more people in need of rescue. He was a good man. Right now William was upstairs in the guest room with Jason and had hopefully persuaded him to get some sleep.

The wake was held at the house. Most of life's other big events had taken place there, and staying home made it easier on Ben. At least here he felt surrounded by Tim, the memories they had made a constant source of comfort. His eyes moved to the pair of paintings on display in the living room. Their home in happier times. Ben was so thankful for that reminder. He refused to feel sorry for himself. Not with a happy past like that to reflect on.

Allison noticed the fresh tears and scooted closer to him on the couch. After handing him a tissue and watching him blow his nose, she gently took hold of one of his arms. "What am I going to do with you?" she sighed. "I promised Tim I'd take care of you. He insisted, not that I needed any convincing."

Ben managed a smile. "He did?"

"Yes. He kept saying I wouldn't need to, but just in case… Tim was obsessed with that promise of his."

"He kept it," Ben said. "As far as I'm concerned, he made it close enough to count."

She studied him for a second, her all-knowing expression only enhanced by age. "You aren't taking your medicine, are you?"

"Can you blame me?" he asked, but he didn't feel the need to defend himself. He knew she wouldn't judge.

"I had similar thoughts when I lost Brian. Of course we weren't so old then, but at the time, I couldn't imagine a life without him. I found one though. Maybe it's not quite the one I had hoped for, but I'm glad I stuck around long enough to become a great-grandmother. I would have hated to miss that."

"I'm glad you stuck around too," Ben said, but he couldn't promise to do the same.

She studied him a moment longer, then reached her own conclusion. "I'll spare you the pep talk. You've been through this before. Still, I have to imagine it's different this round. Seventy years is a long time."

Ben's lip trembled before he got himself under control. "I wouldn't have minded another seventy with him."

"I can't compete with Tim Wyman, *the* hottest guy in high school," Allison said, squeezing his arm affectionately. "But you know you can come live with me. It's a full house right now, and I don't need much excuse to kick the twins out of the nest. It's about time they started fending for themselves. No more being pampered by their nice old granny. If they don't shape up, they're going to meet their wicked grandmother instead."

Ben managed a smile. "Can I be there when it happens? Nothing against them! I love the twins. I just love seeing you kick butt even more."

"That'll bring back a few memories."

"Oh yes!" Ben said with a chuckle. "Except this time, I won't be on the receiving end."

"Don't be so sure," Allison said. "You might be the reason I come out of retirement!"

"I appreciate the offer," he said. "For the living situation, I mean, but I'll be okay here. I won't be on my own. Jason and William are moving in."

"Really? That's thoughtful of them!"

"It is," Ben said. "They suggested we finally keep our vow and get a cabin together. We rented one often enough, but we were all supposed to live out our final days together and... Well, it was a long time ago, and we both know how life can get in the way. It just wouldn't be the same without Tim. What really surprised me is that they want to keep this house. I told them they could sell it when I'm gone, that I wouldn't mind, but between you and me, I'm relieved."

"They're good boys," Allison said. "Enough talk of death. I realize that we're the last two people at a wake, but that doesn't mean we can't have fun."

He looked to her incredulously.

"I'm trying to cheer you up!" Allison said defensively. "That's my job!"

Ben laughed. "If that's your job, maybe I should give you the day off."

"No chance," Allison said. "Best friends never call in sick. Ever. You know I love you. Right?"

He nodded. "I love you too."

"Good." She leaned her head against his shoulder. "I can't say goodbye to you. Not yet."

"I know." Ben shifted to put his arm around her. "Let's just take it one day at a time."

They sat together on the couch, two old friends, and while they seemed to be in the midst of a comfortable silence, their minds were filled with the songs they had sung, the memories they had made, and all the love they had shared over the years.

* * * * *

The only downside to having a brave heart, Ben decided, is that it didn't know when to quit. Four months had passed since Tim's death, and Ben was still alive and… healthy wasn't the right word, although he did experience moments of happiness. Having his son home again after all these years felt good. They brought with them a dog and a cat, and it was almost like the final paintings that Tim had created were a prophecy. Their home was filled with life again—new memories being made, old stories continuing. He liked that. Perhaps a little too much or his body would have given up already. Maybe that's why he found himself standing in the backyard one night, in the same spot where they had taken their vows, but it wasn't the same. Tim hadn't painted Ben in the yard alone, staring up at the sky with tears in his eyes. No matter how happy Ben felt when talking with his son, or while brushing a purring cat on his lap, he still felt homesick, despite spending all his time at home.

Ben returned indoors and decided to call it a night. He paused halfway up the stairs, his breathing labored and his chest spiking with pain. He wanted to sit down and take a break, but that was too complicated a maneuver while on the stairs. Even if he managed, he probably wouldn't be able to get back up again. The last thing he wanted was for Jason to install one of those motorized chairs to get him up and down the stairs, although it *would* be amusing for the first day or so. But no, as he often did these days, he stood there gripping the rail until he had recovered enough to continue.

He made it to his bedroom without having to stop again, taking his time getting undressed and trying not to let sorrow seep into his soul. He wasn't complete. Not without his dearest companion. Funny how Ben longed for Tim most when going to sleep each night. That was a feeling he knew well. Now it had doubled.

He looked to the two photos on the nightstand. One of Jace, the other of Tim, both at about the same age. Ben sometimes took them and acted out little scenes, usually making them fight over him. Just for old time's sake. Tonight he kept it simple.

"Husband number one, husband number two, I miss you both. Please send me nice dreams. If you don't, I'm putting myself back on the market. Do you really want a third guy to compete with?"

Ben chuckled to himself. Then he kissed his fingers and pressed them to Jace's lips, before doing the same for Tim. It was his photo he looked at just before shutting off the light and slipping beneath the sheets. He grimaced, the pain in his chest more irritating than usual as he tried different positions to alleviate the discomfort. Ben was finally dozing off when he felt a hand on his shoulder. It gripped him briefly, then took the blanket and pulled it higher so he wouldn't be cold. Jason had come to check on him, worrying as he so often did these days. Ben tried to gather the energy to open his eyes and reassure him, but the gentle hum he heard was too soothing.

Hum? Fearing something was wrong, he opened his eyes. In the limited light, he saw curved plastic walls, oval windows, and stain-resistant carpet. An airplane interior? Ben sat upright, which for once wasn't difficult. The hand on his shoulder pulled away as he did so. When Ben looked up, he saw a tall man wearing a neatly ironed uniform and the sweetest smile he ever had the pleasure of pressing his lips against.

"Jace?" he said, voice already quaking with emotion.

"In the flesh," came the answer. Then Jace cocked his head, eyes shining. "So to speak."

"Where are we going? Wait, is this a dream?"

"One you never have to wake up from," Jace said, offering his hand.

Then it all came back to him, every time they had met like this, all the conversations they had shared over the decades—a relationship hidden in the twilight hours of the night. But this time, if the promise was true, the dream would last forever. Ben took hold of the hand, noticing that his own was no longer wrinkled or covered in liver spots. He was young again, thank goodness, because he had nearly forgotten just how handsome Jace had been, and how all it took was a simple wink from him to make his heart flutter. Ben let himself be pulled into those arms, enjoying the warm comfort there.

"I've got you," Jace murmured. "You're safe now. No more pain or hard times. From now on, it's just us." An appealing offer, but it wasn't quite right. He pulled back, Jace noticing his concern and chuckling. "Don't worry. Tim is part of that 'us.' So are your friends and family. Eventually we'll all be together again. If that's not the perfect definition of Heaven, I don't know what is."

"Is that where we are?" Ben asked.

"Not quite yet," Jace said. "We could be, but... Well, I've had to wait a very long time for this moment, and I don't want to share it with anyone. I didn't have to ask permission. Tim suggested that I be the one to bring you here." He reconsidered. "Okay, he made me play rock-paper-scissors for the honor, but I'm pretty sure he let me win."

Ben laughed, the tears in his eyes happy. He didn't expect to experience the sad kind ever again, not with the pain of separation having left his heart. He kissed Jace, the experience just as perfect as it had been a lifetime ago. There was no comparison, although he wouldn't mind putting that to the test, and he would just as soon as he and Tim were reunited. Ben could scarcely comprehend the bliss of having the two greatest loves of his life at his side, secure in the knowledge that they would never again be lost to him. For now, he sat in one of the airline seats, pulled Jace down next him, and delighted in the sound of his voice, the touch of his hand, and the joy reflected in his eyes, all while slowly flying toward an eternity filled with promises of love.

Don't mourn this love story.
Go out and live one of your own!

Not ready to say goodbye?

The Woodlands, TX
1997

Ben pressed his back to the bedroom door and bit his bottom lip to stop himself from smiling. He would have to give in eventually, considering who was sprawled out in his bed. Tim had his legs hanging over the edge of the mattress, his body reclined and twisted to one side so he could read the back of a CD case. Alice in Chains, if Ben wasn't mistaken. Okay, so he knew exactly which CD it was and had left it lying around intentionally after Tim had teased him about listening to girl music. Whatever that meant. Was it Ben's fault that the ladies had the best voices? He didn't need to prove his masculinity, but he did want to show that his music tastes were varied, and *Facelift* was one beautifully produced album.

The Something Like… series has officially drawn to a close, but you can still check in on your favorite characters through exclusive mini stories, each accompanied by new illustrations. Read love letters, snoop through text messages, and even vote on what you want to see next! All this and more can be found over on Patreon. Swing by and see for yourself. We've got freebies!

www.patreon.com/jaybellbooks

Something Like Summer has been reimagined as an ongoing web comic series! Join us on this new adventure at: www.gaywebcomics.com

Also by Jay Bell
Kamikaze Boys

True love is worth fighting for.

My name is Connor Williams and people say I'm crazy. But that's not who I am. They also think I'm straight, and mean, and dangerous. But that's not who I am. The stories people tell, all those legends which made me an outsider—they don't mean a thing. Only my mother and my younger brother matter to me. Funny then that I find myself wanting to stand up for someone else. David Henry, that kind-of-cute guy who keeps to himself, he's about to get his ass beat by a bunch of dudes bigger than him. I could look away, let him be one more causality of this cruel world… But that's not who I am.

Kamikaze Boys, a Lambda Literary award-winning novel, is a story of love triumphant as two young men walk a perilous path in the hopes of saving each other.

Hear the story in their own words!

Many of the *Something Like...* books are available on audio too. Listen to Tim's tale while you jog with him, or ignore your fellow airline passengers while experiencing Jace's story again. Find out which books are available and listen to free chapters at the link below:

www.jaybellbooks.com/audiobooks/

Something Like Summer **on the big screen!**

Now you can hear Ben sing and watch your favorite characters fall in love in the *Something Like Summer* movie! Get behind-the-scenes information and find out how you can see it at:

www.somethinglikesummer.com

Made in the USA
Las Vegas, NV
17 July 2022